Samuel Gilm

Contributions to Literature

SALZWASSER
VERLAG

Samuel Gilman

Contributions to Literature

Reprint of the original, first published in 1856.

1st Edition 2024 | ISBN: 978-3-37517-634-1

Salzwasser Verlag is an imprint of Outlook Verlagsgesellschaft mbH.

Verlag (Publisher): Outlook Verlag GmbH, Zeilweg 44, 60439 Frankfurt, Deutschland
Vertretungsberechtigt (Authorized to represent): E. Roepke, Zeilweg 44, 60439 Frankfurt, Deutschland
Druck (Print): Books on Demand GmbH, In de Tarpen 42, 22848 Norderstedt, Deutschland

CONTRIBUTIONS

TO

LITERATURE;

DESCRIPTIVE, CRITICAL, HUMOROUS, BIOGRAPHICAL, PHILOSOPHICAL, AND POETICAL.

BY

SAMUEL GILMAN, D. D.

BOSTON:
CROSBY. NICHOLS, AND COMPANY,
111 WASHINGTON STREET.
1856.

TO

THE CHARLESTON LITERARY CLUB,

WHOSE SOCIAL AND INTELLECTUAL INFLUENCES,

FELT EVEN BEYOND THE PRIVATE SPHERE,

HAVE AVAILED TO CHARM AND RETARD THE AUTHOR'S DECLINING AGE,

THESE

CONTRIBUTIONS TO LITERATURE

ARE RESPECTFULLY AND CORDIALLY INSCRIBED

BY

THEIR ATTACHED ASSOCIATE.

PREFACE.

In the course of an almost absorbing devotion, for forty years, to the duties of the sacred profession, the author of the following pages has indulged in various exercises of a more purely literary character. To such occasional excursions he has surrendered himself, sometimes as his own spirit prompted, but more frequently in obedience to the invitation or the request of others. Venturing to judge from the kind manner in which some of his productions have been received, and inspired by the usual fond ambition of authorship, he is induced to publish a selection from these miscellaneous accumulations of a lifetime. Many of them are now out of print, and several have never been published at all. The author therefore trusts that the present compilation will be regarded by an extensive circle of friends as a welcome memorial, even should it fail of a favorable reception from the public at large.

The different articles have been arranged without reference to chronological order, and indeed on no decided principle of sequence, except a separation of the Poetry from the Prose. The dates of their composition, however, are affixed to the principal articles, partly as a matter of possible interest, partly to explain incidental allusions, and partly to vindicate the originality of some of the thoughts and views.

The examination of the philosophy of Dr. Thomas Brown will be observed to engross a prominent share in this compilation. The works of that remarkable writer seem destined to a higher rank amongst the productions of the nineteenth century than they have as yet generally assumed. Symptoms of returning justice in this respect have appeared in different quarters. Even whilst revising for the press this portion of the collection, the author was happy to recognize the lofty estimate placed on the writings of Dr. Brown, in the recently published conversations and letters of so competent an authority as Sydney Smith.

CHARLESTON, S. C., March 1, 1856.

CONTENTS.

POEMS.

CONTENTS.

MEMOIRS

OF

A NEW-ENGLAND VILLAGE CHOIR,

WITH

OCCASIONAL REFLECTIONS.

BY A MEMBER.

REVISED AND CORRECTED FROM THE THIRD EDITION.

"What though no cherubim are here displayed,
No gilded walls, no cedar colonnade,
No crimson curtains hang around our quire,
Wrought by the ingenious artisan of Tyre;
No doors of fir on golden hinges turn;
No spicy gums in golden censers burn;
If humble love, if gratitude inspire,
Our strain shall silence even the temple's quire,
And rival Michael's trump, nor yield to Gabriel's lyre."

Pierpont's Airs of Palestine.

MEMOIRS

OF

A NEW-ENGLAND VILLAGE CHOIR.

WISHING to present a sketch of manners in New England, and of some changes that have occurred in our taste for sacred music, I have presumed to adopt, for the purpose, a kind of desultory narrative.

The time when the few humble incidents occurred, which are recorded in the following pages, embraced about ten years, bordering upon the last and present centuries. The place was a village, situated not far from the river Merrimac; and for the sake of avoiding any invidious allusions or interpretations, I shall give to the town the fictitious name of Waterfield.

Many years had now elapsed, since any interruption, or indeed anything extraordinary, had happened to the music, that was barely tolerated in the meeting-house at Waterfield. At the period when our memoirs commence, the long established leader, Mr. Pitchtone, had just removed with his family to one of the new towns in the District of Maine, and the choir, which had been for some time in a decaying state, was thus left without any head, or any hope of keeping itself together.

For some Sundays after his departure, not an individual ventured to appear in the singing-seats. Young Williams, the eccentric and interesting shoemaker, who was an apprentice to his father, knew perfectly well how to set the tune, but he had not as yet acquired sufficient self-confidence to pass the leading notes round to the performers of different parts, nor to encounter various other kinds of intimidating notoriety attached to the office. The female singers, besides, had been so long and so implicitly accustomed to their late leader, that nothing could have induced them to submit to the control of so young and inexperienced a guide. And as no other member of the congregation possessed sufficient skill or firmness to undertake this responsible and conspicuous task, the consequence was, that nearly all the performers, at first, absented themselves, not only from the singing-gallery, but even from public worship. Most of them had been so long habituated to their elevated position, and their active duty in the place of worship, that they could not immediately undergo the awkwardness of sitting below among the congregation, and were not a little apprehensive of meeting the stares of mingled curiosity and reproach, which they knew would be directed towards them. In addition to these circumstances, many had not the heart to witness the embarrassment and pain which would naturally be created in the minister and his flock, by the anticipated chasm in the usual routine of worship. Two or three, however, of the more courageous in the late choir, ventured to attend church even on the first Sabbath after the removal of Mr. Pitchtone. They went, indeed, at a very early hour, for the purpose of avoiding notice, and took their seats in some unappropriated pews in a very distant and almost invisible quarter of the gallery.

The entire congregation having assembled, the clergyman waited some time for the accustomed appearance of the sons and daughters of sacred song. It is almost universally the practice, throughout our New England country churches, to commence public worship with the singing of a psalm or hymn. On the present occasion, no person being ostensibly ready to perform that duty, the minister began the services with the "long prayer." Yet, when this was concluded, an imperious necessity occurred of making at least the attempt to diversify and animate the business of the sanctuary, by an act of melody. Accordingly the Rev. Mr. Welby announced and read the psalm adapted to the subject of the sermon which was to succeed. Then, having waited a moment or two, during which a most painful silence and suspense pervaded the congregation, he began, in a voice naturally strong and clear, to sing the psalm alone, still keeping his usual standing position in the centre of the pulpit. Only one voice was heard to support him. It was that of the venerable deacon, who sat immediately beneath, and who hummed a broken kind of bass, without the accompaniment of words, there being scarcely a hymn-book in the lower part of the meeting-house. The same scene occurred in the afternoon, with the slight addition of a female voice in some part of the house, which lent its modest, unskilful, and half-suppressed assistance through the concluding portion of the hymn.

Matters went on nearly in this way for the space of

a month, at the end of which the singing began to improve a little, by the gradual return to church, though not to the singing-gallery, of the stragglers who had composed the late choir, and who were now willing to join in the vocal duties of worship under the auspices of the pastor. At length, when about six months had been thus dragged along, an occasion offered for a return to the deserted orchestra, in a manner which might somewhat shelter the mortification and inspire the confidence of the rallied choristers.

A Mr. Ebed Harrington, who had recently removed into the village for the purpose of studying medicine with the physician of the place, had some pretensions on the musical score. He was an unmarried man, of about the age of thirty years, and had been, until this period, a hard-working laborer on his father's farm, which was situated in an obscure township in New Hampshire. His complexion was of the darkest, his face exactly circular, his eyes small, black, and unmeaning, his form thick-set, and the joints of his principal limbs had been contracted by nature or use into inflexible angles of considerable acuteness. He defrayed the expenses of his board and medical tuition by laboring agriculturally the half of every day, for his teacher, Dr. Saddlebags. The other half of the day, and a large portion of the night, were industriously devoted by our incipient Esculapius to the study of his new-chosen profession, with the exception of a few evenings which he occasionally spent at different places in the neighborhood. It was on one of these visits that he found means to exhibit some imposing specimens of his abilities in the performance of sacred music. And having suggested that he had often taken the lead in the choir of his native parish, he almost immediately received a pressing invitation from some of the most active of the singers in Waterfield, to place himself at their head on the following Sabbath, and thus enable them to supply the lamented vacancy which existed in the apparatus of worship at their meeting-house.

The invitation was accepted. That quarter of the singing-seats devoted to the female sex was filled at an early hour, on the next Sabbath morning, by fair occupants, furnished generally each with her hymn-book, and waiting with some impatience for the other moiety of the choir to arrive, and for the services to begin. The body of male performers gradually assembled at one corner of the building, out of doors, and discussed several particulars relating to the important movement which was now about to take place. One difficulty that staggered the most of them was the manner in which Mr. Ebed Harrington, their new precentor, should be introduced into the singing-gallery. He himself modestly suggested the propriety of being conducted by some one of the gentlemen singers to the spot. But besides that there was not an individual in the circle who conceived himself clothed with sufficient authority, or who felt sufficient confidence in himself to enact so grave a ceremony, it appeared to be the general opinion, that Mr. Harrington, in virtue of his newly conferred office, should march into church at the head of the choir. While they were debating this point with no little earnestness, the time was sliding rapidly away. All the rest of the congregation, even to the last tardy straggler, had entered and taken their seats. An impatient and wondering stillness mantled over the whole assemblage within, and Mr. Welby was on the point of rising to announce the psalm, at the hazard of whatever consequences might ensue, when, by a sudden, spontaneous, and panic-like movement, which I cannot remember who of us began, the tuneful collection without suspended their debate, and rushed in a body into the front door of the meeting-house. Part of us turned off immediately into the right aisle, and part into the left. The stairs leading to the gallery were placed at the end of each of these aisles, at two corners of the building within, so that whoever mounted them was exposed to the view of the congregation. With a hurried and most earnest solemnity, the choristers made their trampling way up these stairs, and soon found themselves in a large octagonal pew in the centre of the front gallery, adjoining an oblong one already filled by the ladies. Each individual occupied the seat which he could first reach, and Mr. Harrington, without being offered the post of honor usually assigned the leader, was fain, in the general confusion and forgetfulness of the scene, to assume about four inches of the edge of a bench contiguous to the door of the pew. Here, while wiping from his brow, with a red dotted calico handkerchief, the perspiration which the anxieties and exertions of the moment had profusely excited, the voice of the clergyman in the pulpit restored him and his fellow-singers to the calm of recollection, and fixed all eyes around upon him as their legitimate guide.

The tune which he selected was well adapted to the hymn announced. Every body remembers "Wells." Mr. Harrington had forgotten to take a pitch-pipe with him to the place of worship, and there was accidentally no instrument of any kind present. He was therefore obliged to trust to his ear, or rather to his fortune, for the pitch of the initial note. The fourth note in the tune of Wells happens to be an octave above the first. Unluckily, Mr. Harrington seized upon a pitch better adapted to this fourth note than to the first. The consequence was, that in leading off the tune, to the words of "Life is the time," he executed the three first notes with considerable correctness, though with not a little straining; but in attempting to pronounce the word *time*, he found that nature had failed to accommodate his voice with a sound sufficiently high for the purpose. The rest of the tenor voices were surprised into the same consciousness. Here then he was brought to an absolute stand, and with him the whole choir, with the exception of two or three of the most ardent singers of the bass and treble, whose enthusiasm and earnestness carried them forward nearly through the first line, before they perceived the calamity which had befallen their head-quarters. They now reluctantly suffered their voices one after another to drop away, and a dead silence of a moment ensued. Mr. Harrington began again, with a somewhat lower pitch of voice, and with stepping his feet a little back, as if to leap forward to some imaginary point; but still with no greater success. A similar catastrophe to the former awaited this second attempt. The true sound for the word *time* still remained far beyond the utmost reach of his falsetto. In his third effort, he was more fortunate, since he hit upon an initial note, which brought the execution of the whole tune just within the compass of possibility, and the entire six verses were discussed with much spirit and harmony. When the hymn was finished, the leader and several of his more intimate acquaintances exchanged nods and smiles with each other, compounded of mortification and triumph,—mortification at the mistakes with which the singing had begun, and triumph at the spirited manner in which it was carried on and concluded. This foolish and wicked practice is indulged, in too many choirs, by some of the leading singers, who ought to set a better example to their fellow-choristers, and compose themselves into other than giggling and winking frames of mind, at the moment when a whole congregation are about to rise or kneel in a solemn act of praise and prayer.

The greater part of the interval between the first and second singing, which was occupied by the minister and the devout portion of his hearers in a high and solemn communion with the Deity, was devoted by Mr. Harrington and his associates above mentioned to turning over the leaves of the Village Harmony, and making a conditional choice of the tune next to be performed, according to the metre of the hymn which might be read. When the time arrived for their second performance, although Mr. Harrington was more happy than before in catching the true key-note of the air, yet, either from some deficiency of science in himself, or from a misapprehension on the part of those who sang bass, this important department of the choir began the hymn with a note which happened to be the most discordant of the whole scale. The consequence was dreadful to every one within hearing, who was afflicted with a good ear. Our Coryphæus interposed his authority to produce silence, by emitting through his teeth a loud and protracted Hush! After some little difficulty, they succeeded in starting fairly, and carried on the performance with due harmony of tones.

In the afternoon, Mr. Harrington was at his post as settled leader of the choir. It is true that he found himself surrounded by only about half the number of assistants who had attended the commencement of his vocal career in the morning. But no one had ventured to insinuate to him his incompetency, and several of the singers charitably ascribed his mistakes to the accidental absence of the pitch-pipe, and to the modest trepidation which naturally arose from his first appearance. His principal mistake, on the latter part of the day, was that of selecting a common-metre tune which ought to have been one in long metre. He perceived not his error until he arrived at the end of the second line, when, finding that he had yet two more syllables to render into music, he at first attempted to eke out the air by a kind of flourish of his own, in a suppressed and hesitating voice. But he was soon convinced that this would never do. Had he been entirely alone, he might in this way have carried the hymn through, trusting to his own musical resources and invention. But it was out of his power to inspire the other singers with the foreknowledge of the exact notes which his genius might devise and append to every second line. They, too, must try their skill to the same purpose, and while the whole choir, tenor, bass, and treble, were each endeavoring to eke out the line with their own efforts and happy flourishes, a tremendous clash of discord and chaos of uncertainty involved both the leaders and the led together. There was nothing in this dilemma, therefore, for him to do, except to stop short at once, and select a new tune.

This he did with much promptness and apparent composure, though that there was some little flutter in his bosom was evident from the circumstance that the tune he again pitched upon, contrary to all rules in the course of a single Sabbath, was "Wells,"—which, however, went off with much propriety, and with none of the interruptions that had marred its performance in the morning.

There are many of the thorough-bred sons of New England, whose perseverance it takes much greater discouragements to daunt than befell the precentorial efforts of Mr. Ebed Harrington on this memorable day. He regarded himself now as the fully instated leader of the choir in Waterfield; a function which he inflexibly maintained, through good report and through evil report, sometimes amidst almost entire desertion, and at other times with a very respectable band to follow his guidance, until his professional studies were completed, and he himself removed from the neighborhood, to plunge into some of the newly settled territories for an establishment, and introduce, perchance, the arts of healing and melody together. I have never heard one word of his destination or subsequent success.

The musical concerns of our parish were not involved in the same embarrassment after his departure, as after that of his predecessor. Young Williams had now increased in years, skill, and confidence. Nature had destined him to be a passionate votary of music. He was scarcely out of mere boyhood, before he grasped the violoncello—or, as we term it in New England, the bass-viol—with a kind of preternatural adroitness, and clung to it with a devoted and ardent perseverance, which very soon rendered him an accomplished performer. Every leisure hour, every leisure moment he could seize, were employed on this his favorite instrument. The first ray of morning was welcomed by the vibrations of its Memnonian strings. Many a meal was cheerfully foregone, that he might feed his ear and his soul with the more ethereal food to which his desires tended. Often too were his musical exercises protracted far beyond midnight, to the annoyance at first of his father's family, who soon, however, could sleep as well beneath the sounds of the lad's bass-viol, as if an Æolian harp were soothingly ringing all night at their windows. As he sat in the solitude of his chamber, a solitude sweetened by his own exquisite skill and the indulgence of his fond taste, he regarded not the cold of winter and not always the darkness of the night. He speedily made himself master of his darling science, as far as such an attainment was possible from the introductions to all the compilations of music within his reach, from Dobson's Encyclopædia,* and from such other appropriate books as the Waterfield Social Library and Mr. Welby's humble collection of miscellaneous literature might supply. His performance was the admiration of all the country round. His father's house was frequently visited for the single purpose of witnessing the display of his uncommon talents. Most willingly did he exhibit his powers before the representative to Congress, or Mr. Welby and his family, or a bevy of admiring girls, or a half-dozen ragged children, who were attracted from their plays in the streets and the fields, to be soothed and charmed and

---

* Dobson reprinted in Philadelphia the Encyclopædia Britannica, referred to in the text.

civilized into silence by our self-taught Orpheus. Now, he would draw tears from every eye by the tremulous and complaining pathos of the string as he wound through some mournful air. Now he would make every soul burn, and every cheek glow with lofty rapture, as he executed the splendid movements of Washington's March, Belleisle March, Hail Columbia, or the much less admirable, but equally popular Ode to Science. Now, by a seemingly miraculous rapidity and perfection of execution, he would exert an irresistible power over the muscular frames of his delighted auditors, putting their feet and hands in motion as they sat before him, and often rousing up the younger individuals who were present to an unbidden, spontaneous dance, to the tune of "The Girl I left behind me," the "Devil's Dream," or an equally magical and inspiring combination of notes that extemporaneously flowed into his own mind on the occasion. During all these scenes, his own fair countenance was rarely ever observed to alter in the least from a certain composed, though elevated and steadfast abstraction. Occasionally, however, the occurrence of a plaintive strain would throw a kind of compassionate softness into his looks, and some sublime movement of melody or new combination of harmony would fill his rolling eye with tears. The motion of his arm and the posture of his body were indescribably graceful. To some persons of extravagant fancy, he seemed, while playing upon his noble instrument, to be sitting on a cloud, that was wafting him about in the atmosphere of sounds which he created. Sometimes the viol and the bow appeared to be portions of himself, which he handled with the same dexterity that nature teaches the soul to exert over its own body. Sometimes agäin you would imagine him in love with the instrument, as if he had no other mistress in the world to fix his serious and impassioned looks upon, and be agitated by her enchantments. For several minutes he would lay his ear down near the strings, and then throw his body far back, and his eye upward, while, in this new position, his head kept time with a gentle motion, and with a sort of unconscious ease. He never refused to play the most common or indifferent air; a circumstance that resulted partly from his good nature, which would not suffer him to be fastidious or disobliging, and partly from his own conscious ability to make music out of a tune which of itself had small pretensions. Indeed, he was one of those few performers, who array in a new and peculiar dress every piece which they attempt to execute. Written notes before him were but a skeleton, which he not merely clothed with a body and animated with a life, but into which he infused a soul and an inspiration that none but the rarest geniuses on earth can cause to exist.

Such was the temporary successor to Mr., or now, more properly speaking, Dr. Ebed Harrington, in the government of the sacred choir at Waterfield. Charles Williams, as I have before observed, was as yet too young to take the lead in the melodious department of public worship, when that interesting and uncouth personage came to reside in the village. But it is very questionable whether the pretensions of the latter to his honorable office in the gallery would ever have been submitted to, during the two years that he remained, had he been destitute of the assistance rendered him by the musical young Crispin whom I have just introduced to my readers. Charles had been almost constantly at his post as leader of the bass, and performer on the violoncello. Sometimes, indeed, on a fine Sunday morning, late in May, or perhaps in midsummer, or early in October, he would take his instrument, and steal alone and unperceived to some retreat about two miles from the village. Here our truant genius would seat himself beneath an oak, and try the effect of mingling the audible sounds of his viol with the *felt* harmony of sunshine, breeze, and shade; interrupting for a moment or two the chirp of the squirrel and the Greek talk* of the blackbird, but then again stimulating them to a more violent little concert in company with his own instrument, and the long, ringing note of the grasshopper, as it hung suspended and motionless over the ground, amidst the calm glare of a burning sun. The delicious enjoyment afforded him by such occasions as these would have tempted him to very frequent indulgences of the kind, had not the music in the meeting-house suffered so much from his absence, and had he not been aware that such conduct was the cause of considerable uneasiness and half-reproachful regret among a large portion of the congregation. Blessed influence of Christian institutions, and of the severe forms of social life, that check the movements of selfishness and eccentricity, and recall the thoughtless wanderer back to the course of duty! Who can complain at the comparatively slight sacrifices which they enjoin, and at the contribution to the common stock of

---

* What schoolboy has not listened with delighted astonishment to the almost exact conjugation of something like a Greek verb, which the blackbird gives him in its Πολλω, πολω, πεπληκα? Has the nightingale itself a better title to Mr. Gray's compliment of "Attic warbler"?

happiness which they demand, in return for the protection, the field of exertion, the inexhaustible sources of enjoyment, and the paths to the attainment of every species of individual excellence, which they so abundantly furnish?

On the elevation of Charles Williams to the seat of leader of the choir, new life was infused into the whole vocal company. Years had done something for him since the period at which our history commences, but experience and the opening native energy of his mind had done much more. Implicit confidence was now reposed in his skill and management, even by the shyest member of the choir. He had occasionally supplied the accidental absence of Mr. Harrington, and had been constantly consulted by that gentleman with peculiar deference in all the business, and mystery, and apparatus, incident to the due administration of his office. It was even whispered round in the singing-pews, that Charles had often been happily instrumental in correcting or preventing several blunders on the part of his superior, not unlike those which I before recorded as distinguishing the outset of that gentleman's career.

With such qualifications, and such a reputation, Mr. Williams entered upon his dignities with the highest spirit and the best prospects of success. The choir was instantly replenished by all the old deserters and by many new recruits. Singing-meetings were appointed in private houses on two or three evenings of each week, for the purpose of practice and improvement. A large supply of the (then) last edition of the Village Harmony was procured, and the stock of good pieces, which all might familiarly sing, was enlarged. The whole number of performers was about fifty. This was one of those happy and brilliant periods, which all our New England churches occasionally enjoy for a longer or shorter term in the musical department of the sacred exercises. I will not contend that the psalms now went off with much science or expression. Charles Williams was fully equal to the task of infusing the best possible taste in these respects into the choir which he led. But he wisely felt that his authority did not extend quite so far at present as to warrant the attempt to introduce among them any nice innovations on the old-fashioned manner of vocal performance. He was not their teacher in the art. He was only one of themselves, and all he could expect to do was to yield himself to the general stream of musical taste and prejudice, with the exception of such little improvements as he hoped to effect by his sole example, or the communication of his ideas in private to some particular friends. He accordingly began and executed the most galloping fugues* and the most unexpressive airs with the same spirit and alacrity that he would have expended on the divinest strains of sacred music.

Notwithstanding, however, these slight unavoidable deficiencies, the present was, as I observed, a bright and happy period in the meeting-house at Waterfield. There was a full choir. It was punctual in its attendance at church. The singing, though a little noisy, was at least generally correct in time and tone. A new anthem was gotten up at the recurrence of each Fast and Thanksgiving Day, and funeral anthems were sung on the Sab-

* A fugue is a piece of music, in which the different parts start one after another, at the interval of a few notes.

bath that immediately succeeded any interment in the parish. There are few who will not acknowledge the luxury of such a state of things, when compared with the necessity of enduring, Sabbath after Sabbath, a feeble, poor, discordant band of singers, or listening to the performance of two or three scattered individuals among the congregation, who go through their duty with reluctance, and seem not so much to be singing praises as offering up substitutes and apologies.

Far different from such a picture were the achievements of our renovated choir. Every tune which they performed seemed to be a triumph over the preceding. Charles Williams was so much in his element, that he inspired all around him with the same feeling.

It is true, there were some peculiarities in the manners and customs of the choir, to which a fastidious stranger might object. In warm weather, Charles assumed the liberty of laying aside his coat, and exhibiting the perfection to which his sisters could bleach his linen, in which practice he was supported by about half the men-singers present. Another exceptionable habit prevailed among us. As soon as the hymn was read, and those ominous preluding notes distributed round, which come before the performance of a psalm-tune like scattering drops before a shower, that portion of the band which sat in front of the gallery suddenly arose, wheeled their backs round to the audience below, and commenced operations with all possible earnestness and ardor. Thus the only part of the congregation which they faced consisted of those who sat in the range of pews that ran along behind the singing-seats.

It was somewhat unnecessary, moreover, that each

individual performer should beat time on his own account. But this was a habit of inveterate standing in the church, which nothing short of the omnipotent voice of fashion could be hoped to frighten away. That voice was not yet heard to this effect in the singing-gallery at Waterfield. But it would have cost many an occupant there a pang to resign the privilege of this little display. Let Mr. D'Israeli and the editor of Blackwood's Magazine inspect the dispositions of men in their handwriting. But as a school for the study of character, give *me* a choir of singers, who are in the habit of beating time, each for himself. How could the most superficial observer mistake these characteristic symptoms? Here and there you might see a hand ostentatiously and unshrinkingly lifted above all surrounding heads, like the sublime and regular recurrence of a windmill's wings. Some performers there were, who studied an inexpressible and inimitable grace in every modification of motion to which they subjected their finger-joints, wrists, elbows, shoulders, and bodies. Some tossed the limb up and down with an energy that seemed to be resenting an affront. Others were so gentle in their vibrations, that they appeared afraid of disturbing the serenity of the circumambient air. Some hands swept a full segment of one hundred and eighty degrees; others scarcely advanced further than the minute-hand of a stop-watch at a single pulsation. The young student at law, the merchant's clerk, and a few others, whom fortune had exempted from the primeval malediction of personal toil, were at once recognized by the easy freedom with which they waved a hand that no sun had browned and the contact of no agricultural implement had roughened.

If, as we have seen, some of the singers were ostentatious in wielding an arm to its full extent, others were equally ostentatious in using only a finger, or a thumb and middle finger joined. To the honor of the choir, however, be it said, that there were several of its members, who performed the duty, which then was customary, of beating time, without any effort or affectation. It should also be ascribed to nothing more than a sense of propriety and laudable modesty, that a great part of the female singers kept time in no other way than by moving a forefinger, which hung down at their sides, and was almost concealed amidst large folds of changeable silk, or of glazed colored cotton cambric. To this a few of them added a slight motion of the head or body, while some of the married ladies openly raised and lowered their hands upon the hymn-books from which they sang.

In addition to the foregoing general imperfections, which prevented the congregation at Waterfield from witnessing the *beau ideal* of a sacred choir, it is to be lamented that there were others, which resulted not from common custom, but from individual peculiarities. The taste and knowledge of music, among all the performers, were far from being uniform. While some sang with great beauty of expression, and a nice adjustment to the sentiment of the happy modulations of a flexible voice, others made no more distinction between the different notes than did the printed singing-book itself, or any lifeless instrument that gives out the tone required with the same strength and the same unvaried uniformity on all occasions. Nothing, too, could be rougher than the stentorian voice of Mr. Broadbreast, and nothing more piercing than the continued shriek of the pale but enthusiastic Miss Sixfoot. I shall not disclose the name of the good man who annoyed us a little with his ultranasal twang, nor of another, who, whenever he took the true pitch, did so by a happy accident; nor of another, who had an ungainly trick of catching his breath violently at every third note; nor of several of both sexes, whose pronunciation of many words, particularly of *how*, *now*, &c., was dreadfully rustic, and hardly to be expressed on paper. Jonathan Oxgoad sang indeed much too loud, but that could have been forgiven him, had he not perpetually forgotten what verses were directed by the minister to be omitted; a neglect which, before he discovered his error, often led him half through an interdicted verse, much to the annoyance of the worthy pastor, the confusion of his fellow-singers, the vexation of the congregation, and the amusement and gratification of Jonathan's too good-natured friends.

There was also a culpable neglect among the male singers in providing themselves with a sufficient number of hymn-books. That it was not so on the other side of the choir, was partly owing to the delicate tact of women, which never suffers them to violate even the minor proprieties of time and place, and partly to their greater attachment to religion. As, in our New-England churches generally, we have no prayer-books to serve as a kind of endearing bond between the public and domestic altars, the vivid imagination and tender affection of the female singer caused her to cherish her hymn-book in such a connection. The more rough, careless, and indifferent habits of our own sex render us less attentive to these sensible memorials for the heart.

Accordingly, in our choir, among the men, the proportion of books was scarcely more than one to four or five performers, so that you might often hear some ardent and confident individual, who was stationed too far from the page to read distinctly, attempting to make out the sentence from his own imagination, or, when he despaired of achieving that aim, filling up the line with uncouth and unheard of syllables, or with inarticulate sounds. It is strange how some little inconveniences of this kind will be borne for a long time without an effort made for their remedy. It was not avarice which caused this deficiency of hymn-books; far from it; it was only the endurance of an old custom, which it occurred to no one to take the proper steps to remove. Was it not thirty years that Uncle Toby threatened every day to oil the creaking hinge that gave him so much anguish of soul,—and threatened in vain?

But I will no longer contemplate the shady points of my picture. On the whole, the blemishes just described were scarce ever offensively perceptible, when compared with the general merit with which the singing was conducted and continued to improve for the space of two or three years. Besides, our supply of good music was equal or superior to the demand. Be it remembered, that we were singing within wooden walls to the edification of an American country congregation, who sprang unmixed from Puritanical ancestors, and not beneath the dome of a European metropolitan cathedral.

It is impossible to look back without some of the animation of triumph upon those golden hours of my early manhood, when I stood among friends and acquaintances, and we all started off with the keenest alacrity in some favorite air, that made the roof of our native church resound, and caused the distant though unfrequent traveller to pause upon his way, for the purpose of more distinctly catching the swelling and dying sounds that waved over the hills and reverberated from wood to wood. The grand and rolling bass of Charles Williams's viol, beneath which the very floor was felt to tremble, was surmounted by the strong, rich, and exquisite tenor of his own matchless voice. And oh! in the process of a fugue, when the bass moved forward first, like the opening fire of artillery, and the tenor advanced next, like a corps of grenadiers, and the treble followed on with the brilliant execution of infantry, and the trumpet counter shot by the whole, with the speed of darting cavalry, and then, when we all mingled in that battle of harmony and melody, and mysteriously fought our way through each verse with a well-ordered perplexity, that made the audience wonder how we ever came out exactly together, (which once in a while, indeed, owing to some strange surprise or lingering among the treble, we failed to do,) the sensations that agitated me at those moments have rarely been equalled during the monotonous pilgrimage of my life.

And yet, when I remember how little we kept in view the main and real object of sacred music, — when I think how much we sang to the praise and honor and glory of our inflated selves alone, — when I reflect that the majority of us absolutely did not intend that any other ear in the universe should listen to our performances, save those of the admiring human audience below and around us, — I am inclined to feel more shame and regret than pleasure at these youthful recollections, and must now be permitted to indulge for a few moments in a more serious strain.

How large and dreadful is the account against numberless ostensible Christian worshippers in this respect! And how decisive might be the triumph of the Roman Catholics over Protestants, if they chose to urge it in this quarter! They might demand of us, what we have gained by greater simplicity and abstractness of forms. They might ask, whether it is not equally abominable in the sight of Jehovah, that music should be abused in his sanctuary, as that pictures and images should be perverted from their original design. For my part, I conscientiously think that there is more piety, more of the spirit of true religion, in the idolatry which kneels in mistaken, though heart-felt gratitude to a sculptured image, than in the deliberate mockery which sends up solemn sounds from thoughtless tongues. How often does what is called sacred music administer only to the vanity of the performer and the gratification of the hearer, who thus, as it were, themselves inhale the incense which they are solemnly wafting, though they have full enough need that it should ascend and find favor for them with the Searcher of all Hearts!

This is a rock of temptation which the Quakers have avoided; in dispensing with the inspiration of song, they at least shun its abuses; and if they really succeed in filling their hour with intense religious meditation and spiritual communion,—if, from their still retreat, the waves of this boisterous world are excluded, and send thither no disturbing ripple,—if no calculations of interest, and no sanguine plans, are there prosecuted, and no hopes, nor fears, nor regrets, nor triumphs, nor recollections, nor any other flowers that grow this side of the grave, are gathered and pressed to the bosom, on the margin of those quiet waters, — if, in short, the very silence and vacancy of the scene are not too much for the feeble heart of man, which, if deprived of the stay of external things, will either fall back on itself, or else will rove to the world's end to expend its restless activity in a field of chaotic imaginations; — if, I say, the Quakers are so happy as to escape these perils, together with the seductions to vanity and self-gratification which music and preaching present, then must their worship, I think, be the purest of all worship, and their absence of exterior forms the very perfection of all forms. But, let me ask of thee, my heart, whether *thou* couldst fulfil these severe conditions? Wouldst thou no longer obtrusively beat and ache beneath the external serenity of a Quaker's composed demeanor and unmodish apparel, and voiceless celebration? Thou shrinkest from the trial, and art still convinced that the road in which thou canst best be trained for heaven lies somewhere at an equal distance between the bewildering magnificence of the Romish ritual, and the barren simplicity of silent worship.

I have long doubted whether, in the prevailing musical customs among our New-England Independent churches, there be not something more unfavorable to the cause and progress of pure devotion, than can be charged against many other popular denominations. The Methodist, and the strict Presbyterian, have no separate choirs. They have not yet succeeded so far in the division of spiritual labor, as to delegate to others the business of praise, or to worship God by proxy. I have often witnessed a congregation of one thousand Methodists, as they rose simultaneously from their seats, and, following the officiating minister, who gave out the hymn in portions of two lines, joined all together in some simple air, which expressed the very soul of natural music. I could see no lips closed as far as I could direct my vision, nor could I hear one note of discord uttered. Was it that the heartiness and earnestness which animated the whole throng inspired even each tuneless individual with powers not usually his own, and sympathetically dragged into the general stream of harmony those voices which were not guided by a musical ear? or was it, that the overwhelming majority of good voices, such as, I presume, if exerted, would prevail in every congregation, drowned the imperfect tones, and the occasional inaccuracies of execution, which most probably existed? It did not offend me that they sang with all their might, and all their soul, and all their strength; for it was evident that they sang with all their heart. I was conscious of hearing only one grand and rolling volume of sound, which swallowed up minor asperities and individual peculiarities. This was particularly the case after two or three verses were sung, when the congregation had been wrought into a kind of movement of inspiration. Then the strains came to my ear with the sublimity of a rushing mighty torrent, and with an added beauty of melody that the waters cannot give. The language was still distinctly intelligible, and the time perfectly preserved. And although, when I retired from the scene, I could not say how expressively this chorister had sung, nor how exquisitely the other had trilled, nor could compliment a single lady on her golden tones, nor criticise the fine science of the counterpoint, yet I felt that I had been thrilled and affected in a better way, and could not but wish that what was really to be approved of among the Methodists might be imitated in those happier churches, where religion is cultivated without protracting her orgies into midnight, and cordially embraced without the necessity of delirious screams and apoplectic swoons.*

Perhaps it may be thought that the good old Presbyterian way of accompanying a clerk, or precentor, who is stationed beneath the pulpit, in front of the congregation, will most generally secure the true spirit and perfection of sacred music. Born and nurtured an independent as I am, I confess that I sometimes feel inclined to the adoption of this opinion, with a few additions and modifications. There is certainly an advantage in imposing upon a single individual the business of leading the melodious part of public devotion. It must necessarily constrain the congregation to unite their voices with his, unless they are totally lost to all sense of the proprieties of the sanctuary. This custom, moreover, must exclude those miserable feuds and other sources of interruption, which will always to a greater or less degree disturb a separately constituted choir.

But in conceding thus much to the children of the Westminster Assembly, I would beg leave to be strenuous in insisting upon a recommendation that may appear very strange as coming from a disciple of John Robinson. I cannot find it in my soul to dispense with

---

* I am happy to testify that these features are growing far less characteristic of the Methodist denomination, than they were at the first publication of The Village Choir.

the glorious majesty of sound with which an organ fills the house of prayer. In the tones of this sublime trophy of human skill, there is something that wondrously accords with the sentiment of piety. We know that martial bravery, love, joy, and other feelings of our nature, have each their peculiar and stirring instruments of sound. The connection between religion and the organ, too, is something more than fanciful. Who has not felt at once inspired and subdued by the voice issuing from that gilded little sanctuary, which towers in architectural elegance over the solemn assembly below, and seems to enshrine the presiding genius of devotional praise?

I am aware that even the united aid of a precentor and organ is insufficient to check certain tendencies to the decline of good singing, which may insidiously creep into a whole musical congregation with the lapse of time. Tunes, it may be said, grow old, and weary the ear; wretched voices may prevail over the better sort; in one pew, a worshipper may always sing the tenor part in a voice of the deepest bass; in another pew, every psalm may be screamed through with one whole note out of the way; a devotion like that of the Methodists, which often seems to make them sing decently in spite of themselves, must not be expected to continue long; a fashion of indifference towards this department of worship may arise and prevail; and especially, the extensive cultivation of secular music in private families may render very many ears so fastidious, as absolutely to frustrate the object of sacred music at church, since the tasteless and indiscriminate clamor necessarily produced by the voices of a mixed congregation must tend to excite in the more refined classes a disgusted and indevout spirit, rather than the sweet and lofty aspirations of choral praise. On all these accounts, it may possibly be argued that our later ancestors have done well in withdrawing from the general congregation the performance of this service, and assigning it to a select choir, who, by concentrating their efforts, and reducing the matter to something of a profession, may keep the stream of sacred song at least pure, though small.

Nearly all these sinister tendencies, however, might, I apprehend, be counteracted by the application of a little care and system. To prevent the repetition of old tunes from palling on the ear, a new one might occasionally be introduced by the clerk, and sung every Sabbath until the congregation were familiar with it. The affliction caused by bad voices might be disposed of by the appointment of a musical censor, or standing committee, whose duty it should be to exercise now and then an act of delicate authority, acquainting the well-meaning offenders with the fact of their vocal disability, and requesting from them in future an edifying silence. As to the decay of devotion, and the increase of indifference among a congregation, these appear to me to be far from good reasons for establishing a separate choir, and are rather proofs that such a choir will effect no sort of good. With respect to the last evil which a select choir is supposed to avoid, the fastidiousness occasioned by the private and profane cultivation of musical taste, I know not why a whole congregation, or at least all the efficient voices in it, may not be systematically taught good church music, and the best and purest taste be made general among them.

But I will candidly allow that some of these schemes of improvement are rather visionary than practical. Sitting at home in one's office, one can easily devise remedies for existing social defects, but in attempting to put them into execution, the science of human nature is found to be ten times more embarrassing than hydrostatics itself. Some obstinate pressure from an unsuspected quarter may burst over the feeble mounds which we are fondly erecting about an imaginary reservoir of beauty and tranquillity. It is a very enchanting employment of the mind to draw sketches of a kind of abstract congregation, where every one present joins in the prayer, and listens profitably to the sermon, and keeps constantly awake, and takes devout part in the psalmody, and where no eye is suffered to wander, nor attention to flag, nor worldly dreams to intrude. But where is there such a congregation on earth? And would even a Handel succeed in tutoring a mixed audience into a celestial choir of angels? On these accounts, I am not disposed to push my censures on my native communion too far. Perhaps novelty and imagination have done a little in recommending to me the practices of other churches, and if I were familiar with the whole history of their musical condition, I might tell as many strange stories of them as I am rehearsing of my own. I am not sufficiently read in Puritanical antiquarianism to know whether the Independents once resembled the Presbyterians in the mode of conducting sacred music, and afterwards found it necessary in the course of time to institute distinct choirs, or whether they on purpose instituted a custom diametrically opposite to that of their rival sectaries, after the fashion in which these last had themselves abolished surplices and organs. Neal* is silent on these curious points. If one may judge from some merry traditions prevalent in New England, our good forefathers had no choirs, but sang under the dictation of one and sometimes two lines at a time from the minister or a clerk. Most of us have heard of singular divisions to which poor Sternhold and Hopkins were subjected by this custom. Thus,

> "The Lord will come, and he will not
> Keep silence, but speak out,"

used to make perplexing sense to the pilgrims, when given out to them by a line at a time; for that such was the manner of uttering it, I have understood from a clergyman who learned it at a Massachusetts Convention dinner twenty years ago, where the agreeable and Orthodox Dr. ——— set the table in a roar by relating the anecdote. It is probable, then, that experience and necessity, in the lapse of time, have forced upon our congregations the present universal custom of assigning to a few individuals the task of leading the praises in public worship. It might now be dangerous, or rather impracticable, to introduce a reformation. If imperfections exist, perhaps they are a choice of the least. Yet still it were to be wished that the choir might not be regarded, so much as it is, the sole medium through which this portion of worship is offered. It were to be wished that our audiences would consider that body as leaders only, not performers; to be followed and accompanied, not to be listened to for luxurious gratification, or fastidious criticism, or as an eked-out variety of the tedious busi-

* Historian of the Puritans.

ness of a Sunday. I can conceive that a choir, if properly instituted and administered, might be exceedingly useful in extending and preserving a true tone of taste, in keeping up a good selection of sacred music, and in acting, so to speak, as the teachers of the congregation, in these and kindred respects. But in the very duty thus prescribed them lies their deplorable danger and temptation. They are unavoidably liable, as was above intimated, to resolve the matter into a mere profession. In the study of sacred music as a science, and the cultivation of it as an art, they forget its ultimate object. Nor could much else be expected from the narrowness of the human mind. Must it not be hard to attend to the thousand little circumstances which a skilful performance requires, and at the same time to keep the heart strained up to a pitch of due devotion? And on the supposition that by practice and habit we can acquire a perfect familiarity with the pieces to be performed, and a mutual confidence can be obtained among all the members of the choir; yet, alas! it is in the very process of cultivating this practice and habit, that the spirit of devotion is apt to evaporate, and to leave us admirable performers rather than cordial worshippers.

This state of things, moreover, has its temptations for the audience at large. The more beautiful the music, the greater is their inclination to listen and admire, rather than to bear a part. It seems a kind of sacrilege to let my indifferent voice break in upon the divine strains which are charming my ear. But the real sacrilege is in my refraining from the duty. Probably, about the most perfect and affecting sacred music in this country is that at the Andover Theological Seminary. Yet who, in listening to the exquisite anthem sung at the anniversary of that institution, does not find himself unconsciously betrayed into an earthly ecstasy of weeping admiration, in which, on analysis, he is surprised and ashamed to find that mere religion has but little, if any, share?

Such always have been and always will be the dangers resulting from the conversion of taste and the arts into handmaids of religion. Perpetual efforts are requisite to keep them from becoming her mistresses at last. I appeal to the consciences of hundreds of congregations, who are in the habit of sitting, Sabbath after Sabbath, with Epicurean complacency, and silently listening to the music above them, as to a gratuitous and pleasant entertainment. I appeal with more confidence to the consciences of a thousand choirs, who are engrossed in the anxious business of carrying a psalm off well, and are distracted with numerous likings and antipathies about different tunes, whether they do not commonly feel cut off, as by a kind of professional fence, from the devotional sympathies and sacred engagements of the congregation in general. Sharing no active or conspicuous part in the other services, but so very active and conspicuous a part in *one*, is it not the case, that they take little, if any, interest in the former, and regard them rather in the light of a foil to set off their own paramount achievements, than as a votive wreath, into which it is their privilege, duty, and felicity to weave a humble flower?

Sorry I am to acknowledge that such were the predominant feelings in the choir at Waterfield at that point of time in its history from which I have been led insensibly so far away by a dull train of digressive reflections.

It is impossible to say how much of this defective sentiment may have been owing to the circumstance of our leader being a gay and rather inconsiderate young man, whom the whole of us were constrained to admire for his musical excellence and many parts of his private character. Certain it is, that Charles Williams had no other holier aspiration or thought at that time, than to acquit himself with applause as the chief of a vocal company. In every other respect, his example would scarcely be recommended on the score of seriousness or piety. A little knot of whisperers was often gathered round him during both the prayer and the delivery of the sermon, who began, perhaps, with discussing some points connected with the common business of the choir, but generally suffered the conversation to stray among still less appropriate and less excusable topics, until the occurrence of a jest or witticism from Charles betrayed them into something more than a smile, and reduced them to the necessity of separating from each other, in order to escape violating the more obvious decencies of the place.

Then, again, it ought not to have been Charles Williams, of all persons, who scribbled with a lead pencil upon every blank leaf of every hymn-book and singing-book within his reach, filling them with grinning caricatures, with ridiculous mottoes, and with little messages to the adjoining pew, some of the occupants of which would blush, when they found themselves glancing with greater eagerness at these irregular and unseasonable *billets doux*, than listening to more edifying productions from the pulpit.

And adieu to the composure of that fair chorister for one morning at least, to whom Charles Williams presented a bunch of dill, a pleasant little herb, resembling caraway, and common in the gardens of New England, the taste of whose aromatic seeds often serves in summer to beguile some forlorn moments that will occur to many attendants at the meeting-houses of this blessed land, as well as elsewhere. Not that a gallant attention of this kind from the hands of my youthful hero occasioned sufficient perturbation in the mind of the receiver to drown her voice and prevent her from performing her part in the musical services. On the contrary, such an incident generally had the effect of inspiring her with more than usual animation, loudness, and expressiveness in her singing, the cause of which could be conjectured by none save such as happened to unite to an accidental observation a sagacious philosophy. No other obvious symptoms of agitation were allowed to escape her watchful self-possession, except perhaps neglecting to keep her snow-white pocket-handkerchief folded up as neatly as usual by the side of her hymn-book, and an inability to recollect the text when she was examined by her decrepit grandmother at home.

Nor were these favors on the part of our leader, in general, very discriminating or partial with respect to their objects. If Charles's bass-viol could have enjoyed a posy of dill, it would often, undoubtedly, have been a successful rival of his more conscious and susceptible mistresses for such attentions. The time had not yet arrived for the tenderest of all passions to become also the most overwhelming and absorbing in his soul. He had indeed too much constitutional sensibility not to find on his hands a succession of weekly or monthly idols of his imagination; but at the same time he had too much juvenile carelessness and too triumphant a presentiment of many exploits yet to be achieved by his genius for music, to allow any very deep and lasting impressions on his heart. Music, praise, and beauty were to him equally intoxicating subjects of contemplation; he had not yet had enough of the first two, to admit of his yielding himself entirely up to the influence of the last.

From the few sketches I have already given of the character of this young man, it will not excite surprise in my readers to learn that his parents, his friends, and himself entertained the wish of changing his present sphere and prospects in life. So much notice had been taken of him in various ways; his general capacity and activity were so conspicuous; and there was something about him so interesting, apart from his eminence as a young musical performer, that it seemed to be almost a defiance of Providence to confine him to the obscure profession of a sedentary mechanic.

I use not the word *ignoble*, nor any other term of disparagement or contempt, as applicable to that vocation. I am too sturdy an American for that. Happily, in our country, we have scarcely a conception of what the epithet *ignoble* signifies, except in a purely moral point of view. The aristocratical pride of Europe accounts for this, by insisting that we are all plebeians together, and of course that distinctions of rank among us are ridiculous. Our own pride, of which we have our full share, accounts for the circumstance on the opposite hypothesis, that we are a nation of high-born noblemen. But this is a poor dispute about names. The truth is, we are neither a nation of noblemen nor plebeians. How can such correlative terms be applied with any shadow of correctness, when the very political relations which they imply do not exist? It is using a solecism to call Americans plebeians, because to that class belongs the conscious degradation of witnessing above them, in the same body politic, an order of men born to certain privileges of which they are destitute by birth themselves. And for a similar reason, it is equally a solecism to regard ourselves, even metaphorically, as noblemen.

Why then did Charles Williams and his friends desire him to emerge from the calling in which his youth had been passed? O, we Americans have our *preferences!* We think it an innocent and a convenient thing to draw arbitrary lines of distinction between different pursuits; otherwise, the circle of one man's acquaintance would often be oppressively large. It is a pleasant employment, too, to clamber over these distinctions in life. Perhaps there is not a country in the world, where occupations are so often changed as in America. We are restless and proud, and since our civil institutions have established no permanent artificial gradations among us, we have devised them ourselves. Yet still it is a matter which we act upon rather than talk about. No American lady would dare to refuse her neighbor's invitation professedly on the score of the other being beneath her in society. Yet her refusal would be as prompt and decided as any lady's in England, towards an inferior in rank.

I do not wish to analyze too minutely the aristocratical leaven among us. I do not exactly understand its principle of operation myself. Pedigree it certainly is not, though that perhaps is one of its elements. Wealth and education have something to do with it. Different vocations in life have much more. Various degrees of softness and whiteness of the hands are perhaps as good criterions as anything. Certain sets of persons do somehow contrive to obtain an ascendency in every town and village. But in the present state of society in our country, this whole subject is extremely unsettled. The mass is fermenting, and how the process will result eventually, time only can decide. Probably some future court calendar will rank among the first class of American citizens all families descended in lines, more or less direct, from former presidents of the nation, heads of departments, governors of States, presidents of colleges, Supreme Court judges, commodores, and general officers. The second class may comprehend the posterity of members of Congress, circuit and state judges, clergymen, presidents of banks, professors in colleges, captains of national vessels, leaders of choirs, and perhaps some others. I have no curiosity to speculate upon inferior classes, nor to determine any further the order in which far distant dinners shall be approached by eaters yet unborn, or future balls shall be arranged at Washington.*

It is a difficult thing to say precisely how much my hero was actuated by mere ambition in his wish to change his course of life. I do not think he despised his paternal employment. *He* had not much reason

* The London Quarterly Review (1835), in commenting on some sentences in the two paragraphs above, which it had somewhere or other picked up, takes them quite *au sérieux*, and makes them the occasion of a grave and rather ill-natured attack on the character of American society!

himself to complain of the proud man's contumely, in his own native village. But there were two strong reasons, besides those before specified, which operated in his father's mind to determine him on the project of dismissing his son from his present occupation. One was, that he was a very unprofitable apprentice. His passion for his favorite art encroached too largely on his time. A round of visits and frolics, to which his musical and campanionable qualities exposed him, absorbed the latter portion of many an afternoon in preparations of dress, and the former part of many a morning in sleeping away the effects of such expeditions. The other reason was, that it seemed to be cruel to confine the lad down to an employment for which he had no inclination, and even no mechanical aptitude. There was little chance of his ever procuring a generous livelihood in that employment, and there were other professions more suited to his excursive and occasionally bookish disposition. These would have been sufficient reasons for his father to make the experiment of some other course of life for his son, more conformable to his taste and character, even if paternal vanity had not whispered into his ear, that his boy was born for very great things yet!

In New England, before the imposition of the Embargo, and in times of peace, there were two ways of rising very high in the world. The one was, to become the clerk of some wholesale or retail merchant in Boston, and the other, to pass through a college. No aspiring lad throughout the country could think of any other avenue to distinction. Charles Williams was not a lover of money or of trade. He was among the very few youths of his native region, who arrive at the age of thirteen without bartering a penknife, or at that of nineteen without cheating or being cheated in the exchange of watches. Accordingly, though he had a distant relative in Boston, who, while yet a minor, had gone four times every year to the market of that metropolis, with a cart full of such assorted commodities as were produced in his native town, and was now one of the wealthiest merchants on the Exchange, Charles obstinately shut his eyes to the prospect of entering this gentleman's counting-house. There was something in literary pursuits much more congenial to the taste and habits of his mind.

With all his follies and eccentricities, he had a warm friend and admirer in the Rev. Mr. Welby, who was for sending *every* young man of the most ordinary capacity to college, that had a soul sufficiently large even barely to meditate on such a purpose. Not that Mr. Welby's object, exactly, was to swell the list of liberally educated persons belonging to the place where he was settled, whenever he should communicate to the Massachusetts Historical Society the topographical and antiquarian account of the town of Waterfield. The propensity in question rather seemed to be with him a kind of weakness, and one, too, with which many of his profession in New England are afflicted. Owing their own importance in life, and their peculiar opportunities for usefulness, to their collegiate education, they have no idea that any greater blessings under the skies can be conferred on an unmarried man, of whatever talents, and at whatever age, than causing him to leave the plough or the workshop, and, after a struggle of seven years between the Latin dictionary and despair, to obtain a degree. It is not surprising, therefore, that the warm-hearted Mr. Welby should offer to become Charles's gratuitous instructor in preparing him for college,—an offer which was gratefully accepted.

Although our hero was far from being so apt a scholar in the niceties of the Greek and Latin tongues, as we have already seen him in the science of music, yet the novelty and dignity of the pursuits which he had now adopted, the definite object proposed for him to accomplish, and the shame of abandoning his aim in defeat, unitedly prompted him to undergo one or two years of pretty severe application to study. During this time he was still a leader of the village choir, though I cannot say that the partial change in his private life and habits operated in correcting many of those reprehensible characteristics which I have before lamented as derogatory to our singing-pew.* And although we had been long taught to anticipate his departure, yet words can scarcely represent the sorrow and dismay with which we bade him farewell on the Sabbath before his setting off for Dartmouth College.

On the next morning at daybreak, a few of us were at his father's threshold to shake hands with him once more. He had already breakfasted, and had mounted the horse which was purchased for the occasion, to be disposed of again, on the best terms possible, when he

* I had some thoughts of describing a few of the effects which Charles's new mode of life, and new topics of consciousness and aspiration, produced on his behavior in private company; but the sketch might clash a little with a picture of a young farmer fitting for college, which now lies by me in an unfinished manuscript history of a country academy in New England, and which may possibly hereafter be presented to the public.

should have entered college. A huge pair of saddlebags, the heirloom of his family for several generations, hung across the horse behind, and contained some changes of wearing-apparel, together with his books, and various articles of pastry for the road, which he owed to the care of his sisters, and some of their female friends. He had already repeated his salutations to his moist-eyed family and acquaintances, and was holding the reins in his left hand ready to start, when, at a signal from him, I reached him his bass-viol, enclosed in a large leathern case made by his good father for the purpose. He received it in his trembling right hand with a look, gleaming through his agitated countenance, which seemed to say, I leave not *every* friend behind,—and spurred off his horse up the margin of the river.

"And who was the next leader of the choir?" is a question, which, (may I humbly hope?) these memoirs have excited sufficient interest for my susceptible readers to propose. With great diffidence I am persuaded to answer, that it was their humble servant. Who or what I am, separately from my once having discharged the honorable function just mentioned, it is of no sort of consequence to know, and it is clear from my anonymous title-page, that I do not think the knowledge would contribute to the eclat of my humble production. If any lines in the following portrait of myself appear to be favorably drawn, let not vanity be ascribed to the act, while I seek to hide the original, and even his very name, from the public gaze.*

* The Village Choir, in former editions, was published anonymously. There were no real grounds, therefore, to ascribe to the author the incidents and attributes enumerated in the text. In fact, he never was the

Previously to the departure of my friend Charles Williams, I had acted as player of clarionet to the choir; not, I fear, always with the greatest reputation; for I scarcely remember a Sunday of my performance, when my instrument did not at least once through the day betray itself into a hideous squeak, as involuntary on my part as if there had been a little evil spirit within the tube, sent there to tempt and torment me. At these agonizing moments, I would cast one glance at the countenance of Charles Williams, and, finding that there was in that image of native civility no mark of fretful reprehension or of tittering infirmity, I proceeded in my part; — nor do I know how I discovered that my fellow-singers were not quite so composed as their leader, unless it were, that while, from alarm and mortification, my face was reddening, and my perspiration flowing, my eyes were enlarged from the same cause, and thus extended the sphere of their lateral vision. But I am no optician, and hazard nothing on this point beyond conjecture. I believe it was instinct that prevented me, on such occasions, from seeing so far as into the adjoining pew. There was one face there, on which, if I had ever seen a smile approaching to derision, I know that it would have broken my heart.

But if I do not deceive myself, the squeak in my clarionet was the only ridiculous thing about me, and was probably but the more amusing from its striking contrast to the general gravity of my deportment. On aying aside, therefore, this instrument of my little dis-

---

leader of a choir in his life, nor ever played on the clarionet, and only introduced his *nominis umbra* to enlarge the dynasty of his choristers, and to complete the varied and veritable history of a Village Choir.

graces, which was a necessary step towards my leading the choir with effect and energy, I trust I had no enormous disqualifications for the office. The authority of Charles had been sustained solely by his transcendent musical talents; mine, I felt, was to be preserved by the most exemplary demeanor, and an assiduous attention to my duty. I could only boast of a mediocrity in musical knowledge and vocal execution. If I was far below my predecessor in accomplishments requisite for the office, I at least avoided the mistakes into which Mr. Harrington had been often plunged. Until a calamitous concurrence of circumstances, soon to be rehearsed, not an individual, I think, left the choir during my administration, with the exception of those whom death or removal out of town subtracted from our number. I loved the office, for it gave me a little importance, and I was, at that time, of no great account in the parish in other respects. Besides, I was extremely attached to public worship, and to all its hallowed decencies, thinking it an honor to exercise the superintendence over so important a department as that assigned to me. With regard to punctuality at meeting, (for so we all call *church* in New England,) the minister himself never outstripped me in that particular. He has more than once, on a stormy day, without commencing service, dismissed my single self, together with one other parishioner, who appeared at meeting only in such weather, and came then, as he whimsically alleged, *to fill up;* and often, on some of our terribly cold and snowy Sundays, when seven or eight worshippers in leggins* would

* A sort of cloth boot used to protect the legs against snow.

well-nigh drown the preacher's voice with the prodigious knocking and stamping of their feet, I was found alone at my post in the singing-gallery, suffering in perfect silence the agony of my frost-bitten extremities, and permitting my attention to be no farther diverted from Mr. Welby, than now and then in watching the dense volumes of congealed vapor, that were breathed out from a few scattered pews in the almost vacant edifice.

So far as I can impartially judge, I was one of the most peaceable and unpretending of men. I gave out always, without the least hesitation, whatever tune was suggested to me by any individual in the choir, sacrificing with pleasure my own little preferences, and what is more, the pride of authority, to the gratification of others. Perhaps the general manners of the choir were improved during my precentorship. Let me with modesty say, and with deference to the shade of my dear friend Charles, who is now no more, that my own example probably contributed to some slight amendment in our body after his departure. I had long since formed a secret resolution in my breast, that no old man in the congregation should be more attentive to the services than myself, and I carried it into effect. This naturally influenced a few of my immediate companions to adopt a similar deportment; and the good order of the rest of the choir suffered at most only a negative violation, from the sleep of some, and the studies of others, who preferred looking over the tunes of the Village Harmony, or reading the everlasting Elegy on Sophronia,* or amusing themselves with the inscriptions

* This Elegy was set to music by I know not whom, and continued to be inserted in some dozen editions of the Village Harmony.

of their late leader, to receiving the benefits which might have been derived from Mr. Welby's excellent sermons.

After a year had glided away very nearly in this manner, some sensation was produced in the choir and congregation, and, ultimately, some disturbance occasioned to my own peace and happiness, by the addition of a gentleman to our number, who, on several accounts, had no small pretensions. He was the preceptor of an academy, situated, if I recollect right, not more than ten miles from the town of Waterfield. He was paying his addresses to a young lady of this last-mentioned place, and therefore seized on the opportunities which a remission of his duties every Saturday afternoon allowed him, to visit the object of his affections. The Sabbath, of course, was spent by him in our village, and, as he was a professed admirer and performer of sacred music, and was a gentleman of liberal education, genteel though forward manners, and a superior style of dress for a country town, he was soon introduced into the singing-pew, and without the least difficulty found a seat at my left hand. Being blest with a happy degree of modest assurance, it did not require a second invitation for him to assume habitually the same place afterwards, as a matter of course.

On the very first Sabbath that he joined us, he started me a little by requesting that *Old Hundred* might be sung to a psalm which the minister had just begun to read. I told him that I should be very glad to oblige him by announcing that tune to the choir, but the truth was, it had not been performed in our meeting-house probably for thirty years;—that there were but four or five singers who were acquainted with it, being such only as had chanced to hear it sung at home by their fathers or grandfathers, and that those few had only practised it once or twice together and in private, from mere curiosity to ascertain how so celebrated a piece of musical antiquity would sound.

"O, if there are four or five," replied Mr. Forehead, (the name of my lofty new acquaintance,) "who know anything of Old Hundred, by all means let us have it. I beg it, sir, as a particular favor, and will give you my reasons for the request after service."

My prevailing disposition to oblige, and the great quantity of time already consumed in our conversation, imposed upon me now the necessity of pronouncing aloud, as was usual just before beginning to sing, the name of this venerable air. No sooner had the word proceeded from my mouth, than there appeared to be a motion of keen curiosity among the congregation below, but in the choir around me there reigned the stillness of incredulity and surprise. All the elder members of the flock, I could observe, looked upwards to the gallery, with the gleams of pleasurable expectation in their countenances. Of our well-filled orchestra, only eight individuals arose, for there were no more among us who possessed the least acquaintance with Old Hundred. And even three out of that number were as ignorant of it as those who continued seated, but ventured to expose themselves, trusting to the assistance they might derive from the voices of the other performers, and from the score of the tune itself, contained in some, though I think not in all, of the copies of the Village Harmony which were present.

The psalm was sung with tolerable correctness; but

accompanied with *such* a fanning on the part of the females, who were all sitting, and *such* a whispering among those of the correlative sex who were unemployed, that I could bode nothing but disturbance and unhappiness for a long time to come in our choral circle.

During the reading of the next psalm, while Mr. Forehead was alarming me with a recommendation to sing St. Martin's, four stout acquaintances of my own pressed forward and whispered with an earnestness that carried the sound over every part of the edifice, "Sing New Jerusalem!" New Jerusalem, therefore, I appointed to be sung, and thus prevented, as I make no sort of question, more than three quarters of the singers from leaving their seats vacant in the afternoon.

At the close of the morning service, I had the promised interview and explanation with my new acquaintance. It seems that since leaving college he had been reading law for a year in an office at one of our seaport towns, and while there had occasionally assisted in the choir of some congregation, into which had been introduced a new and purer taste for sacred music than generally prevailed through the rest of the country. In that choir, as he informed me, no tunes of American origin were ever permitted to gain entrance. Fugues there were a loathing and detestation. None but the slow, grand, and simple airs which our forefathers sang found any indulgence. Mr. Forehead assured me that no other music was worth hearing, and what seemed to weigh particularly with him was the circumstance, that the slow music in question was beginning to be in the fashion. It was under the operation of these ideas that he had been so strenuous in forcing upon our choir the performance of Old Hundred and St. Martin's, in defiance of our helpless ignorance of both of them.

It appeared to me that his zeal on this point was carrying him too far; I saw in his aims quite as strong workings of a conscious superiority in taste and of the fastidious arrogance of fashion, as a love for genuine and appropriate music. I could not but question, too, the propriety of suddenly and violently forcing upon a choir and congregation a species of music to which they were entirely unaccustomed. It occurred to me, besides, that though the most slow and solemn tunes might be executed with good effect when sustained by the accompaniment of an organ, yet it was scarcely judicious to confine the whole music of a *vocal* choir entirely or even principally to that kind alone. But all these suggestions were of no avail in convincing my opponent, and we parted with not the kindest opinions and feelings respecting each other.

In the course of a month, Mr. Forehead's argument, persuasion, and example wrought in a large portion of the choir a very considerable change of taste on this subject. There were some who loved novelty; there were others who yielded to the stranger's assurances respecting the fashionableness of the thing; and there was a third description, who were really convinced of the better adaptation of the ancient tunes to the purposes of worship, and had a taste to enjoy their solemn and beautiful strains. All these classes composed perhaps about a moiety of the choir, and were eager for the introduction of the good old music. The other half were extremely obstinate and almost bigoted in their opposition to this measure, and in their attachment to the existing catalogue of tunes. Disputes now ran high amongst us. Most of us took sides on the question with an inexcusable warmth, and without any attempt at compromise.

I know of nothing more unconquerable and spiteful than the bickerings of a divided choir while they last. In addition to all the ordinary exacerbations of party spirit, there is a most unpardonable offence committed by each side in suspecting the good taste of the other. Thus vanity is wounded to its deepest core, and conscience and conviction are fretted into a fierce perseverance, which is not at all diminished by the circumstance, that the parties must sit, act, and sing in the closest contact, and almost breathe into each other's faces.

In the midst of this unhappy musical commotion, there was one individual who had the good fortune to remain thus far entirely neuter. It was, reader, the humble historian of these transactions,—the afflicted leader of that agitated band. I had long wished, together with my friend Charles Williams, that a better style of music might prevail among us. But we felt that we had neither skill nor authority to effect the exchange. If the tares should be torn up, we knew that the wheat would be liable to come with them. My private opinion, as well as general disposition, led me, therefore, to be as quiescent as possible amid the difficulties now existing. I did not, as I believe, escape all censure from either party, but I received no bitter treatment from any one. Due deference and acknowledgment still continued for some time to be paid me as leader, except perhaps from the pragmatical stranger. But no efforts or prudence on my part could prevent the explosion which was ultimately to ensue.

When it was found that Mr. Forehead had sufficient influence to intróduce a few of his favorite tunes on the settled and customary catalogue, and that the matter had proceeded to something more than a simple experiment, the admirers of fugues looked upon themselves as a beaten party, and took occasion, when two of the obnoxious airs had happened to be given out by me on one Sunday morning, to absent themselves altogether from worship in the afternoon. My feelings in this predicament are not to be described. I regarded myself as a principal cause of this deplorable feud, and lamented that I had not had sufficient strength of mind to resist the encroachments of the active gentleman at my left hand. But the standard was now raised, and war was declared. I felt that it would be ignominious to quit my post. I gave up for a time my arguments with Mr. Forehead on the propriety of singing slow tunes altogether. No attempts were made to effect a reconciliation and return of the absenting party. It was resolved among those who remained behind, to perform no other music than such as we deemed the most genuine, and an express was sent off by the first opportunity to purchase thirty copies of the lately published ******* Collection.

In the mean time, however, the controversy had descended to the congregation. As long as the choir had kept together on terms of seeming decency, it was hardly to be expected that the audience at large would take part in our little animosities. The parish would never have undertaken to control a whole choir, if that choir would have united in any species of music, however contrary to the tastes and habits of those who bore no share in its performance. But when it was found that our little vocal commonwealth had been rent asunder, and that so large a division of malecontents had retired in indignation to a Sacred Mount, the sympathies of brothers, sisters, parents, and friends were at once excited, and musical predilections were enlisted along with the ties of nature to swell the threatening dissatisfaction. For several Sundays I remained firm, supported as I was by all the ostentatious influence and patronage of Mr. Forehead, and the zealous co-operation of his partisans. We persisted every Sabbath in singing these five tunes, Old Hundred, St. Martin's, Mear, Bath, and Little Marlborough, unless the minister varied his metres from that standard; and even then we were prepared with tunes of a similar class. By these means we hoped to awaken a better taste among those of the congregation who were averse to our new style, and eventually to recall a majority of the dissidents, who we trusted would become convinced of the excellence of our improvements, and gradually return to partake of the honor and pleasure attached to them.

But our expectations were disappointed. Our triumph had a date of only about three months, and was even waning while it lasted. We could not force the likings of a prejudiced, and, in some respects, exasperated congregation. The singing in the meeting-house was the constant topic of every private conversation. All possible ridicule and contempt were thrown out against each of the respective styles in question. All sorts of arguments were used, that reason, or passion, or prejudice, could devise. Till at length, I verily believe, our inclinations became so perverted by the mere operation of party feeling, that many of us hated and despised the venerable air of Old Hundred with as much heartiness as they did the toad that crossed their path at twilight, while others regarded the generally very innocent tune of Northfield with the same abhorrence that we bestowed on a snake. Unfortunately for the better side of the argument at this time, the attachment to a rapid, fuguing, animated style of singing was too deeply and extensively seated in the affections of the people of Waterfield, to be eradicated by the impotent perseverance of our diminished choir. Pew after pew became deserted, until we found that we were singing, and Mr. Welby preaching, to almost naked walls. The hoary head was still there, for it loved to listen to the strains which had nourished the piety of its youth. A few families of fashionable pretensions encouraged us, for there was something aristocratical in the superior taste of our newly introduced music, and something modish in its reputation. Nothing but the strongest religious feelings induced a few other scattered individuals to appear at meeting, and it was but too evident that full three quarters of the usual attendants remained at home.

This spectacle produced the deepest effect on my mind. I had a sufficient sense of the blessings of public worship to feel and know that they must not be sacrificed to a mere point of musical taste. I was therefore perfectly willing to resign all my biases for the sake of seeing our beloved meeting-house again filled with its motley throngs, and of feeling the delicious, though perhaps imaginary, coolness excited by the agitations of several hundred fans,—those busy little agents, so lively, so glancing, yet so silent,—and of hearing the full thunder of all the seats as they were slammed down after prayer, though Mr. Welby had frequently remonstrated with earnestness against it, — but, much to my satisfaction, remonstrated in vain, for I scarcely know many sounds more grateful to my ear than this. Whether it is, that it is connected with the idea of a full congregation, which I always loved, or with the close of the prayer, which in early youth I thought insufferably long, or whether it was originally a most agreeable diversification of the inaction and monotony of church hours, I cannot tell; but something has wonderfully attached me to the noise of a thousand falling seats. And this attachment you will find very general in New England. Many a minister there will tell you that his attempts to correct the supposed evil have always been ineffectual; and if you are riding through the land on a summer Sabbath, you may observe that, long before you are in sight of the meeting-house, your starting horse and saluted ear will give decided testimony to the clergyman's complaint, while all the wakened echoes round will inform you that, if you spur forward for a half-mile or more, you will be in season to hear a good portion of the sermon, though you have lost the prayer.*

---

* This passage must indeed be regarded as a record of times and habits that have past. For not only has the nuisance of down-slamming seats been replaced by more quiet and decorous fixtures, but the very posture of the worshippers in prayer has been almost universally exchanged from a standing to a sitting one. Few instances of a change of manners in the course of a single generation are more remarkable than this. Had it been predicted, in the time of the author's youth, that in thirty or forty years a majority of the congregations in New England would sit during prayer, and that too with the cordial assent of the clergymen and the most pious among their hearers, the prediction would have been received with a smile, if not a

I was unable any longer to endure the destitute appearance of the meeting-house, and having consulted with Mr. Welby, who advised me to make whatever sacrifices I could for the restoration of peace, I caused it to be circulated one day in the village, that on the following Sabbath I should return to the kind of music which had lately been abandoned. The necessity for this measure was the more pressing, as I heard it murmured that a town-meeting was soon to be called for the purpose of securing a mode of singing which should be agreeable to a great majority of the parish.

My present associates and supporters, indeed, almost to a man, took umbrage at my determination; and were not seen in public when the Sabbath came. But I was surrounded by all the choristers of the other party, and the meeting-house was crowded, and the down-falling seats rebellowed again to my delighted ear.

And now for several weeks was the full-breathing triumph of the lovers of crotchets and quavers over the votaries of minims and semibreves. The latter faction sullenly absented themselves from the singing-pew, and generally from worship, while the former revelled amid the labyrinths of fugues, believing, to their own happiness, certainly, the order of consecutive parts to be the sweetest of melodies, and the recurrence of consecutive fifths the most delightful of harmonies. In place of the list of ancient tunes above enumerated, were now sub-

---

shudder of incredulous horror. If believed, it would have been considered as indicative of an approaching and lamentable decline of piety. The facility with which the change has taken place, wears an encouraging aspect for the lovers of reform, who may be anxiously awaiting far more important movements in society.

stituted Russia, Northfield, the Forty-Sixth Psalm, New Jerusalem, and others of the same mint. The name of Billings was a sufficient passport of recommendation to any air that was mentioned, while that of Williams or of Tansur was sure to condemn it to neglect. We were encouraged by the looks and voices of all those members of the congregation who were beneath fifty years of age; or if any such declined to accompany us either with a hum or an articulated modulation, they perhaps testified their satisfaction by the visible beating of a hand, whose arm lay along the top of a pew.

But this was to me only a silver age, compared with the golden reign of Charles Williams. I felt that my taste had become much confirmed and purified by my recent study and practice of a better style of church music, and I could therefore the less easily tolerate that which I was compelled now to support. By far the better half of the choir, also, in point of musical skill and execution, refrained from renewing their services, and I was distressed to know what methods I could adopt to allure them back. Even my rival and annoyer, Mr. Forehead, I should have been glad to welcome again at my left hand. His voice had both power and sweetness, and perhaps the only defect in his mode of performing was his perpetual attempt at ornament and trilling, a defect still further enhanced by the circumstance, that, instead of trilling with his tongue, he always attempted that accomplishment with his lips alone, being the veritable original by whom the well-known unhappy change was made upon the word *bow* in the following distich:

"With reverence let the saints appear,
And bow before the Lord."

Nevertheless, I was perfectly willing and desirous to enter into a negotiation with him and his party, for the purpose of procuring, if possible, some mutual compromise and reconciliation, and filling up again the complement of the choir.

But this was an attempt of no little delicacy and difficulty. The exasperation of both parties was too recent and too sore, immediately to admit of an amicable personal union, or to allow the expectation that either side would endure the favorite music of the other. Time, however, which effects such mighty revolutions in the affairs of empires, condescends also to work the most important changes in the aspect of humble villages, and still humbler choirs.

It is the office of this unpretending narrative to record the mutations to which one of the last-mentioned communities is exposed in New England. Whether the train of incidents here exhibited be a specimen of what occurs to many other choirs within the same region, my experience does not enable me to decide. Many of my readers, however, will probably recognize, in these memoirs of a single collection of singers, several features common to all others.

I have often thought that such communities are a kind of arena for the exhibition of some peculiar and specific human infirmities. Every new combination of our social nature, indeed, seems to produce some new results, in the same manner as each species of vegetables nourishes its peculiar tribe of animalcules. I take it that our National Congress elicits from its component members certain specific virtues and vices, and certain modifications of feeling, passion, and talent, denied to us mere readers of newspapers at home. Where but on the floor of the American Capitol would the peculiarities of a certain member's sarcasm, and of another member's sublime statesmanship, be generated and developed?* So in a church choir, there somehow arise certain shades of freaks, certain starts of passion, certain species of whim, certain modes of folly, and let me humbly suggest, also, certain descriptions of virtue, to be found exactly in no other specimens throughout the moral kingdom of man.

May I fondly hope, that these desultory delineations, intermingled though they are with intrusive speculations, and superficial efforts at philosophizing, may at least prove corrective of kindred effects, if such anywhere exist, with those which are here exposed? A mirror sometimes shocks the child out of a passion of whose deformity he could not be convinced except by its disgusting effects on his own face. And if the perusal of these pages, which have been too carelessly thrown together, in order to indulge some juvenile recollections, and to soothe some painful, heavy hours, be instrumental in correcting any imperfections to which our church choirs are liable, I shall feel more than repaid for my anxiety in undertaking the perilous enterprise of authorship. But let us be moving forward.

In a very few months, negotiations were entered into with the body of the other party, of whom some half-dozen individuals of the least zealous had from time to time returned, and given in their adhesion to the ruling powers. The truth was, that, on our part, we felt ex-

* These allusions to Randolph and Webster were perhaps more readily perceived at the first publication of the work, than they may be at this distance of time.

tremely the want of instrumental music, and a few excellent voices on the treble. After Charles Williams had left us, a tolerable bass-viol was played by an elderly storekeeper, a bachelor, who had formerly assisted the choir for several years with that instrument, but had resigned it as soon as Charles became prepared to supply his place. This gentleman with his clerk, who played a fine flute, had participated in the dudgeon of the lovers of ancient melody. But nearly all of them now wished to return, conscious, undoubtedly, of the improvement which it was truly in their power to contribute to our performances, and unwilling that their talents should any longer be hidden in a napkin.

The terms of reconciliation and reunion were settled in the following manner. As our performances were required regularly five times on a Sabbath, it was agreed that the arrangement of tunes throughout the day should be two fugues, two of the slow ancient airs, and one of a different description from either. Neither party could well object to airs of a rapid and animated movement, in which all the parts continued uninterruptedly to the close, as is the case with Wells, Windham, Virginia, and many others. Another class of tunes also were very general favorites, though they avoided both extremes that were the bones of contention among us. I allude to those in which the third line is a duet between the bass and treble, of which St. Sebastian's is a well-known beautiful instance.

For some time, we proceeded together in this new arrangement with as little interruption as could be well expected from existing circumstances. A very few of the most obstinate and paltry-minded, of each side, held out, indeed, for longer or shorter periods, and one or two perhaps never returned till a grand revolution of the whole corps, to be described hereafter, should our history ever reach a second part. For several Sundays, also, four or five Guelphs would contemptuously sit in perfect silence during the singing of the Ghibeline tunes, and as many Ghibelines would return the compliment during the singing of the Guelph tunes. And even when they were compelled to abandon such indecent deportment by the censures to which it exposed them, to my certain knowledge they were silent while standing up with the choir, or moved their lips in a whisper, or sang so very low as to give no sort of assistance to the rest.

However, these little factious symptoms gradually disappeared, and I had at length the happiness of finding myself at the head of my musical flock, with the embers of former grievances well-nigh asleep, and with a decided advantage gained in our taste and selection of tunes. But what struggles and dangers had been incurred in order to arrive at this improved condition! I can resort to no illustration of these events more apt than the kingdom of France, which, as some imagine, derives a faint compensation for the horrors of the revolution, from the amendments effected in some of its circumstances and institutions, that neither despotism nor superstition can in future hope to wipe away.

Yet, amidst these various concussions, it will not be surprising that my own authority should have been completely undermined. It is scarce supposable that I could be a very decided favorite with either of the parties who had frowned so awfully upon each other, since I had in a manner sided with both of them. Although, therefore, I was most scrupulously impartial in selecting such descriptions of tunes as exactly conformed to the terms of the treaty, yet there was not a member of the choir whose friendship was sufficiently zealous to join me in resisting the new encroachments of Mr. Forehead. While that gentleman confined himself to a general selection equally impartial with mine, not a spectator thought of murmuring, when he suggested, as he constantly did, this and that particular tune for any given psalm or hymn; and suggested it, too, with such an air of certainty and confidence, that I was not the man to hold up my head, and say at a single glance, "Sir, I am on my own ground here." When he found that his suggestions were in this way constantly adopted, it was an easy and natural transition for him next to whisper round of his own accord, to the few who sat near him, the name of the tune to be sung, and to whisper it also to me with the same nonchalance, that I might proclaim it to the choir as usual. And then, with as much ease and as calm a face as Napoleon wore when he stepped from the consular chair to the imperial throne, it only remained for him to assume the precentorship at once, by uttering aloud one Sunday, to my amazement, the name of the first tune in the morning, and continuing the practice from that moment until his departure from the choir and the neighborhood.

Thus, my own occupation was gone. On the afternoon of the morning just mentioned, I entered the singing-pew and took my seat at some distance from the post of honor, which I felt was no longer mine. It was of no use to appeal to the members of the choir in my defence. I had suffered encroachment after encroachment to be gradually made upon my authority, until the last act of usurpation was scarcely perceptible. I knew that I could have no enthusiastic supporters of my rights. I had not one personal qualification by which to balance the imposing and overbearing accomplishments of my competitor. I dare say all the choir and all the congregation thought him the best leader, as I confess, on the whole, he was. Probably the precise circumstances under which the exchange was made were not discerned by many among them. Perhaps they might have supposed, that my resignation and transfer of the pitch-pipe were voluntary. Indeed, I half hope they did suppose so. But no, — I am willing they should have known the whole truth. But let the matter rest. It is an era in my biography which I do not like to contemplate.

I am not ashamed, however, that I continued in the choir. I am certain it was not meanness which kept me there, though some at first sight may so interpret it. It was a struggle between pride and duty, in which duty won the victory, — and though pride had indignation for its ally, yet my devoted and disinterested love for those singing-seats came up to the assistance of duty, and decided the contest.

Besides, why should I desert those seats? Should I have felt happier, could I have concealed my mortification better, by sitting with the family below? By no means. I might as well remain where I was, and bury my feelings in the flood of sound with which my own tremulous voice was mingled.

For I considered, that it was always my peculiar lot,

wherever I was, and whatever I did, to have some mortification or other on my hands, or, I would say, on my heart. The squeak of my clarionet was but an epitome of a certain note that has occasionally grated the whole tenor of my fortune and life. I had a disaffected mother-in-law. My schoolmaster was partial to my rival. I was bound an apprentice to an uncongenial employment, which I could not abandon until I was free. I was once jilted. How I was superseded in the choir, has been seen above. I always try to do my best, but am liable to overdo. I have been disinterested and generous to my friends, till I have spoiled them, and they have sometimes become my foes from expecting more than I could or ought to perform. The same out-of-the-way note, I acknowledge, attaches itself to most of my compositions. I have written some things in these very pages of a kin with that portentous strain of my instrument; but I could not help it; and I expect that, with some praises that may be vouchsafed to this production, other things will be said of it that will cut me to the very heart. But I will try to be prepared for them.

And now, reader, you may in some measure understand how I could endure to haunt, like a ghost, the scene of my former triumphs. Remember, however, that I met no scorn on the occasion. Not a soul was there, who would not have regretted my absence. A gentle and quiet exchange of leaders had been effected, and there the matter rested in every mind. The most direct way by which I could have caused it to redound to my ill-reputation and discomfort would have been to make a stir about it. Prudence, therefore, if nothing else, might whisper to me the proper course to be pursued.

Thus a fifth leader of the choir at Waterfield is duly and regularly recorded on these veracious annals. His reign, like that of his predecessor, was stormy and unfortunate. For some weeks, Mr. Forehead adhered inviolably to the articles of union touching the selection of particular kinds of music. But it is the natural tendency of usurped power, when thus easily acquired, to produce security, audacity, encroachment, downfall. The precentor's partialities at length began to burst out, and occasional small violations of the treaty were hazarded with impunity. But when he attempted to advance farther, and one whole Sunday passed without the assignment of a single fugue to wake up the indifferent congregation, an alarm was taken by the lovers of that species of melody. A repetition of former disturbances and irritations was threatened. Some of the choir took no part in the performance; some absolutely left the seats for neighboring pews, and a convulsion was on the eve of again breaking us in pieces.

The amiable Mr. Welby perceived the indications of an approaching storm. He devoted himself, therefore, the ensuing week, to the preparation of a discourse, which he hoped might check the evil in its commencement. Meanwhile, however, the difficulty was provided for in another way. A deputation had called on the existing leader that very evening, and, making the strongest representations of the dissatisfaction which would certainly prevail, if he should continue the course of administration to which he was inclined, extorted from him a promise that he would immediately return to the recent arrangement which had so well secured the harmony of the choir, and the complacency of the congregation.

But Mr. Welby knew nothing of the happy turn that affairs had thus assumed, and the members of the choir, on their part, knew nothing of the benevolent officiousness that was prompting the labors of his study. Even had he been aware that a reçonciliation had taken place, it is probable that he would still have interwoven into his next discourse some gentle persuasives to mutual kindness. His utter ignorance, however, of that happy occurrence, caused his sermon in some places to wear an aspect of unnecessary pointedness and severity. Although it contained but one explicit allusion to the choir, yet it unfortunately was calculated with exquisite skill to meet precisely such a state of excitement as there was every reason to suppose the singers would by this time be wrought up to. But what was meant for exhortation, was now felt as reproach; the more tender and soothing the preacher's language, the more it seemed like oil descending on the flames. The whole choir had come together that morning in a state of jealous irritability; they were ready to break out somewhere; the terms of the last Sunday evening's engagement guarded them from waging battle with each other; the one party were moody and disappointed, the other felt injured and suspicious; "and now to be held up to the congregation, — to be found fault with by the minister, — to be chidden just at the moment when they were all endeavoring to keep peace together!" Such were the exaggerated and unjust reflections excited in their minds by one of the mildest and most beautiful discourses on brotherly love that were ever composed, and in which, as I before observed, only one direct allusion was made to them, wherein the preacher expressed his trust, that they who gladdened the house of God with the harmony of their voices would be particularly careful to cultivate the much sweeter, and, to the ear of Heaven, the much more acceptable harmony, resulting from a union of pious hearts.

But no matter; it gave to those prejudiced and capricious choristers an object on which to exercise their characteristic waywardness, and an opportunity to make themselves of some troublesome importance. Accordingly, to wreak a glorious revenge on the interfering parson, and to impress on the whole world a sense of their immeasurable consequence, not a soul of them on the afternoon of that day appeared in the singing-seats,—with the exception, let me humbly add, of *one*, as unworthy indeed as the rest, but who would never for such a provocation have deserted that gallery until the imitation-marble columns that supported it were crumbling into ruins. Whatever others might have thought of me, however poor-spirited and grandmother-loving I may have appeared, yet if there have been any moments in my life of loftier triumph, but at the same time of more piteous melancholy, than others, they assuredly occurred during the quarter of an hour when I sat perfectly alone in that deserted singing-pew, fixing my eye and face on no other object than my afflicted minister, who was waiting in trembling dismay for the entrance of the rest of the choir.

Never shall I forget the moment when the dreadful truth flashed into his mind, and he perceived, by their protracted absence, the mistake that he must have committed in the morning. Yet it was but an instant of agony, and was succeeded by a high-souled though involuntary look of calmness, and consciousness that he had discharged no more than a well-meant religious and professional duty. The tears were soon wiped away from his face, a decent composure was assumed, a hymn was quickly selected, which Watts, the sweet psalmist of the modern Israel, could furnish him most appropriately for the occasion, and was then announced and read with a tremulousness of voice, that indicated rather a successful effort of firmness, than any yielding weakness of heart.

I had the honor, on that occasion, of setting and leading a tune, which was accompanied by Mr. Welby's modest, though perfect and full-toned bass. We were the only singers for the remainder of that day. The hearts of some among the worshippers were too full, and of others too anxious, to lend us a helping note. From that moment, the closest friendship was formed and cemented between Mr. Welby and myself, and it was but lately that I paid him the last dollar of the money which he liberally advanced to defray more than half the expenses of my college education.

I was "monarch of all I surveyed" in that singing-pew for four months. Mr. Welby of course had no apology to make. Apology indeed! He was in truth the only injured party. Had the whole choir entered the meeting-house on their knees, singing *Peccavimus* and *Miserere*, they would, by such humiliation, have scarcely effaced their violation of sacred proprieties and of the feelings of their pastor. Should Mr. Welby's

Journal of his Ministry, which I know he has copiously recorded, be ever given to the world, I have not a doubt that this transaction will be stated there with ample justice and candor, and make no insignificant appearance among the various trials which a New England clergyman is called to endure.

It was long ere a sense of lingering compunction, together with various other feelings and circumstances, brought the wanderers back to their deserted fold. Meanwhile I continued the discharge of my solitary duty in the gallery, and was most minutely scrupulous in selecting the tunes according to the arrangement prescribed amidst the recent troubles. I was determined to give to no person whatever the slightest cause of offence, but to hold out every encouragement for all who chose to return. Mr. Welby and myself derived occasional assistance from a few voices below, but often the whole musical duties of worship devolved upon us alone. Few indeed of the members of the late choir carried their animosity so far as to renounce attendance at church altogether. Mr. Forehead, I think, was never seen in that meeting-house but once again. Soon after his abrupt retirement from the seats, he married and left the neighborhood, carrying off with him one of the best treble voices in the village.

At the beginning of the following winter, I was compelled to fulfil an engagement that I had incurred, to keep a district-school for three months in the county of Rockingham, New Hampshire. Soon after I had taken my departure for this purpose, Mr. Welby was seized with a troublesome affection of his lungs, which scarcely permitted him to perform even his strictly pastoral services. And now the musical tide in my native congregation was at its very lowest ebb. For two or three Sundays the minister did not even presume to read a psalm, certain that no one present would rise and sing it. Can my readers imagine from what quarter relief was derived in this gloomy state of things? From none other than a few of the very oldest members of the congregation. Four ancient men, the least of whose ages was seventy-three, indignant at the folly and pertinacity of those singers of yesterday, and wearied out with waiting for a return of tolerable music, tottered up the stairs one Sabbath morning with the assistance of the panelled railing, and took their places in the seats left vacant by their degenerate grandsons. Two of them had fought in the old French war, and all had taken a civil or military part, more or less conspicuous, in the struggle for our country's independence. One, indeed, bore a title of considerable military rank. His hair was as white as the falling snow; the other three displayed white or gray wigs, with a large circular bush, mantling over the upper part of the back, like a swelling cloud round the shoulders of old Wachusett. Their voices of course were broken and tremulous, but not destitute of a certain grave and venerable sweetness. They kept the most perfect time, as they stood in a row, fronting the minister, with their hands each holding a lower corner of their books, which they waved from side to side in a manner the most solemn and imposing. Their very pronunciation had in it something primitive and awe-inspiring. Their *shall* broadened into *shawl*, *do* was exchanged for *doe*, and *earth* for *airth*. Their selection of tunes was of the most ancient composition and slowest movement, with the exception, occasionally, of old Sherburne, and the Thirty-Fourth Psalm.

How vividly do I remember the spectacle which they presented to my revering eyes, when I attended the meeting-house late one morning, after having walked on snow-shoes the last five miles of the distance from the place where I was employed in teaching, to pay a short visit to my friends. On entering the beloved edifice, whose white, though bell-less steeple I had for some time gazed on from afar with emotions almost as strong as if I had been absent several years, it was my purpose to ascend immediately to my usual station. But before I had passed the door, unexpected and unaccustomed sounds for that place burst upon my ears, and my curiosity irresistibly led me forward to my father's pew near the pulpit, that I might have a full view of the strange choir which had so magically sprung up during my short absence, and that I might not disturb it by my unnecessary intrusion.

This was not the first nor the last time that I have witnessed extraordinary energy of character, as occasions called for it, displayed by octogenarians of New England. Few of my readers, perhaps, will fail to remember instances analogous to that here recorded. Those apparently decrepit forms, which you see at frame-raisings, confined to the easy task of fashioning the pins, and telling stories of the Revolution, or about the door in winter, mending the sled and gathering sticks for the fire, or drawing the rake in summer after the moving hay-cart, occasionally surprise you by the exhibition of an activity and strength which you would think they must have for ever resigned. Who can tell how much this latent vigor of theirs may be owing to our bracing climate, joined to the effects of their former stirring life, and particularly to the influence of those preternatural exertions, which they, with the whole country, once put forth in the war of independence? I thought I distinctly saw, in the efforts of those seniors of my native parish to supply it with sacred music, something of that spirit which had sprung to arms, when the necessities of their country and the voice of Heaven bade them forego every personal convenience, and take up their march to Charlestown, to Cambridge, and to the heights of Dorchester. Ye laurelled old men! ye saviours of your country, and authors of unimaginable blessings for your posterity! ye shall not descend to your graves, without the fervent thanks, the feeble tribute, of one who often in his thought refers his political enjoyments and hopes to your principle, your valor, and your blood!

How soon will it be ere a Revolutionary veteran will be seen no more among us! It is with a feeling of melancholy and desolation that I perceive their number irrevocably lessening every year. We do not half enough load the survivors with grateful honors.* We ought formally and publicly to cherish them with more pious assiduity. Their pensions are an insufficient recompense of their merits, for the plain reason that they scarcely fought for mercenary considerations. Even those who expected pay, and sometimes could not obtain it from the continental treasury, would have died rather than touch the gold of the enemy. On the anniversaries of

---

* This paragraph, as well as the whole book, was written a year before the Bunker Hill Monument Celebration.

our independence, I would therefore assign to all who had any share in accomplishing the Revolution, a distinct place in our civic processions. The orator of the day should add interest to his performance by an address to their venerable corps. They should be escorted to the festive hall, they should be entertained as honored guests, they should be toasted, and the toast should be drunk standing, and the chaplain of the day should offer prayers for their long and uninterrupted happiness, both in this world and in the next.*

But this last idea brings me round again to the reverend choir, on which was fastened the other end of my chain of patriotic reflections. Those of my readers who are interested as much in the links of a dynasty as in the more general facts of a history, may wish to know who was regarded as the leader among that group of antiques. And the question is pertinent enough. For although they were too far advanced in years beyond the miserable vanities of musical pretension, and were now too much on a level in point of abilities or skill, to be actuated by any aspiring ambition, yet they had also too much experience in the affairs of life not to be aware of the necessity of some ostensible head, in order to manage even the humblest common concern with requisite harmony and effect. The person, therefore, whom, rather by a tacit, reciprocal understanding than any formal nomination or elective acclamation, they made choice of for their conductor, was Colonel John Wilkins, otherwise called Colonel John Ticonderoga, the veteran

* Many of the propositions here presented have since been singularly realized in various public celebrations throughout the United States.

whose hoary locks were above described, and who had been the first to suggest to the others this laudable scheme. Let those who take pride in such humble matters as dates and names remember him, therefore, as the sixth leader of the choir at Waterfield, whose acts are recorded in this faithful chronicle.

My engagement in New Hampshire having expired, I returned home to pursue my studies. Affairs had, by this time, assumed a much brighter aspect. I found, on my arrival, that nearly all the females belonging to the late choir had volunteered a renewal of their delightful services. How difficult it is for woman to persevere in error! Though, physically speaking, the weaker party, yet how often she resists the sinister example of the other sex, and proves herself superior in the strength of her moral powers! The fair ones of my native parish were the first to perceive the unhappy mistake into which they had been betrayed, and the first to acknowledge and practically retract it. Candor requires me to make these statements and reflections, though it were much to be wished that the occasion for it never had existed. But I was willing to forget all the resentment with which I had before wondered at their conduct, when I contemplated the novel and beautiful spectacle that now charmed my imagination. Show me a more interesting picture than reverend and trembling age associated with blooming and youthful beauty in chanting the praises of their common Creator. It struck me as an instance of a kind of *moral counterpoint*, more thrilling to the soul than the sweetest or the grandest harmony of mere sound. Willingly would I have refrained from interposing my indifferent voice, had not duty and persuasion united to reconduct me to the seats.

The experience of life certainly brings every man into strange combinations and juxtapositions with his fellow-beings. Yet, was not mine at the present time rather peculiar? What fate, what hidden sympathy, what kindred gravity of character, drew me into special personal contact and co-operation with four of the most reverend seniors of the land? The contemplation of this new attitude of my presiding genius had sometimes almost too powerful an effect on my imagination. I began to entertain doubts of my own age. At times I thought it my duty to study a new system of ethics and manners, corresponding to my situation. I wished occasionally that Cicero's Treatise on Old Age might be substituted in place of his Orations against Catiline, which I was then reading, as preparatory to my admission into college.

But the dreams of this whimsical hallucination soon fled away, as the months advanced, and Mr. Welby's voice regained its usual health and mellowness, and my venerated fathers in harmony found it too much for their comfort to ascend the stairs on the enfeebling days of spring. Besides, if anything could have restrained the peculiar wanderings of my mind above described, it was the condition in which I was now left. Exposed singly to the fire of a whole battery of eyes and voices from the flower of the parish, and compelled, by my very duty, to maintain constant communications and consultations with them, I was soon reminded, by certain indescribably interesting and perplexing feelings in my breast, that I had many years yet to pass before I could aspire to the honors, the abstracted attention, and the composure of old age.

But though I pretend not to have been exempt from the susceptibilities now alluded to, I call on every scrutinizing spectator (there having been several of that character at church) to bear witness to the unremitted propriety of my deportment during the summer and autumn which I passed in that critical situation. No manifestation of partialities, no encouragement of female frivolities, and no unfeeling neglect or inattention, that I have ever heard of or imagined, were or could be laid to my charge. Our singing, I may confidently say without undue self-flattery, continued to be of no ordinary merit, though we could not welcome one accession to my own side of the choir. Several strong and rich voices on the other side took the tenor or air of each tune, the rest of them united in a melodious treble, and Mr. Welby and myself put forth our whole vocal powers in supporting them with the bass. Such was the uninterrupted method we pursued, until the approach of winter again called me to a distant place, to replenish my little funds with the emoluments of a district schoolmaster.

The destinies of our choir were now provided for in a manner somewhat remarkable, but not, I believe, altogether unexampled elsewhere in our country. The first intention of the ladies was to leave the seats immediately after my departure. Had it been executed, everything might have been thrown back into the deplorable condition in which I had left affairs the preceding winter. Two of my late venerable fellow-choristers were now already gathered to the land of silence, and there were no hopes of obtaining a leader from any quarter. In this emergency, Mrs. Martha Shrinknot proffered her services, and undertook the management of the whole department, until I should myself return and resume it. She was a lady not much past the age of thirty years. Being of an active and inquisitive turn of mind, she had long since made herself acquainted with the mysteries of setting a psalm-tune, knew its key-note at a glance, and had frequently, on private occasions, even before her marriage, given out the leading tones to the different parts, when passing an evening with a few musical friends, who preferred extracting an hour of rational pleasure from the Village Harmony, to the frivolous entertainments of cards, coquetry, and scandal.

It might be out of place here to follow Mrs. Martha Shrinknot home, and exhibit her superintending the best-ordered family and the most profitable dairy in the county. My concern with her now is in her public capacity, and I may say with truth, that a leader of more accuracy, more judgment, more self-possession, and more spirited energy, never took charge of the Waterfield choir, nor, as I think, of any other choir.

Her outset on the first Sabbath succeeded to admiration; and there was every prospect that her reign, though short, would be one of uninterrupted brilliancy and felicity. But an ill star seemed to hover over the spot, and new troubles soon arose to disturb the peace and crush the hopes of the lovers of sacred song.

Among the females of the choir was a young woman of much comeliness, modest demeanor, and an unsullied character, who had been living in one of the richer families of the village, under the denomination of *help*. I approve the feeling which has substituted this word for the offensive one of *servant.* Servant seems to stamp an irretrievable character on the person who bears the appellation. It is less general and vague than the word help. The latter seems to admit into the mind a sense of independence and a hope of rising in the world. As long as Mirabeau's maxim is true, that names are things, let the young heirs of poverty and dependence in free America solace themselves with the substantial comfort of assuming a title which places them, in imagination at least, on a level with their employers, and soothes the sting which may now and then fret their bosoms, when contemplating the unavoidable inequalities of fortune. For alas! not even will this slight change of name secure them from numerous embarrassments and mortifications, as will be seen in the case of Mary Wentworth, the intelligent young woman above mentioned.

The singing-pew for the females contained three long benches, rising one above another, and receding from the front of the gallery. Mary Wentworth had occupied an unassuming seat on the uppermost of these benches for about three years. At her first appearance there, there had been no little stir among certain of the vocal sisterhood; a few airs were put on, a few whispers circulated, a few stares directed at the modest stranger, and the seats of some of the young ladies were vacated for a few succeeding Sabbaths. But most of them returned sooner or later, on better reflection, or on a reviving desire to bear their part in the melodies of the place, and Mary thenceforward was scarcely disturbed by any kind of notice whatever. Nevertheless, her singing was envied by some, and admired by all. To say the truth, she had no equal in this parish, and few elsewhere. Her voice was enchanting in its tones, and astonishing in its compass. She was a perfect mistress of the art, as far as it can reach perfection in the practice of our country choirs. She was fit to bear a conspicuous part in an oratorio, and would have well repaid any degree of scientific cultivation.

Mrs. Shrinknot, who knew not, or affected not to know, the squeamishness respecting rank that was entertained by some of the young ladies, took occasion, on the afternoon of the second Sabbath succeeding her induction into office, to exercise her lawful authority, by inviting Mary Wentworth down to the front seat, and placing her at her own right hand. She wished for the support of her voice, and the assistance to be derived from occasionally consulting her.

On the next Sunday, Mrs. Shrinknot was seized with an illness which prevented her leaving home. She sent for Mary, and, after much persuasion, prevailed upon her to go that day and assume the direction of the choir.

The maiden went early, that she might prepare herself, by time and meditation, with sufficient self-possession, and avoid the flurry of passing by others in order to arrive at the post which had been assigned her. She had not been seated there long, when she observed two young ladies, who had for some years pretty regularly attended the choir, entering into a pew below, with the rest of their family. This was soon followed by several other instances of the same kind, and poor Mary's heart began to sink within her. She looked frequently and anxiously round, in the hope that some, or at least that one individual, would arrive to shield her from the oppression of overwhelming notoriety. In vain! there had been visitings, and murmurings, and resolutions, through the whole of the preceding week, and what with the pride of some, who could not endure that a girl at service should aspire to an equality with themselves,—and the envy of others, whose ears were *pained* (as they used to say, though in a different sense from my use of the word) by the tones of Polly Wentworth's voice,—and the indignation of others, that the long-established order of sitting should be disturbed,—and the pusillanimity of others, who had neither souls nor pretensions large enough to be proud, or envious, or angry, but who quivered on the pivot, and vibrated to whichever side the multitude inclined,—not a bonnet was forthcoming to gladden the eyes of that fair and desolate housemaid.

Yet, though a girl of the most modest and unpretending character, Mary Wentworth had an energy of soul, and a sterling good sense, which enabled her to encounter every emergency with composure, and to act according to the demands of the occasion. Mr. Welby, after waiting a quarter of an hour beyond the usual time, and not knowing himself, poor man, what course he ought to pursue, balancing between his fear of hurting the young woman's feelings, and his duty as a clergyman, at length resolved to commence the services with a psalm, which he read, and proceeded to sing to the tenor part of a tune, that happened to be the universal favorite of the congregation.

Mary Wentworth rose and joined him in the same part. Mr. Welby immediately permitted his voice to slide, with a graceful and almost imperceptible transition, to the bass, with which he continued to accompany her. The air was of a slightly pathetic description, and accorded well with the state of her heart. To say that there was not a *little* effervescence of republican feeling, also, which prompted her on that occasion to put forth the whole blazing extent of her musical powers, would be to arrogate for the fine creature a sort of angelical perfection, and to raise a doubt whether the institutions for which our fathers bled have communicated to every one who moves over the land a sense of individual dignity and importance. Yet, although grief and resentment were both laboring at her heart, her strength of character and her instinctive perception of the proprieties of the place, suffered no more of either to predominate than was exactly sufficient to infuse into her performance that combination of melancholy and animation, which is the last golden accomplishment of the female voice.

In fact, she was surprised at the excellence of her own singing, and this very surprise constantly stimulated her to higher and higher efforts. Her situation and feelings inspired new powers, of which she was unconscious before, and inspiration seemed to create and follow inspiration, like the metaphysical loves in the bosom of Anacreon.

The effect on the audience was prodigious. At first, there reigned the silence of astonishment that she could summon the confidence to sing. This was very soon exchanged for the feeling and the rustling of admiration. A kind of anguish now seized upon the hearts of some of the generous young ladies who had that morning left the choir. They were half willing to be back again there, if for no other purpose than to drown her voice, and dilute the attention so lavishly and improperly bestowed on a human being in the place of worship.

But the impropriety of this admiration appeared to be forgotten by even the gravest and most devout among the audience. As Mary and the pastor proceeded from verse to verse, one after another of their male listeners rose, and turned their faces towards the gallery, so that by the time the psalm was concluded, and Mr. Welby had laid aside his book, to invite his people, in a low and solemn tone, to the worship of God, one half of the assembly were already in the posture assumed by Congregationalists, after the manner of primitive Christians, in the hour of public prayer.

From seeming evil is educed real good. The general compassion and admiration excited by the case of Mary Wentworth now presented an opportunity which had been long desired among the singers of the other sex, to return with a good grace to the seats. By going thither again ostensibly for the purpose of encouraging and protecting a persecuted young woman, they would screen themselves from the mortification of appearing to regret and retract their former conduct. Accordingly, a deputation of ten, on the afternoon of this day, resorted to the spot in the capacity of harbingers or pioneers. In consequence of the continued illness of Mrs. Shrinknot, the females generally declined to follow their example, entertaining in their minds an insurmountable objection against submitting to the substitute whom she had appointed, notwithstanding the overflow of popularity that was now pouring towards that substitute. Not a lady, therefore, was to be seen ascending the stairs in the afternoon, with the exception of Mary herself, who came and resumed her former long-occupied seat on the most retired bench in the singing-pew, from which no entreaties, or arguments, or considerations, urged by Mrs. Shrinknot or others, could ever after induce her to remove. The noble girl saw the hopelessness of contending against a host of jealous and restless prejudices, and cared for nothing in that place so much as peace and good singing.

Mr. Welby was still obliged to act as precentor during the remainder of the day. The new recruits for the vocal service, the sight of whom gladdened his heart, felt unequal to the task of executing that function among themselves. After he had read the first psalm in the afternoon, and they had waited some time for him to begin the singing of it, he perceived what was wanting, and speedily commenced a tune. He did the same with the two other hymns for that day. Mary would instantaneously take the treble, and her companions joined her, one after another, according to their power of seizing the parts belonging to them. After a few trifling mistakes in the bass, which the good ears, however, of those who committed them were able immediately to correct, they succeeded in making themselves all masters of the air before the conclusion of the first verse, and then proceeded with tolerable spirit and correctness to the end of the hymn.

On my return home, I had the felicity to find the choir in a more flourishing condition than it had enjoyed for a long time. About twenty of my own sex occupied the octagonal box, and somewhat less than that number were induced, by the recovery and presence of Mrs.

Shrinknot, and the prudent humility of Mary, to fill the two lower seats of the adjoining pew. These were all in the best training possible under the management of the former powerful lady, who, on receiving the key-note from the bachelor-merchant's bass-viol, immediately sounded forth the melodious fall of fa, sol, la, fa, and distributed the leading notes round to the performers of each of the four parts, — that complement being sometimes effected by an animated counter from the lips of Mary Wentworth.

From this time until the succeeding autumn, when I entered college, I discharged the duties of chief singer without interruption. It was a smoothly spun and brightly dyed portion of the thread of my life. The choir was making constant improvements, and receiving now and then accessions to its numbers, as was to be expected from the exercise of regularity and perseverance in the main body.

Very few occurrences happened to disturb the full cup of satisfaction which I was now enjoying in peace and gratitude. I cannot, however, omit mentioning one momentary dash of bitter, that was casually mingled with its sweets. In the middle of Mr. Welby's long prayer, one July morning, the composure of the congregation was startled by the loud crack of a whip before the meeting-house. Two or three of the younger members of the choir immediately rushed on tiptoe out of the singing-seats to the windows, from which they beheld a gig and tandem approaching rapidly to the door, and saw a pair of gayly dressed gentlemen alight therefrom. In a moment after, we heard the confident and conscious footsteps of their creaking yellow-top boots ascending the stairs, and on turning my eyes, but not my body, in that direction, whom should I behold but my old acquaintance and competitor, Mr. Forehead, accompanied by a gentlemanly-looking friend? They had ridden that morning from Boston, where Mr. Forehead was a successful attorney of much repute in ***** Alley. They both came into the octagonal pew with the same unembarrassed freedom that they would have entered a barroom, and took the first vacant seats in their way; but on reconnoitring, and finding everybody around them in a standing posture, they exchanged smiles of some confusion with each other, and rose again. From Mr. Forehead's familiar nod to me, I should have thought I had seen him but yesterday, instead of parting with him full two years before. I should have returned it with a solemn bow, had not the service which Mr. Welby was now performing made it improper for me to bestow on him the slightest recognition. Their assistance in the tune which succeeded was very fine, and very acceptable to the choir and congregation. They joined us again, however, in the afternoon, and while we were singing the first psalm, they thought proper, instead of lending us their voices, to accompany us with a singular *stridor*, emitted through the nearly closed lips, and resembling something between the sound of a bassoon and the lowest tone of a bass-viol. Some of the choir were frightened, some were shocked, and some very nearly burst out with laughter. My own distress was inconceivable. I felt *haunted* by Mr. Forehead. Rendered absolutely disheartened at the thought of enduring that sacrilegious, though I confess not entirely inharmonious buzz, through the two remaining hymns, I retired from the meeting-house and went home. Mr. Forehead immediately assumed my office, for the afternoon, and his friend, at the request of Mrs. Shrinknot, exchanged his imitative experiments for more natural and appropriate tones.

This, however, was the most disagreeable episode in the present poetic period of my existence. It is doubtful whether at length the separation from my own family caused me a keener pang, than the thought that I must resign, and perhaps for ever, all connection with a little circle, in which I had lately enjoyed, in so eminent degree, the double privilege of receiving happiness and doing good.

After my departure, a variety of causes, unnecessary to be detailed, contributed to the gradual decline and ultimate extinction of the choir on its old foundation. My shorter college vacations I spent at home, and in vain endeavored to arrest this melancholy tendency by the few exertions I could make to rally the scattered members. Sometimes I found that a miserable kind of contest had been waged between Mrs. Shrinknot and the singers of the other sex, who made all the efforts in their power to emancipate themselves from the mortifying dominion of a woman. But they could never succeed, not a man among them possessing sufficient tact, knowledge, and presence, to carry off the business of a leader well. The singing was always decent under her management, but under theirs it was perpetually liable to mistakes, interruptions, languishments, and helpless amazements. There was, however, no open, clamorous warfare between the two parties, but only on one side the restless attempts of pride to repair its own mortifications, and on the other the calm defiance of conscious superiority. They avoided an actual clashing before the congregation. The lady always affected a perfect readiness to yield her authority, whenever there were gentlemen present who chose to set the psalm. But this state of things of course produced frequent embarrassments in the choir. The bowings and the consultations between Mrs. Shrinknot and the gentlemen, occasioned by doubts respecting the propriety of particular tunes and other matters, were frequently protracted long after the minister had read the psalm or hymn, and the congregation would sit waiting and wondering for the music to begin. Meanwhile, as was to be expected, several of the least zealous members of the choir would from time to time steal off from their duties, to sit below, rather than be witnesses and partakers of such pitiable scenes.

The prosperity of my former hobby was still further affected by the introduction of theological perplexities. A flaming young preacher, who carried some points of orthodòxy considerably further than I could then, or can even now approve, had been recently settled in a neighboring town, and exchanged services one Sabbath with Mr. Welby. Tall of stature, cadaverous in aspect, and gloomy in his address as the very depths of midnight, he arose, and after pausing three minutes, during which his eyes were riveted on his book, he gave out the forty-fourth hymn of the Second Book of Dr. Watts, in a voice a full octave below that tone which is commonly called the sepulchral. The hymn is a terrific combination of images respecting the future abode of the wicked, and contains, among others of a similar nature, the two following verses:—

"Far in the deep where darkness dwells,
The land of horror and despair,
Justice hath built a dismal hell,
And laid her stores of vengeance there.

"Eternal plagues, and heavy chains,
Tormenting racks, and fiery coals,
And darts to inflict immortal pains,
Dyed in the blood of damned souls!"

On that day the person who undertook to act as leader of the choir was a middle-aged tinplate-worker, who had lately become a warm convert to the doctrines of Universalism. There were a few of his own persuasion in the singing-seats, and there were some who thought little of the matter either one way or the other, but who would gladly have excused themselves from singing the appointed lines, if others of a milder character could be substituted.

Mrs. Shrinknot was born to be finally an ultra-religionist, but she had not yet taken her decided part in polemics. Her imagination had been much wrought upon at this very moment by the novel phenomenon in the pulpit. She was already an incipient convert; already prepared to yield up her mind to the whole influence of his manner, and the whole demands of his doctrines. When she perceived, therefore, that a majority of singers in the octagon had come to a resolution not to sing the forty-fourth hymn, second book, nor even a single verse of it, her whole soul was inflamed with the spirit of personal and controversial opposition. She turned round to Mary Wentworth, and requested her support, as she was about to rise and commence the hymn, in spite of the fixed resolution of the other side of the choir. Mary shook her head with her usual firmness, and her friend appeared for a moment daunted. But at length, when a sufficient time had elapsed to put the congregation out of all patience, and the young theologian had arisen again from his seat, and was again leaning far over the cushion, with eyes prying into the gallery, to ascertain, if possible, the cause of the delay, Mrs. Shrinknot, at the very moment of her rising to commence the hymn alone, was interrupted and astonished by the following dialogue, which took place between the tinplate-worker leaning over the gallery, and the clergyman leaning over the pulpit.

Tinplate-worker. — "You are requested, reverend sir, to give out another hymn."

Minister. — "Why am I requested to do so, sir?"

Tinplate-worker. — "We do not approve of the sentiments of the hymn you have just read."

Minister. — "I decline reading any other."

Tinplate-worker. — "Then we decline singing, sir."

Minister (after pausing some time, with a look of wretched anxiety, sorrow, indignation, and horror, at what he felt was a sacrilegious violation of his undoubted authority). — "Let us pray."

The congregation obeyed his direction, so far as rising on their feet could be so doing; but had he said, "Let us speculate on the scene that has just occurred," his exhortation would have obtained a far more universal compliance that day than is generally paid to dictations from the sacred desk, and would have corresponded with marvellous exactness to what actually rolled over and over in the minds of the audience, while the minister himself was beginning at the Fall, and going through the whole body of divinity in his prayer, dwelling at much length and with peculiar emphasis on the most dreadful realities of the future world.

Of course, during the ensuing week, the parish was in an uproar. The communing members, technically called the church, who bore omnipotent sway in the internal affairs of the congregation, pressed upon Mr. Welby the execution of this rule, namely, that he should begin at the beginning of Watts's Psalm-Book on the next Lord's day, and, proceeding regularly through that book, cause every verse of every psalm and hymn, without omission or exception, to be sung in their existing order, and never should depart therefrom, — Watts, like the Book of Common Prayer in the Church of England, receiving, in many parts of this region, an equal reverence with the Bible.

But the measures taken to secure sound doctrine were ill calculated to preserve good singing. From this moment my poor choir labored with its death-wound. Occasionally considerable numbers would attend it, and even the tinplate-worker condescended to lend his services, when he could look forward and ascertain that the psalms for the day interfered not with his ultra-latitudinarian creed. But there was no system, no regularity, no zeal, none of that essential *esprit-de-corps* which constitutes the very life of a band of singers. You could more easily calculate on the weather of an approaching Sabbath, than you could on its music. A visit of Mr. Murray, the Universalist preacher, to the neighborhood, was certain to draw three quarters of the choir away. Mary Wentworth departed to keep school at Hampton Falls. Mrs. Shrinknot, disgusted with the moderation of Mr. Welby, who has always satisfied myself with his mild orthodoxy, rode constantly several miles to attend the ministrations of the young divine, who had innocently caused an accelerated decay of the choir. A sense of the unfashionableness of singing at the meeting-house, would at times pervade all the females of the village, and keep them for several months in their pews below. A hundred caprices, a hundred quarrels, rose one after another, in quicker succession, and of more paltry nature, than I can permit myself to describe. The very knowledge of sacred music seemed to be fast decaying. No recruits from the rising generation prepared themselves as formerly to take part in this interesting portion of worship. No movement was started from any quarter to effect a better order of things. All classes were sunk in musical apathy. The Village Harmony, and other Collections belonging to the seats, were carried off and never recovered. Many of the benches in the octagon were broken down by idle boys who went to overlook the doings of town-meetings, and were omitted to be repaired. A feeble attempt was generally made to sing once on each part of the day, but that precariously depended on Mr. Welby's feelings and state of health. And if now and then a scattered worshipper or two straggled into the seats, it was either because they wished to change their places at church for the mere sake of variety, or because they could call no other spot their own.

Such was the condition in which I found the once flourishing singing-pew at Waterfield, when, after having passed four years in Harvard College, and three in a lawyer's office in the county of Bristol, I came and nailed up a professional sign in the centre of my native village. On the first Sabbath, instinct led me to the spot. In going to the meeting-house, I confess I felt too much complacency in the conscious improvement which the preceding seven years had effected in my mind and person. But, alas! this momentary infirmity was full severely punished, when, on approaching the singing-pew, I perceived it too desolate and dusty to be occupied. I passed a mournful day; but better times and better things erelong arose, which I may perhaps be able to recount at some future period, when (if my present essay find favor with an indulgent public, and my leisure from an increasing business permit) I shall attempt the *History of a New-England Singing-School.**

1828.

---

* It has been one of the fond dreams of the author's life to accomplish the task intimated in this closing sentence. The conception of his plan admitted a wide variety of characters, an extensive and diversified field of incident and action, and a representation of many interesting progressive developments of social life in New England. But the imperative demands of a higher path of duty, concurring with several years of impaired health, and somewhat perhaps with his distance from the scene of action, have prevented the execution of an undertaking, to which he would gladly have devoted the vigor of his powers.

THE INFLUENCE OF ONE NATIONAL LITERATURE UPON ANOTHER;

WITH

AN APPLICATION OF THE SUBJECT TO THE CHARACTER AND DEVELOPMENT OF AMERICAN LITERATURE.

That every nation, like every individual, has an intellectual and moral character, original and peculiar to itself, may be regarded as an established axiom. Consequently, the literary productions of every nation must be more or less characterized by the stamp of its peculiar genius. If we could imagine among nations a long-continued abstinence from mutual intercourse, we must also suppose several sorts of resulting literatures, as diverse from each other, in kind if not in degree, as are those of China and Europe of the present day. A state of things like this would assuredly depress the general standard of thought and language throughout the world. No nation, any more than a solitary individual, can be imagined to inherit from nature, and to centre in itself, so proud an affluence of thoughts, emotions, and expressions, as to place it beyond the reach of improvement from foreign sources. In the same manner as the private members of society are induced to lay aside many a rude peculiarity, to suppress many a narrow prejudice, and to catch many a bright idea and generous emotion, by means of constant interchanges in life, so is the intellect of a whole nation, by coming into contact and collision with the intellect of other nations, enabled to elevate its own habits of thought, to seize upon more effective modes of expression, and to winnow its literature from national or accidental imperfections.

It is evident, however, that a process of this kind may be carried too far, and that a nation may indulge so extravagant a passion for foreign models, as to sacrifice that charm and vigor of originality, for which scarcely any acquired accomplishments can be regarded as an equivalent. For, to recur to our comparison drawn from private life, no individual ought to extend his love or deference for society so far, as to sacrifice a certain originality and independence of character. If he only learns to avoid offensive eccentricities, and gives general proof of having breathed the air of good company, his native peculiarities may not only be forgiven, but admired. It is thus in the intellectual intercourse of nations. We shall see, in the historical survey now to be presented as an illustration of these remarks, how nations which have united a firm self-reliance with a suitable degree of flexibility to foreign impressions, have attained the highest literary rank; and, on the other hand, how their literature immediately degenerated, at the moment when they either disdained, or too devotedly sought for, influences from abroad.

The first example shall be drawn from the ancient literature of the Hebrews. That literature is the consecrated drapery of heaven-inspired truths. Yet, as the personal style of Isaiah differed from that of Daniel, or the style of St. John from the style of St. Paul, — as David prophesied in the language of the palace, and Amos in that of the herdman's lodge, — so a reverent and discriminating inspection will not fail to perceive that the Hebrew literature, like that of all other nations, was more or less subjected to the great law of circumstance. Springing forth, as it did, along a line of two or three thousand years, during which the fortunes of the nation were frequently varying, we shall find it approximating to the highest standard of excellence, according as the inspired writers united with the wonderful peculiarities of the Hebrew mind a liberal susceptibility to exterior impressions; and then again receding from that lofty standard, either through an injudicious imitation of foreign models, or an entire exclusion of all foreign influences whatever. Accordingly, behold it first under Moses, the deserved admiration of subsequent ages. To the noble fountain of his own native Israelitish literature and a remoter East, Moses applied a mind, rich, as St. Stephen informs us, in the wisdom and learning of the Egyptians. The union of these two magnificent streams resulted in the production of the Pentateuch; in the same manner as the influence of two mighty rivers sometimes throws up an island, covered with majestic forests and fragrant and beautiful flowers. For what has ever equalled the sublime pictures of creation and nature in the Pentateuch, — the lovely simplicity of its descriptions of patriarchal and pastoral life, — the vivid and graphic reality of its narratives, — its authentic charts of the primitive genealogy of nations, — and the concise, comprehensive, and intelligible texture of its legislative phraseology? To the same period is generally referred the composition of the Book of Job, which vies in literary excellence with the Pentateuch.

To the Mosaic era succeeded the times of the Judges, when intercourse with foreign nations was rigorously forbidden. Accordingly, again, we find a *poverty* of literary documents to be characteristic of this period; no poetry, no didactic treatises, nothing scarcely, in short, save the meagre annals of the commonwealth in war and in peace, until the time of David. With David, and especially with Solomon his son, commenced an entirely new epoch. Conquest and commerce now brought the national mind again into contact with foreign influences. Immediately also advanced the standard of Hebrew literature. The delightful little history of Ruth is the first fruits of a transition from the rude age of the Judges to the enlightened period of the monarchy. To this era, in its subsequent advancement, will the world for ever be indebted for the Psalms of David, that inexhaustible repository of sacred poetry, as varied in its subjects and moods of religious sentiment as were the tones of his own exulting or complaining harp. To the same era belongs also that treasure-house of moral and practical wisdom, the Proverbs of Solomon. Contemporary also with this was unquestionably the Book of Ecclesiastes, a didactic poem, or colloquy, of the highest character, in which the Byron spirit of this world appears to be comparing notes with the Fénelon spirit, respecting their relative opinions and experience of the condition, prospects, and destiny of human nature; the whole closing with that unparalleled lesson for the confident and inexperienced, with this initial sentence, *Remember now thy Creator in the days of thy youth*, — which, while it is adorned with a profusion of ingenious and beautiful imagery, obeys, throughout, the laws of a delicate and scrupulous taste. When were the accumulating infirmities of old age ever described with so much physiological exactness, blended with such fine touches of poetry and pathos?

Nor ought we to forget, in connection with this topic, the inimitable idyl, or series of idyls, entitled The Song of Solomon, combining a perfect tenderness of sentiment with the fascinating simplicity of nature and the most exquisite music of poetry. The truth is, the good old stock of Hebrew intellect was now again released from the confinement and constraint to which it had been for several centuries subjected; a freer and a wider atmosphere was allowed to breathe in upon it; it was stimulated by the fresh contact of a mould different from its own native soil, and the result, as we have seen, was the production of fruits more than usually divine. Traces of Hebrew and Egyptian intercourse are very evident in the sacred literature of this period. Champollion, in his successful studies of the hieroglyphics, was more and more struck by the recurrence of expressions coincident with the language of the Psalms. It is well known that portions of the Song of Solomon refer to the Egyptian princess whom he had married, and who is called his *sister-bride*, in contrast to the Ammonite princess, whom he had previously espoused. Among the recent wonders of Egyptian discovery is a well-identified portrait of that very princess, and near it an inscription of the same expression, *sister-bride*, which occurs in the Hebrew song. In the same Hebrew poem, she is likened also to a *sacred garden*. Every scholar knows that these sacred gardens originated in Egypt, and were guarded by the first order of nuns. The following translation, by an elegant scholar, of the whole passage from the Song of Solomon, will recall the classical descriptions of the same subject as deduced from Egyptian sources: —

"A sacred garden is my sister-bride,
A sacred garden, and a well-spring sealed;
A paradise of sweets, wherein preside
The fairest fruits which spiciest blossoms yield,
Such as in youthful Eden were revealed;
Camphor and spikenard flourish 'midst its flowers,
Spikenard and balsam, cane and cinnamon;
Gem-scattering fountains bathe its fragrant bowers
Of myrrh and incense, balm and origan;
While living waters leap from cedary Lebanon."

The prophets Isaiah and Jeremiah everywhere exhibit manifest indications connecting them with this most classic era in Hebrew literature. With Daniel and Ezekiel the pure standard of Hebraism seems somewhat to decline, in consequence of the extreme Oriental spirit too deeply imbibed from the Chaldeans during the Babylonish captivity. Then came a wide reaction, under the later minor prophets, who, spurning and denouncing every species of foreign influence, fell back upon the narrow intellectual resources of the nation, and were contented with a literary standard considerably inferior to that of the Davidéan era.

During the next four hundred years, as the nation grew in importance, and came in contact with its different conquerors, we see the literature of the Apocrypha and the Rabbis assume a higher character, until at length the Hebrew mind, shone upon by the strong and near effulgence of Grecian and Roman refinement, and still specially breathed on, as in the days of old, by the spirit of God, displayed, in numerous portions of the

Gospels and Epistles of the New Testament, the boldest stamp of literary excellence. The highest degree, and, as it were, the summary exponent and focus of that excellence, I consider exhibited in St. Paul's celebrated definition of Charity, comprising the thirteenth chapter of the First Epistle to the Corinthians, too familiar to all readers to require a repetition. This chapter, to a literary eye, presents a remarkable combination of qualities. To the gorgeousness and fervor of Plato, without his vagueness and mysticism, it unites the strict and acute analysis of Aristotle, without his cold, material, mechanical philosophy. The march, the logical sequence and development of the sentiments, are truly beautiful, while a luxuriant abundance of ideas and images is crowded within the smallest possible compass, like the miraculous economy of an organized human body. The Apostle, seizing upon the Greek term *charity*, brings to its illustration a throng of Jewish recollections and sacred references. In short, the Hebrew mind, in its highest and purest state of inspiration, mingling and struggling with the Roman and Grecian minds, in their palmiest stage of moral and intellectual cultivation, could alone pour out this unequalled strain of divine philosophy, which urges forward the whole human race to the path of its loftiest duty, and the attainment of its brightest ultimate destiny.

The Apostles, with the exception of the Rabbinical authors, were the last writers of the pure Hebrew stock; since Josephus and Philo, who succeeded them by a few years, were content to sacrifice all remains of nationality to the engrossing genius of classic Greece.

The genius of classic Greece suggests the second great example to illustrate the theory which I have undertaken to establish. I am aware how scanty and almost imperceptible are the traces of foreign influence to be actually discerned in the works of the earlier Greek authors. It has been asserted by some of the ablest critics of the day, that the whole body and spirit of ancient Greek literature were perfectly original, — perfectly indigenous; and that it would have been in all respects such as it is, had no other national literature existed. Now I am willing to allow that the intellect of the ancient Greeks was by far the *most* original, the most independent, the most spontaneously active and self-fertilizing, of any in existence. But that it ever did, or could, start forward on its peculiar race of glory without an early and powerful stimulus of exterior influence, is quite contrary to historical facts and probabilities. Greece was surrounded by nations who certainly preceded her in the march of civilization and literary cultivation. The Egyptians on the south, the Phœnicians on the southeast, the Persians on the east, the cultivators of Sanscrit and other Oriental literatures, had all made very considerable advances in science and letters, for ages before a Greek song was sung in the valleys of the Peloponnesus, or a Greek inscription recorded on its rocks. We know that an active commerce was driven by the Phœnicians along the shores of the Peloponnesus. Is it possible that they could refrain from communicating a portion of their intellectual acquirements to so lively, inquisitive, and susceptible a people as the Greeks? We know that the Greeks themselves ascribed to a Phœnician the introduction among them of sixteen letters of their alphabet, and the strong resemblance existing between several letters of the Greek and Hebrew alphabets confirms the tradition. Now, would mere letters be likely to be introduced without a literature? At all events, is not the tradition itself a conclusive proof that the Greek mind, proud as might have been its subsequent literary achievements, was indebted to another national mind for the very instrument by which those achievements were effected, — thus confirming the main positions of this essay? And when we consider, again, those wondrous resemblances between the structure of the Greek language and that of the ancient Sanscrit tongue, — between many portions of the Greek philosophy and the Indian philosophy, — between the gods of Greece and those of India, as demonstrated by Sir William Jones and others, — can we possibly resist the conclusion, that the Greek literature, at a very early period, received an impulse and an impress from some Oriental source, to which it was indebted for many of those infinitely varied qualities that stamped its glorious and triumphant living reign of two thousand years? Did Herodotus travel through so many foreign cities without imbibing something of the various national characteristics which he witnessed? Was he the first of his nation, or the only one of his age, who wandered abroad for improvement? Must there not long have existed between Greece and the surrounding countries, channels of refined intercourse, through which a mental action and reaction must have been constantly reciprocated? Was the Persian court always open to the banished statesmen of Greece, without exercising some influence on her literature? Do we not perceive, in the majority of Greek authors, a certain tinge of Oriental simplicity on the one hand, and Oriental gorgeousness on the other, quite distinct from that masculine, compact, energetic spirit, which may be regarded as the essential characteristic of the Grecian mind? It is no objection to these views of the subject, that we cannot point out allusions to any extraneous literature, or hear the Greeks acknowledging their obligations to other nations, or find them actually quoting by chapter and verse from the sources in question. Do we find such acknowledgments in Virgil, or Terence? And yet do we not know that Virgil and Terence would scarcely have enjoyed a literary existence except by means of the Greek originals from whom they drew their very breath of life? Besides, it is not absolutely necessary for the purpose of my argument that a tangible literature should have preceded the productions of the Grecian mind; that libraries, parchments, and other written monuments, should have been imported at home, or studied abroad. It is enough if personal intercourse and oral communication were frequent and prolific. If Homer or the Homeridæ could ever listen with delight to the wandering or stationary bards of other lands, and treasure some of their strains in their own melodious souls, to be afterwards woven into their own majestic and unrivalled harmonies, my general theory is supported.

It is certainly, moreover, confirmed by the influence which writings in the different *dialects* of Greece exerted on each other. The tribes who spoke those different dialects may be regarded in the light of so many different nations. And who will deny that much of the perfection of the Greek literature was owing to the interchange among those different tribes, — to their borrowing from each other various modes of thought and forms of expression, — to the noble stimulus of mutual example and competition, — and to the power they thus possessed of working up one general literature from the choicest sources and materials? Why else did Herodotus abandon his native Dorian dialect, to write his general history in the Ionic, if processes of this nature were not constantly in action?

The views now urged are still further confirmed by the new and strong impulse which was certainly given to the whole Grecian mind, when Pisistratus had collected the fleeting fragments of the Homeric poetry, for the benefit of his countrymen.

We shall soon see by other examples, in the course of the remaining examination, how a revival of the ancient literature of any country within itself produces similar effects with the introduction and commixture of foreign literatures. Sufficient has now been advanced to warrant the conclusion, that, notwithstanding the self-relying and creative energies of the Greeks, yet even they were benefited by influences from abroad, and that, like their own Apollo, who condescended to accept from Mercury the *caduceus*, or mystic rod of power, wisdom, diligence, and activity, so was even their intellectual character raised by the enlightened genius of commercial intercourse.

The question respecting Roman literature is much more easily disposed of. For some hundred years, that literature was like a savage crab-tree, growing in its own native solitude, and producing fruits, pungent and flavorous indeed, but small, scanty, and unprofitable. At length, the rich scions of Greece were grafted upon it, and not until then did it start up into a prolific and magnificent luxuriance. The Roman literature has been sometimes slightingly spoken of, as a mere echo or reflection of the Grecian. But it is a noble echo, like that which speaks out from a mountain rock; a brilliant reflection, like that which gleams from a mirror in the palace of kings; and who does not always love to contemplate the daring and successful image of a glorious original?

The Roman, however, was far from being a servile imitator, or mere translator. There is a native dignity, a conscious sense of power, in all his movements. It has been happily said of him, that whatever he borrows, he borrows like a conqueror. He appropriates to his own intellectual nature many qualities of the Grecian character, making them entirely his own. Yet perhaps he would have assumed a more commanding station in the domain of letters, had he trusted more to his own resources, and paid a less exclusive and absorbing adoration to the intellect of Greece. He *could* have originated much more, if he had dared. But he generally feared to depart from prescribed forms and models. When he does venture to pour out his soul, as Ovid, or to impersonate the very genius of the commonwealth, as Cicero, or to prosecute independent courses of speculation, as Tacitus, we are made to feel the inherent majesty and energy of the Roman mind. In such cases, the trammels were thrown off; the old traditionary reverence for everything Greek was forgotten; the pupil rose to a level with his master; and the reader, borne onward by the combination of originality and greatness, finds this only to regret,—that the Roman soul had not more frequently thrown itself on the tide of letters, with the same fervor, the same enterprise, the same singleness, the same unconscious and spontaneous nationality, with which it threw itself on the tide of battle and victory.

When letters were beginning to decline in every other part of the Roman empire, they were cultivated with fresh and extraordinary activity at Alexandria. Libraries accumulated, authors were multiplied, and every sort of encouragement was given to the cause of learning. But why did nothing more valuable and impressive proceed from the far-famed Alexandrian school? Why are we only indebted to it for a wilderness of commentary, a body of second-hand and second-rate philosophy, and a mass of literature that merely imitates and counterfeits the literature of olden times? It is because, at this period, there was no nationality, no independent vigor, in Egypt. Her scholars welcomed the flood of materials which came to them from Greece and Rome; but they were at this moment only the insignificant portions of Greece and Rome themselves; they were overborne by the inflowing stream, and had not power to rise up and meet it, to mingle with it, to assimilate it with their own intellectual resources; and for this reason, Alexandria sustains so comparatively low a rank in the community of letters.

Two or three centuries passed away, and, behold, the national mind of Arabia, which had so long slept in solitude and inaction, lighted up by the influence of the Jewish and Christian Scriptures! Mahomet was but the representative or type of his whole nation. The Koran, for which he so largely drew from the Bible, and from old traditionary thoughts, images, and experiences of Arabia, awakened the national intellect to extraordinary vigor. And then again, a few generations later, after the excitement of universal warfare and the orgasm of victory had subsided, and the Arabians were attracted to the treasures of Greek and Roman literature, the genius of the nation took a new and sudden flight. Not only did the Arabians keep the torch of science burning during the Dark Ages, and preserve many literary monuments, which would otherwise have perished, but they themselves effected very considerable achievements in philosophy, history, mathematics, and poetry. To their influence, when they were masters of Spain, has been justly traced the rise of the Troubadours and Trouveurs in France. The tide of conquest at length rolled back; the Arabians were placed on the defensive; they adopted the policy of excluding foreign intercourse, disdaining the ideas and attainments, as well as the society, of other nations; — and where is their literature now?

The example of China also confirms the principles maintained in this essay. The literary monuments of the Chinese are not destitute of considerable talent, ingenuity, and proofs of industry. They have a drama, a history, a poetry, a philosophy, an ethics, and a philology, by no means contemptible. Still, there is a jejuneness, a puerility, a provincial narrowness of grasp, in all the specimens of their literature that have yet reached us, only to be accounted for by the perfect mortmain in which the national mind has been locked up for centuries, and only to be removed by a liberal intercourse with the intellect of other nations.

India surpasses China in almost all the branches just enumerated, and especially in a refined system of grammar and logic. Why so? It is, that she has been formerly, as she is now, the theatre of national collision and commixture, and successive Greek, Mahometan, and Christian conquests have necessarily elevated the standard of her literature.

Persia, again, has a more perfect literature than either China or India. Her central position has blessed her with benign influences from the East and from the West. She has a noble stem of nationality, which has survived the storms of many thousand years; and whenever her soul shall be fully opened to influences of enlightened Christian Europe, she will assuredly take her place among the foremost nations of the earth.

It is now time to survey the progress of the modern Western world, so far as it may be connected with the particular vein of the present discussion.

Long had the mind of Europe been slumbering. The inexhaustible and uncultivated millions of the North had everywhere overspread her surface. The ancient and the recent inhabitants had begun to amalgamate. The young nations that had sprung into being from these admixtures had each a genius peculiar to itself, —a genius capable of great things in its own due time. But as yet there was no manifestation; no development; no creative spark; since the period had not arrived for collision and influence from abroad. But the Crusades mingled the nations of the East and the West together; and soon after the last of the Crusades, we have Dante in Italy, and Chaucer in England, as the glorious fruits. A hundred years later, the scholars of Greece, exiled from their native land by the irruption and oppressions of their Turkish conqueror, spread themselves through the South of Europe, and were everywhere welcomed, not only as Christian brethren in exile, but as the teachers and enlighteners of mind. Immediately revived the general cultivation of ancient literature; and immediately, too, burst forth, not puerile and slavish imitations of the ancients, but original, independent, vigorous national literatures. Italy had already led the way in Dante. Her language arrived soonest at perfection. The mental creations of her Boccaccios, Petrarchs, Ariostos, and Tassos rolled out in full-orbed beauty, at once the heralds and promoters of similar creations in other lands. It is remarkable, that, since the revival of letters, Italian literature has been able to boast of no very splendid era besides this, its earliest development; whereas England, as we shall immediately see, has exhibited four or five such eras at least. The fact may be accounted for, on the principles of this essay, partly by the declining sense of nationality and independence to which the misfortunes of Italy have subjected her, and partly by the restricted intellectual intercourse with other nations, which the policy of her rulers, both religious and political, has imposed upon her. During the last forty years, however, when the aspirations of Italy after a distinct national existence have been frequently revived and encouraged, and she has cultivated with some diligence the different literatures of Europe, her science, her poetry, her history, and her romance have assumed an imposing attitude, and borne very valuable fruits.

At the revival of letters, England first followed in the train of Italy. She received the benefit not only of the awakened cultivation of the Greek and Roman classics, but of the recent emanations of the Italian mind, as well as of several successive translations of the Christian and Hebrew Scriptures. If we can imagine the mind of

England arousing at these voices, and coming forth to mingle in the united progress of Greece, of Rome, of reviving Italy, and of the Bible, we can comprehend the existence of a Shakespeare, a Spenser, and the other prodigies of the age of Elizabeth. It matters not that Shakespeare, personally, was but slightly versed in the original productions of other times and other lands. He needed not the accomplishments of minute or extensive erudition. He was the intellectual type of his age and nation. By the instinct of genius, he knew and felt the essence and spirit of what they knew and felt; and in fact the latest researches have discovered that his education was sufficiently elevated and comprehensive to bring him within reach of the highest sympathies and affinities, so that he might grasp the fruits and results of the learning of his age, although he himself had never delved about its roots.

The same influences which wrought the wonders of the Elizabethan era long continued to operate, and contributed, we conceive, to the formation of a Dryden and a Milton. The national mind then languished for a generation, after the exhaustion of the civil wars. It was awakened to new and brilliant action in the age of Queen Anne, by the copious influx of French literature, which had arisen to its highest tide-mark in the reign of Louis XIV.

Immediately after the age of Queen Anne, we have a school more intensely British in its character, and with many characteristic excellences, consisting of such writers as Fielding, Smollet, Richardson, Chesterfield, Thomson, and Gray. This school was very naturally beginning to languish for want of external stimulus and sustenance; to its dramatic attempts we may well and feelingly exclaim, in one of its own lines, of unfortunate celebrity,—

> "Oh, Sophonisba, Sophonisba, oh!"

while Smollet's history, too unlike his romances, is but a wretched basket of the dryest chips. But as the eighteenth century continued to advance, the power and relations of England also extended. Her intercourse with the several nations of Europe, and with Eastern Asia, attracted her to their literatures. The usual happy reaction on her own mind took place, and the middle and nearly the latter half of the eighteenth century exhibited the splendid constellation of Johnson, Hume, Goldsmith, Junius, Robertson, Gibbon, Warburton, Cowper, Sir William Jones, Horsley, Burke, and their celebrated contemporaries. The whole world was tributary to England, and English literature, in consequence, assumed a kind of majestic metropolitan character, as if speaking for the instruction of many nations, or rather of mankind. But by this very dictatorial attitude it was essentially injured. It became too proud and self-relying. At the commencement of the present century, nothing was more characteristic of England, in every respect, than a sovereign contempt for other nations. This feeling extended itself to her literary relations. She seemed scarcely conscious that any literature but her own was worthy of a thought. She despised the literature of Germany; she despised the literature of France; she despised the literature of Italy; she despised the literature of the East; even her cultivation of the ancient classics was pursued as if it were a kind of old-

English prerogative to know something of Greek and Latin; it was simply hereditary, prescriptive, habitual, mechanical, and was more engrossed by the pedantic mysteries of prosody than by the scope and spirit of those divine productions. And what was the consequence of this state of things? Her own literature became itself contemptible. A Hayley and a Darwin were idolized as poets; a Hoole was endured and was even popular as a translator; an Aikin was submitted to as a critic; a Bisset was listened to as an historian and biographer; and the periodical press was degenerating into the feeblest inanity. But out of this accumulation of insipidity was destined to ascend a new and beautiful creation. The whole energies of England were aroused by her vital contest with the military phenomenon of the age. Her pride, though not indeed subdued, was shaken by her dangers. She began to feel fair sympathies with other nations, and to remember that hers was not the only star in the firmament of mind. Moved by the agitations of the times, the then rising generation of England looked for light from every quarter. The finest geniuses sat at the feet of Germany. Scott, by his translations from Goethe, and Coleridge, by his purveyances from German philosophy, contributed to bring the literary productions of that nation into repute; Roscoe, although then in middle life, awoke a fresh interest in the authors of Italy; the Edinburgh Review called attention to the almost forgotten excellences of the Elizabethan era; Chateaubriand and Madame de Stael extorted respect for the reviving literature of France; Germany was rendered still more fashionable by the captivating commentaries of Madame de Stael; and all these powerful elements, pouring in upon the English mind, already in fervid action, prepared the way for the glories of the first quarter of the nineteenth century,—its Scotts, Campbells, Southeys, Byrons, Wordsworths, Moores, Lambs, Coleridges, Milmans, Crabbes, together with its unrivalled school, or rather schools, of periodical literature.

The original, native vein of the French intellect was a delightful one; lively, precise, penetrating, graceful. It welcomed with the utmost ardor the commixture of Greek and Roman materials at the revival of letters, but for a long time it paid them a too absorbing reverence, forgetting its own glorious capacities, and becoming most ludicrously pedantic. At length the genius of the nation restored itself to a happier equilibrium, and under its influence sprang forth the long line of authors from Montaigne to Voltaire, who have shed so brilliant a lustre around their country's name. Still the French mind has never yet attained its highest destiny. Drinking chiefly from the stream of classical literature, and almost disdaining to be nourished from other sources, it has ever worn a too artificial and antique character. Its whole past literature savors strongly of the classic oil. Rousseau indeed acknowledged his obligations to England, and especially to England's Richardson, who taught him to draw from his own soul and from nature. But Voltaire, who may be called the very genius of France incarnate, could feel no true appreciation or sympathy for Shakespeare, who was equally the incarnate genius of England. The Revolution shook the mind of France from this too narrow and restricted system. She now seeks everywhere with avidity and docility for intellectual sustenance. England, Germany, Italy, and the

East combine to prompt her new and freer impulses; and although of late she has been defiled and tormented with a literature which knows no law, moral, religious, or critical, yet even now she is blessed by some bright, redeeming exceptions. Whenever her political institutions shall be so adapted to her character as to secure her repose, how can we doubt that the country of St. Louis, of Henry IV., of Corneille, of Fénelon, of Madame Roland, and of Lamartine, enjoying the most felicitous position in Europe, and with so much of pure Athenian spirit in her composition, shall yet accomplish her part in the elevation of the whole human mind, and thus fulfil the appropriate destiny of beautiful France?

Spain and Portugal present striking exemplifications of the principles maintained in this essay. The impulse of Greek and Roman literature at the revival of letters was felt in due proportion by these two nations. Their respective minds were aroused at the summons, and spoke out characteristically and impressively. What might not have been fairly expected from the country that produced a Camoens, or from the still greater and nobler nation that could boast of a Calderon, a Lope de Vega, and a Cervantes? But what could those nations do? Shut out by a jealous Index Expurgatorius from the world of letters, they could but vegetate in solitude and darkness. A few plants, peeping here and there through the fissures in the dungeon wall, have caught some rays of the external light, and manifested a corresponding vigor and beauty; and such is the brief story of Spanish and Portuguese literature for the last two or three centuries.

Germany devoted herself so exclusively and intensely

for two hundred years to the cultivation of the classical authors, and of a dogmatic, formal theology, as almost to forget her own nationality, and the abundance and richness of her interior resources. The vast popularity, however, and general circulation of Luther's Translation of the Scriptures, preserved her from the extreme of pedantry, and infused into her earlier literature, subsequent to the revival of letters, a certain solemnity and tenderness. When beginning to awake, at the commencement of the eighteenth century, and to look forth for some new impulse to her powers, she was naturally attracted to the commanding literature of her neighbor, France, which she cultivated with undue admiration and docility. Its spirit was permitted to predominate so much over her own, as to check and overlay the half-dormant energies of her native genius. But as she was still at liberty, — as she could go where she pleased among the nations, for sustenance and stimulants, — she next instinctively turned to the literature of England, to which she gave herself up with her usual fervid assiduity. Hence a very remarkable improvement was effected in her intellectual harvests. Klopstock may be regarded as the representative of this stage of her development. But she still moved on. The untiring and unbounded erudition of her sons brought to light the long-buried treasures of her early popular songs and tales, in which the original germ of the national mind had richly budded; these were studied with a fond ardor by her scholars and poets; an intense German spirit was revived, mysterious like the visions of Walhalla, but delighting as much as ever did Odin or Thor in the materialities of earth. Italy was now visited by the Germans for the effects of her literature and her art; and out of all these combined workings and influences of three hundred years arose the mountain era, of which Schiller, Wieland, Richter, Lessing, and Goethe are among the loftiest summits.

Denmark, Norway, and Sweden have pursued a course very similar to that of Germany. Like her, they long wrote and read in Latin, when they ought to have written and read in their own mother tongues. Like her, they were then seduced by the brilliant example of France, and their literatures were but feeble echoes of that of the great nation. And lastly, like her, they have applied themselves to other European sources of instruction, especially to England; they have revived, and diligently cultivated, the study of their old Icelandic and other Scandinavian treasures; a national spirit is awakened within them, which, however, disdains not to profit from every quarter, and the result appears to be a promising era of fresh, vigorous, and beautiful emanations.

The literary existence of Russia resembles that of an overgrown youth of talents, and therefore hardly comes within the fair limits of the present inquiry. The very alphabet which she uses was the invention and gift of Peter the Great, her representative type, who, by his visits abroad, seems to have been aware of the benefits conferred on the cause of civilization and refinement by foreign impulses. The few specimens of her literature which have been circulated, especially the sublime Hymn to the Deity, translated by Dr. Bowring, and familiar to almost every English reader, are highly creditable to her genius.

I am unable to assign a reason why so little of original

and inventive literature has been presented by Holland to the commonwealth of mind, or at least so little that has attracted general attention. Whether she was too long and disproportionately addicted to classical erudition and severe philosophy under the auspices of her Grotius, — or whether her national elasticity was cramped by her former subjection to Spanish despotism, — or whether she entered with a too absorbing zeal into the theological warfares of the seventeenth and eighteenth centuries, — or whether her language, which is but an ungainly dialect of the German, has repelled the study of it by foreigners, — or whether there be something sluggish and fenny in her powers of invention, — she certainly appears to have made no deep and general impression, although both her position and fortunes have been favorable to great intellectual advancement. During the last century, however, she led the way in the pursuit of classical learning and the sciences, and youth were sent from every part of Europe and America, to acquire the highest education at her universities. I learn also, that, within the last twenty or thirty years, several productions of the Batavian muse, characterized by great refinement and sensibility, have in some measure redeemed the unpoetical reputation of the Low Countries. This happy movement, however, was preceded by a welcome reception into the country of the most choice and brilliant masterpieces of the modern British, French, and German *belles-lettres*.

The principles maintained in this essay are particularly fortified by the example of Scotland. Her *ingenium perfervidum* was intensely wrought upon by the revival of letters, and the introduction of the treasures of Greece and Rome. The admirable Buchanan, alike classical in his Latin prose and poetry, is the type of this stage of Scottish development. Meanwhile, the stir of this and the subsequent periods kept alive that exquisite old vein of Scottish poetry, which the first James had so successfully cultivated, and which awaited its last and most glorious manifestation in the person of Burns; for the poetry of Scott, delightful and peculiar as it is, I deem rather a part of the general movement of the whole British intellect, before accounted for, than of the specific progress of his own native land. It is true that the themes and the scenes of his own country, chiefly, were the proximate stimulants of his wonderful powers; but in the lifetime of Sir Walter the individuality of Scotland was completely merged into that wider one of the whole British mind, and the great author, as he wrote, felt not the pulse, nor addressed the audience, of Scotland alone, but of that mighty empire on which the sun never sets. The intercourse of Scotland with France during the short reign of the unfortunate Mary, seems to have produced no striking impression on the national mind; for France herself at this period was working almost exclusively in the classical mine, and had not yet commenced her peculiarly national literary career. It is said, however, that the dialect and pronunciation of the people of Edinburgh bear marks to this day of the influence exerted by the loquacious and polished court of Queen Mary. During the seventeenth century, the mind of Scotland was principally engrossed by theological exercitations. Exclusively dedicated to the genius of a metaphysical faith, she shared very little in the cultivation of general literature, and scarcely opened her spirit to influences from abroad. But when her union with England was achieved, then commenced the era of her greatest literary glory. The natural effect of external contact, collision, and competition, arising from her rapidly increasing intercourse with England, immediately appeared. While reading Hume, Robertson, Smith, Campbell, Blair, and even Stewart, one almost imagines them sitting in their studies, — or rather walking, for they cultivated the habit of dictation, — moulding every sentence and every chapter so as to fall with the requisite grace and effect on the Southern ears for which they chiefly wrote. Some of them, indeed, are said to have acknowledged, that they composed in English almost with as much difficulty as they would have done in a foreign language. Hume abounded in Gallicisms, as Johnson once truly remarked in conversation. We have seen, in an old European Magazine, a most formidable list of errors against the English language committed by Dr. Blair in the first edition of his Lectures on Rhetoric. Robertson seems to have made a special study of English idioms, which he would sometimes employ as a school-boy selects sentences from a Gradus ad Parnassum. Thus, in the midst of whole pages of elevated, flowing, and dignified history, he would introduce such mosaic-work remarks as that "Mary doated on Darnley to distraction." The whole of Stewart's first volume of The Philosophy of the Human Mind seems to have been composed exactly in the same tone in which he would have aimed to compose an inaugural address in Ciceronian Latin. Still, notwithstanding these disadvantages in point of language under which Scotland labored, the influence of foreign cultivation awakened so much ambition and so much dormant power in her sons, that in her philosophy and her literature, during the latter half of the eighteenth century, she enjoyed the acknowledged pre-eminence of being the instructress, not of England only, but of Europe. And at the moment when mere English poetry, as described in a preceding statement, was at its lowest ebb, were heard the native wood-notes wild of Robert Burns, bursting on the astonished and delighted ear of civilized man, and creating even new schools of thought, of poetry, of criticism, and of philanthropy, founded on the widest basis of human sympathies and human interests. Nay, even Burns himself, however original and idiosyncratic, was moulded under the influences which have just been traced. The finest spirit of English poetry is manifest in a thousand touches throughout his works, equally with the ruder strokes of his own Doric muse. He himself acknowledges the indebtedness of his intellectual growth to some selections from Goldsmith and other English poets, which captivated his young mind at school.

Soon after the commencement of the present century, Scottish literature became completely merged and identified with that of England; though, even so late as the establishment of the London Quarterly Review, that jealous periodical complained that the language, as well as the politics, of England, was continually corrupted by the heresies and solecisms of its Edinburgh rival.

The various problems regarding the ancient literature of Ireland, I pretend not to solve, or at all events to apply to these speculations. Since the conquest, her sons have partaken the intellectual fortunes, and not seldom increased the intellectual glories, of Great Britain.

The populations and the literatures of Europe have sent out their various streams to our own shores, to be reunited and flow on together, in the single channel of American destiny. This new and momentous experiment in the progress of the human mind must deeply interest all who more or less directly participate in its advancement. If the principles advanced in the foregoing pages have been established by a competent induction, every enlightened scholar amongst us must be desirous of effecting and witnessing their faithful application in his own country.

Accordingly, our first aim, we apprehend, should be to cherish in our literature the peculiar qualities of the American character, as an indispensable groundwork for the appropriation of all other materials. And what are these qualities? What are the main, distinguishing characteristics which belong to this vast amalgamation of races, after having been sufficiently long removed from the manifold corruptions, trammels, prescriptions, and artificial distinctions of the Old World, and allowed to spring forth anew with the spontaneity of nature? As we apprehend, they are these, — the free, the intrepid, the excursive, the inventive. We see these attributes in most of the public and private movements of our land, — mingled indeed with sad mistakes, — followed sometimes by disasters, — but finally prevailing over opposition and discouragement. They are discernible in our ceaseless emigrations, — all of us being from the first but a nation of emigrants, — in our daring Revolutionary and subsequent wars, in our ravenous and insatiable appetite for territory, in our mercantile speculations, our religious opinions, our indomitable Protestantism, our camp-meetings, our stump and our legislative oratory, our pulpits, our pleadings, our tribunals, our election-seasons, our periodical press, our multitudinous new inventions, our political expedients, our vices, our various societies to repress them, our laws, our violations of them, our schools, and sometimes in our very amusements, — the most popular exhibition, for instance, at the West, for several years, having been a terrific representation of the infernal regions, with the actual roaring of the flames, and the audible howlings of the damned; while at this moment a picture three miles long, representing the whole valley of the Mississippi, is delighting hundreds of thousands of visitors.

The traces of these same qualities we also perceive in what little national literature we yet can boast of, as having made an impression on the European world. The theologian Edwards, — our state papers, so eulogized by Madame de Stael, — our recent historians, — our eagle-winged Channing, and bird-of-paradise-plumed Irving, — our Brockden Brown, — our other few distinguished novelists, — and the *élite* of Bryant's, Percival's, and other successful American poetry, — all exhibit the possession of these common characteristics.

But as these many qualities are peculiarly liable to excess, abuse, and degeneracy, how can their more perilous tendencies be better resisted than by the assiduous and liberal cultivation of all rich and wholesome foreign literatures?

We have seen, in these remarks, how a resort to such sources, in all ages and climes, has been productive of the happiest effects; how taste has been rectified, and expression improved, and thought fired, and a nation's mind assisted to burst its old shell, and put on new wings. Fortunately, the facilities for such processes are greater in our own country than were ever known before. Different races may approach each other on our common, friendly soil, without having to wait long ages for the removal of national antipathies; and their literatures may be brought together without the necessity of fighting their way through mutual mistake, prejudice, ridicule, and exasperation. The Frenchman and the Englishman sit down side by side on the borders of the same stream, and the German teaches his little son the language of his fathers, while he sends him to the common school provided by their adopted country.

Among modern literatures to be resorted to for these great purposes, the preference should unquestionably be given to the English. Its pages we should turn with daily and nightly hands. It is the well-spring of our language. It embodies a spirit the nearest to our own. Without fear of undue, servile dependence, let us freely consult its past and present monuments; let us listen with patience to its malignant or well-meaning criticisms on our national defects, and let us endeavor to ingraft the choicest mental offshoots of our English ancestry on our own free, intrepid, and vigorous stock.

There are disappointed and jealous American writers, who complain that a disproportionate patronage is lavished among us on English literature. But so dangerous a heresy ought boldly to be met and extinguished. It would be suicidal folly to turn away from the unrivalled treasures of England, out of tenderness for our own authors, however promising and meritorious they may be. We must not renounce the privilege of looking, almost with a fond adoration, to the country where there now exist, and have existed for many a long year, the mighty workings of an intellect the most robust, — a research the most varied, laborious, and successful, a scholarship the most graceful and accomplished, a science the most profound, a genius the most inventive, pathetic, and humorous, a poetry familiar with the loftiest aspirings or the tenderest tremblings of the human spirit, — all sustained by the advantages of a metropolitan position among the nations, a thousand years of traditionary lore and accumulated material, and an intensity of competition, of itself sufficient to call forth whatever powers and excellences lie dormant in our nature. Nothing indeed could better guard us from our national tendencies to a faulty extravagance, than the unwearied and straightforward good-sense of the Anglo-Saxon mind; that mind, by the way, which alone has clung, from the times of the Heptarchy, with a kind of instinctive, yet enlightened and liberal tenacity, to the combined study of the Sacred Scriptures and the pagan classics.

The remarkable fact here alluded to is at once a justification of the leading principle of this essay, and the bequest of an invaluable example for Americans to follow. As for the treasure of the Scriptures, it is already, or may be, in the hands of every American citizen. It contains, beside the waters of eternal life, whatever of æsthetic riches can be found for us in the whole body of the Oriental literatures, without their childish extravagances and defects. The Greek and Roman classics we must continue to study with unflagging, or rather with increasing ardor. We trust that something even of the *utility* of that study has been demonstrated in these remarks. But even though it came short of mere mechanical utilitarianism, and failed to satisfy the political economist, let it be remembered that the alabaster-box of precious ointment may be sometimes substituted for the hundred pence given to the poor. It is cheering to find a general sentiment prevailing in our country, in harmony with this view. Notwithstanding incessant attacks on classical learning, and clamorous appeals against it from every quarter to the principle of utility, the hundred colleges and universities throughout our land have persevered in maintaining the Greek and Roman classics in the foreground of a liberal education. We may have few or no giants in erudition like those of Europe, but it is evident that our standard of classical learning is rising from the point of depression to which it had once sunk. A goodly number of elementary treatises and text-books proceed every year from the press. The best German preparatory works abound more and more among us, in accurate translations. In all our new Territories and States there is a constant demand for teachers of the classics.

Abundant encouragement should next be given to the study of the modern European and other languages, as taste and opportunity may lead the way.

By these means, and by the exercise of an unsleeping discrimination, we may yet hope to build up a literature that shall have something of the primitive and earnest simplicity of the Scriptures, something of the practical good-sense of the English, something of the precision and point of the French, something of Italian smoothness, something of Spanish grandeur, something of German comprehensiveness, and much of the all-pervading, never-dying, perfect taste of the ancient classics, blended with the free, independent, and elastic attributes of our own national mind. Even though these specific foreign ingredients should not be perceived in the new compound of American literature, yet a result may be happily produced no less precious.*

This is a subject worthy of our most earnest contemplation. The literature of a country will sooner or later find its way, for good or ill, to the minds and hearts of its whole population. A Voltaire could loosen the faith of palaces and of *faubourgs*, — a Hannah More could strengthen that of princes and of peasants. Is it not worth while to furnish the humblest individual with accurate and impressive forms of thought and language, which shall convey as nearly as possible the exact truth of things, and awaken the most desirable associations? Is it not worth while to provide, by every possible method, that the resources of the listless and the vacant shall be multiplied, that light shall be afforded to the inquiring, and that the incessant activity of the intellect and the affections should be furnished with the most salutary and palatable food? A literature which accomplishes this for any country, is the greatest of its blessings. Misfortunes may overwhelm her; the tide of invasion or the

* It has been acutely remarked, on the circumstance of one national character arising from the union of any two separate races, that "in morals, as in physics, the commingling of two ingredients appears to produce a third, totally different from the rest. The new substance does not unite the qualities which distinguished its constituent elements while they remained apart, but acquires qualities which were found in neither." — *For. Quart. Rev.*, No. 71.

changes of time may sweep away the accumulated monuments of her wealth and grandeur; her sons may sit down to weep by her broken columns, or, more bitter still, they may be forced to remove in exile from her cherished dust; but if they can still press her immortal literature to their bosoms, they have not yet lost their mother-land, — she lives, and speaks to her children.

1836.

ESSAY ON POSTURES.

WRITTEN FOR AN EARLY NUMBER OF THE NORTH AMERICAN REVIEW.*

"*Sedeant* spectentque." — VIRG.

"In most strange postures we have seen him set himself."
SHAKESPEARE.

MR. EDITOR, —

Among the many ingredients which go to form the complete scholar, all must allow *posture* to be quite pre-eminent. He would deserve a sneer for his pretensions, who affected the literary character whilst at the same time he was ignorant of the rare and difficult accomplishment of sitting with his feet against the wall at a higher level than his head, or of leaning in due contemplative style upon his elbow. But the subject has unfortunately never been reduced to a science. How is it, sir, that the motions of the stars, for centuries to come, have been nicely adjusted to the fraction of a second, — that metals, and alkalies, and gases have been classed and systematized, — that the operations of the mind have been analyzed and developed, — that anatomy, even anatomy, that kindred department, has left almost no region of its own unexplored, — whilst the far

* The North American Review originally included a Miscellaneous Department.

more domestic, human, useful, and every-day business of postures has remained unnoticed and forgotten? To remove this scandal to science is the object of the few humble pages following. The author will be satisfied if he but excite attention to the subject, and will gladly leave the consummation of his attempt to greater adepts in attitude than himself.

Posture, sir, in its most general sense, may be defined, a modification of the body and limbs, for the purpose either of ease or show. It may be divided into standing, kneeling, lying down, and sitting. The first belongs chiefly to the arts of dancing-masters and drill-sergeants; the second, to love and devotion; the third, to ladies of fashion and delicate valetudinarians; it is the fourth and last only which now claims our attention, and that, principally, so far as it respects the sedentary class of people, called scholars. We shall enumerate the several varieties of sitting postures, describing them as exactly as possible, and dwelling on the peculiar advantages which they possess with the quiet votaries of literature.

First. The most universal, easy, and gentlemanlike is denominated the *cross-kneed* posture. All ranks, classes, and ages of males, together with some individuals of the other sex, cultivate this attitude with very happy success. It is no uncommon thing to see as many as sixteen or seventeen in a company, who, throughout an entire evening, most patiently and heroically persevere in this inoffensive mode of arranging the nether limbs. The child of three years of age adopts it among the first imitative accomplishments which excite the joy and admiration of his parents. The aspiring school-boy, by piling one knee upon another, adds a year to his existence, and bodies forth the dignity of the future man. The youth who is just entering the world, who has a letter of introduction to Mr. —— of Boston, or New York, or Philadelphia, would be put to infinite embarrassment if the privilege of crossing his knees were denied him. But without going through every age for the illustration of this division of our subject, I proceed to observe, that the cross-kneed posture is not to be adopted by all persons, at all times, and on all occasions. It is much too nice and trim for every-day use. I know many a respectable farmer who will never sit in this fashion except in his best suit, on a Sunday, or at a board of selectmen, or at the examination of a district school, or when visiting an acquaintance in town. What, sit cross-kneed and erect in a plain frock and trousers, and on a common working-day! Why, sir, it would be as preposterous and uncommon, as to read the Bible on a Monday, or to fix one's thoughts and eyes during the offering up of prayers on a Sabbath.

But this part of our subject is susceptible of a few subdivisions. Of cross-kneed postures there are five kinds:—1. The *natural*, which consists in throwing one knee over the other, and thinking no more about it. This is by far the best, and ought to be recommended universally to your readers. 2. The *broad-calfed*, which is effected by turning the upper knee out in such a manner, as to present as large a face of the inner calf as possible. This was very much in fashion nineteen years ago, but has since that time gradually subsided, and is practised, I believe, at present, only by those who love the fashions of their youth, and a few country-gentlemen in nankeen pantaloons. 3. The *long-legged*, so called, because this posture requires the foot of the upper leg to reach quite down to the floor. It was attempted to be brought into fashion about ten years ago, but it could not succeed, in consequence of the shortness of the limbs of some gentlemen in high ton at that time. It is nevertheless a graceful and elegant posture, and may be practised by your readers, for variety's sake, and with considerable ease, if they will but remember to draw the foot of the under leg in an oblique, retrograde direction, giving the upper an opportunity to descend and meet the floor. I have seen it employed with much execution at tea-parties and morning calls, but it is too much of a *dress* thing to be used on common occasions. 4. The *awkward.* This consists in bringing the upper leg round, and locking it behind the other. Persons of absent habits, or of indifferent breeding, use this posture in company. In private, it is employed when a man gets a little nervous, and is besides almost always assumed unconsciously, when one is engaged in a deep mathematical investigation. Hence, great mathematicians, with some splendid exceptions, are rarely exempt from the habit of sitting in this mode. Lastly. The *bowsprit* posture. This your fashionable, juvenile readers will recognize to be the one which is at present universally in vogue. It consists in extending out the leg as far and as high as the muscle can bear. Two or three years since, our boot-manufacturers — (*shoemakers* is a word quite out of date) — very kindlyas sisted this posture by stiffening the instep of the boot, so that the style in question could be properly preserved without much painful tension.

I am strongly inclined to believe, that the bowsprit

posture was adopted in this country out of compliment to our gallant seamen. It is at present used by about one half of the gentlemen you meet; but so far as my observation extends, appears (probably in consequence of the peace) to be somewhat on the decline.

I would remark, by the way, that the cross-kneed posture is now almost out of use with the other sex. There was indeed an attempt, about five or six years since, to get up the fashion among ladies of adopting this posture, and at the same time of bending over the upper foot, so as to make it form a crescent. She whose foot could describe the most complete curve was envied and admired by all her competitors. But alas! Mr. Editor, there are but few persons whose feet are sufficiently flexible to enable them to shine in this accomplishment. And so it was dropped. Out of a company of twenty-five ladies whom a friend of mine reconnoitred the other evening at a tea-party, twenty-one sat with their feet parallel and together; two, a matron somewhat advanced, and a maiden lady, whose old associations of gentility induced them so to sit, were found in the cross-kneed predicament; and the remaining two, being the youngest of the whole company, had drawn their feet under their chairs, and crossed them there.

But we have too long deferred the more immediate object of this essay, which is to show the connection between posture and literature. At what times, and on what occasions, shall the cross-kneed posture be adopted by the decorous and conscientious scholar? In the first place, let him be sure immediately to assume it on the entrance of a stranger into his study. It is almost as great a mark of ill-breeding to use any other mode of sitting on such an occasion, as it would be to hold your book still open in your hand. I own, that no posture in which you can sit conveys quite so barbarous a hint to your poor visitant as the holding of your book open, which, I regret to say, is sometimes unthinkingly indulged in by scholars, who would be sorry not to be thought gentlemen. But, sir, let me repeat it, the cross-kneed is the posture in which to receive a visitor with whom you are not on terms of considerable intimacy. It gives you time to collect your ideas; it tacitly informs your visitor that he is of consequence enough in your eyes for you to think about the position of your limbs; it thereby conciliates his good feelings, and induces him civilly to present before your face a similar example. When you are thus both seated according to due form and manner, you may interchange thoughts with much facility and effect. But be sure not to abandon the cross-kneed posture till the end of the first half-hour. After that period, you may venture to stretch your feet out, and lean back in your chair. By the end of the second half-hour, you may put your feet over the fireplace, and if your visitor stay two hours, and be somewhat tedious and unprofitable, contrive by all means to get a table between you, and thrust your feet up into his face. Time is valuable, insomuch that the saving of it is one of those few instances where the end sanctifies the means. It often is not enough to pull out your watch, — not enough to sit ten minutes without saying a word to your companion, or even looking at him, — not enough to glance every two minutes at your study-table; no, sir, the only method often which is efficacious is the attitude I have just mentioned, which may be called the assault-and-battery posture, and which exhibits a new and fair illustration of the importance of our subject to the man of letters.

In the second place, let the votary of literature adopt the cross-kneed style in general company. The great advantage of it there is, that it saves him from a thousand ungraceful attitudes, and strange crookednesses, which savor too decidedly of the study, and into which he will be apt almost inevitably to slide, if he ventures beyond the sheltering precincts of the cross-knee. It has too long been the reproach of the scholar, that he behaves like nobody else. For mercy's sake, then, Mr. Editor, since *everybody else* behaves so very well, let us act like them. Let us not bring a reproach upon our profession, and render a life of letters unpopular, by our manner of sitting. A few sacrifices of this nature will cost us no very tremendous effort, and may be of incalculable service to the cause of literature and science.

In the third place, the style in question is to be assumed amidst all kinds of plain reading, where but little attention and study are required. Indeed, so appropriate is it on these occasions, that scholars might very pardonably denominate it the *belles-lettres* posture. How delicious, Mr. Editor, when you have brought the Edinburgh or the Quarterly, and for my own part, let me add, too, the North American, from the bookseller's, all new

"and fresh as is the month of May,"

to take your ivory knife in the right hand, your Review in the left, your cigar, if you please, in your mouth, and at a window, on which the rays of the setting sun are richly, softly falling, and a western breeze is luxuriously blowing, to sit — how? Unworthy he of all these invaluable blessings, who takes any other posture at first than the true belles-lettres-cross-kneed. Or when, in the society of friends, you read aloud the adventures of Conrad, Roderick, or Robert Bruce, or in imagination range through old Scotland with the author of the Antiquary, or visit England, France, Italy, and Greece with modern travellers, — whilst you gracefully hold the book with a wide-spread hand, your thumb and little finger pressing on the leaves to prevent them from closing, your middle finger propping the back, and the other two faithfully employed each to support a separate cover of the book, — do not fail to complete the elegant scene by adjusting one knee above the other in the manner worthy of your employment. Take, generally, this posture, moreover, when you read history, — when you snatch up the Spectator or Mirror to save the odds and ends of your precious time, — when you are reading letters from persons with whom you are not intimately acquainted, (posture not being to be thought of in perusing the epistles of your much-valued friends,) and on all occasions, in short, when your mind only goes out to gather ideas, copiously, easily, freely. So much for this posture, sir, on which I would gladly write pages and pages more, if some other classes did not press upon me with strong claims for consideration.

Secondly. Next to the cross-kneed, that which is most appropriate to secluded, literary characters is the *parieto-pedal* posture. This consists, as will be seen at once from the etymology of the term, in fixing the feet against the wall. This posture was instituted for the relief of literary limbs. However valuable, indispensable, and gentlemanlike may be the cross-kneed, it would be fatiguing and unhealthy always to conform the body strictly to its rules. For this reason, allow the feet of your readers occasionally to make the delicious and grateful transition from the floor to the wall; with this strict proviso, to be transgressed on no condition whatever, that they never shall so sit in the presence of a being of the gentler sex. And here let me expatiate, parieto-pedal posture, in thy praise! At this very moment, while I am assuming thee in languid luxury, holding in my hand a Horace, which is prevented from closing only by my forefinger, unconsciously placed on *Otium Divos*, —here, as, in a direction parallel to the horizon, I station my feet against the wainscot, and, leaning back my chair, fall sweetly and quietly into a rocking, which is more gentle than the cradle-vibrations of half-sleeping infancy, — here let me ponder on all thy excellency. I feel thy influence extending through my frame. I am brought into a new world; the objects around me assume side-long positions; the trains of my ideas are quickened; the blood rushes back, and warms my heart; a literary enthusiasm comes over me; my faculty of application grows more intense; and whatever be the book which I next reach from the table, I find my interest in its contents redoubled, my power of overcoming its difficulties increased, and altogether my capacity of gaining knowledge incalculably enlarged and extended. Mild, and easy, and lovely posture! Let the votary of decorum stigmatize thee as awkward and half indecent; let the physician reproach thee as unnatural and unwholesome; let indigestion, with bleeding at the nose, and personal deformity, shake their hideous fists of threatening out of the mists of the future; — still will I lounge with thee; still shall every room where I reside bear marks of thee, whether they be deep indentations in the floor, occasioned by my backward-swinging chair, or blacker and more triumphant insignia impressed by my shoes upon the wall. Be thou my shelter from the spleen of vexatious housewives, and the harassing formality of ceremony; soothe my full-fed afternoons; inspire my dyspeptical dreams, and let my last fatal apoplexy be with thee.

Thirdly. We come now to the favorite posture of all severe and laborious students. It is simple, picturesque, characteristic. Place your elbow on the table, prop one of your temples with your knuckles, and, if it be excusable to introduce features into this subject, (though I have another treatise partly finished upon literary tricks,) let a slight knitting of the brow take place between your eyes, and you are at once — I will unhesitatingly hazard the assertion — in that position in which Aristotle discovered the categories; in which Pythagoras investigated the properties of the right-angled triangle, and Locke defined infinity; in which Newton balanced the world, Copernicus, like another Joshua, made the sun stand still, and La Place deduced the great motions of our system; in which Bacon sat, while turning the whole course of science, as a pilot turns the course of a ship; in which Stewart was seated, when he detected the error of the French philosophers, and proved that there must be something besides the power of sensation, which is able to compare one sensation with another; in which Bentham unfolded the true principles of legislation, and Berkeley devised the theory of acquired vision; in which Eichhorn made his researches into Genesis, and Paley his into the Epistles; — a posture, in short, in which the greatest energies of intellect have ever been put forth, and by the efficacy of which alone, assure your young readers, they can hope for eminence, or look for almost indefinite advances towards the future perfectibility of our race. Its name is the *delving*.

Fourthly. Now, Mr. Editor, let your *elbow* remain precisely where it was in the last posture; but instead of knitting your brow, and fixing your eyes on the table, let your head turn round, till your open hand is upon the *sinciput;* let your forehead be smooth, as the sleeping surface of a lake; let your eyes be rolling on vacancy, and, *presto!* you are fixed at once in the genuine *attitude poetical.* It is this posture alone which Shakespeare had in his mind, nay, in which Shakespeare must have sat, when he described the fine frenzy of the poet, whose eye glances from heaven to earth, from earth to heaven. It was this posture in which the most interesting portrait of Pope was executed, that has descended to our times. So sat he, I will hazard every poet in my library, when he penned this line,

"And look through Nature up to Nature's God."

So sat Milton, when he described

"Those thoughts that wander through eternity."

In this posture must Goldsmith,

"where Alpine solitudes ascend,
Have sat him down a pensive hour to spend,
And, placed on high above the storm's career,
Looked downward, where a hundred realms appear," &c.

It could be only while thus leaning and thus looking, that Chaucer used to scatter through his poems innumerable refreshing descriptions of those vernal seasons,

"When that Phœbus his chair of gold so hie
Had whirled up the sterrie sky aloft,
And in the Bole * was entred certainly,
When shouris sote † of rain descended soft,
Causing the ground, felé ‡ times and oft,
Up for to give many an wholesome air,
And every plaine was yclothed faire," &c.

What other attitude could our contemporary Campbell have taken, when he leaped in imagination up to those glorious heights on our side of the Atlantic,

"Where at evening Alleghany views,
Through ridges burning in her western beam,
Lake after lake interminably gleam"?

In what other posture could the chaste Tasso have placed himself, when he addressed to the Muse of Christianity that invocation, of which you will excuse the following imperfect version?

"O Muse! not thou, whose meaner brows desire
The fading growth of laurelled Helicon,
But thou, that chant'st amid the blessed choir,
Which pours sweet music round the heavenly throne!
Breathe thou into my breast celestial fire;
O smile, and not thy votary disown,
If truth with flowers I weave, and deck my song
With other graces than to thee belong."

Byron must have sat in this posture, in some cold midnight, when he dreamt his dream of darkness; and Southey must have persisted in the same attitude through a whole vernal season, when he wrote his Thalaba.

So sat Homer and Scott in the conception of their battles.

So sat Virgil and Leigh Hunt in the imagination of their sceneries.

---

* Bull. † Sweet. ‡ Many.

Wordsworth must have arranged his corporeity in the very quintessence of the poetical posture, when he sketched the following outline of his Recluse:

> "For I must tread on shadowy ground, must sink
> Deep; and, aloft ascending, breathe in worlds
> To which the heaven of heavens is but a veil."

So sat his neighbor Wilson, when he described the stream, half-veiled in snowy vapor, which flowed

> "*With sound like silence, motion like repose*";

or the duteous daughter in the sick-chamber of her mother, — she whose feet

> "*Fell soft as snow on snow.*"

So sat Thomson when he wrote this line:

> "Ten thousand wonders rolling in my thought"; —

and Lucan when he wrote these:

> ". . . . . niger inficit horror
> Terga maris: longo per multa volumina tractu
> Æstuat unda minax: *flatusque incerta futuri*,
> Turbida testantur conceptos æquora ventos."

So sat Akenside, when his mind

> "Darted her swiftness up the long career
> Of devious comets, ...
> . . . . . and looked back on all the stars."

So David sat (I would reverently suppose) in his hours of inspiration, when "contemplating man, the sun, moon, and stars." To say nothing of innumerable others.

Fifthly. The *metaphysical posture*. Place both elbows on the table, let the insides of the two wrists be joined together, keeping the palms just far enough asunder to admit the chin between them, while the tips of the little fingers come up and touch the outside corners of the eyes. This posture, sir, from its fixedness, gives you at once an idea of *solidity*. The mutual contact of two of the most tender and sensible parts of the human body, the tip of the finger and the eye, will assist you in making experiments on sensation; and as your whole head is fastened, as it were, into a socket, your eyes must look straight forward, and your train of reflection will be thus more continuous and undisturbed. Keep precisely so for several days together, and you will at length arrive triumphantly at the important and philosophical conclusion, that mind is matter.

Innumerable other attitudes crowd upon my recollection, the formal discussion of which, after just hinting at a few of the most prominent, I must waive, and leave them to be treated by writers of freer leisure, and more enlarged views of posturology. For instance, there is the *dishabille* posture, formed by lying at full length on your chair, crossing your feet upon the floor, and locking your hands upon the top of your head, — very common and very becoming. In conversation, there is the *positive* posture, when you lean your cheek upon one finger; the *sentimental*, when you lean it upon two fingers; the *thoughtless*, when you lean it upon three, thrusting at the same time your little finger into your mouth; and lastly, the *attentive*, when you lean your cheek outright upon your whole hand, bend forward, and stare the speaker in the face. There is the *sheepish* posture, formed by placing your legs and feet parallel and together, laying both hands upon your knees, and contemplating no earthly thing save your own pantaloons. This is to be assumed when you are overwhelmed with a joke, which you cannot for the life of you answer, or when you are attacked with an argument which you have not the ingenuity to repel. There is the *clerical* posture, formed by laying the ankle of your left leg on the knee of your right, and so forming a triangle. Then there is the *lay* posture, made by throwing the legs wide asunder, and twirling the watch-chain. There is the *musical* posture, where you bring one foot round behind the other, and rest the toe most delicately and aerially on the floor. This was used by one of the small band from Bonaparte's court who lately charmed our metropolis with the violoncello and guitar. Why is it not as appropriate to the flute as to the guitar? There is the *monologue* posture, when, in default of a companion, you take another chair, place your feet in it, and hold high converse with yourself. But, Mr. Editor, by far the most independent, lordly, and scholarly style is to command as many chairs for your own accommodation as can possibly come within reach. I had a chum, whilst I was in college, who put in requisition every chair but one in the room. He had one for each of his feet, one for each of his arms, and the last for his own more immediate self. As our whole number of that article of furniture was but half a dozen, I was often perplexed at the entrance of a friend to know how I should economize for the convenience of all seven,— I beg pardon, I should have said, all three of us. After some confused apologies, I used to offer the visitor my own, and betake myself to the window-seat, quite willing, I assure you, to undergo such embarrassments, for the reputation of living with one of the best posture-masters within the walls. Ah, sir, that was the glory of sitting! I cannot describe the silent admiration with which I used to gaze upon the sprawling *nonchalance*, the irresistible ennui, the inimitable lounge, with which my room-mate could hit the thing off after an enormous dinner. I ought here to observe, that the state of mind peculiarly adapted to the posture now under consideration is that of perfect *vacuity*, and that, if I write much longer, I shall probably prepare your readers to assume it. I conclude therefore by wishing them all, whatever may be their favorite mode of sitting,

"The gayest, happiest *attitude of things*."

1817.

INQUIRY INTO THE RELATION OF CAUSE AND EFFECT.*

A WHOLE article of solid metaphysics is a phenomenon that perhaps requires apology as well as explanation. We will therefore briefly submit our reasons for its appearance.

The philosophy of the late lamented Dr. Brown is scarcely known in this country. It was presumed that considerable interest would attach among us to the speculations of the successor of Dugald Stewart, whose own work on the Mind has passed, we believe, through as many editions in the United States as in Great Britain, and who is well known, on becoming *emeritus*, to have warmly recommended Dr. Brown to the chair of Moral Philosophy in the University of Edinburgh. But further, there is a vague belief among those who are but partially acquainted with the nature of the late Professor's speculations, that they coincided too nearly with the dangerous parts of the philosophy of David Hume. A faithful analysis of the work before us will correct this error, and redeem Dr. Brown's reputation. Still further, an unjust

---

* *Inquiry into the Relation of Cause and Effect.* By THOMAS BROWN, M. D., F. R. S. Edinburgh, &c., Professor of Moral Philosophy in the University of Edinburgh. Third edition. Edinburgh. 1818. 8vo. pp. 569.

and indiscriminate censure has overwhelmed the whole system of Hume itself with relation to the doctrine of Cause and Effect. When Professor Leslie, in consequence of having expressed his approbation of certain portions of that system, encountered from the ministers of Edinburgh strong opposition to his pretensions as candidate for a chair in the University, the nucleus of the present volume was published in a pamphlet form, and, by distinguishing what was sound from what was exceptionable in the opinion of Hume, contributed to soften the opposition made to the too honest candidate. The work, in its present very much enlarged state, confirms the points maintained in the pamphlet, and though we profess no love, and but qualified respect, for Hume in his metaphysical capacity, we are willing to assist in removing every unfair stigma from every literary reputation. Besides these reasons, the subject itself, we should hope and presume, however abstruse, will not be deemed entirely devoid of interest and importance. Truth is worth looking after, even among the clouds. A bulky octavo is not written in vain, if it gives the world one clear idea, which otherwise it would not have had. The subject of this work, as the author truly remarks, involves the philosophy of everything that exists in the universe. Hence it must have some practical bearings. Some portions of the treatise before us might be aptly denominated the philosophy of religion. Considerable light is thrown on our relations with the Deity; the idea of our dependence on him is somewhat simplified from that dark and confused mystery which hangs over it; and the clearer the idea, the deeper and better the impression it must make on the mind. The system under review provides also for the admission of the miraculous interference of the Deity, and therefore bespeaks the attention of those who honor revelation; it admits of the doctrine of a particular providence, and must therefore be not unwelcome to the devout. In addition to these reasons, we have considered that the race of lovers of pure old-fashioned metaphysical disquisition is far from being extinct. Edwards on the Will is still the principal rallying-point of our orthodoxy, and Locke* is a general classic among our colleges. The influence of their style and speculations will make us sure of some zealous readers. In the next place, this book is a book of great power. They who read Montorio, Mandeville, Anastasius, Don Juan, for the intellectual energy they display, may here find intellectual energy enough, and not be liable to the suspicion of seeking mere amusement from the narrative, or gratifying a corrupt imagination with the sentiments. Lastly, the improbability that the book will be ever published in this country, united with the high price of the English edition, has induced us to present the ensuing careful abstract to those who may not have access to the original work; while they who have, may be glad of a thread to lead them through a book, which, for the abstruseness of its topics, for refinement in its reasonings, for diffusive amplifications, for winding yet collateral digressions, for long and solemn preambles be-

* Is not a *System of Metaphysics* wanted for our colleges? — something like a history of opinions in that science, with or without the theories of the compiler. Would Locke obtain more than a respectable chapter in such a system? Brucker, Stewart in his Dissertations, and Degerando would furnish copious and valuable assistance in compiling it. The work of the latter is indeed an admirable specimen of what we recommend.

fore the questions discussed are stated, thus creating the suspense of mind which is incident properly to forms of synthetical demonstration, has not many rivals; and yet has no titles to its chapters, no sketch-arguments, no table of contents, no indexes!

Part First of the "Inquiry" treats of the *Real Import* of Cause and Effect.

A cause Dr. Brown defines to be *that which immediately precedes any change, and which, existing at any time in similar circumstances, has been always, and will be always, immediately followed by a similar change.* The object of his inquiry is to prove that there is no hidden, mysterious, connecting link between those antecedents and consequents which we call causes and effects, when we speak of the changes which happen in any part of the material or intellectual universe. The *substances* that exist in nature are *everything* that has a real existence in nature. These substances have no *powers*, *properties*, or *qualities*, separate from themselves, — words adopted by us only for the sake of convenience, and to express the *changes* which we observe to happen around us. A follows B, and B follows C. Now by all the effort which our minds can exert, we can form no idea of anything in these sequences, but the substances A, B, and C, and the sequence itself. We may say, that fire has the *power* of melting metals; but all we mean, and all we know by it, is, that fire melts metals, which expresses only the two substances fire and metal, and the change, called melting, which takes place between them. These abstract terms are indeed of great use in assisting us to avoid circumlocution in our discourse; but we are apt to forget (and the world, Dr. Brown! has pretty well forgotten) that they are mere abstractions, and to regard them as significant of some actual reality. The powers of a substance have been supposed to be something very different from the changes which it operates on other substances, and most mysterious; at once a part of the antecedent, and yet not a part of it; an intermediate link in a chain of physical sequences, that is yet itself no part of the chain, of which it is notwithstanding said to be a link. The most that can be said of these imaginary powers or causes is, that they are new antecedents and sequents thrust in between the former, and requiring themselves as much explanation as the changes which they were brought to explain.

Such we believe to be the substance of Dr. Brown's first section of twenty pages. His elegant paragraphs, his varied and ample illustrations, his occasionally appropriate and eloquent reflections, and even many of his collateral arguments and inferences, though important, must of course disappear before the rugged wand of analysis.

Before proceeding with our abstract, we think proper to notice an obvious objection which has been frequently urged against the foregoing definition of a cause, and to extract our author's reply to it, though occurring in a distant part of his book. If the definition be true, it is asked, why are not day and night reciprocally the cause of each other? Dr. Reid calculated on a great triumph over Hume by pressing this objection. The Quarterly Review, we observe, has repeated it in an article on Leslie's Geometry (No. VII.), and a late number of Blackwood's Magazine, in attempting to justify the incessant attacks of the editors on Mr. Leslie's reputation, has brought it forward again. We shall subsequently, in some strictures of our own upon the definition in question, attempt to show that this objection, and all of the same class, might with great ease have been obviated, if the notion of contiguity in place, as well as proximity in time, had been introduced into the definition. Here, however, we will let our author speak for himself.

"It should be remembered that *day* and *night* are not words which denote two particular phenomena, but are words invented by us to express long series of phenomena. What various appearances of nature, from the freshness of the first morning-beam, to the last soft tint that fades into the twilight of the evening sky, changing with the progress of the seasons, and dependent on the accidents of temperature, and vapor, and wind, are included in every day! These are not one, because the word which expresses them is one; and it is the believed relation of physical events, not the arbitrary combinations of language, which Mr. Hume professes to explain.

"If, therefore, there be any force in the strange objection of Dr. Reid, it must be shown, that, notwithstanding the customary conjunction, we do not believe the relation of cause and effect to exist, between the successive *pairs* of that multitude of events which we denominate night and day. What, then, are the great events included in those terms? If we consider them philosophically, they are the series of positions in relation to the sun at which the earth arrives in the course of its diurnal revolution; and in this view, there is surely no one who doubts that the motion of the earth immediately before sunrise is the cause of the subsequent position, which renders that glorious luminary visible to us. If we consider the phenomena of night and day in a more vulgar sense, they include various degrees of darkness and light, with some of the chief changes of appearance in the heavenly bodies. Even in this sense, there is no one who doubts that the rising of the sun is the cause of the light which follows it, and that its setting is the cause of the subsequent darkness.

. . . . . .

"How often, during a long and sleepless night, does the sensation of darkness — if that phrase may be accurately used to express a state of mind that is merely exclusive of visual affections of every sort — exist, without being followed by the sensation of light! We perceive the gloom, in this negative sense of the term *perception*; — we feel our own position in bed, or some bodily or mental uneasiness, which prevents repose; — innumerable thoughts arise, at intervals, in our minds, and with these the perception of gloom is occasionally mingled, without being followed by the perception of light. At last light is perceived, and, as mingled with all our occupations and pleasures, is perceived innumerable times during the day, without having, for its immediate consequence, the sensation of darkness. Can we then be said to have a uniform experience of the conjunction of the two sensations; or do they not rather appear to follow each other loosely and variously, like those irregular successions of events which we denominate accidental? In the vulgar, therefore, as well as in the philosophical sense of the terms, the regular alternate recurrence of day and night furnishes no valid objection to that theory, with the truth of which it is said to be inconsistent." — p. 387.

The second section proceeds to urge two points; first, that the sort of antecedence which is necessary to be understood in our notion of power or causation, is not mere priority, but *invariable* priority. In the unbounded field of nature there are many co-existing series of phenomena. Just at the moment when the fire melts the metal, the hand may move the metal. In this case it may be said that the motion of the hand immediately precedes, or is an antecedent to, the melting of the metal, but would not in fact be called the cause of it. *Fire* alone *invaria-*

bly precedes such a change, and is thus called its cause. So the sun may rise immediately before the tide rises, but the want of universal invariableness in this sequence prevents us from ascribing to it the relation of cause and effect. These illustrations we have ventured upon of ourselves, the author having strangely introduced none on this most important point, though he could have selected so many, at once rich and impressive, from the wide regions of nature. The second point is an argument in favor of the author's peculiar notion of power; an argument which he calls the *test of identity*, and upon which he relies with much confidence. It is this. How much soever our former habits of thought, or, as the author would have it, our former abuse of language, may lead us to suppose that there is really such a thing as *power*, which operates any change, exclusively of the substances involved in the very change itself, yet the longer we attend to it, and the more nicely and minutely we endeavor to analyze it, the more clearly shall we perceive, that all which we have ever understood, in the notion which we have been accustomed to express with so much pomp of language, is the mere sequence of a certain change, that might be expected to follow as immediately at another time, when the same antecedent recurred in the same circumstances. Thus, when we say that a spark has the *power* of kindling and exploding gunpowder, we say no more and no less than that in all similar circumstances the explosion of gunpowder will be the immediate and uniform consequence of the application of a spark. And because these two propositions communicate the same identical information, the author maintains that the idea of power in the first proposition is perfectly nugatory or rather is a nonentity.

Section third applies the foregoing arguments to all the mental phenomena. We wish to move our limbs, and they move at our bidding. Here is a sequence, and nothing more,—not an atom of power! There is in the first place a desire to move the hand. This is one phenomenon. There is then the motion of the hand, that is to say, the contraction of certain muscles. Thus, reader, you see how magically the author makes the power, which John Locke was pleased to confer on you, slip down into nothing, between these two phenomena. If you doubt it, he calls for his *test of identity*, and asks, Should we learn anything new, by being told that the will would not only be invariably followed by the motion of the hand, but that the will would also have the *power* of moving the hand? He then proceeds to explain the illusion under which the word has been laboring from time immemorial. It seems we have all along supposed such a thing to exist as the will. It is a mistake; there is no such thing. A volition is but a momentary desire. Nature has so disposed of things around us, that innumerable desires are always followed immediately by their objects; of which the infinite varieties of contractions of the muscles in every part of the body are instances. If your desire of wealth were followed by one hundred thousand pounds as immediately as your desire of elevating the eyelid is followed by that muscular motion, you would call that desire will. So, if your will to move a palsied hand were followed by the obstinate quiescence of that hand, your will, with all its boasted energy, its illusive power, would degenerate into, or rather would remain, simple desire. Now it is the rapidity with which the state of things about us has permitted certain changes to follow *some* of our desires and not others, that has led us to ascribe to the former a mysterious quality called power, and to give them a specific name. But the author's acute analysis would seem to reduce into one the two operations of will and desire, and thus to demonstrate that, in all our voluntary actions, there is nothing more than a simple sequence of two phenomena, namely, the will, or a momentary desire, of exactly the same kind with all our other desires, — and the external act. On this head, the author successfully combats the common sophism that the will and the desire may be opposed to each other, and exist so at the same moment of time. When a compassionate judge condemns a criminal to death, he does not at one and the same moment will the criminal's death, and desire his life; the final will to utter the awful award of punishment *succeeds* his compassionate desire, and arises from his belief of a greater good upon the whole which will result from a severe decree. And so of all analogous cases. Be it understood, however, that the author has no quarrel against the term *will;* he allows it to be convenient for the purpose of expressing such of our desires as are immediately followed by their objects; but he will not allow it to express anything more than desire, nor to involve a peculiar notion of power or energy which it has always been supposed to possess.

The next question, into which the author enters with equally unshrinking intrepidity, is, whether what is called the will has any power over the thoughts, or trains of thought, or any states or affections of the mind. To will directly the conception of any particular object is, surely, to have already the conception of that object; for if we do not know what we will, we truly will nothing. To will directly any idea, therefore, is a contradiction in thought, and almost in terms. The author shows also that it is not less absurd to suppose that we can directly will the non-existence of any idea, since our desire to do so would rather render it more lively. Nor is there such a power as indirect volition, or calling up any particular idea by others which we know to be associated in place or time; for if we can effectively will the associated ideas, we can as easily will the unknown idea itself. The fact is, we do not *call up* any of these ideas; but our *desire* of remembering something once told to us, or which once happened to us, &c. *continuing*, the natural order of associate ideas suggests itself, till, sooner or later, the unknown idea of which we were in quest takes its turn to present itself to our mental view. If the preceding views of these mental phenomena be correct, what becomes of the idea of that *power* which has been always ascribed to the *will?*

Some have asserted, however, (we now go on with section fourth,) that from mind alone we derive our notion of power; and that the notion which we thus acquire by the consciousness of our own exertion is afterwards transferred to the apparent changes of matter. This is Mr. Locke's theory. He supposes that when we voluntarily operate any change, we are conscious of exerting *power*; and thus, when we see a loadstone attract or produce a change on iron, we from the analogy of our feelings ascribe power to the loadstone. But if the arguments of the preceding section be right, we have *nothing to transfer* from our own feelings to the operations of matter. We desire the motion of our arm; the arm moves; there is nothing but antecedent and consequent here. So, when the loadstone approaches the iron, the iron moves; here too is antecedent and consequent. In neither case is there a third substance, or a third anything, to be called power. If we have anything to transfer from our own feelings to the motion of the iron, it is desire; which is about as reasonable as to transfer to our own feelings the idea of a motive loadstone. Again, Mr. Hume supposes that the animal *nisus*, which we experience, enters very much into the common idea of the power of one material substance on another. But the author shows, by a copious, elaborate, and beautiful induction, that the universal tendency both of vulgar and scientific minds is never to illustrate the operations of material substances by analogies drawn from mind, but, on the contrary, only to illustrate the operations of mind by analogies drawn from matter. Hence, Mr. Hume's idea is opposed to universal experience. The section is concluded by a most eloquent, and, as we think, triumphant attack upon that imperfect analysis, which has led philosophers to term matter *inert*, as capable only of *continuing* changes, and to distinguish mind alone as active, and capable of *beginning* changes. If mind often acts upon matter, as often does matter act upon mind. The truth is, that certain changes of mind invariably precede certain other changes of mind, and certain changes of matter certain other changes of matter; and also that certain changes of mind invariably precede certain changes of matter, and certain changes of matter invariably precede certain changes of mind. Where then is the advantage of one over the other in point either of inertness or activity? Is it in the *motion* which mind produces on matter? But matter, on its part, produces *sensation* in mind. Even the apparent *rest* of matter, which the author clearly shows is the foundation of our mistaken notion of its inertness, is a sort of action rather than repose. The particles of the seemingly quiescent mass are all attracting and attracted, repelling and repelled; and the smallest undistinguishable element is modifying by its conjoined instrumentality the planetary motions of our own system, and is performing a part which is perhaps essential to the harmony of the whole universe of worlds. So much for the supposed inertness of matter, and for the origin of all our idea of power in the mind alone.

Section Fifth. That original energy, the Omnipotent, the Cause of causes, is the subject of this sublime and unequalled section. But it is only physically that we are here brought to consider the divine power, although, in passing, the author pays to the dignity and interest of our moral relations with that Being a tribute which could have been dictated only by a mind deeply imbued with the most genuine living piety. The author firmly believes in the original dependence of all events on the great Source of being; his conviction is equally strong that he is the providential Governor of the world; but he maintains that God the creator, and God the providential governor of the world, are not necessarily God the *immediate* producer of every change. To suppose that he is himself the real operator and the only operator of every change, is to suppose that the universe which he has made exists for no purpose. In fact, we have ourselves long believed, that, so far from derogating from the glory of our Creator, it actually increases it, to suppose that he has communicated to matter those qualities and laws which produce most of the events that take place throughout creation. The stretch of power and height of wisdom in this view, if we may dare to compare what is in every way infinitely above us, are greater than would be displayed in his universal and immediate interference. Yet it has long been, and is still, the general belief of philosophers, that, besides the physical causes comprehended in the antecedents of those consequences which appear as effects throughout the world, there is an efficient cause that in every case is different from them, and necessary for the production of the effect; an invisible something, which connects each particular consequent with its particular antecedent, or rather is in every case the sole efficient of it. This efficient cause the Cartesians considered to be the Divine Being alone. That idea is now generally exploded; yet still the imaginary efficient cause is retained, though with a less reverent appropriation. Against this theory our author contends that, even if you allow its truth, it only introduces a new operator in every change; it only lengthens a sequence of physical phenomena, and does not produce anything different from a sequence of regular antecedents and consequents. A is invariably followed by C, and I therefore say that A is the cause of C. But you would insert something between, and say that B is the real efficient cause of C. What do you thereby gain? Have you discovered something between A and C which did not appear to me? If you have, you have only analyzed a complex phenomenon more perfectly than I, and I am ready to acknowledge the new link of connection. If you have discovered no such link, but only suppose it, then, whether it be material or spiritual, visible or invisible, you have still to explain how your new cause produces the existing effect, and are driven back to the author's own definition and idea of a cause, founded on the uniform precession of one event to another, and nothing more. Nor will you gain the least triumph over the author, by appealing from his definition to the supposed constant interference of the Deity in every change that exists; for, to say nothing of the utter uselessness, the idle, aimless, cumbrous existence of matter, which this appeal supposes, or the blasphemy involved in making the material objects of creation to be, as it were, only necessary *remembrancers* for the Deity when and where he should act, the author is ready to meet you on your own ground, and he comes prepared with no other weapon than his own simple definition and idea of power or causation. In all those cases, he demands, in which the direct agency of the Supreme Being is indubitably to be believed, *even in that greatest of all events, when the universe arose at his will*, what notion are we capable of forming of such a change? And are we to consider that highest energy to be different, in *nature* as well as in *degree*, from the humble, delegated energies which are operating around us? The author strenuously contends that we are not so to consider it, and that, if we rise to the strongest conception of the omnipotence of God, of which we are capable, still, in contemplating it, we only consider his will as the *direct antecedent* of those glorious effects which the universe displays. This sublime and simple idea he shows to be entirely compatible with our highest conceptions of the intelligence, wisdom, benevolence, free choice, and glory of the Supreme Being, and that to interpose an imaginary link, an intermediary figment, whether we call it by the name of power or anything else, between the will of God and the effect that darts out of it, so far from elevating, would only diminish the majesty of the person and the scene.

With this magnificent conclusion, Dr. Brown terminates the First Part of his Inquiry into the Relation of Cause and Effect. We need not say how forcibly the devout believer in revelation must be struck by the coincidence of this result with the celebrated description of the creation of light and of the world in the beginning of Genesis. Surely, if nothing more, it is at least an interesting fact in the history of metaphysical philosophy, that during the last hundred and fifty years, and in that portion of the globe in which the Hebrew Scriptures have been universally laid open, and more generally read than any other book; — while busy, restless, and ambitious thinkers without number have agitated their systems and theories, theologians frowning on philosophers, not so much for refusing to be taught by the Bible as for picking flaws in *their* schemes of divine power and agency, and philosophers sneering at theologians for defending a book which happened to contain no trace of their own refined views of the connection of cause and effect, of power and result; — at last, a philosopher equal to any of his predecessors for severe and logical habits of thought, for intellectual education and metaphysical genius, and superior to them in the advantage of coming later into the world, — an inquirer whose professional duty it was to search for truth among all their systems and theories, and who unquestionably was fully equal to the task of examining, analyzing, estimating, and deciding on them, — an author, too, who has carried mere *refinement in reasoning* as far as it was ever carried before, — perhaps but just short of a fault, — has at length finished this vain and tumultuous circle of philosophizing, by coming round to the precise point where Moses began, and demonstrating that the founder of the Jewish polity and literature has, at the very outset, laid down an ultimate truth, which he has so beautifully amplified and illustrated in his immediately succeeding emblematical picture of creation. So true it is, that the progress of philosophy, like that of social civilization and genuine refinement, is continually tending in its results to the original dictates of divine inspiration, acting on pure and unsophisticated nature.

Of the notes on this part of the Inquiry it would be unmerciful in us to attempt to convey an idea by means of a detailed abstract. They contain criticisms on Mr. Hume's definition of a cause; an argument reducing what are called *final causes* to real *prior causes* in the mind of the Deity; additional considerations to show that the qualities of a substance are not separate from the substance itself; remarks on the universality of a belief, in all ages, of something like an imaginary efficient cause; a long essay on the true nature, and in defence of the possibility, of miracles, against the arguments of Hume, but on principles different from those of all Hume's former opponents, which the author thinks to have been inadequate; another long essay, demonstrating the perfect possibility, but the very high improbability, of a particular providence, maintaining the reasonableness of the doctrine, but refuting its necessity; and two or three other notes, which confirm or illustrate some portions of the text. An abstract of the two long essays on miracles and a particular providence, however interesting in themselves to a majority of our readers, might perhaps serve with more propriety as an article for a theological journal.

To those who have become convinced by the reasonings of the preceding part, the question will naturally occur, How has it happened that the world has been so long deceived? Why that universal concurrence of mankind in every age in supposing certain causes always to exist separately from the substances in which changes are constantly seen to take place? This question is too imposing to be passed over. Accordingly, the author devotes to it the whole of his Second Part, entitled, "Of the Sources of Illusion with Respect to the Relation of Cause and Effect." We avoid only one error, he tells us, in knowing that we have been deceived; but we may avoid many errors in knowing how that one has deceived us.

The sources of our error, in supposing causes to have an existence separate from the substances which produce any change, are of two kinds: first, certain arbitrary forms of language; second, the very nature of things.

Under the former head, the author first enumerates various metaphorical phrases, which have been employed to express the regularity of the antecedence and consequence of certain phenomena. We speak of events as *connected* or *conjoined;* and we speak of their *bond* of connection, as if there were something truly intermediate. Now, so far as a bond is a sign of *proximity*, so far the word is a very good metaphor to express causation; but inasmuch as it also implies something intermediate between two substances, the frequent use of this metaphor leads to the supposition that the bond connecting two *events* is also something intermediate; and the author, with great acuteness, remarks, that our very ignorance of anything really intervening will only render more mysterious what, obscure as it may be in our conception, we yet believe not the less to exist. Hence the mystery which is often attached to efficient causes, so called.

Another way in which our language tends to deceive us in this respect, is the necessity which we are under of having some terms to express invariable sequence, and others to express casual sequence. Now it so happens that we have rigidly appropriated cause and effect to express the former, and priority, succession, and other terms for the latter. For convenience' sake, we never confound them. We use the word *cause* so exclusively to express the great circumstance of invariableness, while the word *sequence*, or its concrete, *to follow*, is so often used to express mere casual succession, that they assume to our minds the appearance of essential dissimilarity, and even opposition, so that we revolt when we come to hear the words *effect* and *sequence* coupled as synonymous; a feeling which the addition of the important qualifying adjective *invariable* to the latter is not able wholly to remove.

There is yet another form of verbal influence, in some of the most common, unavoidable modes of grammatical construction, which seems to have greatly favored the mistake in question. When, in compliance with the analytical forms of grammar, we speak continually of the powers *of* a substance, or of substances that *have* certain powers, in the same manner as we are accustomed to speak of the birds *of* the air, of the fish *of* a river, of a park that *has* a large stock of deer, or of a town that *has* a multitude of inhabitants, we gradually learn to consider the power *of* a substance, or the power which a substance *possesses*, as something different from the substance itself, inherent in it indeed, but inherent as something that may yet subsist separately. And here follows one of the author's very happiest, yet quite characteristic illustrations. Indeed, though but an illustration, it carries in itself the appearance of a triumphant argument. In the ancient philosophy, he observes, this error extended to the notions both of form and power. In the case of form, however, though the illusion lasted for many ages, it did at length cease; and no one now regards the figure of a body as anything but the body itself. It is probable that the similar illusion with respect to power, as something different from the substances that are said to possess it, would in like manner have ceased, and given way to juster views, if there had not been, in the very nature of things, many circumstances of still more powerful influence to favor the illusion in its origin, and subsequently to foster and perpetuate it.

These circumstances, therefore, will next deserve our consideration.

The first is the seeming latency of power, at times when it is said to be not exerted. We say that there is in cold, unkindled fuel a latent power of liquefying steel; that a man has the power of moving his arm, whenever he chooses to move it; and so forth. With these expressions, as popular and convenient forms of language, the author finds no fault; but he argues at much length, and with considerable, though, as we think, just refinement, that they are utterly incompatible with the results of philosophical analysis. What is permanent in our imagination of objects may be very far from being permanent in the objects themselves which are imagined by us. If power, according to the reasoning in the first section of the First Part of this treatise, express nothing more than the changes which actually take place in substances, there is no power in the intervals of what is termed exertion, because there is no change, nor tendency to change. The power, in short, is wholly contingent on certain circumstances, beginning with them, continuing with them, ceasing with them. In the intervals of recurrence of these circumstances, however, — or, to use the ordinary popular language, in the intervals of *exertion* of the supposed latent *power* of a substance, — we may think of the circumstances in which its presence is productive of change; and knowing that, as often as these circumstances recur, the change too will recur, we may transfer to the substance, as if permanent in it, what is truly permanent only in our thought, which, in the absence of the circumstances of efficiency, imagines them present. But a very slight attention, surely, ought to be enough to convince us that it is by our imagination only we thus invest the substance with a character of continued power which does not belong to it. For example, a very high temperature is necessary for the liquefaction of steel by wood. Let them lie for ever in their natural state in the closest proximity, and the power of one over the other will be undeniably non-existent. When their circumstances become changed by the application of heat, at that very moment, and not till then, exists the change of fusion, and consequently the power of fusion, which are therefore equally words without meaning where the necessary temperature is not present. Thus also with regard to the supposed latent power which a man has of moving his arm. Is the man who is now before us, who has his limbs all in a quiescent state, with no intention at all stirring in his mind, — is he, in fact, one and the very same complex being with *the man who wills* just previously to the motion of his arm? In philosophical strictness, he clearly is not. The addition of the state of volition changes the compound individual, as much as the addition of heat to ice changes that individual substance to water; only in the one case a visible alteration takes place before our eyes, and we give the changed substance a new name, and ascribe to it new powers; whereas, in the other case, there is the same living body before us, at different moments, unaffected in its external conformation by the accession of a state of *willing*, although, until that change takes place, the ascription to the living being of an actual power to raise its arm is confessedly absurd, since the arm does and must for ever lie still where the will is not. Our error lies in falsely ascribing a unity and sameness of physical character to substances in all the changes of circumstances in which they can be placed, and in consequently referring to them in all circumstances what is only referrible in certain circumstances. Power, then, is not something latent in substances, that exists whether exercised or not. What is termed the exercise of power is only another name for the presence of the circumstances in which, and in which alone, there is the power of which we speak; as power not exerted is the absence of the very circumstances which are necessary to constitute power. Now, from this fallacy of believing that the powers which substances *exhibit to us in certain situations* are *latent at all times* in those substances, and yet separate from them, arises the error of supposing that there are mysterious *causes* of all the phenomena we behold constantly latent in the substances around us, and yet distinct from the substances themselves.

The author closes this Second Part by discussing one more great source of the error in question, namely, *the imperfection of our senses.* What at first seems to be the immediate cause of many of our sensations, we afterwards learn is only the first antecedent of a long train of antecedents and consequents, reaching from the outward object to our perceptive faculty, which were at first imperceptible, but which some finer analysis evolves and presents to our search. Hence we are led habitually to suppose, that, amidst all the changes perceived by us, there is something latent which links them together, and, though concealed from our view at present, may be discovered perhaps by some analytic process that has not yet been employed. He who for the first time hears a bell rung, if he be ignorant of the theory of sound, will very naturally suppose that the stroke of the tongue on the bell is the cause of the sound which he hears. By subsequent analyses, however, he successively arrives at various intermediate agencies, — vibrations excited in the particles of the bell itself, — the elastic medium of the air, — the auditory nerve, — the whole mass of the brain. All these phenomena, from the imperfection of his senses, were taking place before him unobserved. He suspects, therefore, that in phenomena the most familiar to him there may be, in like manner, other changes that take place before him unobserved, the discovery of which is to be the discovery of a new order of causes. This constant search, this frequent detection of intermediate causes before unknown, irresistibly induces us to suppose that in every case whatever in which we behold the antecedent and consequent of a change, there lies between them a connecting link, a separate cause, yet undiscovered. Yet it is evident, that, between the antecedent and consequent which we at present know, we must at length come to some ultimate change, which is truly and immediately antecedent to the known effect. Do we gain anything by saying, that this last antecedent has the *power* or is the *cause* of producing the last effect? Is it not equivalent to saying simply that it uniformly precedes the effect? For the supposition of a bond or a cause in this last sequence is necessarily out of the case. The truth is, we see only parts of the great sequences that are taking place in nature. If our senses had originally enabled us to discern all the minute changes which happen in bodies, if we had never discovered anything intermediate and unknown between two known events, a *cause*, in our notion of it, would have been very different from that mysterious unintelligible something, between entity and nonentity, which we now conceive it to be, or rather of which we vainly strive to form a conception; and we should have found little difficulty in admitting it to be, what it simply and truly is, only another name for the immediate, invariable antecedent of an event.

The object of the Third Part of this Inquiry is to explain *under what circumstances* the belief of power arises in the mind. What leads us to suppose that one thing is the necessary cause of another, or, in other words, that any particular antecedent, under the same circumstances, is, has been, and always will be followed by a particular change? This is a highly curious intellectual fact; the observation of a single moment often suggesting to us a belief which extends through all past and all future time.

Power, as we have seen, necessarily involves the expectation of a future change of some sort, that is to be exactly similar as often as the preceding circumstances are exactly similar.

Is this expectation built on the ground of *experience* only? Does it imply always, that the consequent has been known to us, as well as the antecedent; or is there, in the appearance of the antecedent itself, before the attendant change has even been once observed, what might enable us to anticipate that change, as about to take place in instant succession? The author decides this question entirely in favor of experience. He shows that we have no knowledge of the qualities of bodies *a priori*, and therefore no knowledge of the effects which they must produce. Nothing, for instance, in the appearance of iron or loadstone indicates to us that these two bodies will rush together on being made to approach each other. Neither their color, nor their hardness, nor any other quality they possess, would suggest such an effect to our minds. Nor is there anything in the color, weight, and other sensible qualities of grains of mustard-seed and grains of gunpowder, which would enable us to predict that a spark, which falls and is quenched on a heap of the one, would, if it had fallen on a heap of the other, have kindled it into rapid and destructive conflagration. Nay, the most universal and familiar of all phenomena, those namely of gravitation, admit of no readier prophecy. We expect an object to fall to the ground, not from examining its color, or shape, or hardness, but because we have frequently observed the event to happen. It is the same too with all the phenomena of the mind, except our instincts, where the knowledge is not in us, but in the great Being who formed us. Nothing *a priori* assures us that certain motions of our limbs will follow certain desires of our minds, or that the sight of wretchedness will cause in one breast no emotion, but will melt another into pity. Experience alone teaches us these and all other mental phenomena.

But experience informs us only of the *past*, while the relation of power is one that comprehends the past, the present, and the future. Something else, therefore, besides mere experience enters into that operation of the mind which adjudges to any antecedent in a sequence the attribute of power or causation. Is it by a process of *reasoning*, then, that we are enabled, as it were, to see with our mind what is invisible to our eyes, and thus to extend to an unexisting future an order of succession, which, as future, is confessedly, at the time of our prediction, beyond the sphere of our prediction? The author maintains that reasoning does not enter at all into the matter, but that it is nothing more than an *intuitive* and irresistible *belief*, which leads us to anticipate the recurrence of the same consequent, following the same antecedent, whenever the circumstances remain unaltered. When we say that B will follow A to-morrow, because A was followed by B to-day, we do not *prove* that the future will resemble the past, but we *take for granted* that the future will resemble the past. The past fact and the future fact are not inclusive the one of the other, and as little is the proposition which affirms the one, inclusive of the proposition which affirms the other. There is no logical absurdity in supposing, that the one proposition may be true, and the other not true; however difficult it may seem to us to believe the one, without believing the other. We may use the *forms* of reasoning in such a case; yet the belief will always be found to be involved in the very process. A chemist may say, that because a certain gas has just extinguished a lighted taper plunged into it, it *therefore* will extinguish it now. This may seem a fair logical enthymeme. But the major proposition is assumed without proof. It is taken for granted that a lighted taper plunged into the gas will always be quenched, which is the very thing that a semblance of reasoning is brought forward to prove. So when we say that a loadstone will continue to attract iron because it is magnetical, there is only a show, and not the reality, of reasoning. Belief, and belief unaccounted for, is all that is involved in the whole process; because, as the very term *magnetical* implies the quality of attracting iron, we might as well have said that iron will attract iron because it will attract iron. Therefore *reasoning* has no concern with the operation of the mind in question.

It is supposed by some, however, and especially by certain mathematical writers, that there are a few exceptions to the conclusion just drawn. They would seem to contend, that there is a class of facts which are capable of being inferred, even before observation or experience, with complete and independent certainty of the result. The inertia of matter, and the phenomena of the composition of forces, and of equilibrium, have been urged as instances of this kind. The argument of the sufficient reason has been called in to demonstrate these facts, with a triumphant reliance on its perfect adequacy. The following is D'Alembert's argument to prove the inertia of matter as far as it is comprehended in the continued *rest* of bodies. "A body at rest," he says, "must continue in that state till it be disturbed by some foreign cause; for it cannot determine itself to motion, since there is no reason why the motion should begin in one direction rather than another."* "Since there is *no reason*"! an assumption of the very thing to be proved. To be capable of asserting that there is no reason why the motion should begin in one direction rather than another, is already to possess the largest conceivable measure of experience, to know all the conditions of existing things, with all their mutual influences. What is or is not a sufficient reason, experience, and experience only, can show. We believe, indeed, that a body will not quit its state of rest, if all circumstances remain the same; for this, from the influence of that general law of thought which directs our physical anticipations of every kind, it is impossible for us not to believe. But if the irresistible force of this general faith be wholly laid out of account, and if, in affirming that it cannot quit its state of rest and move in one particular direction, our only reason be, that we see no cause why the body should not begin equally to move in some other direc-

* *Traité de Dynamique.*

tion, we, in the very supposition that the motion in the particular direction is without a sufficient cause, beg the question which we yet profess to demonstrate. How can we presume that we know, at any moment, what physical circumstances may, or may not, be about to determine some particular motion of the body, since we are equally unacquainted with the efficacy or inefficacy of all the circumstances? And if we suppose ourselves to know previously the efficacy or sufficiency of some of these circumstances, and the inefficacy or insufficiency of the others, and must therefore know, before any reasoning from the abstract principle, whether a change is or is not to take place, why do we ascribe to the result of the subsequent reasoning the knowledge which was essential for the understanding of its very conditions or terms?

But our author stops not here. He shows that the argument of D'Alembert, allowing its force and legitimacy in other respects, does not exhaust all the possible conditions of the case. Is *rest* the only state which a body can assume, even granting that there is no possibility, because there is no reason, that it should move one way rather than another? Recollect that the argument is not about a mathematical point, or an elementary atom, but about the bodies which actually exist in nature around us. Why, then, may not a change take place in the quiescent mass, similar to what we term explosion when a mass of gunpowder, previously at rest, is kindled? Here there is no particular motion of the elementary particles, east, west, north, or south, but motion in all these directions.

The author attacks with equal success a similar argument of D'Alembert with respect to the other case of inertia in bodies, namely, their continued motion when no foreign force interferes to put them to rest.

So also with regard to the *uniformity* of their motion; when it is attempted to be demonstrated that "the motion must be uniform, *because* a body cannot accelerate nor retard its own motion," the very point in dispute is obviously taken for granted.

The author wishes it carefully to be remembered, that he does not deny the inertia, nor the other properties and phenomena of matter, which have been attempted to be made the subjects of abstract demonstration; on the contrary, they appear to him as indubitable as any other instances of the regularity of events. He only objects to our supposed power of predicting these facts independently of experience.

By far the largest section in the book is devoted to strictures on several demonstrations of this kind, given by D'Alembert, Euler, and other mathematicians, who, we apprehend, have been pressed somewhat too hardly by our acute and ingenious author. It should be recollected, we think, that these writers did not aim at quite such ultimate, abstract, and metaphysical statements of the case, as alone would justify the torrents of argumentation which are here poured down upon them. They were simply mathematicians. They were engaged in constructing and writing systems of mixed mathematics, in which some general views of matter must necessarily be given, although the principal object of their treatises was only the measurement of abstract quantities. To preserve a scientific form throughout, and indeed to lay a foundation for the whole train of their mathematical reasoning, it was natural that they should throw into theorems, and definitions, and forms of demonstration, against the delusive solemnity of which our author inveighs, some of those general laws and properties of matter which are made known to us *by universal experience.* Even in doing this, we think, they tacitly appealed to experience, and would have revolted as much as Dr. Brown himself at the idea of establishing abstract propositions, independent of the knowledge we already have of the external world. Nor are we much afraid that the apparent solemnity and formality of those demonstrations have deluded so many persons as Dr. Brown imagines, into the error which he is combating. D'Alembert would probably have been willing to let the afore-cited argument run thus: "Since there is no reason *that we know of* why," &c. This little clause would have rested the whole matter on experience, and have rendered Dr. Brown's lengthened strictures entirely unnecessary. Now we venture to say, that the French writer had a tacit condition of this kind in his mind, and supposed that every one of his readers had it. Little prepared was he to expect, that the thunders of chemistry would be brought to bear on an argument, of which the application was meant to be confined solely and entirely to the measurement of weight and motion. The demonstrations of this nature given by all these writers were good enough for their purpose; they were never intended to be applied in any form whatever beyond the systems to which they were originally attached, and Dr. Brown himself has not uttered a hint that the mathematical superstructures erected upon them sustain the least injury from the unsoundness or incompleteness of the foundations. We are willing to allow, that the reasonings in question are merely verbal; that they are built on that very experience of which they seem to preclude the necessity; and that they partake perhaps largely of that display which is characteristic of the style of the modern Continental mathematicians. But that they were ever brought forward under the least pretension of assuming ultimate metaphysical truths, we no more believe, than that the subsequent long and intricate demonstrations founded upon them were intended as models of oratorical argument. We protest against these quixotic digressions, in which writers in one science try by their own principles the writers in another. What would be thought of an astronomer, who should go far out of his way to overwhelm with confusion the compiler of an Ephemeris, for heading his columns, in defiance of the demonstrated truth of the Copernican system, with *sun rises* and *sun sets?* Had our author shown in a few words, as he might have done, and in a passing way, that the language of mathematicians, if received without due caution, in its whole metaphysical extent, is not strictly true, he would have fully answered his object in the treatise before us, and furnished a very appropriate and sufficient illustration of the necessity of *experience* in predicting the usual phenomena of matter. But to devote eighty pages of unrelenting and triumphant ratiocination against mathematicians, and that too in the forced character of metaphysicians, was by far too much. We would rather have seen the same space expended on those glaring faults of style, that carelessness, that obscurity, that pomp and exuberance of demonstration where all is plain, that obstinate silence or oracular brevity on points of intrinsic difficulty, and, in short, that total deficiency of didactic skill,* which have made the elementary treatises of so many mathematicians but sealed books to numberless students, who have reluctantly and desperately sunk into the mortifying conclusion that they were not born for the mathematics, when the truth of the case was they were not born to understand writers who studied not, or knew not, how to express themselves.

We have before hinted at our author's doctrine which makes *intuitive* and *irresistible* belief to be the basis, after experience, of our idea of causation. His view of it is this: whatever antecedent we have observed to have immediately and uniformly preceded any consequent, we *cannot possibly avoid believing* will precede it again and always, when placed in exactly the same circumstances. This belief is just as natural to us as to perceive external things when they are presented to our senses. The following extract contains the amount of the argument brought to prove this point:—

"Perception, Reasoning, Intuition, are the only sources of belief; and if, even after experience,—for experience is in every case necessary,—when we believe the similarity of future sequences to the past which we have observed, it is not from perception, nor from reasoning, that our confidence is derived; we must ascribe it to the only other remaining source. We certainly

* It is our most serious belief, that a new chapter is wanted in Campbell's Philosophy, and other treatises of Rhetoric, which shall prescribe rules for writing works on the mathematics. Thus, one rule might be, not to sum up the doctrine of surds in the most concise manner possible, and as if the object were only to refresh the memories of veteran mathematicians, while pages are devoted to the easiest and most obvious portions of the doctrine of *plus* and *minus*.

do not perceive *power*, in the objects around us, or in any of our internal feelings; for perception, as a momentary feeling, is limited to what is, and does not extend to what is yet to be: and, as certainly, we do not discover it by reasoning; for, independently of our irresistible belief itself, there is no argument that can be urged to show why the future should exactly resemble the past, rather than be different from it in any way. We believe the uniformity, in short, not because we can demonstrate it to others or to ourselves, but because it is impossible for us to disbelieve it. The belief is in every instance intuitive; and intuition does not stand in need of argument, but is quick and irresistible as perception itself." — p. 314.

Another of the author's finest passages is the following, which is brought to defend and illustrate his peculiar views of this subject, and closes the Third Part of the work. It will evince, moreover, how far his speculations were from those atheistical tendencies of which they have been suspected.

"That, with a providential view to the circumstances in which we were to be placed, our Divine Author has endowed us with certain instinctive tendencies, is as true as that he has endowed us with reason itself. We feel no astonishment in considering these, when we discover the manifest advantage that arises from them; and of all the instincts with which we could be endowed, there is none that seems, I will not say so advantageous merely, but so indispensable, for the very continuance of our being, as that which points out to us the future, if I may venture so to speak, before it has already begun to exist. It is wonderful, indeed, — for what is not wonderful? — that the internal revelation which this belief involves should be given to us like a voice of ceaseless and unerring prophecy. But when we consider WHO it was that formed us, it would, in truth, have been more wonderful if the mind had been so differently constituted that the belief had not arisen: because, in that case, the phenomena of nature, however regularly arranged, would have been arranged in vain; and that Almighty Being, who, by enabling us to anticipate the physical events that are to ensue, has enabled us to provide for them, would have left the creatures, for whose happiness he has been so bounteously provident, to perish, ignorant and irresolute, amid elements that seemed waiting to obey them, — and victims of confusion, in the very midst of all the harmonies of the universe." — p. 319.

The Fourth and last Part is employed in an examination of Mr. Hume's Theory of our Belief of the Relation of Cause and Effect. If our readers will lend their attention to a few succeeding statements, they will perhaps find that clear ideas of Mr. Hume's philosophy have not hitherto prevailed, and that Dr. Brown's system of Cause and Effect, although corresponding with a portion of Mr. Hume's, yet departs as widely as possible from it on every exceptionable point. We shall take considerable pains to set these assertions in a convincing light; — both because we regret to have learned, that an opinion was not long since entertained, by most illustrious authority in England, that Dr. Brown had been endeavoring to set up a theory of causation, which was ill understood by himself, and which differed not materially from the theory of Hume, — and because, as our author is now laid where he cannot reply to a surmise against the soundness and correctness of his writings, we would try, with at least as fond a reverence as strangers may be supposed capable of feeling, to efface every stain that may unjustly attach to his literary reputation.

Mr. Hume commenced the statement of his views on

this subject by reviving some hints that former writers had suggested as to the doctrine of a *conjunction*, rather than a *connection*, of the events that are constantly succeeding one another in the world of nature around us. In this simple doctrine, how much alarm soever a misstatement or a misapprehension of it may have once excited, there was not the semblance of a dangerous tendency. It still left the existence of every object and every event in nature as real and as certain as they were before. In resolving those incessant changes, that are everywhere happening, into a long train of antecedents and consequents, it did not deny, but rather confirmed, the necessity of an antecedent for every consequent, and thus furnished a strong argument for the existence of some great First Cause, — some necessary antecedent of all the effects in the universe. It still left to this great invisible Being the ability to will into existence every substance that is, and the wisdom of *arranging* that eternal continuity of successive phenomena, which is all the time developing such astonishing results of order, harmony, beauty, and happiness. There was nothing truly sceptical about this doctrine, if by *sceptical* we mean any quality of an opinion which fairly leads to an irreligious conclusion. The question related purely to a physical matter of fact, which, in whatsoever way decided, leaves all the great truths of natural and revealed religion as sacredly guarded as they were before. As for Philosophy, *she* certainly had a right to demand the evidence for that supposed invisible link which connects each change with the substance that produces it. On the absence of that evidence, Hume, trusting to the evidence of the senses which God had given him, and perceiving by those senses nothing more than a succession of changes, advances his leading doctrine, that we can have no other idea of causation, than a bare precession of one event to another, without involving anything that intervenes between the antecedent and consequent. Dr. Brown, perceiving the strong ground of nature and the senses on which Hume stood, embraces the doctrine, states and defends it at much length in the First Part of this treatise, insists that every new link which is discovered between the two parts of a sequence, such, for instance, as an inflammable gas between the heat of yon candle and the combustion of this pen, becomes only a new unlinked antecedent to the visible effect; — and not only this, but in his Second Part assigns several satisfactory reasons why the world should have been so long deceived in imagining, and giving a name to, a nonentity.

The next doctrine of Hume was equally free from the character of scepticism. It was, that the human mind has no capacity of predicting, previously to experience, the particular consequents that will result from any given antecedent, or, in other words, that we are unable of ourselves to divine any of the powers of nature. It required but little reflection to adopt this opinion, which, to our minds, is perfectly independent of the former doctrine, and might be true, whatever theory of causation be so. Accordingly, Dr. Brown, as we have seen, in this Third Part, maintains that experience alone is the ground of those predictions which we are every day forming of the future effects of objects now existing around us. Thus far our two philosophers go together. But from this point they separate; they diverge widely and irrecoverably.

Having hitherto agreed with each other, when they come to ask, *On what principle of the human mind* we predict, after experience, the consequences of causes? Dr. Brown answers the question, *By intuitive and irresistible belief.* On thrusting this pen into the candle's blaze, we believe it will burn; but we arrive at this belief, not from any process of reasoning, but because, having before seen the same effect proceed from the same cause, *we cannot help believing it.* This simple and clear statement of an ultimate fact, so consonant to the most approved rules of the Baconian philosophy, terminates Dr. Brown's system. And whether his system be right or wrong, we do earnestly crave leave to insist, that, if ever there was one which deserved to be called intelligible, compact, consistent, simple, it is this. Even before Dr. Brown wrote, we were confessedly all in the dark about causation. He does not pretend to reveal the mystery of it to us, but only to check our impatient and unavailing struggles after a figment of our own fancy, to exhibit the limits of the human mind on this subject, and to confine our reasoning and imagination entirely to the visible side of the curtain of our existence, on which are wrought no other figures, nay, out of which peeps not a thread, but those of experience. If the author himself was so unfortunate as not to understand his own system, he certainly has had the signally good success of causing *some* readers — humble, and without authority, we allow, but as conscientiously attentive to the train of his reasonings as their capacities would admit — to comprehend it to their most entire satisfaction. Nor, until we find some hint in his writings, or hear of some declaration that passed his lips, revealing a consciousness of the unintelligibility of his speculations, can we possibly admit or conceive that he did not understand them himself.

Let us now turn to Mr. Hume, and see if he has really gained in our author an implicit and unqualified follower.

Instead of allowing, or perhaps perceiving, the force and authority of that great principle of intuitive belief which terminates Dr. Brown's speculations, he lays extraordinary stress on the following maxim, which, in hands as dexterous as his own, may lead into the most licentious, extravagant, and dangerous scepticism.

"In all reasonings from experience, there is a step taken by the mind, which is not supported by any argument or process of the understanding."

At the enunciation of this portentous proposition, the mind involuntarily stands aghast. All the realities and well-grounded expectations of life seem to be sinking, like fragments of floating ice, under our feet. The truth of the proposition itself you cannot deny; that is, if you allow that the business of life is carried on by "reasonings from experience." It is but too evident that from no quarter on earth have we got the information that *the future will resemble the past*, which is the assumed step that Hume refers to. Hence one feels that he has no right to introduce that assumption into any reasoning which is to guide his future operations. The consequence is, he may proceed to beat his head against a rock, with all the calmness in the world, and still be a very reasonable man; and why? Because he has no right to assume that *the future will resemble the past!* and therefore the rock may, as likely as not, meet his head with the softness of a pillow of down. A wanton assassin may be justified in rushing out of his den, and stabbing a whole virtuous population one by one through the body; because, if he supposes that his dagger will sever their souls from their mortal tenements, he most illogically assumes a step in his reasoning for which he has no authority, namely, that *the future will resemble the past.* Not to multiply examples of this kind, which must press on the imaginations of our readers as numerously as on our own, we will yet instance only religion, which, by the magical waving of this dialectic wand, is made to evaporate into air, along with all other solid realities. For why should you rely on any one attribute of Jehovah, — why should you trust in his mercy, hope for his bounty, pray for his blessing, nay, expect his existence or your own one moment longer, — since in so doing you assume that step for which you have no imaginable authority, which is, that the future will resemble the past?

This is the slough to which Hume would conduct us. It seems a cruel fatality, that the man who has taken off the bandage from our eyes, by which we might have been betrayed into the midst of this miry scepticism, and who has shown us the rock on which we may safely and surely rest our foot far this side of the disastrous results of the maxim of Mr. Hume, should have been suspected of coinciding in the main with that insidious philosopher. Brown asserts that we expect an effect to follow any given cause, or the future to resemble the past, only in consequence of *an irresistible and intuitive belief*, which God has wrought into our very constitutions, and which we can no more avoid than we can avoid perceiving a visible object when we open our eyes. Hence, the mind of itself assumes no step in the above-mentioned reasonings, if reasonings there be; it is God himself who assumed it, when he so created us that there should be a perfect correspondence between our own minds and the onward progress of rolling events around us. From this view of the subject, not one dangerous or shocking consequence flows. It utterly excludes the idea of an arbitrary or unappointed arrangement of things, since we find, in millions of instances, events to take place according to our expectations, and in the few instances where they do not, it is in consequence of the error of our expectations, arising from a limited experience. So far, moreover, from its involving scepticism, it is quite plain that it justifies and encourages a universal and confident belief, as directly opposite to scepticism as pole to pole. And as to exciting any distrust towards the Deity, or any irreligious affections whatever, we have already learned in the beautiful passage which closes the abstract of the Third Part of this book, that, in impressing on our minds this unavoidable, this instinctive belief, the Deity has manifested for us a signal tenderness, which must touch every susceptible heart. When we recollect, that, were it not for this truly vital principle in our mental constitution, we must every moment be liable to be crushed by the masses and powers that are resistlessly and incessantly in action all around us; that we must be constantly exposed to being caught in the wheels of that mighty machinery, whose operations we can now intuitively predict; or that we must sit still and starve amidst this world of plenty and joy into which we are born; we may literally say of our Creator, with Moses, *As an eagle stirreth up her nest, fluttereth over her young, spreadeth abroad her wings, taketh them, beareth them on her wings, so the Lord* hath condescended to take care of his creature man.

Yet Mr. Hume, writhing beneath the tortures of his own absurd conclusions, sets about with all his metaphysical might to extricate himself from them, although in so doing he only wanders still further from the simple upward path of Dr. Brown.

Instead of resorting at once, with our author, to an ultimate principle of our mental constitution, an intuitive belief, which would have untied the knot that puzzled him, he makes the affair of *the gratuitous step* in our reasonings from experience a very intricate process, which he would explain to the following effect, as summed up in the Inquiry.

"When two objects have been frequently observed in succession, the mind passes readily from the idea of one to the idea of the other: from this tendency to transition, and from the greater vividness of the idea thus more readily suggested, there arises a belief of the relation of cause and effect between them; the transition in the mind itself being the impression, from which the idea of the necessary connection of the objects, as cause and effect, is derived." — p. 391.

We can afford but some very short commentaries on this passage, which will, however, be sufficient to demonstrate its astonishing absurdity, and will still further evince that Hume and Dr. Brown do not go hand in hand so affectionately together.

1. Hume begins, "When two objects have been *frequently* observed in succession," &c. He here implies, that we do not expect that one thing is to be the cause

of another, or that the antecedent will again produce the consequent, or, in other words, that the future will resemble the past, until after *repeated* observations of the sequence. But our belief arises on a *single* observation, according to Dr. Brown, who instances a vast number of cases in which there can be no doubt, such as the stinging of a bee for the first time, or the smell of a new flower, which we immediately believe will in all future time produce the same effects. Our author reconciles to his principle those cases which seem to contradict it; but we must not stop to show how. The difference between the two writers is our principal object here.

2. "The mind," continues Mr. Hume, "passes readily from the idea of the one to the idea of the other." There is something so hypothetical, so unphilosophical, in this assumption, that we need not contrast it with our author's simple, open theory of *immediate and intuitive belief*. Surely there is some difference between stating an ultimate intellectual operation, as Brown has done, without attempting to explain it, and gratuitously representing the mind as skipping backward and forward from idea to idea, as a bird does from twig to twig.

3. One would have thought the preceding assertion of Mr. Hume quite shadowy enough; but next comes a statement, which is evanescent and impalpable as the shadow of a shade. "From this tendency to transition, and from the greater vividness of the idea thus more readily suggested, there arises a belief of the relation of cause and effect between them." Whoever can grasp the meaning of this *tendency*, and then combine it, somehow or other, with the *vividness of an idea*, so that the union of the two together shall make up the operation

of belief, must be blessed with a truly metaphysical genius. Even on the supposition that the statement is clear and intelligible, our author demonstrates its falsity by a long course of arguments, combating particularly the error that the *vividness* of an idea is essential even to the strongest belief. This is at least a *third* minor difference.

4. "The transition in the mind itself being the impression, from which the idea of the necessary connection of the objects, as cause and effect, is derived." A *transition in* the mind, an *impression on* the mind! — a singular absurdity! Yet this is the very keystone of the theory which would explain our expectations of the future, or our belief in causation, on any other principle than *intuitive* belief.

We leave this passage now to the reflections and the judgment of our readers, and will not attempt to abstract more copiously the hundred pages in which our author exposes its fallacies, its assumptions, its absurd consequences on the one hand, its inconclusiveness on the other, and the various theories and considerations brought to defend it. The whole topic may perhaps be regarded as an excrescence on the simple exposition of the theory before us. Indeed, the author himself somewhere apologizes for its introduction, by observing that Mr. Hume's opinions on the subject have had so powerful an influence on this abstruse but very important part of physical science, that it would be injustice to his merits, to consider them only with incidental notice, in a work that is chiefly reflective of the lights which he has given.

Before dismissing our author, we shall venture to offer one or two strictures on the leading doctrine and definition contained in his book.

We apprehend that both he and Mr. Hume have overlooked an essential element which enters into our idea of a cause, and which, if introduced into their definition, would at least have made it more easily comprehended and received. *A cause* Dr. Brown defines to be *that which immediately precedes any change*, &c. This definition involves only *immediate succession*, or *proximity in time*. Is not *contiguity in place* equally a part of our notion of causation? Must not the antecedent in our idea be locally *present* with the consequent? It is an axiom, which, at its very first announcement, everybody — child, peasant, philosopher — believes and acknowledges, that no power can act where it is not present. It is true we have an idea of remote causes, as well as proximate causes. But every remote cause is supposed to act upon something immediately near it, and then that something to act upon another as immediately near, and so on, till we arrive in idea at the proximate cause, which, to produce the last effect, is believed to be near it, even to actual contiguity. We think that the omission of this idea has led Dr. Brown, as well as Mr. Hume, into considerable embarrassment, when they came to apply their principle to the innumerable *coexisting sequences* of phenomena, which at every moment are taking place throughout nature. They have both left that point in an unsatisfactory state, Mr. Hume to Dr. Brown, and Dr. Brown to us. If nothing more than immediate precession in time is admitted into our idea of causation, then why is not the acorn, which is planted at the same time with the cherry-stone, regarded as the cause of the fruit-tree, as much as it is of the oak? Admit into your definition the necessary circumstance of contiguity in place, as well as immediate precedence in time, and you escape this objection. We are aware that Dr. Brown has in a manher provided against it by a somewhat cumbrous and not very easily comprehended paraphrase. After beginning his definition, by declaring a cause to be that which immediately precedes any change, he adds, *and which, existing at any time in similar circumstances, has been always, and will be always, immediately followed by a similar change.* We would not exclude this portion of the definition, but would only submit, whether the introduction of contiguity of place as well as proximity in time would not have imparted to the definition more precision, universality, and tangibility.

That this circumstance of *contiguity* always forms part of our strict and simple notion of causation, the more we reflect upon it, the more we are inclined to believe. We wish, therefore, that Dr. Brown had called in this idea,* and wrought it up throughout his treatise in his own admirable manner. It is possible that, in so wishing, we do not look round and through the subject with the comprehensive survey of thorough-going theorists. Yet we cannot but think, that the proposed improvement would have materially assisted him in keeping his main object in view, and prevented many laborious circumlocutions in fortifying his positions against a throng of difficulties and objections, that perpetually arose upon him as he advanced.

---

* When our author speaks of the term *bond of connection* as being adopted to express proximity in time, it is remarkable that he did not perceive how much more appropriate it is to imply proximity in place.

Our author, in the definition before us, seems to us to have revealed just so much of the truth as is conveyed in telling a man in what parallel of latitude his ship is sailing on the ocean. Had he brought in the circumstance of contiguity in place, we think that this would have been like drawing his line of longitude; it would have reduced the difficulty to a specific point, and given to our floating, mysterious idea of a cause a fixed, intelligible, and definite relation. Observe, too, that the objectionable notion of an *invisible link* would be equally excluded by this as by the other form.

What then would be *our* definition? *A cause is that which immediately precedes and is immediately present at any change.* If very hardly pressed, we might call in the closing phraseology of our author's definition. Yet we think we could do without it.

Will our readers briefly analyze this our definition along with us? Think of any change, any phenomenon whatsoever. Think now of an object or event which is in so close proximity to it as to exclude the contact of everything else existing. If this object or event exist in this closest contiguity immediately previous to the change, what else is your idea of a *cause?*

N. A. Review, 1821.

REMINISCENCES OF A NEW-ENGLAND CLERGYMAN AND HIS LADY,

LIVING AT THE CLOSE OF THE LAST CENTURY.

IMAGINE, nearly fifty years ago, a youthful widow left with four small children in the town of Gloucester, at the head of the harbor at Cape Ann, one of the arms enclosing Massachusetts Bay. Her husband had been a very successful merchant in that place, but had recently died insolvent, his insolvency arising from the capture of several vessels by the French in our war of 1798 with that nation. She had heard of an excellent academy in the township of Atkinson, New Hampshire, not far from the boundary line between that State and Massachusetts. Thither she resolved to carry her son, her "only son," the writer of these memoirs, who was then about seven years of age, — not as Abraham carried Isaac, to the altar of sacrifice, but with the purpose of obtaining for him the blessing of an education. She had learned much of the parental and benevolent character of the minister of the town and his lady, whose house was filled with boarders in attendance at the academy, of which, however, the clergyman was not the preceptor, but only the leading patron and trustee. So, one summer morning, she leaves the sea-shore with a horse and chaise, taking her boy as her only companion, over an untried and intricate road of forty miles. She passes through the pleasant town of Ipswich, so quiet at that time, that the whimpering of their chaise's whippletree, and the occasional hammering of the village blacksmith in the sultry noon, were the only noises which they heard; and then, leaving Newburyport far to the right, arrives late in the day at the beautiful village of Haverhill, on the Merrimac, with its noble bridge over the river, and situated on the northern boundary of Massachusetts. Six miles farther north, through a perpetually ascending region, conduct her to the wished-for mansion of the venerable and hospitable clergyman. Here she tells her story of sorrow, declares that she must return the next day to seek by trade a livelihood for herself and her little ones, confesses that she owns not at present a single dollar for their support, and waits to learn the determination of her reverend new acquaintance. The answer is not long in coming. "Madam," said he, in tones which still ring musically in the ears of the writer, and with a cordial smile which seems to shine on the memory as but of yesterday,— "Madam, leave your little boy with us. He shall be one of our family, and enter the academy. If Providence blesses your efforts to secure for yourself a livelihood, well and good; you may remunerate us in the usual way. But if you are doomed to struggle with adversity, be not anxious about your son; here you may be sure that he shall have a home and an education." The charming though elderly lady of the clergyman, who sat silently knitting in the corner of the room during the conversation, with an elegant cap on her head, which won my boyish admiration, and a more attractive countenance beneath it, smiled all along in perfect approval of her husband's generous proposal, and closed the interview by a few kind and precious words of assent and comfort. Romantic as this incident may seem, since the widow had not the slightest claim of any kind on her new-found friends, nor had even her name been known to them until that very day, yet is the relation literally true.

The next morning, the stranger, with a face beaming with joy, eyes glistening with tears, and a heart filled with gratitude and hope, re-ascended the chaise to pursue her homeward journey alone. Such instances of female enterprise are not at all uncommon in New England, even at the present day. The subsequent exertions of our adventuress in trade were abundantly favored by that benignant Being who, throughout the volume of revelation, so frequently and tenderly promises his especial protection to the widow and the fatherless. During the space of ten or twelve years, every one of her children enjoyed, for a greater or less period, the advantages of the family and the institution at which she had placed her son, and she ever regarded it as one of the most cherished blessings of her life, that she was amply enabled to remunerate her disinterested benefactor. To him, and to all connected with him, let us now return. I will do what may be in my power, before we part, to make my readers well acquainted at least with good old "Sir Peabody" and his lady.

The township of Atkinson is one of those numerous subdivisions, of about six miles square, into which nearly the whole of New England is parcelled. The inhabitants of each township form a distinct corporation, all its fiscal, police, and general affairs being conducted by a body called the Selectmen, usually consisting of three persons elected at an annual town-meeting, which assembles at the church, or rather the meeting-house. Atkinson, though far below the summit of that granite territory which swells gradually upward from the Merrimac River until it reaches the Monadnock and White Mountains, still occupies a most commanding position. Looking round on its immense horizon to the south, you might easily fancy yourself on the central apex of the land. With an ordinary telescope you can discern steeples some fifteen or twenty miles distant, counting more than a dozen of them within the whole field, while those of Haverhill, only six miles removed, seem lying comparatively at your feet; and when a warm, gentle south wind prevails, they send up the faint yet clear tones of their distant evening-bells, so magically soft, that you know not whether they are floating from earth or heaven. To the north, or back of the settlement, appear ascending forests and cleared lands, with here and there a distant steeple, until the eye rests at last on the shadowy outline, scarcely distinguishable from the sky itself, of the Grand Monadnock Mountains. What an object for the daily contemplation of an enthusiastic, imaginative youth! How they speak to him of eternal solidity and repose! How they grow into and become a part of the stamp of his being, their dim and far-off grandeur shedding a mystic influence on his soul, which no remoteness of years or situation can efface! When, after dwelling for a long time in some level country, he again sees their forms or similar ones near the horizon, he thrills with the sensation of a new return to life.

There is in Atkinson nothing, properly speaking, like a village. No stream collects there a factory's little population on its banks. The houses are scattered over the whole domain, generally within sight of each other. Every variety of architecture prevails, from the low red cottage, to the ambitious, white-painted, and very sizable mansion; there being, I presume, even here, as in other parts of New England, aspiring souls, who, when about to erect a dwelling-house, might possibly go by night and measure the exact length of their neighbor's residence, for the pleasure of boasting that their own should be six inches larger. The gable-roofed meeting-house, without a steeple, and painted in fading white, stood on an elevation which commanded a large part of the town. At the distance of half a mile on one side appeared the academy, of more modern and ambitious pretensions, and surmounted by a well-proportioned cupola. The township was set off from some adjoining settlements, and incorporated a few years before the Revolution, receiving its name from the Hon. Theodore Atkinson, at that day one of the leading men in New Hampshire. The population has been nearly stationary for half a century, and an idea of its fixed character may be conceived from the fact, that in 1830 it amounted to 555, and in 1840 to 557. Thus Atkinson seems to stand like some individual being, and we may well suppose certain original peculiarities to be developed from this unchanging and undisturbed position. There are, I believe, few smaller towns in the State. The gazetteers represent the ground as uneven in its surface, but as being of a superior quality and well cultivated, and state that the cultivation of the apple has received much attention there; a fact to which I can testify by many savory juvenile reminiscences. The gazetteers also mention a remarkable floating island on a bottomless pond, near the outskirts of the town; but they do not mention the large and delicious cranberries growing upon it, which concur with the very danger of the enterprise in tempting many an adventurous youth to explore its perilous recesses. Hard by the meeting-house stood, and I trust stands yet, the modest but not inelegant mansion of the pastor, — rather the handsomest, perhaps, in the whole town, — with a neat court-yard before it, surrounded by lilacs and roses, various snow-white articles of apparel surmounting the fence on every washing-day, and with a small fruit and flower garden extending still in front of that, on the opposite side of the road. This house will be the central point of interest in our sketches. Few private dwellings in our country, I imagine, have sent out more genial and extensive influences, or have gathered to themselves a richer abundance of delightful recollections and elevated sympathies.

Its occupant and proprietor, Rev. Stephen Peabody, possessed a character so remarkable, and in some respects so unique, as to deserve being rescued from gathering oblivion. He was a native of Andover, Massachusetts, ten miles to the south of Atkinson. He graduated at Harvard College in 1769, in the same class with the celebrated Chief Justice Theophilus Parsons, and with Colonel Scammell, a brave soldier and early victim of hostile treachery in our Revolution. Mr. Peabody delighted, like a true son of his own and of every other

Alma Mater, to take down his College Catalogue from the nail behind the door, on which it hung with the Farmer's Almanac, and entertain all who would listen with the individual biographies and characters of his classmates. He would sooner dispense with his humble salary (to be hereafter mentioned) than fail of his annual visit to Boston and Cambridge during every Commencement week. It was customary, up to the time of the Revolution, to arrange in the printed Harvard College Catalogue the names of the alumni belonging to each class, not in alphabetical order, but according to their rank in society. Every modern edition of this document, even in our own time, preserves the same arrangement in the lists of the older classes; so that whoever may have had an ancestor that graduated at that college, can easily learn his relative social position by consulting the Triennial Catalogue. My venerable clerical friend was certainly not at the summit of his class in this respect, neither was he quite at the bottom of the scale of respectability. I have heard him describe the pecuniary difficulties and struggles he was obliged to undergo, in order to procure his education. His sisters had kindly made him up twelve very important articles of linen, and at the beginning of each term he would take them to Cambridge in his saddlebags, all clean-blanched by their own fair hands, and would wear each of the garments one week, bringing the whole number home again at the end of the term, in a condition fit for the purifying cares of his affectionate laundresses. Throughout his college life, he secured his own diet by waiting on his classmates at table; an office which has been borne by some of the most eminent men in our country, and was not abolished from our colleges until a recent date. He felt the disadvantage of commencing his literary career late in life, being nearly thirty years old at the time of his graduation, and having borne among his classmates the title of *Pater omnium.*

Those were not the favored days of Theological Seminaries, or of charitable Education Societies. He therefore entered, as was customary for divinity students, into the family of some distinguished minister of the Gospel, on whose farm he labored for his board, and defrayed his other expenses by teaching a winter school. While he was yet a candidate for the ministry, the Revolutionary war commenced, and Mr. Peabody served for a time as chaplain in the regiment of Colonel Poor of New Hampshire. There might be some affinity between the name of this officer and Mr. Peabody's subsequent settlement at Atkinson, since that town abounds in the name of Poor, which, together with those of Page and Noyes, used to comprise about one half of the inhabitants. Towards the close of the war, he was ordained as the first minister of the town. His salary was eighty pounds, or about two hundred and fifty dollars, per annum, with the addition, I believe, of a few cords of wood; and it was never increased one farthing during his ministry of more than forty years. It was his custom, on a particular day in the year, to wait at his own house on his parishioners, for the purpose of receiving their minister's tax. As he had open accounts with almost all of them, for labors rendered him, or provisions supplied, or articles manufactured, during the year, the cash balance which he was enabled to sum up and count over after their departure would rather amuse him by its exceeding littleness, or nothingness, than weigh upon his conscience for services overpaid. His farm contained about fifty acres. To liquidate his debt for it, which I believe he was never quite able to effect, the severest privations and hardest toils were cheerfully borne by himself and his first wife, who was renowned for the number of rolls of wool and flax which she would card in a given time. The early years of his ministry must have been well illustrated (I do not mean paralleled) by a picture I have somewhere seen of a poor English curate, and described underneath by the following lines: —

"Though lazy, the proud prelate 's fed,
This curate eats no idle bread:
His wife at washing, 't is *his* lot
To pare the turnips, watch the pot.
He reads, and hears his son read out,
And rocks the cradle with his foot."

I have heard him mention, that, after having wrought in the field the whole day, he has often sat up all night to compose and finish his sermon; which, by the way, he wrote in a small, distinct, and beautiful hand.

In person Mr. Peabody was large and commanding, having attained full six feet in height, and being otherwise of very portly dimensions. His eye was black, and his face was swarthy but well-proportioned. His hair was bushy and curling, swelling out to an ample rotundity behind, like that of Mirabeau. I believe he never followed the coxcombry of our reverend forefathers in wearing a bush-wig, or a wig of any other kind. Though in general courteous and bland in his address, yet when he heard profane language, or received a personal insult, an awful shadow would gather on his visage, his eye would roll fiery glances in every direction, and the dauntless volley of rebuke would be poured from his lips. His passions were naturally strong, and he feared no human being alive. Had any of his parishioners dared to attack his person (since he had his quarrels sometimes), I have not the least question that they would have bitterly rued the moment, for his physical powers were mighty, and in his youth he had been the invincible wrestler of many parishes round, and being now fresh from the Revolutionary war, he had not yet learned to identify the higher Christianity with non-resistance.

His conversation was enlivened with innumerable anecdotes, which he related with surpassing glee and humor, reserving the contagious laugh until the closing point, and using all sorts of dramatic accompaniments, frequently rising from table in the midst of a meal, and taking the floor, if he could thereby set off the action to better advantage.

His musical powers and habits were extraordinary, and he almost revelled through life in an atmosphere of sweet sounds of his own creating. On rainy days, when unlikely to be disturbed by captious or narrow-minded visitors, he would take out his golden-toned violin from a little closet, and draw from its strings the richest and most bewitching notes, a sweet and serene half-smile all the time playing over his lip and cheek and eye. His voice was of vast compass, and exquisitely flexible. He was at home in every part in music. When there was no choir in the meeting-house, he led the singing himself; and when there was one, he supplied the deficient parts, rolling out a mellow and deep-toned bass, or warbling with his treble or counter over the whole concert, like an animated mocking-bird. He sang on week-days at his work, and sometimes talked aloud to himself most agreeably. He would sing on his rides about the town, or when travelling in his chaise, alone or accompanied, by night or by day; and all the solitudes and echoes of that region have many a time rung with his loud and melodious voice. He was most fond of sacred music, but did not disdain a scrap now and then of secular. He would sing you, in perfect taste, with graceful gesture and a happy look, either sitting or standing, various extracts from the delightful old anthems of Arne or Purcell, or from the oratorios of Handel. Coming home from public worship, if a favorite tune had just been sung there, he would repeat it over and over as he entered the house, stopping you in a companionable way, looking you smilingly in the face, and asking if it was not beautiful. He would, except on Sunday mornings, awaken the whole household of sleepers at sunrise, or as soon as he had made the fires, by singing up and down stairs, "The bright, rosy morning peeps over the hills," "The hounds are all out," or some other hunting-song equally stirring. He would take into his lap a little round, favorite dog, and, commanding it to sing with him, he would begin by roaring some tune aloud, the dog immediately joining in with a louder and responsive roar. The only inconvenience from this practice was that the dog one Sabbath followed his master unperceived to the meeting-house, and up to the platform of the pulpit-stairs, and too zealously practised there the musical lessons which he had been taught at home. On some warm summer afternoon, when all the windows of the house were open, and one of his young boarders, far up in the garret at his studies, might happen, for variety's sake, to burst out in some cherished tune or strain, such, for instance, as old St. Anne's, his venerable friend, in the lower story, awaking from his transitory nap, would fall in with his mellifluous bass, and so would they sing for a long time together, until, looking out of their respective windows, they would smile upon each other, as who should say, "Were there ever two better friends than we?"

He was, indeed, the soul of good nature, particularly with the young, and seemed never so happy as when four or five of them were clambering about his person, taking and yielding unrestrained liberties in turn. Like the Apostle Paul's charity, he was "easily persuaded," and you had rarely to ask him more than once to tell one of his inimitable anecdotes, or take down the violin from the closet on a rainy day, or perform his duet with Watch, the overgrown little dog. If a poor and promising young man in the parish was desirous of a liberal education, Mr. Peabody's purse was open for his assistance, with a very distant and precarious chance of being repaid. His hospitality was ungrudging, to the utmost extent of the Apostolic and New Testament standard. Not a day passed that some welcome addition failed of being made to our already crowded table. The parishioner coming to return his book to the Social Library,— the old, familiar acquaintance,— the professed old acquaintance, too, whom the host was sometimes puzzled to recognize,— the travelling brother-minister, stopping with his horse for a week or two,— the passing belated stranger, too far from the tavern for his dinner,— all were cordially invited to partake of the fare for the day. The very doors of the mansion were left unfastened at night, — as, indeed, they scarcely needed locks in that primitive society, — and many a winter traveller from Vermont and Upper New Hampshire, going down in his loaded sleigh to the markets on the sea-board, has come in to warm himself by the midnight bed of embers, held long and pleasant conversations with Mr. Peabody as he lay in an adjoining bed-room, and then retired, the parties being destined never to see or imagine each other's appearance, or to hear each other's voice again.

The titles by which he was designated among his acquaintances were various, according to the degrees of affection, or respect, or indifference, with which he was regarded. By some he was called "Priest Peabody," by others "Parson Peabody," by others "the Reverend Mister," by others again plain "Mister Peabody"; but from all the family, and from all those who were more or less intimately connected with or attached to him, he received the endearing appellation of "Sir Peabody," by which he will generally be distinguished in the remainder of these sketches.

As a divine, he was far from being eminent, though he certainly held in his constitution the elements of a popular preacher, and he exercised, by the force and decision of his character, considerable influence in his own little section of the ecclesiastical world. He was occasionally called on to preach a sermon at an ordination, and once before the legislature of the State; and his few published discourses on such occasions are quite respectable in point of style and matter. In his pulpit manner there was frequently a good deal of animation. He had often heard Whitfield in his youth, and he would sometimes in private imitate that celebrated orator with impressive effect, calling upon the angel Gabriel not to fly back to heaven without carrying with him the tidings of at least one converted sinner,—looking at the same time, in the manner of Whitfield, afar off to the sky, as if he saw the lessening wing of the departing seraph. Approximations to such passages, however, were very rare indeed in his own public performances. In doctrine, he had always been an inveterate Arminian, showing no mercy to Calvinism, or to Hopkinsianism, or Universalism, wherever they might be found. In later life, he advanced still farther into what is denominated Liberal Christianity, having purchased and perused Noah Worcester's "Bible News" with satisfaction, recommending and lending it to his friends, and reading Buckminster's Sermons with delight at his Sabbath family services.

His library, if it deserve such a name, was marvellously small. Besides Matthew Henry's Commentary on the Scriptures, and Cruden's Concordance, I do not think he owned thirty theological books, nor more than that number of any other kind, except a small closetful of the pamphlets of forty years, from which one could catch tolerable glimpses of the political and ecclesiastical matters of New England during that period of time. While studying my Greek Testament at home, to be recited to my teacher at the academy, I always applied in vain to Sir Peabody for a solution of my grammatical and other difficulties, since he candidly confessed that he had grown somewhat rusty on that score. He read some compact and valuable annotations on the Bible (Cappe's, I think,— not Newcome Cappe) at daily morning prayers, and a choice sermon from President Davies, Witherspoon, or some other approved divine, at the Sunday evening family service. Great was the pleasure among the youthful portion of his auditory, when for these divines he would substitute Hannah More's Cheap Repository Tracts. Sweetly even now on the memory descends "The Shepherd of Salisbury Plain," blended with the recollection of those calm Sabbath sunsets. Our friend's acquaintance with English literature was respectable, though rather stationary, being sustained by the attentive reading of a few solid volumes, which might be taken from the Haverhill Library, or from the small, well-selected Atkinson Social Library, of which he was the founder and librarian. To this establishment about twenty or thirty farmers and others were subscribers, who would carefully return its books wrapped in their pocket-handkerchiefs, and an intelligent shoemaker in the parish could boast that he had perused every volume it contained. Sir Peabody had a good habit of reading aloud a paper in the Spectator, every morning, to the female members of his family, while they were engaged in those earnest cares and gentle mysteries which necessarily succeed the refreshments and exercises of the breakfast-table. The newspapers which he took (for I deem that the newspaper one habitually reads is a constituent part and parcel of the very man) were, first and foremost, the Columbian Centinel, printed semi-weekly at Boston, which was the favorite organ of the old Federal party, and therefore of almost the whole clergy of New England, and whose venerable editor, Benjamin Russell, survived at Boston to a green and bright old age of more than eighty years; next, the weekly Haverhill Observer, on the same scale of politics, but about which the partisans of the opposite side would mercilessly pun, in pronouncing it a truly *weakly* paper; and lastly, as the violence of party and a general intellectual activity more and more prevailed, The Boston Repertory, established with the main design of personally and politically opposing Thomas Jefferson. Mr. Peabody occasionally contributed an anonymous political essay to the Haverhill Observer; but in vain was his name concealed from his prying parishioners of the opposite party, who recognized the style and sentiments which he had reiterated among them in private, and who made his lucubrations the subjects of much ill-natured comment and sarcasm in little groups at the shoemaker's or the tavern.

Our friend was not one of those selfish lords of the household, who engross in silence the first reading of the wet sheet, and bury the news of the day or week in their own uncommunicative spirits. He faithfully read aloud and in order the whole contents to the family, whatever might be our want of interest in some of the columns; and if an article, however long, particularly pleased him, we were doomed to hear the reading of it repeated, more perhaps than once or twice, to some winter-evening visitor. He kept a minute journal of the particulars of every day, which amounted, at the close of each year, to a thick duodecimo volume. Those forty or fifty volumes, which I have often seen as they lay piled up in the top of the closet, if still preserved, and explored by some competent inquirer, would unquestionably furnish materials for a curious and valuable memoir of their writer's life and times. At the end of each annual journal, a list was kept of all the deaths which had occurred during the year in the circle of his acquaintance; and the melancholy catalogue, which, as it gradually increased under his hand, called forth from him a sigh of recollection, or a tribute to departed worth or friendship, or a religious reflection, generally contained more than one hundred names every year.

He would once in a while compose an elaborate letter to some distant acquaintance, containing his opinions and strictures on the prevailing tendencies of the day. They were written with much wisdom and point, and, before being copied off for the post, were read with considerable formality to some members of the family for their criticism or concurrence.

He was given sometimes to deep metaphysical discussion; and I have seen him, at a protracted breakfast hour, apparently succeed in convincing ladies who had brought their children to board with him, that the Divine "decrees" were in some way consistent with the perfect freedom of the will. His fair guests had nothing to say in defence of Jonathan Edwards, and listened to his assailant's remarks with as little impatience and distress as can well be imagined.

He found opponents, however, less courteous and submissive in certain members of the Association of Ministers, who met in turn about once in two years at his house. There, though sometimes everything went off pleasantly, yet often arguments, words, and feelings ran high; Calvinist and Arminian conflicted in the fierce tug of war; countenances darkened and eyes flashed on both sides; constrained and hurried adjournment was made to the meeting-house, where a few lay-women and fewer laymen were waiting for the public service; a dinner, crowned with many a luxury, was partaken with feelings of mingled acrimony and festivity; the very grace, before and after meat, by different ministers, was criticised in little knots of whispering malecontents; parties separated for their homes, foreboding disastrous days to the Church; — and all are now reposing in the arms of that sovereign, universal peacemaker, whose dominion extends just five or six feet below the wars and passions and jealous alarms which rage on the verdant overlying surface.

To return to our friend in his pastoral relation, — his sermons were regularly divided, although the divisions never reached the *nineteenthly* or *twentiethly* with which the discourses of olden time are often reproached. After a short introduction, he almost always laid out his matter into four partitions, the last of which was to contain a variety of practical conclusions; and these, I must confess, were occasionally multiplied and protracted, to the consternation of some among his younger hearers at least. He would often introduce very long extracts from Matthew Henry's Commentaries, and I think from one or two other writers, honestly intimating how far the extract extended, by closing it with "Thus Mr. Henry," or, more briefly, "Thus he."

His public prayers were invariably the same, and it might be owing to this circumstance, and a well-disciplined mental piety, that he was enabled to conduct that part of public worship with fluency, and I have no doubt with sincerity also, while his nearly closed eyes would follow some entering stranger, or late straggler at service, till he reached his pew.

His funeral services were deeply impressive and affecting, and, as he loved his parishioners warmly, his own tears would generally lead the way for the tears of others. When, on these occasions, the throng of attendants from the neighboring towns was large, he would take his stand near the bier out of doors beneath some tree; and there his sonorous voice, ejaculating ardent intercessions for the mourners, and solemn admonitions for all, was heard at a very great distance.

On wedding occasions, with his extraordinary social qualities, he was of course the life of the evening. Even when the parties came to his house, he entertained them with sportive anecdote and sound advice, and on one particular occasion was not the less amusing and instructive, although the avaricious bridegroom, in lieu of one dollar, the legal fee for the ceremony, tendered him exactly one quarter of that amount.

For the last thirty years of his life, I doubt if he composed on an average four new sermons annually, though he faithfully revised, corrected, and modified his old ones, even if the weather gave him reason to expect no more than half a dozen attendants at service.

There must have been considerable power and unction in his ministrations, since, notwithstanding a great variety of opinions and denominations prevailed in the town, he brought their adherents together in pretty full congregations almost to the last, arresting the fixed attention of infidels, Methodists, Baptists, and Universalists, as well as those of his own immediate persuasion. I have seen men, who I knew were not believers in Christianity, fastened as by a spell to his discourses from the beginning to the end. I have known the hardened sinner who came to him in private, subdued and softened into tears, and gently guided by his counsels and prayers into those green pastures and by those still waters where his soul would find enduring rest. Men who had long violently opposed his views, and had been harrowing thorns in his side, yet who constantly attended his services, I have found from time to time, in my subsequent visits to Atkinson, become, much to my surprise, as Sauls among the prophets, most affecting instances of calm, fervent, and habitual piety, and dying at last in the full faith and hope of a blessed immortality. There were two or three hardened individuals, indeed, who would never appear inside the sacred walls, except when they had lost one of their own family by death; and then they would attend and hear the funeral sermon, submitting even so far to public opinion and custom as to offer up a note for the prayers of the congregation. How many ways have God's grace and providence to subdue to himself the stubborn will of man! I take no notice here of the habitual drunkards of the parish, nor of a few sorry individuals who really had not souls large enough to know how to find themselves within a meeting-house. They remind me of a sublime saying which Sir Peabody himself used to quote from one of his shrewd parishioners with uproarious approbation, that if a million of such souls were to dance together on the point of a fine cambric-needle, they would fancy themselves to be revelling in infinite space!

Mr. Peabody's communion-table was attended by the usual proportion of professors. How observable and lamentable, that just about the same undue proportion still continues in nearly all the congregations throughout the land at the present time! With a fearless hand he held the keys and wielded the rod of discipline, excommunicating from the church the flagrant offender, and then perhaps influencing him in private, until he was brought again into the pale, with the agony of repentance at his heart, and the petition for re-admission on his lips. There were occasions, in the course of his preaching, when the blackening cloud and fiery flash which I have before described would overcast his countenance. In his annual sermons, for instance, on New-Year's or Thanksgiving day, while enumerating the blessings of the preceding year, the peace and quiet which the town had enjoyed, and the general satisfaction which the people had expressed in his ministry, his voice would lower and his countenance change, as he remarked, after a momentary pause, "—a few incendiaries alone excepted!" Here he alluded to some sectarian or infidel opponents who had disturbed his ministry and interrupted the harmony of the town. Every one knew the individuals to whom he alluded, even if he himself did not look down, as it is altogether likely he would, with glaring eye, over his spectacles, into the very pews of the offenders.

Once I saw his Christianity most severely put to the test in his public services. It was on a very inclement day, and there were but few worshippers in the meeting-house. When he had reached about the middle of his sermon, a strong perfume of tobacco-smoke became distinctly perceptible to every one in the building. He paused for a little while, gazed round, and, not being able to discover whence it proceeded, resumed his discourse. In the mean time the mysterious odor grew stronger and stronger, and the house was soon filled with a dense vapor. Again and longer did he pause. And as, with spectacles now raised to his forehead, his eye explored every part of the edifice, both on the floor and in the galleries, he at length saw ascending from the bottom of one of the gallery pews three separate streams of smoke, in fast-repeated puffs, as if they were issuing for a wager, or were determined to exhaust themselves, in spite of the notice which they had now evidently attracted from the minister and the congregation. "Is it possible," exclaimed the grieved and exasperated divine, —"Is it possible that such sacrilegious impiety as that which I see should take place in this house of God? Let it stop instantly, or if conscience and religion can be of no avail, an appeal must be made to the strong arm of the law." A pause of still and solemn wonder mantled over the thin congregation. Not a word was spoken, not an object stirred, save the three continued streams of puffs, which persevered in their daring outrage, in defiance of every awful or constraining sanction. "Squire Vose!" at length exclaimed Sir Peabody, addressing himself in a determined, authoritative voice to the preceptor of the academy, who was also a justice of the peace, and whom on other occasions he simply called Mr. Vose, "I desire that you would proceed to the pew in the gallery from which that smoke is issuing, and put down the offence immediately, and that to-morrow you would take measures to have the offenders prosecuted and punished to the utmost extremity of the law." Accordingly Mr. Vose proceeded to the gallery, extinguished the source of the disturbance, and the service then proceeded quietly to the close. The next day, the culprits, who proved to be three apprentices and farmers' boys,—though, to his shame, one of them, at least, was of a manly growth,—becoming alarmed at the threatened consequences of their thoughtless sacrilege, were induced, if I rightly recollect, to make penitent acknowledgments and promises of better conduct for the future, and so were forgiven.

This leaning to the authority of the civil power contributed perceptibly, I apprehend, to characterize much of Sir Peabody's ministerial deportment. There still existed at that time in New England a sort of palpable connection between Church and State, which subsequent legal enactments and alterations of constitutions have everywhere done away. There also prevailed towards clergymen, as somehow connected with the resistless majesty of the civil law, a traditionary reverence, handed down not only from our English ancestors in the times both of the Kings and the Commonwealth, but also from our puritanical Pilgrim fathers, whose policy, it is well known, went far to combine the rod of the magistrate with the pastoral crook. This feeling of reverence, no doubt, was considerably prevented from decaying by the sympathy and co-operation which the New-England clergy exhibited with the popular party throughout our whole Revolutionary struggle,—as, indeed, it was afterwards very much undermined and diminished by the zeal with which they espoused the principles of the Federal party, in the times that followed the French Revolution. For the payment of Mr. Peabody's salary, the law permitted him to look to the whole corporate town, and not to any voluntary assemblage of friends and partisans. It was thus guaranteed to him by the power and authority of the State, and, no matter how many sects abounded in Atkinson, they were all obliged to contribute to the minister's tax equally with the Congregationalists or Independents, to whose communion he himself belonged, and who were the direct descendants from Oliver Cromwell's own denomination. No combination of enemies could avail to eject him from his pitiful living. We believe that New Hampshire threw off these slight fettering relics of the ancient order of things several years previously to Massachusetts, and that Sir Peabody experienced not a little the moral effects of the change before his death. Perhaps the three burners of false incense in the gallery were among the earliest symptoms of the rising spirit of Young New England to question and to break the spell. Such was not, however, the general tone of the transition period which I am endeavoring to portray. The traditionary, mystic influence which the minister exercised over his parishioners went even, I think, in many cases, beyond the legitimate powers he possessed, and would have been stoutly resisted, could it have been encountered and analyzed by some daring hand. It was something like the sway which one of the Speakers of the House of Commons wielded over that assembly in the third quarter of the last century. Long after the royal authority had been shorn of its formidable prerogatives, this gentleman had the skill to intimidate many an adventurous orator who had dared to treat lightly the proceedings of the House, by exclaiming, "Let the honorable gentleman beware of what he says, or he shall assuredly be reported!" That word *reported* fell on the ears of Parliament like some mysterious denunciation from the invisible world. On one of these occasions, however, some intrepid and independent champion of the popular cause is said to have replied, "And to whom, in the name of wonder, Mr. Speaker, am I going to be reported?" Whereupon this was the last time the threat was ever uttered.

Sir Peabody was, in many analogous respects, this Right Honorable Speaker of his parish and his day. In his very person he would on some rare occasions stand out as the embodying representative of the grand conceptions and reverences of the past. Methinks I see his form even now, as it impressed itself on my youthful imagination, looming afar off in the road, on the hill-top, against the sky. He may be going to pay some very formal visit. As he descends the hill with an animated and vigorous, but not hurried pace, I discern more distinctly his elaborate and imposing old-time dress, — his high three-cornered beaver hat, — his large single-breasted coat, sweeping down on each side with an ample curve, — his vest, "full twice the length of these degenerate days," ending on both sides with large pockets and lappets, — his snow-white plaited stock, under a smoothly shaven, expanded chin, and fastened behind with a silver buckle, — his nether garment terminating at his knees, and fastened there also with small silver buckles, — his long black-silk stockings extending from the knee to the foot, — the whole being finished and consummated by shining, square-buckled shoes. He draws still nearer, and with something of the old erect, military air which he had caught in the camp, something of that conscious lingering majesty of church-and-state authority about him which I have hinted at in the preceding paragraph, something of the man of the world, and much more of the sociable, good-humored, busy, Christian pastor, he makes to those whom he meets a graceful, ceremonious bow, yet accompanied with a smile, and a hearty "Good day," and passes on.

This, however, belongs to my earlier and more palmy recollections of him. As age advanced, and means perhaps were straitened, and post-Revolutionary fashions prevailed, his dress and appearance, even in his best array, became less picturesque, aristocratic, and awe-inspiring. Silk would now give way to worsted, and the shoe-buckle be replaced by the plain galloon or plainer leathern string.

But far more astounding the change exhibited, even at the former brilliant period, by the very same individual, when engrossed by the labors of some busy season of the year; — holding perhaps the plough; or hoeing the cornfield until the latest shade of twilight; or urging forward the various processes of haymaking; or grafting his trees; or gathering in the autumnal harvest; or pressing out his year's stock of cider from immense apple-heaps; or shaking and gleaning the apple-trees, all of which he mounted for that purpose himself; or laying up the choicest kinds of fruit in his extensive apple-cellar, to bring them out every day through the winter with profuse and hospitable pride; or butchering a beeve, or butchering a swine, — operations, every detail of which he executed with artistic dexterity, though I imagine he was the only butcher who never sacrificed a lamb without repeating aloud to himself or to the by-standers those four lines of Pope, —

> "The lamb thy riot dooms to bleed to-day,
> Had he thy reason, would he skip and play?
> Pleased to the last he crops the flowery food,
> And licks the hand just raised to shed his blood."

Amidst toils like these came forth the large flapped, weather-stained, round, and low-crowned hat, which had commenced its brighter days of service in a very different shape some dozen years before,—the unshaven face, neglected, at some very busy periods, from one Sabbath morning to another,—and the old service-beaten gown, tied up about the waist, or probably no upper garment at all save the reeking shirt that covered his bending frame.

For his years, he was one of the most laborious men in his parish. With the occasional exception of a hired workman or two, and a small apprentice-boy, he carried on the operations of his farm alone. The whole fuel for several fires in the house, through the long Northern winter, was often chopped and supplied by his stalwart arm alone.

When polished visitors arrived from the seaport towns or elsewhere, give him but an hour at his toilette, and again he is metamorphosed into the well-dressed, hospitable entertainer, betraying no complaint at the interruption of his most urgent toils, and carrying on animated conversations for hours together. In short, it would now almost appear that he preferred talk to work, that he would rather play the gentleman than the hard laborer, and that he gladly seized the agreeable duties of hospitality as an excuse to escape from the overwhelming drudgeries of the farm. I well know that such insinuations were maliciously whispered about against "Priest Peabody" by the mean, insurrectionary spirits of the parish.

Perhaps there was greater plausibility in the regrets which his more serious friends would sometimes express, that the demeanor of Sir Peabody now and then savored of an apparent worldliness and carelessness, hardly consistent with the strict proprieties of the ministerial character. Such regrets may have been somewhat justified by his exuberant animal spirits, his love of a busy, bustling life, his exceeding proneness to social intercourse, and the debts, expedients, and multiplied managements, far and near, to which, with a currency changing in value, he was obliged to resort, in the voluntary task of sustaining a family of twenty boarders.

He used to relate an anecdote of himself with his peculiar humor,—that having once fattened a first-rate calf for market, he sent it by one of his parishioners to the town of Haverhill, anxious to obtain for it the highest price. "And what shall I tell the people of Haverhill," said his friend to him, "in order to persuade them to come up to your mark?" "O, tell them," replied Sir Peabody, "that the calf belongs to a poor man who is maintained by the town of Atkinson." The stratagem, although originally intended as nothing more than an innocent joke, succeeded very well, and Mr. Peabody frequently afterwards had his laugh in person against the purchaser.

It will be regarded as a striking symptom of the change in public opinion, and even in the spirit of our laws, that Sir Peabody was the acting manager of a public lottery for the benefit of his cherished Atkinson Academy, disposing of the tickets all over the country wherever he was able, and himself personally superintending the drawing, while the whole proved an embarrassing concern, on account of the incomplete sale of tickets, or some other unfortunate mismanagement. It cost him two or three journeys to Boston in the depth of winter, in vainly endeavoring to procure the consent of the Massachusetts legislature, that the tickets might be sold in that Commonwealth; and sadly did the family feel, as we all flocked around him at the opening of a fresh Columbian Centinel, and then heard him read with Christian and philosophic calmness from the journal of the legislature, that "the Rev. Mr. Peabody had leave to withdraw his petition."

Whether all these possible deficiencies from a high pastoral standard were the operating cause of that rebellious sectarism which broke up his little town into fragments, and for many years prevented the ordination there of any officiating minister, the Searcher of hearts and Former of spirits can alone determine. I have myself often breathed a wish, in subsequent years, that it had been my lot in early youth to receive my religious impressions from a clerical example of greater spirituality and a more decidedly preponderating piety. But then, again, I have almost immediately recoiled from the thought, as if I had rendered a kind of sacrilegious injustice and ingratitude to the memory of my old, warm-hearted, unvarying friend. The recollection of his many whole-souled virtues, which I have already enumerated in this sketch, and the positive religious good which I know his ministry in many cases produced, are amply sufficient to redeem it from any deep-stained reproach of inefficiency. Where is the man, and especially among those whose natural constitution prompts them to much outward activity, — where is the man whose character is entirely free from some practical inconsistency? I know that such inconsistencies are to be lamented and condemned, and everybody shall do it for Sir Peabody who does it in a thorough-searching, thorough-cleansing manner for himself.

The most prominent characteristic about this very peculiar man was, it seems to me, that he was a true son of nature. No child of the forest, no hero of antiquity, ever stepped forth before his fellows with more freshness and freedom of action. There was little or no self-discipline or self-training about him; but whatever part of his character had not been formed and moulded by the stringency of outward circumstances was just as it came from the hand of God. If he had little about him of the loftier and self-denying qualities of the highest spiritual Christianity, so, on the other hand, he had nothing about him artificial, or simulating, or pretentious.

As I have ventured with a free hand to draw a light-and-shade portraiture of my friend, I ought, in concluding it, to observe, that none had better opportunities than myself of testifying to the reality and solidity of his piety. Having listened to his morning prayers for several years together, after the Bible had been duly read by the whole family around in turn; having joined his evening devotions at an hour when the distinct, solemn ticking of the clock united with the surrounding darkness and stillness to impress every word on the attention; having witnessed a certain sweet and gracious sanctity which always pervaded his countenance and manners on the Sabbath; having heard him, hundreds of times and on every variety of occasion, both when alone and with children whom he desired to impress, utter serious reflections on the vanity and precariousness of life, and the religious responsibility of man; having visited his bedside at night, under the youthful struggles of an agitated experience derived from perusing Doddridge's "Rise and Progress," or Edwards's "History of Redemption," or the Bible itself, — books which he had himself carefully recommended to me to read, — and having there received, in that solemn, though not fearful darkness, his tender, judicious, fatherly, guiding lessons; — I may not hesitate, while acknowledging in his case the existence of imperfections incident to our common humanity, to claim for him the merited appellation of — to me at least — a man of God.

He sleeps in the small grave-yard behind his meeting-house. Journeying a few years since from Boston on purpose to visit the spot, and standing by his grave while the bleak wind of New Hampshire murmured against his tombstone, and the grand, blue, shadowy Monadnock, unchanged as ever, waited afar off behind me, I could not repress the gushing ejaculation, — "O venerated spirit! It was long mine to witness thy busy, faithful, efficient activity and influence in the scene that outspreads yonder before us; I fear not to pray that it may also be mine to meet thee and share thy destiny, whatever it may be, in the dim and distant eternity."

At the same moment, my arm was resting on another monumental stone. It was that of the blessed lady who, in my penniless boyhood, had joined her husband in welcoming me to her home, and who acted towards myself and a hundred others of both sexes the unstinting part of a friend and mother. Mrs. Peabody, — or "Madam Peabody," as some called her, — or "Ma'am Peabody," — so all who loved her pronounced it, as a kind of correlative appellation to "Sir," — had died a few years previously to her husband; an event which contributed more than anything else to change the appearance and ways of her aged, declining partner. He would sometimes try afterwards to repeat his ancient anecdotes, but accompanied them with only a faint smile, instead of the old infectious and irresistible laugh. Mrs. Peabody was allowed by all who enjoyed the happiness of her acquaintance to stand in the very foremost rank among the daughters of America. She was one of three celebrated sisters; the other two having been Mrs. Adams, wife of the elder President Adams, and Mrs. Cranch, mother of the present Judge Cranch of Washington. I apprehend that by the numerous surviving relatives and admirers of those two accomplished ladies it will be considered no disparagement to their just claims, if I assert that Mrs. Peabody was the most interesting woman of the three. She was the daughter, with them, of the Rev. Mr. Smith, of Weymouth, near Boston, and was educated under the best ante-Revolutionary influences of that vicinity.

Her conversational powers were of a superior order. She was adequate to any theme that custom has brought within the range of the female mind. Possessing the charms of a fine person, a delicate, transparent complexion, and a beautiful, speaking eye, with manners highly polished and courtly, a retentive memory, choice and fluent language, and an anxious pressure, a constantly inquiring upward tendency towards the right, — towards some indefinite point of moral and religious progress, — how could she do otherwise than produce a deep impression on all within her sphere, kindling within them a love and reverence for the capacities of human nature;

and earnest desires to make it better both in themselves and in others?

Scarcely ever did the youthful flock that gathered around her sit down at table, that she did not introduce some pleasing or improving topic of conversation, which she would embellish with apt and admirably recited passages from Shakespeare, Dryden, Pope, Addison, Young, Thomson, and Cowper. Her annual visits to her Boston and Quincy friends kept up her stores of refined cultivation, and she always returned prepared to communicate her interesting observations on society, manners, and even the music and scanty painting of the day. Her vigilant eye kept an incessant watch over the conduct and character of her boarders; sweetly would she rebuke, delicately would she warn, affectionately would she advise. Many a young man did she render thoughtful; in many a young woman did she awaken lofty aspirations after excellence. And when they left her house with her lessons warm on their memory, she would deepen and protract the impression by sending after them her carefully composed and richly laden correspondence, which, if it could be collected and published, would justify the tribute I now delight to pay.

Not that she always appeared in this refined and elevated full-dress of character. Too well for that did she know the household duties of a New-England clergyman's wife. She was almost as absorbingly devoted to the labors of her own department as we have seen that Sir Peabody was to his. Combing a dozen heads every morning, and shearing them when necessary, — mending innumerable stockings and *et ceteras*, — superintending large broods of various poultry, — achieving the house-work which her one small maid must necessarily leave unfinished, — making those miscellaneous preparations for a large family dinner which might not come within the grasp of her one solitary cook, — and everywhere, from true Christian principle, not from sordid thrift, gathering up the fragments that nothing might be lost, — could she be justly charged with fastidiously playing the lady? And though her morning dress could never, of course, be compared with the slouching, nondescript array which I have tried to suggest as appertaining to Sir Peabody, — inasmuch as woman always contrives, amidst the lowest occupations, to keep herself in more decent trim than man, — yet would I often witness with admiration and reverence the metamorphosis which she also underwent in the latter part of the day. The agitated and agitating housewife of the forenoon would be now in full court-dress, sitting erect in her rocking-chair, and reading Paley's Moral Philosophy, or some work of an equally elevated description, which "Sir" in fact could rarely find time to peruse.

Now can it be wondered at that I should regard her as the beau-ideal of womankind? Her image is at this moment in my mind's eye, with that selfsame peculiar, elaborate cap which had appealed so strongly to my boyish imagination the first moment I saw her. Why, indeed, may not the character of a lady be very much interpreted from the contour and structure of her head-dress? For instance, — to appeal to a diametrically opposite kind of example, though it is logical, I believe, to do so, — could any reader of Dickens possess one half the depth of insight which he now enjoys into the qualities of Sally Brass, had the author deprived her of that specific yellow cap, with which he could not avoid surmounting her head, if he wished to convey a complete conception of her character? And in like manner I am certain that those snow-white folds within folds, those muslin-depths of soft bluish tint, those interwoven advancing and retiring festoons of fine thread-lace, and that general poetic effect of outline, position, and air which adorned the majestic crown of my revered and beloved friend, were only so many external symbols, types, and representatives of that matchless purity of heart, those mystic and winning graces, and those exquisite intellectual adornments, which lay, like a substratum of vital, productive reality, within the recesses of her noble spirit beneath.*

Her first husband was the Rev. Mr. Shaw of Haverhill. I know little of the character or ministry of Mr. Shaw, except that he was generally regarded as a very worthy man, and faithful in his sacred vocation. Bating some economical arrangements imposed by the stress of hard necessity, their house was the centre of an elegant little society for twenty years after the Revolution; some of the most cultivated residents of Boston and its vicinity delighting in a pilgrimage to Haverhill, where they could enjoy the charms of Mrs. Shaw's presence and conversation.

---

* A portrait of this lady, executed by Stuart in his best style, with her queenly head-dress and all, and realizing everything that has been said in the text respecting her personal appearance, is now in the possession of Mrs. Felt of Boston, the surviving daughter of Mrs. Peabody; to whom and her husband, the Rev. Joseph B. Felt, the whole of this sketch has been submitted in manuscript, while their friendly suggestions have been gratefully and faithfully adopted.

In reference to her second marriage, I must relate a curiously interesting anecdote, communicated to me by an old female domestic of Mrs. Shaw's family, herself one of the excellent of the earth, and who followed the fortunes of my friend in both her marriages. Mrs. Shaw had a cousin, Rev. Isaac Smith by name, a man of an excellent and lovely character, an accomplished scholar, a finished writer, and a polished gentleman of the old school. He had visited England, where he had been intimate in the family of the celebrated Miss Hannah More. He was now preceptor of the very respectable Dummer Academy at Byfield, near Newburyport, from which he would make excursions through the country in a one-horse chaise, kindly ready with his services to his ministerial brethren. Much later in life he removed from Byfield to the town of Boston, where he became chaplain of the almshouse, keeper of the Theological Library, and moderator, by seniority in age, of the Boston Association of Ministers, in the discharge, I believe, of which three offices he died, at the advanced period of eighty years. I there happened to enjoy for a considerable time the pleasure of the good old gentleman's acquaintance, when commencing life myself, and prosecuted together with him some agreeable tasks in theological literature. But I must now go back many years to the date of my anecdote. While Mr. Smith was preceptor of the Byfield Academy, and riding benevolently round the country, in middle life, Mrs. Shaw of Haverhill became a widow. Mr. Smith was one of several gentlemen who, according to common report, now aspired to her hand. I think my good-hearted informant assured me that he had entertained, even in his earlier years, similar fond pretensions to his fair young cousin. But owing to some diffidence, or delay, or accidental absence on his part, he had been precluded even then from the attainment of his hopes by his more successful rival, Mr. Shaw. He sought in no other quarter for the consolation of his wounded affections, but remained just as he was, until a mingled Providence again apparently opened for him an avenue to the former object of his regard. But it so happened that Mr. Peabody of Atkinson was a widower, of about the same standing in that isolated condition with Mrs. Shaw herself, and was now meditating a second connection in life. He had visited her house too long and frequently, and was too well acquainted with the rare virtues and attractions that centred in her character, not to perceive that a prize so near and so precious ought by no means to be snatched from his grasp without a seasonable effort on his part to secure it. By a singular coincidence, Mr. Smith and Mr. Peabody both selected one and the same day, of violently pouring rain, to secure, by the offer of their hands, the consummation of their glowing and honorable hopes; just as two eagles, o'erwearied with gloomy earth, might choose, unknown to each other, the moment of a driving storm to ascend into the serene and bright upper heaven. The choice of such a day, however, might possibly have been made by either party to preclude the probability of any rivalry or other officious interruption. Be that as it may, they both started from their homes after an early dinner, Mr. Peabody having six miles to ride in a southern direction, and Mr. Smith fifteen in a northern. Somewhat after dark, Mr. Smith's chaise, with all the deliberation of conscious security, enters the yard behind the favored residence, and stops, as usual, at the door in that part of the house. Lydia, my kind and true-hearted humble friend, being the domestic there, appears immediately at the door, with a look of peevish anxiety and agitation uncommon to her. She had long been encouraging Mr. Smith to take the present step, and much preferred that her mistress should join her destinies to him, to her union with any other man. She had ever pitied the frustration of his early pretensions, which she held to be still valid, and she considered, besides, that the superiority of his refined and gentlemanly manners, together with the respectability of his connections, entitled him, more than any other aspirant, to the envied hand. But when did ever match-maker succeed in outwitting the wiser decrees of destiny? My well-meaning gossip was obliged, in conclusion, to say, while in after-days, in a low voice, so as not to be heard in the Atkinson parlor, she recounted these incidents to a group of wondering school-boys, — "I am afraid, boys, that when I went to the door, I spoke more sharply to Mr. Smith than I ought to have done; for I said to him, 'You are altogether too late, sir; Mr. Peabody has long ago dried his coat by this kitchen-fire, and has been sitting now with Mrs. Shaw for a whole hour in the parlor.'" Where or how Mr. Smith spent that evening, I never had the irreverent curiosity to inquire. I only know that the remainder of his long life was passed in a meek and acquiescent celibacy, tinged with a soft shadow of sadness, of which few knew the cause;* and I believe as

* Rather recently, a surviving friend of Mr. Smith has obligingly communicated to me a somewhat different history of that excellent gentleman's affections in later life. So that my closing impressions in regard to his declining experience may have been tinged with the shadows of my imagination.

firmly as that I am writing here, that he is now in that blessed world where there is neither marrying nor giving in marriage, and that he is, along with his two excellent friends, what he certainly seemed always and everywhere to be while here on earth, as one of the angels in heaven.

What kind of a treasure Sir Peabody thus obtained, has been already in a good measure portrayed. She was in general duly appreciated in her new place of residence, as she was always received with joy, also, in her frequent visits to the old; and I am not mistaken in saying, that, with few exceptions, she was looked up to by all the parishioners of both sexes in Atkinson, as a kind of superior being. I have observed the stamp of her bland and gracious manners on the good ladies of the place, even after the lapse of twenty years from her death. Can any one forget that dignified and winning expression with which, at the close of public worship, she followed her husband out of the meeting-house? According to a custom in that town, which I do not recollect to have observed in more than one other part of our country, and I know not whence it originated, the minister was the very first person to depart from the sanctuary, the whole congregation silently standing until he and his lady had passed the threshold of the door. It was at least a respectful and impressive custom. What a contrast to the indecent haste, and scramble, so to speak, with which many congregations start off for home; as if the benediction were like the dropping of a signal pocket-handkerchief on a race-course! Why, at least, might not all remain for a brief space, while the organ is enunciating its solemn and spirit-stirring *finale*, which is scarcely heard or appreciated under the present arrangement, and so depart one by one, as varying moods might prompt, consistently with the sanctity of the spot and the occasion? Nothing, indeed, can be more worthy of imitation than the custom of Episcopalian assemblies, in closing their public services with silent personal prayer. Next to the solemn effect of such a practice was that reverential repose with which we all used to stand waiting, while "Sir" descended the pulpit-stairs and passed along the broad-aisle, bowing alternately on each side with elaborate ceremony, and solemn, expanded eyes, and "Ma'am" immediately followed him out of the pew at the foot of the pulpit-stair, with her look cast down to the floor, as though *she* had no prerogative to bow, and with a modest, incipient smile on her visage, as if conscious that the pious love of many eyes were directed upon her. Reverence! whither hast thou fled? Since these thine external manifestations have disappeared, hast thou left behind, in the unfettered soul within, a growing love for the substantially true, and right, and holy, and beautiful, and venerable, and eternal?

But the same malignant spirits, who had fastened upon and magnified the defects of Mr. Peabody, were not wanting to espy or devise faults in his lady. I pass over the more contemptible of her maligners, who complained, that at her tea-visits abroad she preferred white to brown bread, and whom I only mention as indicating one feature of the manners of the times, which I trust has long since for ever disappeared. But the more plausible and decent of "Ma'am's" detractors levelled their shafts at much higher game. Among these, the favorite whispered scandal was, that she was a woman of towering pride, and over fond of dress. Of pride she had no more than an angel from heaven, who stoops to protect and sympathize with the poorest and humblest, while he approaches the loftiest and haughtiest with a calm, conscious sense of his own celestial dignity, which mean spectator-angels might possibly construe into pride. With regard to her alleged attachment to dress, so profound is my reverence for her whole character, that I have no doubt she conscientiously mingled her practice on this point with the purest sentiments of duty. Perhaps that characteristic emblematical cap of hers might seem to a cynical observer occasionally decked out with superabundant ornament. I remember reading in modern ecclesiastical history, that the Huguenot ministers of the sixteenth century had the greatest difficulty in preventing the pious, lovely, and noble Madame Du Plessis, and several other ladies of high rank, from offending in the very same particular, and were finally compelled, like the Methodist divines of a later day in their war against ribbons, to decline the contest. Perhaps some adornment of the kind is essential to the highest type of a lady of the Caucasian race. Perhaps, too, the very angel from heaven, to whom I just now alluded, may sometimes view with too much complacency the lustre of his own pruned, ethereal wing. But let that pass. Could I even be convinced that in my sainted friend the refinement of an elevated nature ever faded down into feminine infirmity, I would but seize the occasion to remember and inculcate that absolute perfection belongs only to ONE.

1847.

CRITICAL ESSAY ON THE ORATORY OF EDWARD EVERETT.*

PUBLISHED IN THE SOUTHERN QUARTERLY REVIEW FOR APRIL, 1851.

As Mr. Everett needed no accession to his reputation, this re-production of his brilliant life on the rostrum may be considered as a gratuitous present to the public. It will be thankfully welcomed, not only as in itself a choice contribution to American literature, but as something like an historical monument of the progress of our national culture. The author's life has been coeval with a peculiarly vigorous and critical stage of American development, whose tendency to absorption in gross, material interests or coarse political excitements, he has successfully resisted, while he has aided, as much as any man living, to impart to it a refined and intellectual direction. Gifted with extraordinary powers of mind, which almost from childhood produced upon his native community a kind of mysterious impression, he has incessantly sought to "magnify his office," by communicating a healthy and generous impulse to the spheres within his reach. His large and active ambition, disdaining everything eccentric or illegitimate, has invariably been baptized in a

* *Orations and Speeches on Various Occasions.* BY EDWARD EVERETT. In two volumes. Second Edition. Boston: Little and Brown. 1850.

pure and wholesome element, and confined itself within the limits of immediate usefulness. Pandering to no low or transient tastes, he seems always instinctively to have proceeded on the conviction, that the public mind could be moulded and guided by influences adapted to its better nature; and the result has shown how well founded was his conviction. If the pursuit of literature is cherished with any fondness in these United States, if the name of scholar is honorable among us, no person, probably, can lay claim to so large an agency in producing the happy effect, as Edward Everett. It is a curious and gratifying circumstance in his very imposing career, that in three widely separated regions, — on our Atlantic coast, by our Western waters, and in the mother country, — processions and festivals have been formed to do him personal honor, — not for his political influence, or leadership in any movement of exciting reform, but purely from the milder fame of his admirable and well-directed scholarship. We know of no similar contemporaneous example, nor, in fact, anything like it since the early and enthusiastic days of modern literature.

As apposite to these observations, we subjoin an extract from the little work of a tourist, published at New York, in 1838. The authoress is describing a Commencement occasion at Harvard College in 1836, at which Mr. Everett was present, in his official capacity, as Governor of Massachusetts.

"It was seventeen years," she observes, "since I had previously attended this celebration; my thoughts chiefly rested on the audience, and were drawn away from the speakers by the throng of memories that clustered so richly over the scene. There were many changes. The old Puritan meeting-house was gone, and had given place to one of elegant and classical structure.

. . . . . .

"After musing awhile on these things, until the voices of the speakers sounded, dream-like, amid the deeper voices of the past, my attention was riveted by one conspicuous individual. I had seen that subdued glance years ago, at his first college exhibition; it was the same, — the same slow raising of the clear blue eye, the same deferential bow at honors conferred. The cheek of the man was pale, on the boy's was a crimson spot, where genius seemed feeding; time had laid his hand on the head of the man, the boy's fair hair was glossy and full; the limbs of the man, though not large, were firm, the boy was slender, so slender that it was feared mind would master him, and that he would be one of those plants that die early. Why God so often takes the prematurely ripe, we know not; but we know that the responsibilities of such moral agents, when he permits them to remain, are fearfully great. The eye of Heaven must look searchingly down on the individuals it has gifted so unsparingly.

"At the Commencement of 1811, he again appeared, still a boy, bearing off the honors of a man. There was another lapse of time, and he stood before the Phi Beta Kappa Society as a poet; and the lips of the fair opened in praise, and friends gathered and fluttered like butterflies around the opened flower, and old men shook their heads in pleasant surprise, or gazed upon his modest brow, and bade him God speed. A few years passed, and he stood to be ordained in the holy character of a Gospel minister. I shall never forget that day. As his fathers in the ministry laid their hands on his head, he looked too slight for so tremendous a charge; but when, at the close of the service, he pronounced a blessing on the audience, there was a tremulous depth in his voice which spoke of ardent communing with duty.

"Another period elapsed, and he visited Europe, to glean from its fields pleasure and improvement. In the Chapel of Harvard College, on his return, I heard his first discourse. It was a brilliant summary of interesting things. Since then he has walked the halls of statesmen; his various orations have risen like a line of beautiful hills on the literary horizon, and he has been crowned with civil honors." *

A very mistaken and superfluous regret is sometimes expressed by Mr. Everett's admirers, that he has not devoted his powers to some grand, continuous work, but has employed them on such fragmentary productions as compose the two volumes before us. We think there is in this regret more sentimentality than good sense. If some creating spirit chooses to give us for our refreshment a whole grove of noble palms, we will not quarrel with him for refraining to bestow in their room a solitary gigantic oak. If an architect overspreads the land with beautiful and commodious churches, to which many neighborhoods resort for edification and delight, we will not ask him, Why have you spent your life upon these, rather than upon a single towering cathedral? The truth is, an almost epic unity and interest pervades these volumes, notwithstanding the piecemeal nature of their ingredients. They tell an eventful story, as they proclaim the life-like movement of the country in its varied historical, political, material, intellectual, moral, and spiritual relations. Even had Mr. Everett reserved his powers for one huge work, we presume he must have divided and subdivided it into chapters and sections. Now here *is* a huge book, divided not indeed into chapters, but into profound and brilliant orations and addresses, which grew so, as it were, by nature, and were not artificially cut and carved out by the book-maker's hand. When high merit is presented to us in one form, why should we

---

* Poetry of Travelling in the United States, by Caroline Gilman.

complain of that form, and wonder that it comes in no other? Must Shakespeare be arraigned for working up his plots into five dramatic acts, instead of expanding them into the twelve books of a Paradise Lost? or shall Horace be disparaged, for not assuming the exact individuality of Maro? Mr. Everett has met the demand of his generation, by assisting to shape and direct its mighty but vague aspirings. If he has not written a treatise in three volumes, let him console himself with the thought that he has been doing something better,— he has not thrown his life away,— he has aided to stamp an age! We give all honor to the meritorious producers of three, six, or nine connected volumes. But we suspect several of these fortunate writers will be among the first candidly to confess that Mr. Everett did something to stir the atmosphere which breathed or summoned their fine creations into life. Such boast he may make with Coleridge, but not, like Coleridge, lament his abused and misdirected powers. There are some judicious observations on a subject allied to this, in Lord Jeffrey's article on the Memoirs of Sir James Mackintosh. They were, perhaps, intended as an indirect justification of the critic's own literary career, as well as that of the writer reviewed; and Mr. Everett himself is entitled to apply them to the multifariously detailed labors of his past literary life. Speaking of Sir James's deferring the execution of his larger projects, in order to enlighten the public mind through the pages of reviews and other journals, Lord Jeffrey says:—

"For our own parts, we have long been of opinion, that a man of powerful understanding and popular talents, who should devote himself to the task of announcing principles of vital importance to society, and render the discussion of them familiar, by the medium of popular journals, would probably do more to direct and accelerate the rectification of public opinion upon all practical questions, than by any other use he could possibly make of his faculties. His name, indeed, might not go down to posterity in connection with any work of celebrity, and the greater part even of his contemporaries might be ignorant of the very existence of their benefactor. But the benefits conferred would not be the less real; nor the conferring of them less delightful; nor the gratitude of the judicious less ardent and sincere."

But even as a substantive literary treasure, we regard these volumes as equally honorable to the American press with other more consolidated productions. Why should not a collection of orations possess a value as positive and absolute as a history or a treatise? Could classical literature, for instance, endure the extinction of the speeches of Demosthenes and Cicero, any more than of the writings of Thucydides and Seneca? Proud as we are of the histories of Sparks, Prescott, and Bancroft, yet we cannot admit that, as a whole, the addresses of Mr. Everett are at all less creditable to the country, or less beneficial in their tendency. They were composed and delivered under circumstances eminently adapted to stimulate the utmost efforts of the intellect. At the celebrations and *dies fasti* which called them forth, their author was not invited as a mere portion of the pageant, or to play an assigned part to secure the ceremonial from failure. The whole surrounding community looked to him for an instructive expression of the very spirit of the occasion, as well as of their own cherished and unspoken interest and sentiments in regard to it. The range of time embracing the production and delivery of these addresses, may well be regarded as a brilliant epoch in the history of New England. The announcement, that Mr. Everett was to be the speaker for the day, awakened unusual anticipations far and near. The audiences, crowded to overflowing, were in a large measure composed of the most distinguished men in the country, of every profession, with all that was attractive and accomplished, in the best degree, of the other sex. No tinsel oratory, no commonplace declamation, could send audiences like these to their homes in a mood of perfect gratification. Nor were the charms of delivery, — the severe simplicity, yet graceful elegance of manner, — the voice, that could glide at will between trumpet-tone and an almost feminine pathos, — the eye, that could at once command multitudes with its fiery gaze, and yet seem to search the thoughts of every individual,* — and, especially, the exhibition of a glowing enthusiasm, ever ready to break forth, but ever repressed and chastened by the reins of a firm self-control, — at all adequate, of themselves, to satisfying the demands of the particular audiences whom the occasions in question assembled together. There must be discussion and speculation ; the philosophy of the subject in hand must be probed to its depths ; there must be novelty in the facts and reflections presented, but without antics or extravagances of

---

* The portrait prefixed to these volumes presents, in many respects, a happy resemblance. But every distinguished orator ought to be consigned to some effigies *in action*. The birds of Audubon, the sculpture of Chatham, belonging to the city of Charleston, and the Belvidere Apollo, suggest the immense difference in art between repose and activity. How would the admirers of Mr. Everett prize a likeness of him, taken in the act of lifting, as it were, from their feet, a crowded audience in Faneuil Hall !

thought; there must be sympathetic, but reasonable appeals to that consciousness of a high future destiny, which is the irrepressible sentiment of American bosoms. With all these requisites Mr. Everett came well prepared, from the stores of his immense cultivation, and the workings of his fervid genius, to represent the teeming thoughts of the day. Called upon a hundred times for the performance of these arduous tasks, he has never failed to gratify the public expectation. In the facility with which he has ever consented to appear before his fellow-citizens, he has shown equal kindness and intrepidity, for it is long since he could expect to increase his reputation, or incur no risk of possibly diminishing it. Such are some of the circumstances which may enable us, in part, to form a due estimate of the volumes we are examining.

They whose good fortune it is to have been present on most, or many, of these occasions, enjoy a rare advantage in perusing the present publication. The excitement of recollection here surpasses in its effects the excitement of novelty. Very many of the addresses are associated with the idea of gala-day triumphs, — of delightful anticipations previously cherished, — of refined and densely crowded assemblages, — of the electric sympathies inspired by such scenes, — of the pride and admiration felt for the orator by whole communities, — of the curiosity experienced by those who were strangers to his person, — of the intense and never-wearied attention which listened to the last, and would have been glad of more; and then, of the separation, often to distant homes, with the memory of what had been heard prolonging the pleasure, and renewing it afterwards for many days, as an era or privilege in life. For our own part, stationed here at the remote South, we necessarily have enjoyed but few opportunities of personally listening to these performances. But most of them we perused at their first publication, and now, as we read them again in their collective form, we seem to be renewing a pleasure, as it were, but of yesterday, so deep was the influence which many years ago they exerted upon our minds.

Nor must it be understood that our orator affected to produce impressions only on refined and brilliant assemblages. Many of his happiest essays were prepared for the laboring classes of society. His addresses to these classes, combined with Dr. Channing's Lecture on Self-Culture, were as opportune as they were elaborate, and probably did as much, in proportion, to satisfy and elevate the toiling, yet questioning masses of the community around, as was effected with more "observation" in a larger field by the religious zeal of Whitfield and Wesley. We cannot imagine how the Socialist question can be more convincingly met, than in Mr. Everett's Lecture on the Workingmen's Party.

In preparing these publications anew for the press, we perceive that the author has very diligently and conscientiously employed the critical pruning-knife. Seldom have we known such unrelenting judgments passed by a writer of mature life upon the style of his earlier years. Some of the compositions, in fact, may be said to be in a degree rewritten. It must have been entirely a matter of personal interest with himself, for we presume the public would not have demanded the numerous emendations in question, and we have never known his writings characterized as loose or incorrect. We understand that some critic in a New Orleans paper, in a notice of the present publication, stigmatizes this dressing up anew of one's printed lucubrations as an unwarrantable liberty. The censure seems to us unfounded. Surely the purchasers of previous editions have no right to complain, for they have enjoyed a fair *quid pro quo* in the best which the author had to give them at the earlier period. Nor is the existing public in any manner abused, for Mr. Everett ingenuously announces that the productions of his youth required some amendment, which he has here endeavored to bestow upon them. The only parties we can imagine as likely to be aggrieved are the booksellers, who may possibly retain copies of the uncorrected addresses on their shelves. But we much doubt whether copies enough remain to inflict severe injury in this quarter, at least beyond what can be more than repaid by a supply of the same article in a fresh and improved condition. With regard to the general question, as a point of mere literary ethics, we believe that the practice adverted to can be defended by various considerations. Certainly a writer may be supposed anxious to transmit his productions to posterity in a state as near perfection as possible. The inquiry of the future reader will be, not at what age in life they were composed, but by whom they were composed, and if they were finally published or not with the author's sanction. A writer of high and generous aims will naturally wish his works to produce the most beneficial impression, whether his name be connected with them or not. If the name accompany them, he must wish it associated with as much literary excellence as he can personally and fairly confer.

The world has never yet, that we have learned, complained of "new and improved editions." The practice of the brightest and most revered authors of ancient and modern times can be alleged, if it were necessary, in defence of the instance before us. And as to German authors, their little fingers are thicker, in this respect, than Mr. Everett's loins. Nothing is more common with them, than to rewrite successive editions of the same work, until at length it would be hard to recognize an identity between the earlier and later issues. We remember to have once translated a rather bulky treatise of Eichhorn on the Pentateuch, and being, a few years later, solicited to furnish it for a well-known periodical, we found that subsequent editions had so far changed the individuality of the original work, as to require, not a revision, but an absolutely new translation.

It may be interesting to our readers to compare a paragraph or two, in which Mr. Everett has called up to his side his earlier self, to inspect and correct the young gentleman's exercises. Perhaps they will think, with ourselves, that in some, though not in all instances, the pupil's phraseology may be preferred to his preceptor's. We will take the first example from the opening page.

EDITION OF 1824.

"Mr. President and Gentlemen: — In discharging the honorable trust of being the public organ of your sentiments on this occasion, I have been anxious that the hour, which we here pass together, should be occupied by those reflections exclusively which belong to us as scholars. Our association in this fraternity is academical; we engaged in it before our Alma Mater dismissed us from her venerable roof, to wander in the various paths of life; and we have now come together in the academical holidays, from every variety of pursuit, from almost every part of our country, to meet on common ground, as the brethren of one literary household. The professional cares of life, like the conflicting tribes of Greece, have proclaimed to us a short armistice, that we may come up in peace to our Olympia.

"But from the wide field of literary speculation, and the innumerable subjects of meditation which arise in it, a selection must be made. And it has seemed to me proper that we should direct our thoughts, not merely to a subject of interest to scholars, but to one that may recommend itself as peculiarly appropriate to us. If 'that old man eloquent, whom the dishonest victory at Chæronea killed with report,' could devote fifteen years to the composition of his Panegyric on Athens, I shall need no excuse to a society of American scholars, in choosing for the theme of an address on an occasion like this, *the peculiar motives to intellectual exertion in America.* In this subject, that curiosity which every scholar feels in tracing and comparing the springs of mental activity, is heightened and dignified by the important connection of the inquiry with the condition and prospects of our native land."

EDITION OF 1850.

"Mr. President and Gentlemen: — In discharging the honorable trust which you have assigned to me on this occasion, I am anxious that the hour which we pass together should be exclusively occupied with those reflections which belong to us as scholars. Our association in this fraternity is academical; we entered it before our Alma Mater dismissed us from her venerable roof; and we have now come together, in the holidays, from every variety of pursuit, and every part of the country, to meet on common ground, as the brethren of one literary household. The duties and cares of life, like the Grecian states in time of war, have proclaimed to us a short armistice, that we may come up in peace to our Olympia.

"On this occasion, it has seemed proper to me that we should turn our thoughts, not merely to some topic of literary interest, but to one which concerns us as American scholars. I have accordingly selected, as the subject of our inquiry, *the circumstances favorable to the progress of literature in the United States of America.* In the discussion of this subject, that curiosity which every scholar naturally feels in tracing and comparing the character of the higher civilization of different countries, is at once dignified and rendered practical by the connection of the inquiry with the condition and prospects of his native land."

The next specimen is from a subsequent oration.

EDITION OF 1825.

"Fellow-Citizens: — The voice of patriotic and filial duty has called us together, to celebrate the fiftieth anniversary of an ever-memorable day. The subject which this occasion presents to our consideration almost exceeds the grasp of the human mind. The appearance of a new state in the great family of nations is one of the most important topics of reflection that can ever be addressed to us. In the case of America, the interest, the magnitude, and the difficulty of this subject are immeasurably increased. Our progress has been so rapid, the interval has been so short between the first plantations in the wilderness and the full development of our political institutions; there has been such a visible agency of single characters in affecting the condition of the country, such an almost instantaneous expansion of single events into consequences of incalculable importance, that we find ourselves deserted by almost all the principles and precedents drawn from the analogy of other states. Men have here seen, felt, and acted themselves, what in most other countries has been the growth of centuries.

"Take your station, for instance, on Connecticut River. Everything about you, whatsoever you behold or approach, bears witness that you are a citizen of a powerful and prosperous state. It is just seventy years since the towns, which you now contemplate with admiration as the abodes of a numerous, increasing, refined, enterprising population, safe in the enjoyment of life's best blessings, were wasted and burned by the savages of the wilderness; and their inhabitants by hundreds — the old and the young, the minister of the Gospel, and the mother with her new-born babe — were awakened at midnight by the war-whoop, dragged from their beds, and marched with bleeding feet across the snow-clad mountains, — to be sold as slaves into the corn-fields and kitchens of the French in Canada. Go back eighty years farther; and the same barbarous foe is on the skirts of your oldest settlements, at your own doors. As late as 1676, ten or twelve citizens of Concord were slain or carried into captivity, who had gone to meet the savage hordes in their attack on Sudbury, in which the brave Captain Wadsworth and his companions fell."

EDITION OF 1850.

"Fellow-Citizens: — The subject which the present occasion presents to our consideration is of the highest interest. The appearance of a new state in the great family of nations is one of the most important topics of reflection that can ever be addressed to us. In the case of America, the magnitude and the difficulty of the subject are greatly increased by peculiar circumstances. Our progress has been so rapid; the interval has been so short between the first plantations in the wilderness and the full development of our political system; there has been such a visible agency of single characters in affecting the condition of the country, such an almost instantaneous expansion of single events into consequences of incalculable importance, that we find ourselves deserted by the principles and precedents drawn from the analogy of other states. Men have here seen, felt, and acted themselves, what in most other countries has been the growth of centuries.

"Take your station, for instance, on Connecticut River. Everything about you, whatever you behold or approach, bears witness that you belong to a powerful and prosperous state. But it is only seventy years since the towns which you now contemplate with admiration, as the abodes of a numerous, refined, enterprising population, safe in the enjoyment of life's best blessings, were wasted and burned by the savages of the wilderness; and their inhabitants, in large numbers, — the old and the young, the minister of the Gospel, and the mother with her new-born babe, — were awakened at midnight by the war-whoop, dragged from their beds, and marched with bleeding feet across the snow-clad mountains, to be sold as slaves to the French in Canada. Go back eighty years farther, and the same barbarous foe is on the skirts of your oldest settlements, — at your own doors. As late as 1676, ten or twelve citizens of Concord were slain or carried into captivity, who had gone to meet the Indians in their attack on Sudbury, in which the brave Captain Wadsworth and his companions fell."

Whatever correction our author might see fit to apply to his writings, he is at least to be congratulated for having avoided the affectations into which some of his contemporaries were betrayed. He confesses and laments having made Johnson and Burke his models in composition; yet rarely, if ever, is their faulty manner conspicuous in his productions. On the other hand, he may owe to his study and admiration of those great masters his unsurpassed flow of pure and nearly perfect English diction. Although he had lived several of his most imitative years in Germany, and had perused with youthful fervor the popular authors of that country, yet we find in his style no trace of German influence. He was just as much tempted as others have been, and perhaps, by reason of his mode of education, more so, to dress up a feeble or commonplace thought with oracular obscurity or fantastic outlandishness; but he disdained the unworthy foppery, and renounced in advance the feverish and unnatural popularity which, in some quarters, such arts are apt to gain. In his most ambitious flights, he is never "transcendental"; in his most pointed sentences, never otherwise than purely idiomatic. We doubt whether he ever calls Washington, in the affected ethical slang of twenty years ago, "a true man," and are pretty confident that he does not talk of the "mission" of America among the nations. Steeped as he has been all his life in every variety of foreign literatures, the indigenous redolence of his style is remarkable. The only paragraph in these volumes, so far as we remember, of which the savor is not as essentially English as that of Mr. Clay himself, is the following, which reminds us, though not offensively, of the piquant vivacity of Voltaire, or some other French philosopher, applied to a grave and profound subject.

"The first king was a fortunate soldier, and the first nobleman was one of his generals; and government has passed by descent to their posterity, with no other interruption than has taken place when some new soldier of fortune has broken in upon this line of succession, in favor of himself and of his generals. The people have passed for nothing in the plan; and whenever it has occurred to a busy genius to put the question, By what right is government thus exercised and transmitted? the common answer, as we have seen, has been, By divine right; while, as the great improvement on this doctrine, men have been consoled with the assurance that such was the original contract."

It is common to hear Mr. Everett characterized, in an exclusive way, as "a magnificent declaimer." In the better sense of the word the appellation is correct, although it conveys but a very partial account of his oratory. Declamation is one of those terms to which disparaging ideas have been attached, in consequence of the spurious and inadequate attempts that are every day made to exhibit the excellent reality. Genuine declamation has in all ages been among the highest efforts of human art. It is an appeal to the nobler passions and sentiments of an audience, when reason is supposed to have accomplished its office. It invests familiar or forgotten truths with their due grandeur and importance, and enkindles an interest in them, which is otherwise too apt to languish. There is room for the display of transcendent skill and power, in the topics, the phrases, the methods, which a speaker employs for these purposes. Declamation is the poetry of eloquence. The declamatory passages of the ancient orators are impressed on the memory of every reader of the classics. The Old and New Testaments also abound in the happiest instances. The volumes before us present several admirable specimens. But we are surprised to observe, in a continuous perusal of the whole, how very rare, comparatively, is the declamatory element; we mean, of course, only in its higher sense, the inferior sort never having, that we know, been charged upon the author. Mr. Webster himself, even in his deliberative speeches, to say nothing of his efforts on the rostrum, is more of a declaimer than Mr. Everett. The predominant, nay, almost the entire character of the volumes before us, is didactic. The author enters, as we have already intimated, into the philosophy of every subject; and, besides, if his theme be an historical event, he brings forward a new store of illustrative facts and incidents, unknown to the current generation, whom he thus renders as familiar with it as if they themselves had been among its busiest actors. Then, when he indulges in declamation, the fervid language springs as naturally from these speculations and verities, as the gorgeous emblazonment of the clouds round the setting sun proceeds from his illumining rays.

The versatility and scope of the author's mind may be conceived from the immense variety and importance of the topics which he has been called upon to discuss for the benefit of his fellow-citizens. It seems as if they had supposed he must know and could talk about everything that is experienced beneath the circuit of the sun. For instance, he investigates, at Harvard College, in an original vein, the circumstances favorable to the progress of American literature, — traces, at Plymouth, the vast consequences that flowed from the first settlement of New England, — describes, at Concord, with the graphic pencil of a contemporary, the earlier battles of the Revolution, — elucidates, at Cambridge, the distinctive principles of the American constitutions, — institutes, in Faneuil Hall, by a happy stroke of genius, a parallel between the lives and characters of Adams and Jefferson, whose twin-death, on one and the same day, furnishes a sort of key-note with which the eulogy harmonizes throughout, — takes occasion, in one of his Fourth of July orations, to give a general and learned history of Liberty itself, — erects a literary monument, at the dedication of one in stone, to the memory of John Harvard, — addresses, while on a tour in the Western States, three large assemblies in different places, with something specifically appropriate to each occasion, — characterizes, at Charlestown, with the fondness of a son of Massachusetts, the primal settlement of his native State, — then, with equal familiarity, discourses, before several rising Institutes, on the importance of scientific knowledge to practical men, and on the encouragement to its pursuit, his style being here in beautiful keeping with his subject-matter, no longer elaborate and ornate as elsewhere, but plain, simple, *affectionate* even,—lectures, at Charlestown, on the Workingmen's Party, among which, with adroit ingenuity, he succeeds in ranking every decent class in the community, placing, as we have heard, an effectual extinguisher on some threatening agrarian agitations of the day, — expatiates again, and mostly in new trains of thought, on the advantage of knowledge to worldly men, — exhausts, at Washington, the subject of African Colonization, — demonstrates, at a meeting in St. Paul's Church, Boston, the importance of assisting education in the Western States, — urges on, at Faneuil Hall, in what we regard as the most Demosthenéan of his speeches, the completion of the Bunker-Hill Monument, — compresses into a lecture, at Salem, the whole merits of the great Temperance question, — unfolds, in an oration at Worcester, the intimate connection between the Seven Years' war and the war of our Independence, — discusses, at Yale College, in what is perhaps, in point of style, the most finished performance of the collection, the education of mankind, — discriminates, before the Massachusetts Agricultural Society, the peculiar advantages of the American farmer, — pronounces, at the request of the young men of Boston, a very elaborate eulogy on the life and character of La Fayette, evincing here a felicitous talent for narrative, — talks over, in Lexington, like an actor in the scene, the Revolutionary fight at that place, introducing some curious and apposite memorials of John Hancock and other worthies of the time, — singles out, for his theme at Beverly, the youth of Washington, which he demonstrates to have been a remarkably providential preparation for that hero's subsequent career, — argues, at Amherst College, in a fine vein of philosophy and with large inductions from the history of science, the favorable influence of education on liberty, knowledge, and morals, — exhibits, at South Deerfield, in commemoration of the battle of Bloody Brook, the same familiarity with the Indian wars, that he has elsewhere shown with the battles of the Revolution, and ingeniously defends the Indian policy of the Pilgrim Fathers, — sketches, before the Boston Society for the Diffusion of Useful Knowledge, the boyhood and youth of Franklin, and here indulges, contrary to his wont, in a sportive, conversational strain of wit and humor, — maintains, on the Fourth of July, at Lowell, that the prohibition of colonial manufactures by the mother country was one of the chief grievances that resulted in the American Revolution, — defends, before the American Institute of the city of New York, the principle of protection to manufactures, which he shows to have been a favorite policy in all periods of our country's history, — comes, in Faneuil Hall, to the rescue of the languishing subscription for the long Western Railroad, in a somewhat dashing speech, which shows, however, a very minute and extensive knowledge of the subject, — elucidates, at Springfield, the influence of the religion of the Pilgrims on the institutions of our country, — contends, in after-dinner speeches, at Boston and Charlestown, for the continuance of the militia system, holding now the office of Governor of the State, which he continues to occupy several years onward, — personates, in an address at the Harvard Centennial Celebration, the venerable Winthrop proposing to the government of the infant Colony a tax in behalf of the College, probably, as the orator thinks, the first ever laid for the support of public education, — strikes some appropriate and happy chord, on each occasion, when toasted at an anniversary celebration in Dedham, at a cattle-show in Danvers, and at a festival of the Irish Charitable Society in Boston, — eulogizes, at a meeting of the Boston Prison Discipline Society, the special objects of that institution, — descants, at Williams College, in a tone of unusual elevation, on the advantages both of superior and of popular education, — acknowledges, at a public scholastic examination, his indebtedness to the Boston schools, which had been the best friends of his youth, — speculates, before the Massachusetts Charitable Mechanic Association, in a profound, but familiarly illustrative way peculiar to himself, on the vast importance of the mechanic arts, — then speaks Indianee, officially, with an Indian delegation, — then renders an affecting tribute to Dr. Bowditch, — then another to the surviving Revolutionary heroes, — describes Education, in a convention at Martha's Vineyard, as the nurse of the mind, — indulges in tender, boyish reminiscences at Dr. Abbott's jubilee in Exeter, — brings out, with great power and clearness, before the Boston Mercantile Library Association, various fundamental ideas on accumulation, property, capital, and credit, — illustrates the importance of education in a republic, at a School Convention at Taunton, where he introduces, with so much effect, the celebrated letter of Elihu Burritt, — pronounces a gallant speech at a Centennial Anniversary of the settlement of Barnstable, — recommends at Barre, to the citizens of

Massachusetts, with exceeding plainness and force of language, the system of Normal Schools, — celebrates at Springfield, in words of jubilant gratulation, and with spirited, yet true sketches of the approaching future, the opening of the great Railroad, which he had before done something at Faneuil Hall to promote, — speaks, to the Scots' Charitable Society, with more than common elegance, tenderness, point, and enviable reminiscence, — delivers, at the opening of the first course of Lowell Lectures in Boston, a long and interesting sketch of its founder, whose testamentary munificence was equally honorable to his native city and to his own memory, — acquits himself, on fourteen different occasions, while Ambassador in England, with much grace and propriety, but with more diplomatic generality of phrase, and less eloquence and impressiveness, than he is accustomed to display at home, — renders twice at Plymouth, after his return to his native land, fresh tributes to the memory of the Pilgrims, — signalizes his inauguration into the Presidency of Harvard College, by a rich, solid, and well-timed tractate on university education, — presents some fine views on medical education at the opening of the new Medical College in Boston, — pleads, in Faneuil Hall, in behalf of the starving Irish, — solicits aid for the colleges of Massachusetts before committees of the Legislature of that State, in two successive speeches, the latter of which appears to us the strongest and closest piece of argument in the collection, — obeys the call of the same Legislature in pronouncing before them a comprehensive and adequate eulogy on John Quincy Adams, — indulges in a strain of familiarity and good humor at the opening of a High School in Cambridge, — despatches, at a dinner of the American Scientific Association in the same city, some current objections against such institutions, — commends, at a cattle-show in Dedham, the life of the farmer, — commemorates again the nineteenth of April at Concord, exactly one quarter of a century after his graphic oration at that place among the earliest of his celebrities, and indulges chiefly in conciliatory sentiments towards England, — and, lastly, proves, before the Massachusetts Bible Society, the intimate connection, in all ages and nations, between vital Christianity and the use of the Scriptures in the vernacular tongues.

What a life to have led! Or rather, what fruitage falling from the topmost boughs of a tree, whose life below must have been so busy in exhausting rich soils, assimilating all finer elements, and expanding beneath the happy influences of opportunity and Providence!

We regret much that no index of subjects was prepared and affixed to the present publication. It would have contributed largely to the future convenience of many a reader, and would have conveyed a more complete idea of the author's labors than the mere general announcement, in the table of contents, of an oration pronounced here, and an address delivered there. The lack of such an index is quite imperfectly supplied by the preceding *catalogue raisonné* of the topics discussed in these volumes.

Having thus, as we trust, with sufficient readiness and fulness, attested the eminent merits of this collection, we shall now, with some diffidence, animadvert on what we are constrained to regard the defects, though few, which the perusal of it has brought to our notice. Dealing with a writer of less mark, we should probably have declined the unwelcome task; but if there are certain popular errors and corruptions of style, which may be likely to take shelter and sanction beneath Mr. Everett's example, so much the more is it the critic's duty to point them out, and rescue our literature from the dangers that threaten it.

A profound writer, in a late number of the Edinburgh Review, closes a long article on the History of the English Language with the following impressive exhortation: "When we reflect on the enormous breadth, both of the Old World and the New, over which this noble language is either already spoken, or is fast spreading, and the immense treasures of literature which are consigned to it, it becomes us to guard it with jealous care, as a sacred deposit, — not our least important trust in the heritage of humanity. *Our brethren in America must assist us in the task.*" Let the ensuing criticisms be accepted as a very brief response, on our part, to this earnest and flattering challenge.

We would first notice a few phrases, probably of American origin, against which we have long cherished an instinctive suspicion, as trespassers on the domain of pure English. They are such expressions as "*in our midst,*" "*reliable,*" "*in this connection,*" "*acquit my duty,*" &c. As they have been but recently introduced into the language, and are in general carefully avoided by the purest writers, while sound philological reasons, as we presume, might be arrayed against them, we dismiss them, without further remark, as slips of the author's pen.

We observe that Mr. Everett seems quite attached to the French form of speech, in such expressions as *being arrived, we are arrived, I am come*, corresponding to *étant arrivé*, etc. We are aware that these phrases are justified by very extensive and authentic usage, and by the Gallic element which still, here and there, lingers in our tongue. But this use of the substantive verb before neuter participles with a passive termination, is so much in conflict with the general habitudes of our syntax, that we have no doubt it will gradually retire before a more complete and symmetrical growth of the language. The very circumstance, that it attracts attention as an exceptional form, is a proof that it is felt to be not quite natural, — and, since a more purely English expression can always be substituted for it, and, in fact, even now enjoys as wide and reputable an acceptation as its rival, the time, we think, is not distant, when the more vernacular phrase must be exclusively employed. We can conceive of no advantage in retaining the foreign form, except as a memorial of the toils of our distant juvenile forefathers, in conning their French conjugations.

Another favorite habit of the author is to employ the words *doctor* and *doctors* for *physician* and *physicians*. Except in very colloquial and domestic usage, this phraseology, we believe, is nearly extinct. As doctors of every name have now become so profusely multiplied, the term seems too general, as a means of formally specifying our excellent friends of the profession.

These verbal discussions require no apology, for all allow that the highest and dearest interests of humanity may depend upon the correct and logical use of the terms we employ. The establishment of right grammatical rules is but the establishment of channels of clear and accurate thought, and sustains a nearer relation to everlasting principles than is ordinarily imagined. Many a valuable bequest has been successfully contested, through some loophole of ambiguous phraseology, and the destinies of the Christian Church have more than once hung on the definition of a term. The most interesting to man, of all the appellations applied to the Deity himself, is THE WORD.

To go, however, from the criticism of words to that of things, though such transition crosses no very wide gulf: We perceive (Vol. I. p. 319) that continued currency is allowed to the old story of Shakespeare's getting his livelihood by holding horses at the door of a theatre. We had thought that this anecdote had been exploded by the researches of modern editors; but so fluctuating often are these questions of literary history, that it is possible our author may have found some good reason still to regard the account as canonical.

While in this criticising mood, we may observe that a few more explanatory notes would have rendered the edition more valuable. A brief description, for instance, of the particular occasion on which the oration at Lexington was delivered, would have elucidated some of its allusions for many readers, who are now comparatively in the dark about them. Some method, also, might have been devised, consistent with the author's known modesty, to intimate at times the different official relations borne by him. The point of several addresses is in some degree lost, for the want of such information. For the same reason, it should have been mentioned that the Fourth of July celebration at Fanueil Hall, in 1838, was conducted for the first time on principles of total abstinence.

Generally, Mr. Everett well exhausts the subjects of

his discussions. In his masterly address before the Mercantile Library Association, on accumulation, property, capital, and credit, while defending the claims of capital, we thought that he omitted one important principle in laying down what he considers "the whole doctrine of interest." He says nothing of the *risk* attendant on loans of money and other capital, which must evidently enter, as a considerable element, into the theory of interest. A percentage, representing such a risk, being easily calculated in ordinary times, may most fairly be charged for the use of the principal, on all who share its advantages and who occasion the risk, even though the capitalist be regarded as nothing more than a steward, acting for the public benefit.

We expected the pleasure of re-perusing here the author's speech before the Horticultural Society, pronounced immediately on his return from his embassy to England. Both the occasion and the remarks appeared to us much more interesting than those appertaining to several addresses actually introduced. Some explanation, at least, of the circumstance would seem to be required, as there is so free an admission of other matter.

We have already acquitted Mr. Everett of a tendency to German transcendentalisms, or other over-refined speculations. If any portion of his two volumes must enforce a reluctant exception to this acquittal, it will perhaps be found in the following somewhat mystical sentence, which came upon us with a rather startling effect. "It may be," says he, "that the laws of the material universe, gravitation itself, may be resolved into the intelligent action of the minds by which it is inhabited and controlled, empowered to this high function by the Supreme Intellect." * This dictum of philosophy is quite beyond our grasp. According to all common experience, the farther matter recedes from any connection with life and thought, the more subjected it becomes to the power of gravitation. Still, we should feel ourselves groping less dimly after the meaning of this proposition than after that of Mr. Emerson's on the same subject-matter, who looks for the time when the world shall see "the identity of the law of gravitation with *purity of heart*"! It is difficult enough, to be sure, to identify, with Mr. Everett, the eternally fixed, uniform, and mechanical operations of gravitating matter with the boundless impulses, the absolute, spontaneous freedom, of the mind; but to go further, and identify the same operations with the moral emotions and unspeakable breathings of the responsible spirit, is, to us, much like smelling the essence of a contradiction, or laying hands on sound, as it escapes fluttering from the string.

We have cheerfully accorded to Mr. Everett the praise of an unvaryingly pure taste and chastened imagination. But there are one or two passages which we hesitate to include in our comprehensive encomium. One, in particular, occurring near the commencement of the address on the battle of Bloody Brook, strikes us as somewhat overstrained. Amply, however, we repeat, are these few falsetto notes redeemed, throughout the rest of the addresses. Generally speaking, never was a series of popular harangues cast in a finer mould of good sense, correct taste, sound reasoning, wholesome sentiment,

* Vol. II. p. 220.

and unaffected diction. Everything is said in the right way and the right proportion, as if the Elysian spirit of the classics had, in these pages, once more visited the upper air; vivacity and solidity blend with and temper each other; the presiding, the pervading genius, seems everywhere to be wisdom; nothing is spoken for mere effect; nothing is far-fetched, yet nothing commonplace; there are no ekings-out of deficient trains of thought, no admission of superfluous ones; but all is natural, — all full, calm, self-poised, onward-sweeping, transparent, and luminous, like a broad upland river, swollen even with its banks, on a bright vernal day.

Fain, now, in conclusion, would we present our readers with a copious series of the "Beauties of Edward Everett." But, out of the twenty or more passages which we had marked, in the vain hope of extracting them at length, the most daring presumption of a privileged contributor may venture only upon a few, referring cursorily to the remainder.

The following combines two of the author's prominent excellences: in the first division, the power of bringing out unconsidered truths into broad and clear relief; in the second, a happy talent for illustrative narrative.

"Nothing is wanting to fill up this sketch of other governments, but to consider what is the form in which force is exercised to sustain them; and this is a standing army, at this moment the chief support of every government on earth except our own. As popular violence — the unrestrained and irresistible force of the mass of men long oppressed and late awakened, and bursting, in its wrath, all barriers of law and humanity — is unhappily the usual instrument by which the intolerable abuses of a corrupt government are removed, so the same blind force, of the same fearful multitude, systematically kept in ignorance both of their duty and of their privileges as citizens, employed in a form somewhat different, indeed, but far more dreadful, — that of a mercenary standing army, — is the instrument by which corrupt governments are sustained. The deplorable scenes which marked the earlier stages of the French Revolution have called the attention of this age to the fearful effects of popular violence, and the minds of men have recoiled from the horrors which mark the progress of an infuriated mob. They are not easily to be exaggerated. But the power of the mob is transient; the rising sun most commonly scatters its mistrustful ranks; the difficulties of subsistence drives its members asunder, and it is only while it exists in mass that it is terrible. But there is a form in which the mob is indeed portentous; when, to all its native terrors, it adds the force of a frightful permanence; when, by a regular organization, its strength is so curiously divided, and, by a strict discipline, its parts are so easily combined, that each and every portion of it carries in its presence the strength and terror of the whole; and when, instead of that want of concert which renders the common mob incapable of arduous enterprises, it is despotically swayed by a single master mind, and may be moved in array across the globe.

"I remember — if, on such a subject, I may be pardoned an illustration approaching the ludicrous — to have seen the two kinds of force brought into direct comparison. I was present at the second great meeting of the populace of London, in 1819, in the midst of a crowd of I know not how many thousands, but assuredly a vast multitude, assembled in Smithfield Market. The universal distress was extreme; it was a short time after the scenes at Manchester, at which the public mind was exasperated; deaths by starvation were said not to be rare; ruin, by the stagnation of business, was general; and some were already brooding over the dark project of assassinating the ministers, which was not long after, matured by Thistlewood and his associates, some of whom, on the day to which I allude, harangued this excited, desperate, starving assemblage. When I considered the state of feeling prevailing in the multitude around me, — when I looked in their lowering faces, heard their deep, indignant exclamations, reflected on the physical force concentrated, probably that of thirty or forty thousand able-bodied men, and, added to all this, that they were assembled to exercise what is in theory an undoubted privilege of British citizens, — I supposed that any small number of troops who should attempt to interrupt them would be immolated on the spot. While I was musing on these things, and turning in my mind the commonplaces on the terrors of a mob, a trumpet was heard to sound, — an uncertain, but a harsh and clamorous blast. I looked that the surrounding stalls in the market should have furnished the unarmed multitude at least with that weapon with which Virginius sacrificed his daughter to the liberty of Rome; I looked that the flying pavement should begin to darken the air. Another blast is heard, — a cry of 'The Horse-Guards!' ran through the assembled thousands; the orators on the platform were struck mute; and the whole of that mighty host of starving, desperate men incontinently took to their heels, in which, I must confess, — feeling no call on that occasion to be faithful found among the faithless, — I did myself join them. We had run through the Old Bailey and reached Ludgate Hill before we found out that we had been put to flight by a single mischievous tool of that power, who had come triumphing down the opposite street on horseback, blowing a stage-coachman's horn." *

See here, how a wanton charge can be retorted, and forced to contribute to the honor of the slandered party: —

"A late English writer has permitted himself to say, that the original establishment of the United States and that of the colony

* Vol. I. p. 116.

of Botany Bay were pretty nearly modelled on the same plan. The meaning of this slanderous insinuation is, that the United States were settled by deported convicts, in like manner as New South Wales has been settled by transported felons. It is doubtless true, that, at one period, the English government was in the habit of condemning to hard labor, as servants in the Colonies, a portion of those who had received the sentence of the law. If this practice makes it proper to compare America with Botany Bay, the same comparison might be made of England herself before the practice of transportation began, and even now, inasmuch as a considerable number of convicts are at all times retained at home. In one sense, indeed, we might doubt whether the allegation were more of a reproach or a compliment. During the time that the colonization of America was going on the most rapidly, some of the best citizens of England, if it be any part of good citizenship to resist oppression, were immured in her prisons of state, or lying at the mercy of the law.

Such were some of the convicts by whom America was settled, — men convicted of fearing God more than they feared man; of sacrificing property, ease, and all the comforts of life to a sense of duty and the dictates of conscience; men convicted of pure lives, brave hearts, and simple manners. The enterprise was led by Raleigh, the chivalrous convict, who unfortunately believed that his royal master had the heart of a man, and would not let a sentence of death, which had slumbered for sixteen years, revive and take effect after so long an interval of employment and favor. But *nullum tempus occurrit regi.* The felons who followed next were the heroic and long-suffering church of Robinson, at Leyden, Carver, Brewster, Bradford, Winslow, and their pious associates, convicted of worshipping God according to the dictates of their own consciences, and of giving up all — country, property, and the tombs of their fathers — that they might do it unmolested. Not content with having driven the Puritans from her soil, England next enacted or put in force the oppressive laws which colonized Maryland with Catholics and Pennsylvania with Quakers. Nor was it long before the American plantations were recruited by the Germans, convicted of inhabiting the Palatinate, when the merciless armies of Louis XIV. were turned into that devoted region; and by the Huguenots, convicted of holding what they deemed the simple truth of Christianity, when it pleased the mistress of Louis XIV. to be very zealous for the Catholic faith. These were followed, in the next century, by the Highlanders, convicted of the enormous crime, under a monarchical government, of loyalty to their hereditary prince, on the plains of Culloden; and the Irish, convicted of supporting the rights of their country against what they deemed a foreign usurper. Such are the convicts by whom America was settled.

"In this way, a fair representation of whatsoever was most valuable in European character — the resolute industry of one nation, the inventive skill and curious arts of another, the courage, conscience, principle, self-denial, of all — was winnowed out, by the policy of the prevailing governments, as a precious seed, wherewith to plant the American soil." *

Next follows a remarkable passage, conceived and executed, unconsciously of course, in the best manner of Macaulay: —

"If we would, on a broad, rational ground, come to a favorable judgment, on the whole, of the merit of our forefathers, the founders of New England, we have only to compare what they effected with what was effected by their countrymen and brethren in Great Britain. While the fathers of New England, a small band of individuals, for the most part of little account to the great world of London, were engaged, on this side of the Atlantic, in laying the foundations of civil and religious liberty, in a new

* Vol. I. p. 159.

commonwealth, the patriots of England undertook the same work of reform in that country. There were difficulties, no doubt, peculiar to the enterprise, as undertaken in each country. In Britain, there was the strenuous opposition of the friends of the established system; in New England, there was the difficulty of creating a new state, out of materials the most scanty and inadequate. If there were fewer obstacles here, there were greater means there. They had all the refinements of the age, which the Puritans are charged with having left behind them; all the resources of the country, while the Puritans had nothing but their own slender means; and, at length, all the resources of the government, — and with them they overthrew the Church, trampled the House of Lords under foot, and brought the king to the block. The fathers of New England, from first to last, struggled against almost every conceivable discouragement. While the patriots at home were dictating concessions to the king, and tearing his confidential friends from his arms, the patriots of America could scarcely keep their charter out of his grasp. While the former were wielding a resolute majority in Parliament, under the lead of the boldest spirits that ever lived, combining with Scotland, subduing Ireland, and striking terror into the Continental governments, the latter were forming a frail union of the New-England Colonies, for immediate defence against a savage foe. While the 'Lord General Cromwell,' (who seems to have picked up this modest title among the spoils of the routed aristocracy,) in the superb flattery of Milton,

> 'Guided by faith, and matchless fortitude,
> To peace and truth his glorious way had ploughed,
> And on the neck of crowned fortune proud
> Had reared God's trophies,'

our truly excellent and incorruptible Winthrop was compelled to descend from the chair of state and submit to an impeachment.

"And what was the comparative success? There were, to say the least, as many excesses committed in England as in Massachusetts Bay. There was as much intolerance on the part of men just escaped from persecution, as much bigotry on the part of those who had themselves suffered for conscience' sake, as much unreasonable austerity, as much sour temper, as much bad taste, as much for charity to forgive, and as much for humanity to deplore. The temper, in fact, of the two commonwealths was much the same, and some of the leading spirits played a part in both. And to what effect? On the other side of the Atlantic the whole experiment ended in a miserable failure. The Commonwealth became successively oppressive, hateful, contemptible, — a greater burden than the despotism on whose ruins it was raised. The people of England, after sacrifices incalculable of property and life, after a struggle of thirty years' duration, allowed the general who happened to have the greatest number of troops under his command to bring back the old system, — king, lords, and church, — with as little ceremony as he would employ in issuing the orders of the day. After asking, for thirty years, What is the will of the Lord concerning his people? What is it becoming a pure church to do? What does the cause of liberty demand, in the day of its regeneration? there was but one cry in England, —What does General Monk think? What will General Monk do? Will he bring back the king with conditions, or without? And General Monk concluded to bring him back without.

"On this side of the Atlantic, and in about the same period, the work which our fathers took in hand was, in the main, successfully done. They came to found a republican colony. They founded it. They came to establish a free church. They established what they called a free church, and transmitted to us what we call a free church. In accomplishing this, which they did anticipate, they brought also to pass what they did not so distinctly foresee, — what could not, in the nature of things, in its detail and circumstance, be anticipated, — the foundation of a great, prosperous, and growing republic. We have not been just to these men. I am disposed to do all justice to the memory of each succeeding generation. I admire the indomitable perseverance with which the contest for principle was kept up, under the second charter. I reverence, this side idolatry, the wisdom and fortitude of the Revolutionary and Constitutional leaders; but I believe we ought to go back beyond them all for the real framers of the commonwealth. I believe that its foundation stones, like those of the Capitol of Rome, lie deep and solid, out of sight, at the bottom of the walls, — Cyclopéan work, the work of the Pilgrims, — with nothing below them but the Rock of Ages. I will not quarrel with their rough corners or uneven sides; above all, I will not change them for the wood, hay, and stubble of modern builders." *

The following peroration of the address last cited may venture comparison with some of the finest passages, embodying local associations, in ancient literature: —

"Yes, on the very spot † where we are assembled, — now crowned with this spacious church, surrounded by the comfortable abodes of a dense population, — there were, during the first season after the landing of Winthrop, fewer dwellings for the living than graves for the dead. It seemed the will of Providence that our fathers should be tried by the extremities of either season. When the Pilgrims approached the coast of Plymouth, they found it clad with all the terrors of a Northern winter.

'The sea around was black with storms,
And white the shores with snow.'

"We can scarcely think now, without tears, of a company of men, women, and children, brought up in tenderness, exposed, after several months' uncomfortable confinement on shipboard, to the rigors of our November and December sky, on an unknown and barbarous coast, whose frightful rocks even now strike terror into the heart of the returning mariner, though he knows that the home of his childhood awaits him within their enclosure.

---

* Vol. I. p. 243. † Charlestown, Massachusetts.

"The Massachusetts company arrived at the close of June. No vineyards, as now, clothed our inhospitable hill-sides; no blooming orchards, as at the present day, wore the livery of Eden, and loaded the breeze with sweet odors; no rich pastures, nor waving crops, stretched beneath the eye, along the way-side, from village to village, as if Nature had been spreading her floors with a carpet fit to be pressed by the footsteps of her descending God! The beauty and the bloom of the year had passed. The earth, not yet subdued by culture, bore upon its untilled bosom nothing but a dismal forest, that mocked their hunger with rank and unprofitable vegetation. The sun was hot in the heavens. The soil was parched, and the hand of man had not yet taught its secret springs to flow from their fountains. The wasting disease of the heart-sick mariner was upon the men, and the women and children thought of the pleasant homes of England, as they sank down, from day to day, and died at last for want of a cup of water, in this melancholy land of promise. From the time the company sailed from England, in April, up to the December following, there died not less than two hundred persons, — nearly one a day.

"They were buried, say our records, about the Town Hill. This is the Town Hill. We are gathered over the ashes of our forefathers.

"It is good, but solemn, to be here. We live on holy ground; all our hill-tops are the altars of precious sacrifice.

"*This* is stored with the sacred dust of the first victims in the cause of liberty.

"And *that** is rich from the life-stream of the noble hearts who bled to sustain it.

"Here, beneath our feet, unconscious that we commemorate their worth, repose the meek and sainted martyrs whose flesh sunk beneath the lofty temper of their noble spirits; and there

---

* Bunker Hill.

rest the heroes who presented their dauntless foreheads to the God of battles, when he came to his awful baptism of blood and of fire.

"Happy the fate which has laid them so near to each other, — the early and the latter champions of the one great cause! And happy we, who are permitted to reap in peace the fruits of their costly sacrifice! Happy, that we can make our pious pilgrimage to the smooth turf of that venerable summit, once ploughed with the wheels of maddening artillery, ringing with all the dreadful voices of war, wrapped in smoke and streaming with blood! Happy, that here, where our fathers sank, beneath the burning sun, into the parched clay, we meet, and assemble, and mingle sweet counsel and grateful thoughts of them, in comfort and peace!"*

The following is the way in which Adam Smith might have speculated on the wonderful connection and interdependence between the labors of science and the labors of art: —

"But we may go a step farther, to mark the beautiful process by which Providence has so interlaced and wrought up together the pursuits, interests, and wants of our nature, that the philosopher, whose home seems less on earth than among the stars, requires, for the prosecution of his studies, the aid of numerous artificers, in various branches of mechanical industry, and, in return, furnishes the most important facilities to the humblest branches of manual labor. Let us take, as a single instance, that of astronomical science. It may be safely said, that the wonderful discoveries of modern astronomy, and the philosophical system depending upon it, could not have existed but for the *telescope*. The want of the telescope kept astronomical science in its infancy among the ancients. Although Pythagoras, one of the

---

* Vol. I. p. 245.

earliest Greek philosophers, is supposed to have had some conception of the elements of the Copernican system, yet we find no general and practical improvement resulting from it. In fact, it sunk beneath the false theories of subsequent philosophers. It was only from the period of the discoveries made by the telescope that the science advanced with sure and rapid progress. Now, the astronomer does not make telescopes. I presume it would be impossible for a person who employed in the abstract study of astronomical science time enough to comprehend its profound investigations, to learn and practise the trade of making glass. It is not less true, that those employed in making the glass could not, in the nature of things, be expected to acquire the scientific knowledge requisite for carrying on those arduous calculations applied to bring into a system the discoveries made by the magnifying power of the telescope. I might extend the same remark to the other materials of which a telescope consists. It cannot be used to any purpose of nice observation, without being very carefully mounted on a frame of strong metal, which demands the united labors of the mathematical-instrument maker and the brass-founder. Here, then, in taking but one single step out of the philosopher's observatory, we find he needs an instrument to be produced by the united labors of the mathematical-instrument maker, the brass-founder, the glass-polisher, and the maker of glass, — four trades. He must also have an astronomical clock, and it would be easy to count up half a dozen trades which, directly or indirectly, are connected in making a clock.

"But let us go back to the object-glass of the telescope. A glass-factory requires a building and furnaces. The man who makes the glass does not make the building. But the stone and brick mason, the carpenter, and the blacksmith must furnish the greater part of the labor and skill required to construct the building. When it is built, a large quantity of fuel, wood and wood-coal or mineral coal, of various kinds, or all together, must be provided; and then the materials of which the glass is made, and with which it is colored, some of which are furnished by commerce from different and distant regions, and must be brought in ships across the sea. We cannot take up any one of these trades without immediately finding that it connects itself with numerous others. Take, for instance, the mason who builds the furnace. He does not make his own bricks, nor burn his own lime: in common cases, the bricks come from one place, the lime from another, and the sand from another. The brick-maker does not cut down his own wood; it is carted or brought in boats to his brick-yard. The man who carts it does not make his own wagon, nor does the person who brings it in boats build his own boat. The man who makes the wagon does not make its tire. The blacksmith who makes the tire does not smelt the ore; and the forgeman who smelts the ore does not build his own furnace (and there we get back to the point whence we started) nor dig his own mine. The man who digs the mine does not make the pick-axe with which he digs it, nor the pump which keeps out the water. The man who made the pump did not discover the principle of atmospheric pressure, which led to pump-making; that was done by a mathematician at Florence (Torricelli), experimenting in his chamber on a glass tube. And here we come back again to our glass, and to an instance of the close connection of scientific research with practical art. It is plain that this enumeration might be pursued till every art and every science were shown to run into every other.

. . . . .

"Not a little of the spinning machinery employed in manufacturing cotton is constructed on principles drawn from the demonstrations of transcendental mathematics, and the processes of bleaching and dyeing now practised are the results of the most profound researches of modern chemistry. And if this does not satisfy the inquirer, let him trace the cotton to the plantation where it grew, in Georgia or Alabama; the indigo to Bengal;

the oil to the olive-gardens of Italy, or the fishing-grounds of the Pacific Ocean; let him consider Whitney's cotton-gin, Whittemore's carding-machine, the power-loom, and the spinning apparatus, and all the arts, trades, and sciences directly or indirectly connected with these, and I believe he will soon agree that one might start from a yard of coarse printed cotton, which costs ten cents, and prove out of it, as out of a text, that every art and science under heaven had been concerned in its fabric." *

The following beautiful passage comprises, in our opinion, the whole doctrine of physical and moral good. The union, here, of profound with familiar reasoning, is quite characteristic of the author.

"But I am met with the great objection, *What good will the monument do?* I beg leave, sir, to exercise my birthright as a Yankee, and answer this question by asking two or three more, to which I believe it will be quite as difficult to furnish a satisfactory reply. I am asked, What good will the monument do? And I ask, What good does anything do? What is good? Does anything do good? The persons who suggest this objection of course think that there are some projects and undertakings that do good, and I should therefore like to have the idea of *good* explained, and analyzed, and run out to its elements. When this is done, if I do not demonstrate, in about two minutes, that the monument does the same kind of good that anything else does, I will consent that the huge blocks of granite already laid should be reduced to gravel, and carted off to fill up the mill-pond, — for that, I suppose, is one of the good things. Does a railroad or a canal do good? Answer, Yes. And how? It facilitates intercourse, opens markets, and increases the wealth of the country. But what is this good for? Why, individuals prosper and get rich. And what good does that do? Is mere wealth, as an ulti-

* Vol. I. p. 297.

mate end, — gold and silver, without an inquiry as to their use, — are these a good? Certainly not. I should insult this audience by attempting to prove that a rich man, as such, is neither better nor happier than a poor one. But as men grow rich they live better. Is there any good in this, stopping here? Is mere animal life — feeding, working, and sleeping like an ox — entitled to be called good? Certainly not. But these improvements increase the population. And what good does that do? Where is the good of counting twelve millions, instead of six, of mere feeding, working, sleeping animals? There is, then, no good in the mere animal life except that it is the physical basis of that higher moral existence which resides in the soul, the heart, the conscience, in good principles, good feelings, and the good actions (and the more disinterested, the more entitled to be called good) which flow from them. Now, sir, I say that generous and patriotic sentiments, sentiments which prepare us to serve our country, to live for our country, to die for our country, — feelings like those which carried Prescott, and Warren, and Putnam to the battle-field, are good, — good, humanly speaking, of the highest order. It is good to have them, good to encourage them, good to honor them, good to commemorate them, and whatever tends to animate and strengthen such feelings does as much right down practical good as filling up low grounds and building railroads. This is my demonstration. I wish, sir, not to be misunderstood. I admit the connection between enterprises which promote the physical prosperity of the country and its intellectual and moral improvement; but I maintain that it is only *this connection* that gives these enterprises all their value, and that the same connection gives a like value to everything else, which, through the channel of the senses, the taste, or the imagination, warms and elevates the heart." *

We must find room for a piece of literary criticism,

* Vol. I. p. 359.

of the very highest order. The author thus argues the influence of pure spiritual knowledge on the progress of poetry.

"Not a ray of pure spiritual illumination shines through the sweet visions of the father of poetry. The light of his genius, like that of the moon, as he describes it in the eighth Iliad,* is serene, transparent, and heavenly fair; it streams into the deepest glades, and settles on the mountain-tops of the material and social world; but, for all that concerns the spiritual nature, it is cold, watery, and unquickening. The great test of the elevation of the poet's mind, and of the refinement of the age in which he lives, is the distinctness, power, and purity with which he conceives the spiritual world. In all else, he may be the observer, the recorder, the painter; but in this dread sphere he must assume the province which his name imports; he must be the *maker:* creating his own spiritual world by the highest action of his mind, upon all the external and internal materials of thought. If ever there was a poetical vision calculated, not to purify and to exalt, but to abase and to sadden, it is the visit of Ulysses to the lower regions.† The ghosts of the illustrious departed are drawn before him, by the reeking fumes of the recent sacrifice; and the hero stands guard, with his drawn sword, to drive away the shade of his own mother from the gory trench, over which she hovers, hankering after the raw blood. Does it require an essay on the laws of the human mind, to show that the intellect which contemplates the great mystery of our being under this ghastly and frivolous imagery, has never been born to a spiritual life, nor caught a glimpse of the highest heaven of poetry? Virgil's spiritual world was not essentially superior to Homer's; but the Roman poet lived in a civilized age, and his visions of the departed are marked with a decorum and grace which form the appropriate counterpart of the Homeric grossness.

---

* Homer's Iliad, VIII. 551.

† Odyssey, XI.

"In Dante, for the first time in an uninspired bard, the dawn of a spiritual day breaks upon us. Although the shadows of superstition rested upon him, yet the strains of the prophets were in his ears, and the light of divine truth, strong, though clouded, was in his soul. As we stand with him on the threshold of the world of sorrows, and read the awful inscription over the portal, a chill, from the dark valley of the shadow of death, comes over the heart. The compass of poetry contains no image which surpasses this dismal inscription in solemn grandeur; nor is there anywhere a more delicious strain of tender poetic beauty, than that of the distant vesper bell, which seems to mourn for the departing day, as it is heard by the traveller just leaving his home.* But Dante lived in an age when Christianity, if I may so speak, was paganized. Much of his poem, substance as well as ornament, is heathen. Too much of his inspiration is drawn from the stormy passions of life. The warmth with which he glowed is too often the kindling of scorn and indignation, burning under a sense of intolerable wrong. The holiest muse may string his lyre, but it is too often the incensed partisan that sweeps the strings. The 'Divine Comedy,' as his wonderful work is called, is much of it mere mortal satire.

"In 'Paradise Lost,' we feel as if we were admitted to the outer courts of the Infinite. In that all-glorious temple of genius inspired by truth, we catch the full diapason of the heavenly organ. With its choral swell, the soul is lifted from the earth. In the 'Divina Commedia,' the man, the Florentine, the exiled Ghibelline, stands out, from first to last, breathing defiance and revenge. Milton, in some of his prose works, betrays the partisan also; but in his poetry we see him in the white robes of the minstrel, with upturned though sightless eyes, rapt in meditation at the feet of the heavenly muse. Dante, in his dark vision, descends to the depths of the world of perdition, and, homeless fugi-

* "Del Purgatorio, Canto VIII."

tive as he is, drags his proud and prosperous enemies down with him, and buries them, doubly destroyed, in the flaming sepulchres of the lowest hell.* Milton, on the other hand, seems almost to have purged off the dross of humanity. Blind, poor, friendless, in solitude and sorrow, with quite as much reason as his Italian rival to repine at his fortune and war against mankind, how calm and unimpassioned is he, in all that concerns his own personality! He deemed too highly of his divine gift, to make it the instrument of immortalizing his hatreds. One cry, alone, of sorrow at his blindness, one pathetic lamentation over the evil days on which he had fallen, bursts from his full heart. There is not a flash of human wrath in all his pictures of woe. Hating nothing but evil spirits, in the childlike simplicity of his heart, his pure hands undefiled with the pitch of the political intrigues in which he had lived, he breathes forth his inexpressibly majestic strains, the poetry not so much of earth as of heaven.

" Can it be hoped that, under the operation of the influences to which we have alluded, anything superior to 'Paradise Lost' will ever be produced by man? It requires a courageous faith in general principles to believe it. I dare not call it a probable event; but can we say it is impossible? If, out of the wretched intellectual and moral elements of the Commonwealth in England, imparting, as they did, at times, too much of their contagion to Milton's mind, a poem like 'Paradise Lost' could spring forth, shall no corresponding fruit of excellence be produced when knowledge shall be universally diffused, society enlightened, elevated, and equalized, and the standard of moral and religious principle, in public and private affairs, raised far above its present level? A continued progress in the intellectual world is consistent with all that we know of the laws that govern it, and with all experience. A presentiment of it lies deep in the soul of man, spark as it is of the divine nature. The craving after excellence,

* " Dell' Inferno, Cantos IX., X."

the thirst for truth and beauty, has never been, never can be, fully slaked at the fountains which have flowed beneath the touch of the enchanter's wand. Man listens to the heavenly strain, and straightway becomes desirous of still loftier melodies. It has nourished and strengthened, instead of satiating, his taste. Fed by the divine aliment, he can enjoy more, he can conceive more, he can himself perform more.

"Should a poet of loftier muse than Milton hereafter appear, or, to speak more reverently, when the Milton of a better age shall arise, there is yet remaining one subject worthy his powers, — the counterpart of 'Paradise Lost.' In the conception of this subject by Milton, then mature in the experience of his great poem, we have the highest human judgment, that this is the one remaining theme. In his uncompleted attempt to achieve it, we have the greatest cause for the doubt, whether it be not beyond the grasp of the human mind, in its present state of cultivation. But I am unwilling to think that this theme, immeasurably the grandest which can be contemplated by the mind of man, will never receive a poetical illustration proportioned to its sublimity. It seems to me impossible that the time, perhaps far distant, should not eventually arrive, when another Milton, — divorcing his heart from the delights of life, — purifying his bosom from its angry and its selfish passions, — relieved, by happier fortunes, from care and sorrow, — pluming the wings of his spirit in solitude, by abstinence and prayer, — will address himself to this only remaining theme of a great Christian epic." *

In the next extract, we seem to be reading one of Addison's own shorter Spectators.

"Consider the influence on the affairs of men, in all their relations, of the invention of the little machine which I hold in my hand, (a watch,) and the other modern instruments for the meas-

* Vol. II. p. 224.

urement of time, various specimens of which are on exhibition in the halls. To say nothing of the importance of an accurate measurement of time in astronomical observations, nothing of the application of time-keepers to the purposes of navigation, how vast must be the aggregate effect on the affairs of life, throughout the civilized world, and in the progress of ages, of a convenient and portable apparatus for measuring the lapse of time! Who can calculate in how many of those critical junctures, when affairs of weightiest import hang upon the issue of an hour, prudence and forecast have triumphed over blind casualty, by being enabled to measure with precision the flight of time in its smallest subdivisions! Is it not something more than mere mechanism which watches with us by the sick-bed of some dear friend through the livelong solitude of night, enables us to count, in the slackening pulse, nature's trembling steps towards recovery, and to administer the prescribed remedy at the precise, perhaps the critical, moment of its application?

"By means of a watch, punctuality in all his duties, which, in its perfection, is one of the incommunicable attributes of Deity, is brought, in no mean measure, within the reach of man. He is enabled, if he will be guided by this half-rational machine, creature of a day as he is, to imitate that sublime precision which leads the earth, after a circuit of five hundred millions of miles, back to the solstice at the appointed moment, without the loss of one second, no, not the millionth part of a second, for the ages on ages during which it has travelled that empyreal road.* What a miracle of art, that a man can teach a few brass wheels, and a little piece of elastic steel, to outcalculate himself; to give him a rational answer to one of the most important questions which a being travelling towards eternity can ask! What a miracle, that a man can put within this little machine a spirit that measures the

* "It is not, of course, intended that the sidereal year is always of precisely the same length, but that its variations are subject to a fixed law. See Sir John Herschel's Astronomy, § 563."

flight of time with greater accuracy than the unassisted intellect of the profoundest philosopher, — which watches and moves when sleep palsies alike the hand of the maker and the mind of the contriver, nay, when the last sleep has come over them both!

"I saw, the other day, at Stockbridge, the watch which was worn on the 8th of September, 1755, by the unfortunate Baron Dieskau, who received his mortal wound on that day, near Lake George, at the head of his army of French and Indians, on the breaking out of the Seven Years' war. This watch, which marked the fierce, feverish moments of the battle as calmly as it has done the fourscore years which have since elapsed, is still going; but the watchmaker and the military chieftain have now, for more than three fourths of a century, been gone where time is no longer counted. Frederic the Great was another, and a vastly more important, personage of the same war. His watch was carried away from Potsdam by Napoleon, who, on his rock, in mid-ocean, was wont to ponder on the hours of alternate disaster and triumph which filled up the life of his great fellow-destroyer, and had been equally counted on its dial-plate. The courtiers used to say that this watch stopped of its own accord when Frederic died. Short-sighted adulation! for if it stopped at his death, as if time was no longer worth measuring, it was soon put in motion, and went on as if nothing had happened.

"Portable watches were probably introduced into England in the time of Shakespeare; and he puts one into the hand of his fantastic jester as the theme of his morality. In truth, if we wished to borrow from the arts a solemn monition of the vanity of human things, the clock might well give it to us. How often does it occur to the traveller in Europe, as he hears the hour told from some ancient steeple, — That iron tongue in the tower of yonder old cathedral, unchanged itself, has had a voice for every change in the fortune of nations! It has chimed monarchs to their thrones, and knelled them to their tombs; and, from its watchtower in the clouds, has, with the same sonorous and impartial stoicism, measured out their little hour of sorrow and gladness, to coronation and funeral, abdication and accession, revolution and restoration, victory, tumult, and fire. And with like faithfulness, while I speak, the little monitor by my side warns me back from my digression, and bids me beware lest I devote too much of my brief hour even to its own commendation." *

The lovers of the Bible shall be entertained and edified by a choice extract.

"When the appointed time had come, the writings of Moses, of David, and Isaiah; locked up in a dialect which was wasting away in the cities of Judah and on the hills of Palestine (a region at best not as large as our New England), were transfused into the far-reaching, widely spoken tongue, which had become the language of government, of commerce, and of philosophy, from the mouths of the Rhone to the Indus. And in this language, and at this critical juncture of religious history, though their authors were Jews, the books of the New Testament were written in Greek. When another stupendous revolution, or rather series of revolutions, had transferred the sceptre of empire to Rome, and the Latin language had acquired an almost exclusive predominance in Western Europe and Northern Africa, with some extension in the East, among the first intellectual phenomena of the new order of things we find the old Italic version of the Hebrew and Greek Scriptures, the parent of the Vulgate and so many subsequent translations. In this way, by means of the Roman language, which did not exist as a dialect on the lips of men when the earlier books of the Old Testament were written, — the language of a people who, in the days of Moses and David, were wandering a wild clan along the banks of the Tiber, —

* Vol. II. p. 250.

through this singular medium, — rather let me say this awe-inspiring instrumentality, — these old Hebrew voices, mute and unintelligible as originally uttered, are rendered audible and significant to the Western Church and world. And then, as we descend the line of history, as the Latin and Greek, great world-dialects, become obsolete, — dying, dead languages, as we significantly call them, — and new tongues are created by the mysterious power of the vocal faculty, we are to behold, as was so well observed by Mr. Hill, as an invariable consequence, often as the first result of the change, a new translation of the Scriptures. Nowhere is this so sure to be the case as in the great national stock to which we belong. Gothic and Saxon antiquity has handed down to us, through the wreck of the Dark Ages, nothing older than portions of the paraphrases and versions of the Scriptures, which were made in those dialects respectively, not long after the introduction of Christianity into Germany and Britain. Indeed, in the ancient Gothic tongue I am not sure that anything has survived but portions of the translation of the New Testament.

"Thus great and wide-spread families of men have been broken up or have silently passed away, and the tongues they spoke have ceased to be a medium of living intercourse; hordes of indigenous shepherds (indigenous we call them) grow up into enlightened states; wild tribes of nomadic conquerors pour down from the North, and ripen into polished commonwealths; undiscovered continents and islands, filled with strange races, are made, as it were, to emerge from the deep; languages that are dying out mingle on the canvas of human fortune with languages that are coming in, like the melting images of the illusive glass, till it is impossible to tell where one begins or the other ends; but the word of God is heard along the line of the ages, distinct amidst the confusion, addressing an intelligible utterance to each successive race in the great procession of humanity. The miracle of Pentecost becomes the law of human progress, and nations that have sprung into being cycles of ages since Moses and the

Prophets and the Apostles wrote, still hear them speaking, every man in his own language." *

Here the contributor looks to the indulgent editor, as if asking, May we go on? The decided, yet kindly shake of the head puts it out of the question, and we can only *wish* that there were space to introduce passages, on the right foundation of government, Vol. I. pp. 112, 113; on the proclivity of despotic rulers to wars, illustrated by a masterly outline of modern wars, 124–126; on the Indian policy of the Pilgrims, 238, 239; on the tendency of civilization to reproduce and expand itself, 273–275; on the impulse given to the industrial arts by the mere publications of Walter Scott, who probably never did a day's work in his life, in the ordinary acceptation of the term, 302; on the superiority of the Bunker Hill Monument to books in perpetuating the memory of the battle, 359, 360; on the unsurpassed moral heroism of La Fayette, 507, 508; on the discoveries yet to be effected by the growth of science, 617–619; on the enviable condition of these United States, so truly and fairly described, that the author, in his preface, needed not to apprehend the charge of over-strained nationality, 400, 401; on the favorable influence of science upon the loftier kinds of poetry, Vol. II. 216–219; on the relative conditions of mankind the day before and the day after the discovery of printing, 240, 241; on the magical and evil-absorbing influences of the steam-engine, 245; on the momentous privileges attached to the elective franchise, 316, 317; on the decay of the primitive simplicity of school-boy manners in New England, 603; and on

* Vol. II. p. 669.

the superiority of the Christian Scriptures to other books assuming the character of sacred, 672.

We will but touch upon one topic more. It is interesting and even curious to observe how thoroughly *American* Mr. Everett is in his favorite themes and speculations. He seems as one born to think and to speak for his native country. Rarely does he go beyond her limits, in search of subjects on which to exert his commanding powers. Like those animals whose color is extracted from the ground they grow on, he seems blended and identified with his natal soil. What is the spirit of our institutions? What is the plastic life of our nation's history and being? How may these be developed and carried out? These are the inquiries towards which his face is invariably set. Even his addresses while he was ambassador abroad, dwelt more on the land of his birth than on the brilliant and exciting scenes around him. Cambridge there reminded him of his own humbler Alma Mater; the cattle-shows of England carried his thoughts and fancies home; and a compliment to himself brought forth some plea for America. Most of his writings correspond with this patriot tendency. It is familiarly known that a series of articles in defence of this country from his youthful pen, in the earlier numbers of the North American Review, attracted respectful attention abroad, and silenced a swarm of travellers and reviewers, whose richest capital consisted in slandering and depreciating everything American. In accordance with this darling passion of his life, or rather this bent of his nature, the two volumes which we are now to dismiss may be regarded as essentially a picture of the best and brightest side of American existence, reflected as it is from the character of the various occasions commemorated, from the orator's own manner of dealing with them, and from the approving sympathy and interest which followed him. It is not so much Mr. Everett as our own United States that produced these volumes; most other books written among us might have been composed by strangers as well as by Americans; but these, never. They are one with the country, and apart from the country could not have been. If we wished to acquaint a foreigner with what our life and institutions are doing, and may do to achieve their happier destinies, — what are the prevailing wishes, aims, tastes, thoughts, and habits of our more established population, — what we think of our duties and dangers, — what topics will arrest our attention and engage our interest, — what appeals will stir our hearts, — what, in short, are the most hopeful phases of our condition and prospects, — we would not so soon point him to the journals even of impartial and kindly disposed tourists, as to these unconsciously representative, but only so much the more faithful, pages of Edward Everett. His country owes him a debt of gratitude and honor, which she must take care to pay.

1850.

PERCIVAL'S POEMS.*

Mr. Percival has now given to the public three volumes of poetry, and has acquired a flattering distinction in our land. All allow the force and brilliancy of his genius, and the skill of his versification. All have at times felt a pensive chord in their bosoms responding to the sweep of his melancholy lyre. Yet what is the reason that he is not received with quite that measure of general enthusiasm which would fairly correspond to his merit, and constitutes the choicest outward reward of every poet? It lies, we fear, somewhat deeper than the inelegant typography of his first volume, the indiscriminate profuseness with which he makes up his contents, the submissiveness of his imitations, or his frank defiance of public opinion in matters of religion; though even these objectionable points have undoubtedly had their force with different classes of readers.

But the most formidable obstacle to Mr. Percival's general popularity is the same, we apprehend, which has hitherto prevented the multiplication of editions of Southey and Wordsworth; we mean, a disinclination in

* *Clio*, Nos. I. and II. By James G. Percival. Charleston and New Haven.

those authors to consult the precise intellectual tone and spirit of the average mass to whom their works are presented. Theirs is the poetry of soliloquy. They write apart from and above the world. Their original object seems to be, the employment of their faculties and the gratification of their poetical propensities; after which, the world is indulged with the favor of listening to the strains that have charmed and soothed their own solitude. A few congenial souls, indeed, will always be found to sympathize with such effusions, and none may be inclined to question the genius from which they proceed; and sometimes, as is frequently the case with the present author, the inclinations of the poet himself may coincide with the general taste by a happy chance, and thus produce compositions, which deserve immediate, extensive, and permanent popularity.

But we do not wonder that the success of poets of this stamp is frequently incomplete. We have little faith in this abstracted and unsocial sort of poetry. Science may be prosecuted very successfully, without the least reference to any general standard of taste and feeling abroad. Hardly so with literature. One cause, we presume, of the literary excellence and lasting admiration attained by the works of the ancients, was the practice of reciting them before an audience. Being composed with this view, they must have possessed more life and energy, more direct appeals to human sympathy, the power of being seized more vividly and readily by the average comprehension, and especially, to a greater degree, the happy art of awakening and playing with the attention so as never to push it to the borders of ennui, than if the author sat apart in his own closet, and sang for no other object than the gratification of his own ear, and in reverence for his own standards of criticism alone. Thus, might it not have been because Homer charmed in person the ears of all Greece, that he has reached the hearts of all ages? Herodotus read his Muses at the Olympic games. The masterpieces of the Augustan era were rehearsed in the court of the emperor. Boileau, Voltaire, Rousseau, Marmontel, produced most of their matchless compositions under the immediate expectation of reading them to coteries or individuals. We cannot but persuade ourselves that such a practice must be extremely efficacious, in securing a more general reception and popularity for works written under their influence, than for those written without it, all other circumstances being equal. The genius of a writer may be overwhelming; his learning prodigious; his ear attuned to the finest influences; his taste fastidiously pure; and his glances "from earth to heaven" as bright and as quick as inspiration can make them;—yet if he does not often glance too "from heaven to earth"; if he does not study the common susceptibilities of the mass of his readers, and industriously tune the key-string of his own soul, till it vibrates nearly in unison with the compounded note sent up from the general breathing of human nature, he may lay his account, and perchance find his consolation, in being the poet of the few rather than of the many. To the cause thus imperfectly set forth, we are inclined to ascribe the limited circulation of Mr. Percival's Clio, which certainly contains some of the best poetry that has yet been sung by "degenerate Americans."

It may be asked, Would you have poetry written entirely in the spirit of *vers de société?* Shall the poet slavishly abandon himself to the tastes and ideas of others? Shall he not even aim at elevating the general standard as nearly as possible to ideal excellence? Shall he refuse to draw his chief resources from the workings of his own soul, thus imparting to his productions a peculiarity, a characteristic individuality, which shall touch some of the finest springs of curiosity and interest in his readers? Shall his profession be that of a dancer, in which every step and posture which is taken is calculated for show and effect? No, certainly: that were to rush into the opposite extreme. It is the fault which places the poetry of Moore so many degrees below the point of perfection. Scott might probably have failed in the same quarter, and Byron in the opposite, the *quartier solitaire*, had not a certain native tact or address, resembling what in common life is called a knowledge of the world, taught them to resist their respective constitutional tendencies, and hit the true point of nature and popularity. Our ideas may be a little further illustrated by instancing the French and German schools of poetry, which severally verge towards the extremes we allude to. Shakespeare, whose single name may be cited in company with schools of literature, will quickly occur to every reader, as maintaining the desirable mean, in perfection. This is the true taste. While the bard is duly independent of extraneous influences, and pours into his strain all his own native fire and force, we would have him at the same time aware that there is an ear of scrutinizing and impatient taste abroad which is listening to him,—an ear which will certainly be dissatisfied if he wastes his music on preludes, and voluntaries, and symphonies of his own wayward devising, and confines not himself within some modulated movement, to which the feelings of all his readers shall beat time, like the heads in the *platea* of an Italian opera-house.

The Last Minstrel was not in our opinion the worse bard, because,

> "Gazing timid on the crowd,
> He seemed to seek in every eye
> If they approved his minstrelsy."

Still, the poets of the soliloquist school may possibly complain that we do not faithfully represent their case. They may disclaim the disinclination which we charge upon them to consult and to hit that happy medium of taste and propriety which awakens the interest, fastens the attention, and secures an eager perusal from the reading world. They may appeal to their love of applause and to their vanity, as being quite equal to what is felt by more popular poets. They may contend that their mortification at ill-success, and their restlessness under criticism, are as acute and troublesome as those writers can possibly endure who pen every line with the image of a staring public directly before their eyes. Very true. But is not this mortification and restlessness produced by the circumstance that the world and the critics refuse to come up to your standard, and not that you have failed in attaining to theirs? Is there not a kind of feeling of insulted graciousness, of repulsed condescension, which you experience, rather than of humbling acquiescence, at finding that what has pleased and delighted yourselves in the composition, and been permitted to go abroad in public, has failed to please and delight everybody in the perusal? And when you appeal, as Mr. Southey and others sometimes do, to posterity, say fairly whether you would not wince a little, if you could learn that posterity also will neglect you; and whether you would not then appeal to a more remote posterity still, for your reward, and so on, till posterity and poetry shall be no more.

If, after all, the recluse fraternity should strenuously deny the truth of our position; if they insist that they are as anxious as others to seize upon that mysterious medium of style, sentiment, spirit, and expression, which shall instinctively correspond to the tastes of the wide world of readers, and that they are willing to make every sacrifice to attain this end; — then they do but force a more disagreeable alternative upon their good-natured critics, who are endeavoring to account for the circumscribed popularity which awaits their excellent productions. Must we not reluctantly ascribe to them an inaptitude or inability to infuse into their writings a tone precisely harmonizing with the natural inclinations and principles of taste implanted in the general mind? Certain early intellectual tendencies, voracious and undiscriminating habits of reading, seclusion from varied intercourse, or a partial feebleness or obliquity in the power of observation, may have prevented them from discerning, either in their own minds or those of others, the exact limit where delight ends and weariness begins, in the perusal of works of the imagination. Or Nature, in bestowing on them nearly all her rarest and most precious gifts, may have envied them the last, and so withheld that delicate tact, which would have enabled them so to employ their talents as invariably to produce fascinating results. Hence, in perusing the writers whom we are attempting to characterize, we are liable to be annoyed by a disproportionate stress laid upon certain ideas and sentiments; or, a strain of thought is dwelt upon too long, — longer than we are willing to follow it out; or our minds become cloyed by an unsparing profusion of beautiful images and poetical luxuries; or they are often strained and confused by the writer's breaking off from some leading track of thought to run into by-paths and labyrinths, thus holding the faculties in a painful suspense, until we are again brought back to the onward path. There is too little attention paid to those graceful transitions and natural juxtapositions of the thoughts, which carry the reader forward imperceptibly, and enable him to follow the poet in his highest flights without a wearied effort. A heavy, indescribable weight will sometimes come over the eyelids, which are all the while dazzled with beauties, and offended with but few faults. Our minds are constantly rousing themselves up to the task of pursuing pleasure; and the incipient nod is now and then only checked by our starting and exclaiming, How beautiful!

Whoever has attempted a fair sit-down to any of Mr. Percival's volumes must, we are confident, recognize most, if not all, of the peculiarities above specified, and ascribe to their influence the frequency with which he has laid aside the book, and achieved a complete perusal only by repeated assaults.

Yet we will venture to say, (for here closes the unwilling and unenviable portion of our task,) that he who has examined to any considerable extent the poetry of our author must have received an ample reward, and found abundant and splendid exceptions and balances to the defects above enumerated. There certainly reigns in many parts of it the true ethereal spirit. The vein is often as rich as any we have ever known. The pieces are not few in which the soul of the author, rising as he proceeds, involves itself and the reader in a cloud of delicious enchantment. He possesses the rare and divine art of imparting to language those mysterious and unearthly influences which come to us from the strings of an Æolian harp. Without employing our senses as instruments, he can yet diffuse through our frames something like the result of all the sweetest sensations. Other authors often obtain admiration and fame from the excellence and beauty of separate ideas and sentiments, and the skill with which they arrange them. These gifts are enough to make the fine writer; they may produce the deepest immediate impressions. But to these Mr. Percival adds the power of exciting in the mind a pervading and continuing charm; an aggregate effect, separate from the original one, analogous to a secondary rainbow. As you wander through the garden of his poetry, you enjoy something more than the pleasure of gazing on individual specimens, or inhaling their successive sweets, or surveying gay beds and fairly ordered parterres; for the air itself is occupied with a spirit of mingled fragrance. As mere music often speaks a sort of language, so our author's language breathes a sort of music. We are convinced that it is true poetry, since in reading it we have had exactly the same feeling as in surveying admired objects in the sister arts of painting and sculpture.

To descend, however, to praises a little more particular and discriminating, the author's wide command of the English language deserves honorable notice. His rhymes are unhackneyed, yet always very natural. He has scarcely a trick of the mere versifier. We meet with few inversions of the common order of syntax. He has drunk deeply of the best undefiled springs.

We are next pleased with his intimate familiarity with classical literature. It is evidently of a kind not borrowed from Lemprière. It generally appears in incidental allusions, which are rather forced upon him from a well-stored memory, than sought after for the purpose of display. It is doubly gratifying to meet with this accomplishment in our author; both as it furnishes a proof that the race of ripe classical scholars is flourishing among us, and also that the stock of classical images and ornaments is far from being exhausted. We are persuaded, moreover, that Mr. Percival has caught, from the study of Greek models, a certain Attic purity and severity of style, conspicuous in some of his best-wrought pieces.

Besides this quality, we also observe, in every part of these volumes, proofs of very extensive and profound general knowledge. There is an almost encyclopedic familiarity with many departments of modern science. It is this ample store of images and illustrations, joined with his happy mastery of them, which gives us confidence in the ultimate splendid success of Mr. Percival's authorship. He is not to be named with those poets who set up with a small stock of ideas and a pretty talent, and soon write themselves out. We regard his powers and resources as inexhaustible, and if his spirit be elastic enough to try them all successively, condescending at the same time to feel and be guided by the pulse of public taste, (we do not mean merely the public of to-day,) he will acquire for the literature of his country and for himself an enviable renown.

Another agreeable peculiarity in these pages is the felicitous art of weaving into the texture of a composition the names of common and vulgar objects, which a poet of ordinary powers would despair of introducing with success. Mr. Percival overcomes in a moment the repulsive or unpoetical associations attached to such words, and invests them with an unwonted dignity and purity.

The scenery of our country, too, has to thank him for consecrating some of its objects in his verse. The following address has scarcely a fault that we can discern. It may possibly be thought that the picture is not sufficiently individual, and that when travelling about with it in your memory, you shall not recognize by it the Seneca Lake distinct from any other fine sheet of water. But this is a precarious objection. The author may not have meant it for a picture of that particular lake, but for a record of his feelings while accidentally gazing, at different hours, on one of the most beautiful of natural objects. But whatever may be the truth of this objection, surely every line of the piece presents a distinct image of beauty, and is in perfect keeping with the spirit of the whole, which was caught from the softest breathing of nature. But we are affronting our readers thus to enact so long the part of a Cicerone.

"TO SENECA LAKE.

"On thy fair bosom, silver lake!
The wild swan spreads his snowy sail,
And round his breast the ripples break,
As down he bears before the gale.

"On thy fair bosom, waveless stream!
The dipping paddle echoes far,
And flashes in the moonlight gleam,
And bright reflects the polar star.

"The waves along thy pebbly shore,
As blows the north-wind, heave their foam,
And curl around the dashing oar,
As late the boatman hies him home.

"How sweet, at set of sun, to view
Thy golden mirror spreading wide,
And see the mist of mantling blue
Float round the distant mountain-side!

"At midnight hour, as shines the moon,
A sheet of silver spreads below,
And swift she cuts, at highest noon,
Light clouds, like wreaths of purest snow.

"On thy fair bosom, silver lake!
O could I ever sweep the oar,
When early birds at morning wake,
And evening tells us toil is o'er!"

This extract reminds us that it is now time to introduce others from the two small volumes before us, which we shall do partly for the sake of exemplifying and defending the criticisms already advanced, and partly to adorn our own pages.

In the following crowded, classical, and animated picture, the occasional resemblance to Lord Byron ought not to be called an imitation so much as a successful attempt at rivalry: —

"LIBERTY TO ATHENS. ODE.

"The flag of freedom floats once more
Around the lofty Parthenon;
It waves, as waved the palm of yore,
In days departed long and gone;
As bright a glory, from the skies,
Pours down its light around those towers,
And once again the Greeks arise,
As in their country's noblest hours;
Their swords are girt in virtue's cause,
Minerva's sacred hill is free; —
O may she keep her equal laws,
While man shall live, and time shall be!

"The pride of all her shrines went down;
The Goth, the Frank, the Turk, had reft
The laurel from her civic crown;
Her helm by many a sword was cleft;
She lay among her ruins low;
Where grew the palm, the cypress rose,
And, crushed and bruised by many a blow,
She cowered beneath her savage foes;
But now again she springs from earth,
Her loud, awakening trumpet speaks;
She rises in a brighter birth,
And sounds redemption to the Greeks.

"It is the classic jubilee, —
Their servile years have rolled away;
The clouds that hovered o'er them flee,
They hail the dawn of freedom's day;
From heaven the golden light descends,
The times of old are on the wing,

And glory there her pinion bends,
  And beauty wakes a fairer spring;
The hills of Greece, her rocks, her waves,
  Are all in triumph's pomp arrayed;
A light that points their tyrants' graves
  Plays round each bold Athenian's blade.

"The Parthenon, the sacred shrine,
  Where wisdom held her pure abode:
The hill of Mars, where light divine
  Proclaimed the true, but unknown God;
Where justice held unyielding sway,
  And trampled all corruption down,
And onward took her lofty way
  To reach at truth's unfading crown:
The rock, where liberty was full,
  Where eloquence her torrents rolled,
And loud, against the despot's rule,
  A knell the patriot's fury tolled:
The stage, whereon the drama spake,
  In tones that seemed the words of Heaven,
Which made the wretch in terror shake,
  As by avenging furies driven:
The groves and gardens, where the fire
  Of wisdom, as a fountain, burned,
And every eye, that dared aspire
  To truth, has long in worship turned;
The halls and porticos, where trod
  The moral sage, severe, unstained,
And where the intellectual god
  In all the light of science reigned:
The schools, where rose in symmetry
  The simple, but majestic pile,

Where marble threw its roughness by,
  To glow, to frown, to weep, to smile,
Where colors made the canvas live,
  Where music rolled her flood along,
And all the charms that art can give
  Were blent with beauty, love, and song:
The port, from whose capacious womb
  Her navies took their conquering road,
The heralds of an awful doom
  To all who would not kiss her rod;—
On these a dawn of glory springs,
  These trophies of her brightest fame;
Away the long-chained city flings
  Her weeds, her shackles, and her shame;
Again her ancient souls awake,
  Harmodius bares anew his sword;
Her sons in wrath their fetters break,
  And freedom is their only lord."

"CONSUMPTION.

"There is a sweetness in woman's decay,
When the light of beauty is fading away,
When the bright enchantment of youth is gone,
And the tint that glowed, and the eye that shone
And darted around its glance of power,
And the lip that vied with the sweetest flower
That ever in Pæstum's * garden blew,
Or ever was steeped in fragrant dew,—
When all that was bright and fair is fled,
But the loveliness lingering round the dead.

* Biferique rosaria Pæsti. — *Virg.*

"O there is a sweetness in beauty's close,
Like the the perfume scenting the withered rose;
For a nameless charm around her plays,
And her eyes are kindled with hallowed rays,
And a veil of spotless purity
Has mantled her cheek with its heavenly dye,
Like a cloud whereon the queen of night
Has poured her softest tint of light;
And there is a blending of white and blue,
Where the purple blood is melting through
The snow of her pale and tender cheek;
And there are tones, that sweetly speak
Of a spirit, who longs for a purer day,
And is ready to wing her flight away.

"In the flush of youth and the spring of feeling,
When life, like a sunny stream, is stealing
Its silent steps through a flowery path,
And all the endearments that pleasure hath
Are poured from her full, o'erflowing horn,
When the rose of enjoyment conceals no thorn,
In her lightness of heart, to the cheery song
The maiden may trip in the dance along,
And think of the passing moment, that lies,
Like a fairy dream, in her dazzled eyes,
And yield to the present, that charms around
With all that is lovely in sight and sound,
Where a thousand pleasing phantoms flit,
With the voice of mirth, and the burst of wit,
And the music that steals to the bosom's core,
And the heart in its fulness flowing o'er
With a few big drops, that are soon repressed,
For short is the stay of grief in her breast:
In this enlivened and gladsome hour

The spirit may burn with a brighter power ;
But dearer the calm and quiet day,
When the heaven-sick soul is stealing away.

" And when her sun is low declining,
And life wears out with no repining,
And the whisper that tells of early death
Is soft as the west-wind's balmy breath,
When it comes at the hour of still repose,
To sleep in the breast of the wooing rose ;
And the lip, that swelled with a living glow,
Is pale as a curl of new-fallen snow ;
And her cheek, like the Parian stone, is fair,
But the hectic spot that flushes there,
When the tide of life, from its secret dwelling,
In a sudden gush, is deeply swelling,
And giving a tinge to her icy lips
Like the crimson rose's brightest tips,
As richly red, and as transient too,
As the clouds in autumn's sky of blue,
That seem like a host of glory met
To honor the sun at his golden set :
O then, when the spirit is taking wing,
How fondly her thoughts to her dear one cling,
As if she would blend her soul with his
In a deep and long imprinted kiss !
So, fondly the panting camel flies,
Where the glassy vapor cheats his eyes,
And the dove from the falcon seeks her nest,
And the infant shrinks to its mother's breast.
And though her dying voice be mute,
Or faint as the tones of an unstrung lute,
And though the glow from her cheek be fled,
And her pale lips cold as the marble dead,

Her eye still beams unwonted fires
With a woman's love and a saint's desires,
And her last fond, lingering look is given
To the love she leaves, and then to heaven,
As if she would bear that love away
To a purer world and a brighter day."

In the lines to the Houstonia Cerulea, and the address to Seneca Lake, our author comes into competition with Mr. Bryant, as a fine observer of nature, a pensive moralist, and a true poet. We recognize in the former a spirit kindred to that which dictated the Lines to a Waterfowl. The admirers of Mr. Bryant must admit that Percival's lines on Self-Devotion to Solitary Studies, and on the Prevalence of Poetry, are not unworthy of the genius that produced Thanatopsis, having, we think, no greater resemblance to Akenside than that exquisite and much quoted production has to the Grave of Blair.

The second number of Clio is not equal to the first. We can only take from it The Coral Grove, highly original and imaginative.

"THE CORAL GROVE.

"Deep in the wave is a Coral Grove,
Where the purple mullet and gold-fish rove,
Where the sea-flower spreads its leaves of blue,
That never are wet with falling dew,
But in bright and changeful beauty shine,
Far down in the green and glassy brine.
The floor is of sand, like the mountain drift,
And the pearl-shells spangle the flinty snow;
From coral rocks the sea-plants lift
Their boughs where the tides and billows flow;

The water is calm and still below,
  For the winds and waves are absent there,
And the sands are bright as the stars, that glow
  In the motionless fields of upper air:
There, with its waving blade of green,
  The sea-flag streams through the silent water,
And the crimson leaf of the dulse is seen
  To blush, like a banner bathed in slaughter:
There, with a light and easy motion,
  The fan-coral sweeps through the clear, deep sea;
And the yellow and scarlet tufts of ocean
  Are bending, like corn on the upland lea:
And life, in rare and beautiful forms,
  Is sporting amid those bowers of stone,
And is safe, when the wrathful spirit of storms
  Has made the top of the wave his own:
And when the ship from his fury flies,
  Where the myriad voices of ocean roar,
When the wind-god frowns in the murky skies,
  And demons are waiting the wreck on shore,—
Then far below, in the peaceful sea,
  The purple mullet and gold-fish rove,
Where the waters murmur tranquilly,
  Through the bending twigs of the coral grove."

Could the published poetry of Mr. Percival be reduced to a single volume of moderate size, and printed in a style worthy of the contents, it would, we have thought, be an acceptable present to the world, honorable to our country, and valued by posterity. But already, we understand, another work is announced from the same prolific pen; and as long as Mr. Percival will continue to write, our experience of the past raises so high our hopes of the future, that we do not ask him at present to divert his energies from composition to revision and reduction. By and by, in the calm and leisure of his days, he will, we presume, take pleasure in revising his works sternly and impartially, and fastidiously select from them fewer perhaps than the world would do, on which to fix the seal of immortality. In the mean time, may we entreat him to let no false sense of independence, or inordinate admiration of Lord Byron, tempt him any more to flout the Cross, or to throw doubts on the soul's immortality. Religion may not be wanted by so ethereal a race as the poets. But reviewers and other common men very much need it in the course of their numerous temptations. What would become of the wretched herd of authors, if reviewers were freed from some higher motives and restraints than are to be found among the miserable elements of this world? Let poets be careful, then, how, by the acuteness and philosophy lent them in some inspired moment of disappointment and hypochondriasis, they overthrow the labors of the Lardners and Paleys, falsify the demonstrations of the metaphysicians, and disappoint the dearest and most universal sentiment of mankind!

He must not complain of the severity of these sarcasms, who, besides throwing suspicion on the beautiful enthusiasm for virtue, the perfect purity of sentiment, and even the occasional eulogiums on religion which adorn the other portions of his works, has deliberately, in two or three disloyal stanzas, cut more than one humble believer to the heart.

N. A. Review, 1823.

A WEEK AMONG AUTOGRAPHS.

A RECENT visit to the mansion of I. K. Tefft, Esq., of Savannah, furnished me with an unaccustomed entertainment, in describing which, I may hope to reproduce it, in a faint degree, for others. This gentleman has devoted a portion of his leisure for several years to the collection of Autographs, or specimens of original handwriting by eminent persons of various ages and countries. It it were not otherwise known that his literary tastes and habits had peculiarly fitted him for such an occupation, the fact would be sufficiently evident from the actual fruits of his researches. His compilation of manuscripts, by different writers, nearly all of whom have been persons, in one way or another, of considerable distinction, amounts to about five thousand articles.* They thus constitute a very rare curiosity, or rather assemblage of curiosities, which few can even partially inspect without strong feelings of surprise and gratification. They present, too, a striking testimony of the extraordinary results that may be achieved by di-

---

* This number has probably been much more than trebled since the first publication of the essay.

recting one's attention and energies to a particular pursuit, whatever it may be.

Nor can such a collection be simply regarded as a curiosity. It deserves, in many respects, the higher praise of usefulness. The inquiries and exertions necessary to its formation must often bring to light some valuable literary or historical document. It is not mere signatures, or scraps of handwriting, that Mr. Tefft has been so sedulously collecting. He has intended that each specimen should consist, if possible, of an interesting letter, or some important instrument. Must it not be readily allowed, that a series of only single epistles from all the eminent men who were active, both in a civil and military capacity, throughout our Revolutionary war, would of itself constitute an interesting volume, and throw a desirable light on the history of that period? Yet such a series might be culled with great ease from the collection we are now contemplating.

Very few large autographic collections are known to exist. They are among the last intellectual luxuries grafted on a high growth of refinement and civilization. Here and there some peculiar taste or bias determines an individual to the pursuit, and he experiences the innocent delight of beholding his treasures rapidly incease, while his friends and acquaintances, in the mean time, are permitted to enjoy many an hour of deep interest and pleasure in reviewing the results of his quiet yet enthusiastic labors. In our own country, besides Mr. Tefft, there are but two very extensive collectors, the Rev. Dr. Sprague of Albany, and Robert Gilmor, Esq. of Baltimore. Dr. Sprague's collection has attained considerable celebrity, and amounts to more than twenty thousand articles. Mr. Gilmor's, also, is particularly valuable; and a printed list of the most important specimens has been circulated by him for the convenience of himself and his friends. His American is separated from his Foreign collection, and is thus classed: Civil and military officers before the Revolution,—military officers of the Revolutionary war,—military officers since the Revolution,—naval officers,—signers of the Declaration of Independence,—worthies of the Revolution,—signers of the Constitution of the United States,—presidents and vice-presidents,—secretaries of state,—secretaries of the treasury,—secretaries of war,—secretaries of the navy,—attorneys-general,—post-office department,—governors of States and Territories,—members of Congress,—diplomatic,—law,—divinity,—medicine,—literary,—scientific,—artists,—miscellaneous, which includes all that cannot properly be placed under one of the other heads. The foreign autographs in the same collection are subjected to a similar arrangement. The accomplished Grimké, during the last few years of his life, paid much attention to this subject, and has left a considerable collection of autographs, which, had he been longer spared, would undoubtedly have soon been greatly enlarged. Among the most distinguished collectors abroad are Rev. Dr. Raffles of Liverpool, the well-known author of the "Life of Spenser," and Rev. Mr. Bolton of Henley-upon-Thames. It would thus appear that clergymen have a particular partiality for this pursuit, though by what affinity I presume not to determine.

Few autographs, comparatively, have reached our country from the continent of Europe, nor is Mr. Tefft acquainted with any collector in that part of the world. That there must be such, however, is highly probable, particularly in France, Germany, Holland, and Italy. The English Encyclopædias contain no information on the subject, though it would seem to deserve a place in their miscellaneous records. The Encyclopædia Americana, which is partly a translation from the German, dismisses the article with the tantalizing remark, that "some collections of autographs of famous men are very interesting." I should apprehend that there is a sufficient number of autograph-collectors in the world to justify and support an annual publication on the subject. Such a work would be invaluable to the fraternity. It should contain catalogues of all existing collections. It should give an account of new and interesting discoveries. It should present fac-similes of the rarest and most valuable subjects. By this means, every collector might compare his own deficiencies with the redundancies of others, and an equilibrium be everywhere maintained at much less trouble and expense than are incurred at present.

Mr. Tefft has succeeded in forming his large compilation without incurring any direct expense. Through the liberality of many persons in our country who have held choice autographs in their possession, he has always on hand duplicates of considerable worth, by the exchange of which with persons, either at home or abroad, he has been enabled to confer so peculiar a value and extent on his collection. Having amassed five thousand specimens, it may be supposed that he has nearly exhausted the range of distinguished names; and accordingly, when some obliging friend from a distance sends him a parcel, he finds, on looking it over, that it scarcely contributes a single new name to his collection, though the whole may be otherwise valuable and interesting. Some of his most curious specimens he has received gratuitously from friends in Great Britain, although, as might be expected in a very artificial state of society, they would often command considerable prices in that country. The poet Campbell raised forty-five guineas for the Poles by autographs; and visiting a lady who had notes from distinguished people on her table, he advised her to conceal them, or they would be stolen. Brougham's autograph was valued at five guineas. Distant, undoubtedly, is the day when the casual holder of a few bits of paper in America will think of extorting a compensation from the gentle and devoted collector of autographs.

One of the most interesting features of this occupation consists in the personal correspondence between the autograph-collector and individuals who are in possession of the desired articles. Between the collectors themselves not only an acquaintance is formed, but often a warm and substantial friendship. If one could imagine the mutual regard entertained between two persons who are in the habit of interchanging a few Birds of Paradise, or a real Phœnix, or a consignment of the most delicious tropical fruits, or a goodly specimen of Georgia gold, one might understand the emotion felt at the reception of a long-sought-for scrap by one of the signers of the Declaration, or perchance the veritable signature of some foreign name,

"Wherewith all Europe rings from side to side."

Again, nothing can exceed the obliging and courteous language and actions of several distinguished men who have been applied to for autographs within their control. My Savannah friend has rarely, if ever, had the misfortune to be met with neglect in answer to applications of this kind. His letters from such men as ex-Presidents Madison and Adams (both father and son), Professor Silliman, General Lafayette, Washington Irving, Duponceau, Joseph Buonaparte, Dr. Mitchell, Mr. Grimké, Basil Hall, Dr. Raffles, and many others, exhibit their private characters in a truly amiable light. When thus not merely the nature of this occupation, but its external circumstances, are of so agreeable a description, we cannot wonder at the zeal with which it is pursued.

The science of the autograph-collector is not without its higher and peculiar mysteries. By much experience and exercise, he acquires a skilful discernment which belongs not to common eyes. He will tell you of correspondences between the handwriting and the mental disposition of individuals, about which he is rarely, if ever, mistaken. He will speak of immediately discerning, amidst a hundred new specimens, and before inspecting the signatures, those which have been written by the most eminent persons. And why should it not be so? Perhaps it will be found more philosophical to credit such pretensions, than to ridicule or distrust them. For if we often judge of a character, with no little precision, by a single tone of the voice, by a single motion of the body, by an instantaneous glance at the physiognomy; and if, which is yet more to the point, a *nation* has its peculiar style of writing, so that a French manuscript is as easily discernible from an English one as are the respective dialects of the two countries; if the manuscripts of the same nation at different eras are also perceptibly different, so that a writing of the sixteenth century is no more like one of the eighteenth than are the dresses of those two periods like each other; if the chirographies of the two sexes are almost always immediately distinguishable, so that a brother and sister, educated under the same circumstances, and taught by the same writing-master, shall yet unavoidably reveal their respective styles; and if, lastly, different *classes* of persons shall be known by their different handwritings, so that a mere child could pronounce which is the mercantile clerk's, which the lawyer's, and which the leisurely gentleman's, — let us beware how we rashly discredit the experienced inspector of autographs, who deduces from the signature of an *individual* the qualities of his mind.

The occupation we are describing (I find it easier to speak in the plural) is sometimes enlivened by moving adventures, hair-breadth rescues, and joy-inspiring discoveries, which the uninitiated world knows nothing of; and sometimes it is damped by the most cruel disappointments. A manuscript is often sought for with anxious diligence for years; and when perhaps all hope is abandoned, and something like acquiescence or resignation is beginning to compose the spirits of the baffled inquirer, not only the desired signature, but (precious and ample reward for all past labors and regrets!) a whole letter by the same hand, is sent in from some unexpected quarter. Mr. Tefft was long in pursuit of an autograph of Kosciusko. He received from a Northern friend a scrap of paper containing the simple signature of that warrior's name, with an expression of regret that nothing more under his hand could be found.. Some time afterwards, he received from another friend an entire letter of Kosciusko, with the exception of the signature. On comparing the two papers, with trembling anxiety, it was found that they both originally constituted one and the same letter. Sometimes an ignorant descendant of renowned ancestors will be unwilling to part with any of their manuscripts, through an inability to comprehend the collector's object; sometimes a heaping trunk is committed by a vandal hand to the flames, or, if rescued, its contents are perhaps found to be ruined by the moulds and damps of age.

But we have perhaps been too long detained from examining the valuable collection which has occasioned these preliminary remarks. We find the manuscripts in excellent preservation, being arranged and classed in six volumes, after the manner of Mr. Gilmor's collection, already described. There is, besides, a box of miscellaneous autographs. Let us first open this. A very courteous letter from Captain Hall lies on the top, enclosing an engraved fac-simile of the letter written to him by Sir Walter Scott when detained at Portsmouth by the wind in 1831, and giving some account of Sir Walter's own favorite production, "The Antiquary." This letter has been already published in several American newspapers, and we will dismiss it by simply remarking that Sir Walter's first sentence has been erroneously deciphered and printed, as we ourselves had the pleasure of discovering. He does not say, "My dear Captain Hall, as the wind seems *determinately* inflexible," but he says, far more clearly and forcibly, "as the wind seems *determinedly* inflexible."

Next is an invaluable document. It is a communication from the son of Dr. Currie of Liverpool, the biographer of Burns, covering a long and interesting letter from that immortal poet to the celebrated Dugald Stewart. It is written in a large, bold, perpendicular, and slightly angular hand, not unworthy the author of "Tam o' Shanter."

A distinguished professor of a Northern institution, in a very kind letter, thus writes: "We have in Yale College a very remarkable autograph, or rather auto-delineation: it is a sketch of himself with a pen, made by Major André, a few hours before his execution. There is also a lock of his hair, taken from his grave. In the sketch, he is represented as sitting at a table; the portrait is full length, and about the size of the palm of your hand. It came into the possession of Lieutenant Nathan Beers of the Connecticut Line, then on duty, and who stood near to André, as a member of the guard, at the moment of execution. Lieutenant Beers is my near neighbor, and, at eighty years of age, enjoys his faculties perfectly, except hearing. Colonel Talmadge, a very gallant and distinguished cavalry officer, was charged with the immediate custody of André's person, and upon his arm the unfortunate man was leaning, on his way to execution, when he first saw the preparation for what he deemed a dishonorable death. He recoiled a moment at the sight, and asked with emotion if he must die in that manner. Colonel Talmadge is still living, and cannot even now relate that tragedy without tears."

As a happy pendant to the foregoing, we have next a letter from, our Lafayette, dated in 1832, saying: —

"With much pleasure I would gratify your autographic inclinations, but have for the present no European writings to offer, excepting a note from the King of the French, which I enclose. As for this letter of mine, which you are pleased to call for, I hope it will be placed in the *American* part of your collection. I beg you to remind me to my friends in Savannah, and to believe me most sincerely yours.

"LAFAYETTE."

We soon take up a letter, apparently from a London merchant or banker, dated 6th April, 1676, to his friends in the country. It is curious by reason of mentioning that King Charles II. was then at New-Market, "and 't is said," continues the letter, "his Majesty in Counsell did on Sunday was seavenight past order that the chimney money should be assigned for payment of the bankers." This chimney-money probably corresponded to the house-duty of modern times. It is sometimes called *hearth-money* by the historians. The same letter contains the following passing touch of private life:—"Matt. H. and little Kitt were both invited through Easter to Sir Wm. Bucknall. The hinmost was not there, but the foremost was, and questionless the orange was well squeezed."

Another document is an order, dated in 1724, for the payment of a dividend on the South-Sea Stock, celebrated in history as the cause of such widely extended ruin.

There is also an original letter written by Miss Elizabeth Scott to her father. The chief interest about it is, that Dr. Doddridge once cherished the hope and effort to marry Miss Scott, but without success. She was a lady of great talents and accomplishments, and the author of some poems. The letter before us is only remarkable for a deep tone of piety and filial affection. The writer seems to have been a great bodily sufferer. One little thing about the exterior of her letter bespeaks its feminine authorship, and carries us back, as by a magic power, through a hundred years. Some thirty or forty *pin-holes* are made in the wafer of the letter, the fair and worthy writer apparently not having a seal at hand. The privilege of seeing pin-holes, made in a wafer by the fingers of a lady to whom Dr. Doddridge was attached, is one of no small value. If she could have found it in her heart to favor the fond divine more indulgently, doubtless she would have been able, instead of a pin, to have used a seal, with the device of a blazing heart, and the initials P. D. beneath it. As to the superscription, directed upside down, we know not what to say.

Turning over a number of interesting articles, which we cannot possibly specify, we come to a manuscript sermon of Cotton Mather. It is written half unintelligibly, in the finest and closest hand, on three very small leaves, the latter part of it seeming to be only notes or hints for extemporaneous enlargement. The text consists of the words, "Blessed be God." An instance of Mather's bold and poetic imagination occurs near the middle of the discourse. Describing the life and character of the Apostle Paul, who had such valid reasons to bless God for his conversion, he says: "A vile sinner *against* God may become a high servant of God. As they said, Is Saul among the prophets? thus they could say of another Saul, Is he among the Apostles? A fierce persecutor of our Lord Jesus Christ may become a rare ambassador for him." At this point he inserts in the margin, as an after-thought, which he felt necessary to crown his climax of antitheses, "and a firebrand of hell may become a bright star of heaven."

As this autograph of Mather is among the oldest in the collection, I may here mention that the *very* oldest is dated in 1665, and that on one sheet of paper are fastened four small documents written in New England between the years 1665 and 1689. Thus the collection is not yet peculiarly rich in antiquities.

We now turn over a considerable number of articles, consisting of letters, dinner-notes, orders, and signatures from the most conspicuous Americans of past and present times. However piquant it may be to the curious in such matters to inspect the hasty undress and confidential billets of living Presidents and Ex-Presidents, members of Cabinets and Congress, and various other eminent characters, the laws of decorum must not be violated by transcribing and blazoning them here. But see! we arrive at a mutilated letter from Benedict Arnold. It is written in a large, clear, bold, regular hand, and contains a complaint of his character having been cruelly and unjustly aspersed; concluding thus: "I have the honor to be, with the greatest respect [here some one has written in pencil, *a Traitor*], Your Excellency's most obedient and very humble servant. B. ARNOLD."

Soon following this is the rough draft of an animated Address to the young men of Boston, dated Philadelphia, 1798, by the elder President Adams. It begins thus: "Gentlemen, it is impossible for you to enter your own Faneuil Hall, or to throw your eyes on the variegated mountains and elegant islands around you, without recollecting the principles and actions of your fathers, and feeling what is due to their example." After alluding to the dangers of the country, he writes, "To arms, then, my young friends; to arms!" — and concludes in an equally characteristic strain. Some sheets after, we find a letter from the same pen, written from Philadelphia to Boston as early as 1776. It is addressed to a certain Miss Polly Palmer, in a style of playful gallantry. The whole of it is so interesting, that it shall be extracted here entire.

"PHILADELPHIA, *July* 5, 1776.

"MISS POLLY: — Your favor of June 15, 1776, was handed to me by the last post. I hold myself much obliged to you for your attention to me, at this distance from those scenes, in which, although I feel myself deeply interested, yet I can neither be an actor nor spectator.

"You have given me (notwithstanding all your modest apologies) with a great deal of real elegance and perspicuity, a minute and circumstantial narrative of the whole expedition to the lower harbor, against the men of war. It is lawful, you know, to flatter the ladies a little, at least if custom can make a thing lawful; but, without availing myself in the least degree of this license, I can safely say, that, from your letter, and another from Miss Paine to her brother, I was enabled to form a more adequate idea of that whole transaction, than from all the other accounts of it, both in the newspapers and private letters which have come to my hands.

"In times as turbulent as these, commend me to the ladies for historiographers; the gentlemen are too much engaged in action, — the ladies are cooler spectators. There is a lady at the foot of Pens-Hill, who obliges me from time to time with clearer and fuller intelligence than I can get from a whole committee of gentlemen.

"I was a little mortified at the unlucky calm which retarded the militia from Braintree, Weymouth, and Hingham. I wished that they might have had more than half the glory of the enterprise; however, it satisfies me to reflect, that it was not their fault, but the fault of the wind, they had not.

"I will enclose to you a DECLARATION, in which all America is remarkably united. It completes a revolution, which makes as great a figure in the history of mankind as any that has preceded it: — provided always that the ladies take care to record the circumstances of it, for, by the experience I have had of the other sex, they are either too lazy, or too active, to commemorate them.

"A continuance of your correspondence, Miss Polly, would much oblige me. — Compliments to Papa and Mamma, and the whole family. — I begin now to flatter myself, however, that you are situated in the safest place upon the continent.

"Howe's army and fleet are at Staten Island. But there is a very numerous army at New York and New Jersey, to oppose them. Like Noah's Dove, without its innocence, they can find no rest.

"I am with much respect, esteem, and gratitude, your friend and humble servant,

"JOHN ADAMS."

The autograph-inspector must not, however, flatter himself that he can always find a very interesting document, apart from the mere signature or handwriting of the eminent individual to whom it belonged. The every-day correspondence, even of heroes themselves, is not particularly heroic. You will turn over many a precious relic of the officers engaged in our Revolutionary war, and find perhaps nothing more important than an order upon a quartermaster-general, or the detail of accidents unworthy of a permanent record. Yet sometimes a few hastily written lines will transport you in imagination to the heat and bustle of the contest; as where Lord Stirling enjoins Colonel Dayton, "besides watching the motions of the enemy along the Sound, to get some certain intelligence from Staten Island and New York of their preparations or intentions; and I will be with you in the morning, but say nothing of that"; — or where Archibald Bullock, the first republican Governor of Georgia, begs Colonel M'Intosh, commander of the Continental Battalion, in a letter which is quoted by M'Call, the historian, immediately to withdraw a sentinel from his door; "since," he continues, "I act for a free people, in whom I have an entire confidence and dependence, and would wish upon all occasions to avoid ostentation"; — or where Thomas Cushing of Boston, in 1773, invites Elbridge Gerry to a meeting of the Committee of Correspondence, to prepare for the possibility of approaching war; and says in a postscript, "It is thought it will not be best to mention abroad the particular occasion of this meeting"; — or when M'Henry writes to Governor Hawley, that he had sat up two nights to produce two numbers of some address to the people, and adds: "We go against Arnold, but let us not be too sanguine. He is covered by entrenchments. War is full of disappointments," &c.; — or where Rawlins Lowndes writes to Governor Houston of Georgia, "I hope you will be able to keep off the enemy until succors arrive to your assistance. General Lincoln set off this morning, and the troops are on their march."

It is curious, however, to observe the turn taken by the correspondence of the same class of men as soon as the great struggle for independence was over. They enter now upon the field of local or general politics; or they look after their private affairs, which have evidently been deranged by their long devotion to public service; or they order from an artist, an eagle, the badge of the Cincinnati; or they inquire into the value of grants of land voted them by legislatures; or they solicit the office of sheriff; or they take measures to establish academies, and improve society around them.

We now open the box lettered Distinguished Foreigners. And first greets the eye a precious parcel containing several autographs of Sir Walter Scott. We have this note to his favorite publisher and friend, James Ballantyne: "Dear James, You have had two blank days, I send you copy from fifty-two to sixty-four, thirteen pages." We have an entire and closely written leaf of the History of France in Tales of a Grandfather. We have a billet without direction, sent probably to some one waiting at the gate of Abbotsford, and couched in these terms: "Sir Walter is particularly engaged just now. Andrew Scott is welcome to look at the arms, and Sir Walter encloses a trifle to help out the harvest-wages." We have an order on a bookseller in this fashion: "Mr. Scott will be obliged to Mr. Laing to send him from his catalogue

9373 Life of J. C. Pilkington,
9378 Life of Letitia Pilkington."

And lastly, we have the solitary signature, Walter Scott, which will no doubt be worth its full guinea before many years. One peculiarity distinguishes the manuscripts of this author from all others. It is that he never dots an *i*, or crosses a *t*, or employs punctuation of any kind, except, now and then, a solitary period. In this respect his writing strongly resembles the inscriptions of the ancients.

On comparing the sheet of copy which he furnished for the printer with the published History of France, I find a number of essential variations. The probability is, that James Ballantyne, who was an accomplished scholar, or perhaps the press-corrector, who, in Europe, is often possessed of no mean acquirements, treated Sir Walter's manuscripts pretty much after his own pleasure. The magic weaver had dismissed his fabric, wrought indeed in the firmest texture and the most beautiful figures and colors. But the *finisher* went carefully over the whole, adjusted the irregular threads, removed the unsightly knots, stretched out every part to an agreeable smoothness, and thus rendered the wonderful commodity more fit for the general market.

Reluctantly laying aside these memorials of the Great Enchanter, we take up a very polite letter from Joseph Bonaparte, enclosing the autograph of his far more renowned brother. It is on the outside of a note addressed by Napoleon to Joseph, when the latter was a member of the Council of Five Hundred. It is written on a thick, firm piece of paper, which has been clumsily and hastily sealed with red sealing-wax. The seal is inscribed with the name of Bonaparte, in the French, not the Italian mode of spelling it; and bears the device of a female figure leaning on a lictor's axe and rods. The superscription is this :—

"Concitoyen
Joseph Buonoparte
deputé au conseil
des 500
Paris."

Thus the autograph fixes its own date before 1800, the Council of Five Hundred having been dissolved on the 9th of November, 1799. In fact, it is not at all impossible that this very envelope covered a note from Napoleon to his brother, penned during that agitating week which preceded the death-blow of his country's liberties.

If ever handwriting was characteristic, this little superscription is decidedly so. Were a painter of genius employed to represent a field of battle by a few lines and dashes of a pen, he could not execute a closer resemblance than this. It is difficult to inspect it without being almost induced to stop one's ears. The *i*'s and *j*'s indeed, unlike those of Scott, are dotted; but the dots look exactly like flying bombs. The *t*'s are all duly crossed; but they are crossed as was the bridge of Lodi; and that imagination must be slow indeed, which does not perceive that the hand which produced even this little specimen was guided by a soul whose congenial elements were power, rapidity, confusion, victory.

What next has found its way to this little world of Autographs?

Lafayette's toast: "The Holy Alliance of Nations in the cause of equal rights and universal freedom." Then follows the same in French, all in his own handwriting.

Next is an order of Southey the poet, on a bookseller, for Aretino and Strabo.

Next, a note from Wordsworth; but who will credit its being entirely concerned with the letting of land, the laying down of crops, and the productiveness of a certain blacksmith's shop?

There is a characteristic scrap from John Wesley,

though a few of the words are unintelligible. The readable part of it is this: —

"Within a few months I am brought much forward. A few more, and I shall be no more seen. May I . . . . .

"Your affectionate friend and brother,

"J. Wesley."

Two sonnets by Bowles, in his own handwriting, will gratify the lover of poetry, and remind him of the high testimony of Coleridge to the merits of that elegant writer.

Next, a manuscript of two pages by William Cobbett, which appears to be a diatribe against the English government for its conduct towards America during the last war.

Next, the beautiful lines of John Bowring, entitled, "Whither shall my spirit fly?" written in his own hand, and marked by his own signature.

Next, a note from Lady Byron to her bookseller, ordering a number of theological works.

Next, a letter from Adam Clarke, inviting a distinguished clergyman of South Carolina, who was then in London, to visit him.

Next, a long and interesting letter from Whitfield on the subject of his school for orphans.

Dr. Franklin, in a letter lying near, says of Mr. Whitfield himself: "I knew him intimately upwards of thirty years. His integrity, disinterestedness, and indefatigable zeal in prosecuting every good work, I have never seen equalled, I shall never see excelled."

In turning to a large parcel of American autographs, we observed the following valuable remark in a letter of Gouverneur Morris. Speaking of a distinguished Southern politician, he says: "He seems to me one of the best of men, who, even if they begin life wrong, soon get right; and let me tell you, this thing is much more rare than experienced men suppose."

A letter from Bartram, the celebrated botanist, now attracts the eye. It is dated Charleston, S. C., April, 1775. To what friend it is addressed does not appear; but it is evidently dictated by a heart in which the love of goodness and of botany are both prevalent. "I wrote yesterday," he says, "to your son John, at Jamaica. I begged him to associate with the best characters, and at the same time I begged of him to take notice of the plants and other natural productions of the island, and to send you the seeds and fruits. I am resolved to take another scout in the Indian countries. Believe I shall go among the Cherokees; thence through the Creek nation to West Florida. I want to see the western and mountainous parts of these Colonies, where I hope I shall pick up some new things. It 's look'd upon as hazardous, but I think there 's a probability of accomplishing it."

Of Spurzheim, all that could be obtained was one of his printed lecture-tickets, on which he wrote the date, and on which he also stamped his favorite seal, "*Res, non verba quæso.*" Every relic of this distinguished man has been in great demand; and unfortunately the supply was diminished by the application of his heirs for every scrap on which he had written.

Despairing, however, to present anything approaching an adequate idea, or even complete catalogue, of the various treasures of this collection, we will only further remark, that the curious in these matters may here inspect entire letters or notes of James Hogg, General Braddock, Haydon the distinguished painter and writer, Lord Brougham, of whom there are two specimens, Tennant author of Anster Fair, Dr. Chalmers, John Galt, Lucy Aiken, Dr. Parr, John Wilson (a note to William Blackwood), Granville Sharp, Clarkson to Joseph Lancaster, Thomas Campbell, Shee the poet and artist, Rogers the poet, Martin the painter, Mrs. Grant of Laggan, J. R. M'Culloch, Mrs. M'Lehose the Clarinda of Robert Burns, Dibdin the bibliographer, Wilberforce, Dr. Wardlaw, Rev. Rowland Hill, Wiffen the excellent translator of Tasso, Marshal Ney, William Godwin, Miss Jewsbury the late Mrs. Fletcher, Godoy the Prince of Peace, Miss Frances Wright, Rev. Matthew Henry the Bible commentator, the Duke of Wellington, Matthews the comedian, Francis Jeffrey, Mr. Alison of Edinburgh, Leigh Hunt, Scoresby the Arctic navigator, Robert Owen, William Roscoe, Mrs. Hemans to a friend on songs and song-writing, Lockhart, Napier the present editor of the Edinburgh Review, Baron Humboldt (an elegant letter of introduction to the late Stephen Elliott, written in French), George Canning, General Oglethorpe when in Georgia, Dr. Fothergill to John Bartram, De Quincey the opium-eater, James the novelist, General Moreau, Miss Edgeworth, and Miss Martineau.

The collection which we have now attempted partially to describe is liberally open to the inspection of every respectable inquirer. Any important contribution to it is received with gratitude by the proprietor. Should the present essay awaken attention to the subject, the writer will recur with increased pleasure to his "Week spent among Autographs."

ANOTHER WEEK AMONG THE AUTOGRAPHS.

Several valuable acquisitions have been made to the collection of I. K. Tefft, Esq., and his kindness permits the following notices of them to be communicated to the public.

We have, first, a letter from John Pynchon to his son in London, dated Boston, May 18, 1672. This was forty-two years after the settlement of Boston. The sight of this manuscript carries us back to "the day of small things" in that now populous and extended city. We see in imagination its three or four churches scattered among the three hills of the place. We see its few crooked streets (a quality which they still possess) winding about to accommodate the gathering settlers. Boston at this period contained probably three thousand inhabitants. Even then they were a noble set of men. Only eleven years after the date of this letter, when the Colony of Massachusetts fell under the displeasure of Charles II., who issued a decree against its charter, a legal town-meeting of the freemen was held, and the question was put to vote, whether it was their wish that the General Court should resign the charter and the privileges therein granted, and it was resolved in the negative unanimously. Soon after, Sir Edmund Andros was appointed the first royal governor; and his administration proving arbitrary and oppressive, the people took forcible possession of the fort in Boston, and of the Castle in the harbor, turned the guns upon the frigate Rose, and compelled her to surrender, seized the Governor, and held him a close prisoner under guard in the Castle.

These were evidently the true progenitors of those sons who, in 1765, resisted the Stamp Act, and in 1773 emptied the tea-chests into the dock.

The letter before us, however, which begins with "Son Joseph," is only an effusion of anxiety and complaint from a loving father, who had heard no tidings of his son for a long time. He seems to have resided at Springfield, Mass., and to have made a journey all the way to Boston to hear something of his son. Though short, the letter is full of religious expressions. How different in this respect from most letters in modern days! The writer prays that his son may be delivered from the tempest of the times, and so with his earnest prayers he leaves him to the Lord.

The next specimen (we take them promiscuously, without classification) is of high value. It is no less than a long letter from the celebrated poet Wieland, author of Oberon. It is addressed to Pfeffel, himself a jurist and diplomatist of considerable eminence. Many an enthusiastic German collector would cheerfully give a small bit of his little finger to be possessed of this treasure. It is observed by Menzel, one of the ablest living German critics, that "it was Wieland who first restored to German poetry the free and fearless glance of a child of the world; a natural grace, a taste for cheerful merriment, and the power of affording it. The cheerful, amiable, refined Wieland," he continues, "a genius exhaustless in grace and lightness, in wit and jest, banished the unnatural from German poetry, discovered nature in the world as it is, and taught the national mind to move easily, firmly, and in harmony." If we trusted this description alone, we might suppose that a German would value an autograph of Wieland as highly as an Englishman would prize one of Pope or Addison, or an American one of Irving. But, unfortunately, the delicate wit, sparkling fancy, and fascinating style of Wieland are, in too many of his works, brought into the service of an Epicurean and sceptical spirit. It does not diminish, but rather enhances, the value of the specimen before us, that it was written when Wieland was quite a young man, — only about seventeen years old; for we have examples enough of his composition at more advanced periods, and our curiosity is particularly gratified by seeing how the youthful poet and scholar expressed himself, so long before he felt the public eyes of admiration and criticism fastened upon him. The letter itself is of sufficient interest to be extracted entire. We make use, with a few immaterial alterations, of a translation furnished to Mr. Tefft by some German friend.

"GÖTTINGEN, *April* 16, 1750.

"DEAREST AND BEST AULIC COUNCILLOR:* —

"I have been waiting three or four days for the departure of the mail, to give you some account of my journey and happy arrival at Göttingen. Our fate, as far down as Durlach, you have learned from Mr. Wild. I arrived safely at Frankfort, where I stayed the greatest part of the time with Mr. Sarasin, and after three days went to Cassel, where I experienced a kind reception from the Countess. She desired me to let the mail-coach proceed, and promised to procure me a private conveyance for Göttingen. An acquaintance of hers conducted me through the whole town, and gave me a sight of everything remarkable. I had her invitation for supper, breakfast, and dinner. I related

* An Aulic Councillor was a member of the Imperial Council, who also exercised the functions of judges of the Supreme Court of the German Empire.

to her the conduct of her son, — his faults, his indolence, — without the least reserve. She was much pleased when she heard that, notwithstanding all of them, he still retained the affection of yourself and Mr. Lerfe. She promises to aid you in some suitable method to effect his correction. Full confidence is placed in your skill and experience in education, and she will shortly write to Colmar. The letter I received at Frankfort from the Count gave her a great deal of uneasiness, as it spoke of a rising upon his right shoulder. It was her wish that he should drink beer in lieu of wine at his meals. May I beseech you, my dearest Mr. Pfeffel, to console her on these two points in your next monthly letter. She truly deserves all the attention and pains that you can take on her account. She is the noblest woman, the best mother, — so without all pretension, and full of kindness. Never have I seen so many good qualities united in one woman. Do not consider this a blind judgment of mine; on the contrary, I was fully prejudiced against her ere I knew her so completely, and I feel persuaded that, after the visit she intends paying you, you will be of the same opinion with me. The Count, as much as I esteem his good heart, is not worthy of such a mother. May you soon be able to give her better news of him. She expects none before the expiration of three months; but flatters herself that her contemplated measures, together with his governors, will produce a change of mind. She gave me a letter of introduction to the Pastor Feder, and desired me to write to her from time to time.

"Monday, the 10th, I arrived here at Göttingen. Your son is perfectly well. We board together with young Stonar (an excellent youth), Escher from Zurich, and Zwickig; and as our chambers are close together, we can always be in company. He has given me his entire confidence, and I think we shall continue in the closest harmony. How great is my good fortune to cultivate that friendship with the son which his noblest father has honored me with! To-morrow our lectures commence, four of which we have in common, and we can recite together.

"I cannot express my thanks for your letters of introduction to Mr. and Mrs. Less, and the kindness and indulgence you have favored me with. It is my daily wish that an opportunity may occur to enable me by deeds to show that I am not ungrateful.

"I am much pleased with this city and its establishments, but never walked a more costly pavement. The purse must be continually in hand, and everything is paid for fourfold.

"May you, my dearest and best Aulic Councillor, continue in uninterrupted health. Remember me in the circles of your amiable friends, your dearest consort, Mr. Lerfe, Luce and his worthy companion, the country counsellor, most kindly; and accept assurances of my everlasting attachment and regard. Your obedient friend and servant,

"WIELAND."

The next is a truly precious memorial,—a note to Alexander Cunningham from Dr. Hugh Blair, author of the "Sermons" and "Lectures on Rhetoric." Both the authorship and the subject-matter induce us to extract it entire, although it has already been printed in Currie's Life of Burns.

"DEAR SIR,—As you told me that you had in view in the new Edition of Mr. Burn's works to publish some of his Letters, I now send you enclosed, (as I promised you,) his Letter of thanks to me upon his leaving Edinburgh. It is so much marked by the stroke of his Genius, that I thought it worth while to present it, among letters from some other persons. If you think it proper to be published with other Letters of his, I have no objection. You will please take a copy of it, and send me back the Original, which I mean to keep. I would have called with it, but I am still confined by some remains of the Gout, and by a Cold which I contracted on coming to town.

"Yours, most faithfully,

"HUGH BLAIR.

"*Argyle Square, Friday, 2d December.*"

It will be seen here that Dr. Blair in a few instances retains the antique fashion of beginning his nouns-substantive with capital letters. Another peculiarity, and identical with Sir Walter Scott's, which we formerly noticed, is, that he rarely dots an *i* or crosses a *t*, and is much too sparing of his punctuation. Out of the thirty-eight small *i*'s occurring in the note, to say nothing of several neglected *j*'s, only five are dotted. What could have been the secret cause of this distinction? Was it mere caprice, or was it everlasting principle? Perhaps a few dots were conscientiously sprinkled here and there to preserve the just rights of this excellent little letter from utter prostration. The *t*'s fare a great deal worse, for they have not the sign of a cross from the beginning to the end of the note. There is nothing, not even a difference in length, to distinguish them from the lofty *l*'s. The entire note, however, is written in a large, bold, legible hand; indeed, almost wonderful for a man of about eighty years of age, which Dr. Blair must have been at the time of writing it. Do we then see before us the actual chirography in which were penned those beautiful and admirable Sermons that have charmed so many thousand readers of taste and pious sensibility, as well as those far-famed Lectures, which, in spite of some defects, have formed and guided the taste of the last and present generations of English and American scholars? Emotions, at once classical and sacred, may well be excused for overflowing at the sight of a relic like this. Nor can we be induced to dismiss it without fondly lingering over it a little longer, and detecting even the slightest peculiarity which may transport us in imagination into the familiar presence of the much-honored dead.

Behold, then, the highly decorated flourish of the initial *H* in the signature of Hugh Blair! See the long and graceful dash which the hand of the octogenarian struck forth upon the superscription of the note! Who can fail to perceive, even in these minute characteristics, the external traces of that elegant mind which had so long been employed in the fervent contemplation of beauty in all its forms and manifestations?

We must also notice the large, thick, black wafer, which mutely tells the story of some recent bereavement in the family of the venerable sage. The irregular folds, which considerably differ from a perfect parallelogram, shall be charitably ascribed to the trembling hand of age, or to the unavoidable hurry of the moment. Doubtless the writer had many billets to answer, and many attentions to respond to, on his occasional visits to town. Nor shall criticism be severe on the slight mistake at the beginning of the note, where, in the expression "Mr. Burn's works," by a wrong location of the apostrophe, the poet's name is written as if it were Burn instead of Burns. We remember that some enemy of the Doctor during his lifetime, goaded by the fact that ten editions of the first volume of his Sermons were called for in one year after their publication, malignantly sent forth to the world an appalling list of all sorts of errors discovered in that single volume of a Professor of Rhetoric and Belles Lettres in the University of Edinburgh. A far different feeling, even a sacred and reverent curiosity, has actuated us in thus examining, as it were, the very shreds and dust of this hallowed instrument, which we now reluctantly dismiss.

Following this, we take up what must be allowed on

all hands to be quite an autographical gem. It is the superscription of a note, addressed by Frederic the Great to his confidential friend and correspondent, the distinguished Baron de la Motte Fouqué. The paper employed by his Majesty was of a thick, coarse, bluish-white. But what had the greatest warrior of the age, when writing to one of his greatest generals, to do with pink-colored, hot-pressed, wire-wove, gilt-edged, billet-doux fabrics? The superscription is written in a noble and beautiful style, — bold, grand, flowing, as if executed by a hand accustomed to the victories of the Seven Years' War, — at the same time, however, perfectly distinct and legible, as if characteristic of a monarch who was equally inclined to the pursuits of literature and taste. The leading address is in French, after this fashion: —

"To my General of Infantry,
The Baron de la Motte Fouquè,
at
Brandenburg."

At one corner of the superscription is written in the German language this announcement: "Accompanied by a box of cherries, and two melons."

On another fold of the paper is written in French, in Fouqué's handwriting, which confers on it a high additional value, the following notice: —

"Sans-Souci, July 5, 1766.
Invitation to come to Sans-Souci,
together with the reply."

The autograph is still further enriched by a distinct and finely preserved seal of the royal coat of arms. The device is gorgeously beautiful.

Two intelligent Germans, to whom we have shown the whole specimen, much doubt whether, after all, it contains the veritable handwriting of the renowned monarch. They assert that Frederic, having only had a French education, was incapable of writing such correct German as the inscription in the corner of the note. They think it probable that the whole direction proceeded from the pen of the royal secretary. If these suggestions should prove correct, of course the delightful visions of our imagination respecting the correspondence of the handwriting with Frederic's character must be dispelled into air, unless we suppose that the secretary himself, by long and intimate acquaintance with his master, had imbibed or unconsciously imitated some of his lofty qualities.

There is next a very curious historical document, penned by the Earl of Annandale in the year 1707, in the midst of the troubles which distracted Scotland at that period. Many a letter has been printed far less interesting than this. It transports us to the very field of battle, where we are told of prisoners coming in and Highlanders threatening attacks, and the Duke of Argyle having returned to the camp, and eight score of the enemy having just been seen climbing the hills, &c., and all written on a piece of paper so small as to show the extreme scarcity of that article even in the government camp.

Lo! another precious relic! A leaf from the Diary of Henry Kirke White, the poet. We all remember that poor Henry passed some time in an attorney's office before he was assisted by Mr. Wilberforce to prepare for a university education. While breathing that ungenial atmosphere, he committed to paper this brief skeleton-record of a few of his unhappy days. The very sight of it is dreary and melancholy, like the writer's heart. All that we here learn of his occupations is, that on Saturday, the 8th of some month, he was engaged in "entering up the Hall books; on Monday, the 10th, copying all the morning certain letters for Mr. Enfield; on Wednesday, fair-copying a schedule of fines and amercements; on Thursday, do. do. another copy on unstamped parchment; on Friday, the 14th, drawing advertisement of two heifers, the property of Edward Musson, being stolen or strayed out of his close in the parish of Radford. Attending the printer therewith," &c., &c.

One blessed blank appears amidst these worldly details. It is that of Sunday the 9th. Nothing is recorded under this date, except the simple day. And one cannot but vividly sympathize with such a being as Kirke White for this short though happy respite from labors which he must have loathed. Henry Kirke White's Sabbath! It is almost a subject for a poem. Imagination follows him to his closet, to his church, to his lonely evening walk, to the long portion of his night spent over his Bible, his Milton, or some of England's noblest divines. The handwriting of this specimen is manly, and elegantly plain.

This is succeeded by another rarity, — a letter from the celebrated George Whitfield, dated London, June 13, 1755, then in the forty-first year of his age, to his nephew James Whitfield, at Savannah in Georgia. It is so characteristic, that it must here be inserted entire.

"My Dear Jemmy, — I wrote to you a few days ago by a Carolina ship, and since that have received your two letters, which convinced me that you was not ungrateful. May this crime of crimes in respect either to God or man, be never justly laid to your charge! Remember your present, as well as future and eternal all, in a great measure depends on the improvement of a few growing years. Be steady and diligent and pious *now*, and you will find that God will do wonders for you. The Captain is mightily pleased; and your father, notwithstanding his affection to see you, is glad you are provided for. Your sister Fanny will soon be married, and Fanny Greville is already disposed of. Her husband (a young attorney of Bath) has sent me a very obliging letter. Oh that my relations were born of God! I hope you will not rest without it. To encourage you in outward matters, I have sent you, in *part of payment*, some loaf-sugar, which I thought would be a good commodity. Your father also hath sent you some buckles, knit breeches, and a dolphin cheese, with a letter. All which I hope will come to hand. Write often; work hard, and pray much, and believe me to be, my dear Jemmy,

"Your affectionate uncle and assured friend,

"G. W."

Following this is a curious affair, which appears to be enveloped in a little mystery. It is something like a mourning-card, containing an inscription by the celebrated Lavater. It was lately given to Dr. Sprague of Albany by Lavater's son-in-law, at Zurich, in Switzerland, the birthplace and residence of the great physiognomist. The following is an exact translation of the whole inscription: —

"To a Friend after my Death.
Let everything be a sin to thee, and that
alone, which separates thee from the
Lord. 18th November, 1794. L."

The sentiment is so excellent, that we will attempt to give it here a metrical clothing: —

Detest as sinful, and detest alone,
Whate'er removes thee from the Eternal One.

Another card succeeds, of a different kind, but of still more value, probably, as an autograph. It is from the celebrated Goethe, who asks of Professor Riemer the loan, for a short time, of the Bohemian Grammar. This, by the way, is an excellent method of borrowing books. The card is a kind of substantial acknowledgment, which leads at once to the recovery of a missing volume, often of more value to its owner than money. When will the borrowers of books exercise consciences void of offence in this matter, and be as scrupulous in restoring to the proprietor some cherished author, or the fragment of some precious set of twelve or twenty volumes, as they are in honoring a note at the bank, or discharging the bill of a flourishing tradesman? Until a more scrupulous punctuality on this subject shall prevail, the morality and the civilization of literature will be far from perfect. To return to Goethe's card, we have only further to observe, that the signature alone appears to be the handwriting of the great magician-poet, while the rest of the manuscript probably proceeded from his amanuensis.

Mr. Tefft has recently received, from a friend at the North, an original manuscript letter of William Penn, which he regards as one of the most valuable autographs in his collection. Letters written by this distinguished man are extreme rarities at the present day, Mr. Tefft having hitherto never been able to procure more than a bare signature, cut out from some parchment document. This letter is precious on more than one account, — not only as being a veritable original from the hand of the far-famed Quaker, but as exhibiting the characteristic qualities of the man. We see in it his downright simplicity, his quaintness of style, his remarkable force of mind, his rare mingling of religious humility with a bold and decided line of policy. The reader may be reminded that Penn, at the date of the letter, was forty-two years of age. Only four years previously, he had purchased, settled, and visited his colonial establishment in America. He had now returned to England, and had taken lodgings near the court of King James II., to exercise his influence with that monarch in behalf of his philanthropic schemes. In this situation, it seems, he had heard of some unhappy disorders that had disturbed his infant colony in America. The letter before us is chiefly occupied in suggesting measures to suppress them. Carolinians will be interested in the allusion to the respectability and substantial condition of many of the original settlers of their native State.

Thomas Lloyd, to whom the letter is addressed, succeeded William Penn as President of the Colony. He appears to have been an unsalaried officer. Judging from several of Penn's expressions, we should conjecture that he was dissatisfied with Lloyd's want of energy in suppressing the disturbances, though he shrinks from preferring any direct complaint. His mind certainly seems to have been wrought up into a sad gust of perplexities and anxieties. But now for the letter itself. The orthography is exactly transcribed.

"Worminghurst, 17th 9 mo
1686.

"DEAR THO: LLOYD

"Thyn by way of new york is with me, & first I am extreamly sorry to hear that Pennsilvania is so Litigious, and brutish. The report reaches this place with yt disgrace, yt we have lost I am told, 15000 persons this fall, many of ym men of great estates yt are gone and going for Carolina. O that some one person would in ye zeal of a true Phinias & ye meekness of a Christian spirit together, stand up for our good beginnings, and bring a savour of righteousness over that ill savour. I cared not what I gave such an one, if it were an 100£ or more out of myn own pocket, I would and will do it, if he be to be found, for ye neglect such a care of ye publick might draw on his own affaires. but I hope to be ready in the Spring, my selfe, and I think, with power and resolution to do ye Just thing, lett it fall on whom it will. O thomas, I cannot express to thee ye greif yt is upon me for it. but my private affaires as well as my publick ones, will not lett me budge hence yet; tho I desire it with so much zeal, and for yt reason count myself a Prisoner here.

"I waite for answear of yt about ye laws; for yt of ye money, I am better satisfied, tho' Quo warrantos at every turn have formerly threatened. I hope some of those yt once feared I had to much powr will now see I have not enough, & yt excess of powr does not ye mischief yt Licentiousness does to a State, for tho ye one oppresses ye pocket, the other turns all to confusion; order & peace with poverty is certainly better. It almost tempts me to deliver up to ye K. [King] & lett a mercenary Gover'r have ye taming of them. O where is fear of god & common decency. pray do wt thou canst to appease or punish such persons, & if in office, out with ym, forthwith. If J. White and P. Robson be of ym, displace them Immediately. *Thom. think not hard of it because of charge in comeing, being and goeing. I will be accountable for yt,* if thou please but to do yt friendly part. lett T. Hor: J. Har: J. Clap, R. Tur: J. Good: T. Sim, see this & who else thou pleasest. if you have any love to me, & desire to see me & myn with you, o prevent these things that you may not add to my exercises. If a few such weighty men mett apart & waited on god for his minde & wisdom & in ye sense & authority of yt, you appeared for ye honour of god, ye reputation of the governour & credit & prosperity of ye Country, to check such persons, calling ym before you as my ffds [friends]; men of Credit with me; & sett your united Shoulder to it, methinks it may be better. to ye Lord I leave you saluting you all in endless Love, being & remaining,

"Your true and loving
ffriend

"WM. PENN.

"Salute me to thy Dr
wife, tell her she must
remember her name in
my business. also to
thy children.

"give my love to ye Gover'r * &c.

"P. S.

"Ffor Balt. & Sas-quhanagh [Susquehannah] I have not ended, being otherwise stopt too, I waite my time, but doubt not being upon good terms. lett none be brittle about my not being there yet, I come with all ye speed I can; tho I must say, twere better all were in another order first; for these disorders — strike ym back I have had some regard to in staying; which is a sad disappointment to me & ye country.

* Who this Governor was, it is difficult to imagine. The historical records of Pennsylvania mention no presiding officer as being there at this time, except Thomas Lloyd himself. He is designated, however, as "President," and there may have been a magistrate subordinate to him with the title of Governor.

"The East Jersey Prop'rs believe thy report about my letter to yee. I am not with ym once in two months. they meet weekly. they are very angry with G. Lowry. Salute me to Frds There away, old Lewis & wife; also to Capt. Berry, I have sent his letters as directed. press him about land for me in East Jersey. I shall fall heavy on G. L. if I live, for denying him in my wrong, till all be taken up yt is desirable. Speak to G. L. thyself about it, for wt he has done will be overturned (I perceive) by ym here, & he served. Vale.

"Myn salute yee."

Allusion has already been once or twice made to Dr. Alexander Murray. This gentleman was Professor in the University of Edinburgh, and the greatest Oriental scholar of his day. He died about the year 1813. He was author of a "History of the European Languages," "Life of Bruce the Traveller," and other works. We have before us a few extremely interesting memorials of his genius and pursuits. One of them is a sheet of paper crowded in every part with some of the exercises of the great linguist in acquiring a foreign tongue. Among his other accomplishments, he was an elegant poet; and accordingly, we have here a few rough but very curious sketches from his Muse. The following unfinished stanza, which appears to be the commencement of a song intended for some festive club, will strongly remind us of the daring, reckless tone of Robert Burns:—

"Though whingean' carles should vex their hearts,
And ca' our social meetings sin,
Awa! we ken their halie arts!
An honest man defies their din.
When brithers twelve in Session sat,
And HE was HEAD that ken'd them a',
The Deil came ben, and claim'd his debt,
The *sourest* man ———"

Probably he was here about to write *amang them a'*. But perceiving that it would make a false rhyme, he threw by the whole affair, which has thus remained incomplete.

On another scrap of paper, we find a few elegiac stanzas, quite unfinished, and full of interlineary corrections and erasures, but intermingled with beautiful touches of poetry.

A gentleman of Charleston, S. C. has recently presented Mr. Tefft with a letter addressed to him seventeen years ago, by the celebrated Macaulay. It was written when both himself and his correspondent were members of the University of Cambridge in England, and bears evident marks of that resplendent talent which has since so frequently dazzled and delighted Europe and America.

Another gentleman of Charleston has contributed a signature of General Moultrie, attached to some public instrument, and accidentally found in the street. Moultrie had a curious device or flourish with which he ornamented his signature. It resembled more than anything else a *fortification*, with its bastions, its salient angles, its retreating angles, its squares, compartments, &c. Might not one fancy that there was always about him a kind of unconscious memory of the most important crisis of his life, and which outwardly expressed itself in this very characteristic manner?

We have already mentioned the collection of the Rev. Dr. Raffles of Liverpool. We are now permitted to present the following extract of a letter from that gentleman to Mr. Tefft, respecting some portion of his collection, and we must confess that the extraordinary value and magnificence of its contents far surpass our utmost previous conceptions.

"You ask me about my collection of Autographs, my method of arrangement, &c., &c. I have several series. The first and principal series consists of the autographs, chiefly letters, of eminent and remarkable persons of all classes and countries, from the time of Henry VII. of England to the present day. These are put upon tinted paper of folio size; one leaf of the paper containing the autograph, and the other the portrait, or something else illustrative of the history of the individual: — for instance, with Addison's autograph you will find his portrait after Sir Godfrey Kneller, and an original number of the Spectator. With Dr. Johnson's, you will find a view of the house in which he was born, at Litchfield, and the house in which he died, &c. This collection I hope soon to bind, and expect it will amount to twenty volumes. To this I intend adding a supplementary volume of Biographical Notices. This volume is alphabetically arranged.

"2d. My *American collection.* This is not yet arranged. It contains the Signers of the Declaration of Independence, — one of which alone is wanting,* — all the Presidents, with many of the Vice-Presidents and Governors of States; Divines, and other public characters, — civil, naval, military, and miscellaneous. I have not yet determined as to the way in which I shall arrange these; but if on folio tinted paper like the others, I should think that it would amount to eight or ten volumes.

"3d. *Authors.* I have a large collection of letters of authors of all kinds, which I intend to bind up alphabetically, with portraits in quarto, leaving a blank leaf between each letter for biographical notices. This will contain many duplicates of such as are in the first-mentioned series, and to these I may perhaps add Artists.

---

* George Taylor.

"4th. *Nobility.* Containing duplicates of such as are in the first collection by reason of their celebrity, or in the third in consequence of their being authors; or such as, having nothing but their *rank* to distinguish them, are already in neither of the above series.

"5th. To the above classes I may add several distinct and separate volumes, which are complete in themselves; e. g.: —

"A volume containing one hundred and twenty autographs, letters of the late Rev. Andrew Fuller, — quarto.

"A volume containing letters of Fuller, Ryland, Fawcett, Pearce (of Birmingham), &c., — folio.

"A volume of letters to George Whitfield, all indorsed by himself, — folio.

"Do. Do. — quarto.

"The entire MS. of James Montgomery's Pelican Isle, with other poems, composing his last published volume, — quarto.

"The entire MS. of Wiffen's translation of Tasso, — 2 vols. quarto.

"The Church Book of Oliver Heywood, the rejected Minister. — An invaluable little book, written wholly with his own hand, containing his covenant, and that of the church, and biographical notices of the members.

"A Thesis, by Dr. Watts.

"A Manuscript (Algebra), by Abraham Sharp of Bradford, the friend and correspondent of Sir Isaac Newton, — a 4to vol.

"A considerable collection of foreigners, not included in the first series.

"A collection of Notes, which will form several volumes octavo.

"A folio volume of documents on vellum.

"A folio volume of *franks* of the Peers at the coronation of George IV., &c., &c., &c.

"I am, sir, &c.

"Thos. Raffles."

In a letter recently received, Dr. Raffles says: "Pray, are your *Signers complete ?* I look with mingled emotions of sorrow and hope upon the only *hiatus* I have in mine."

We formerly inquired why so considerable a proportion of Autograph-collectors appear to be clergymen. Might not a phrenologist account for it by the disposition to reverence, which may be supposed to be common between both descriptions of persons ? The same sentiment which conducts the mind to the venerable records of Scripture, and to the Ancient of Days, may guide them also to other relics of antiquity, and every surviving memorial of greatness. The following paragraph from the newspapers exhibits the taste for autographs in a rather curious form : —

"The Rev. Dr. Cotton, Ordinary of Newgate, has, for a long series of years, been devoting his attention to the collection of dying speeches, trials, &c. of celebrated criminals, as well as their autographs; and whenever they could possibly be obtained, of their portraits also. The Rev. Ordinary likewise possesses an extraordinary collection of Chinese drawings, representing the torments in after-life upon evil-doers, according to Chinése belief."

In our first essay on Autographs, we complained that the English Cyclopædias contained very scanty and trivial notices of the subject. A friend has since kindly sent to us a volume of the "Dictionnaire de la Conversation et de la Lecture," from which we translate the following article, as an appropriate conclusion to our autographic lucubrations.

"AUTOGRAPH, from the Greek *autos*, self, and *grapho*, to write, signifies a writing from an author's own hand. If the men of former generations had attached the same value that we do to autograph manuscripts of great writers, to letters, and to the signatures of celebrated personages, we should neither be compelled to regret the loss of so many Greek, Latin, and French productions, of which there remain scarcely the titles or even a melancholy remembrance, nor the destruction of so many letters, memoirs, and diplomatic documents, which might have assisted in dissipating the darkness and the contradictions that envelop the history of ancient times and the Middle Ages, and in filling up the chasms with which it abounds. In countries where elementary instruction is as yet but little diffused, in ages when it was unknown, and even at very recent epochs, when it was too much neglected, avaricious, ignorant, or superstitious heirs sold by weight, or delivered to the flames, without scruple and without examination, all papers which had been transmitted to them by deceased relatives. This is no longer the case at the present day, especially at Paris. The preservation of papers and of autograph writings has become the object of a special anxiety, of a sort of idolatry, which among some individuals has degenerated into a mania, a folly. From this state of things has resulted a new kind of commerce, which traffickers and speculators openly undertake for the sake of profit. Letters, autographic documents, signatures affixed to diplomas, to public acts, or to receipts, upon paper or parchment, are taken clandestinely from public libraries, from various archives, and from other literary and political depositories, by unfaithful officers or unscrupulous amateurs. They are sought for, they are discovered, among grocers and dealers in goods. Purchased for a mere trifle, they are resold to the curious at a very high price. The search for these kinds of manuscripts has also produced a new branch of industry. As comparatively few persons are wealthy enough to form expensive collections of autographs, the defect is supplied by engravings, and by the still more economic processes of lithography. *Fac-similes*, traced after the originals, have been published, either separately or in new editions of our best classic authors, Corneille, Racine, Boileau, Bossuet, Fénelon, Lafontaine, Madame de Sévigné, Voltaire, J. J. Rousseau, &c. They have been inserted in picturesque travels and other works. But it is principally in collections devoted to the purpose, that they are found in the greatest number. One of the most prominent is the work entitled '*L'Iconographie Universelle*,' (Universal Likeness-Magazine,) where the *fac-simile* of the handwriting of each illustrious personage is subjoined to a biographical notice of him, accompanied by his portrait. It is especielly in *L'Isographie des Hommes célèbres* (*Handwritings of celebrated Men Imitated*), published in thirty-one numbers in quarto, from 1827 to 1830, that we find the most curious and the most numerous collection of fac-similes of autograph letters and signatures. It contains not less than seven hundred, of which the originals were borrowed from the library of the King, from those of Vienna, Prague, Munich, &c., from the archives of the kingdom and of the different bureaus of administration, and from private cabinets. Lithographic collections of autographs have likewise appeared in England and in Germany; but they are neither so complete, nor so well arranged, nor so well executed. The Royal Library of Paris possesses an immense collection of manuscripts, autograph letters, and signatures of kings, princes, ministers, warriors, scholars, and illustrious persons of both sexes, whether French or foreigners, from the thirteenth century to the present time. Conspicuous among them are the voluminous correspondences of Marguerite of Valois Queen of Navarre, of the Dukes of Guise, the Constable de Montmorency, the Mareschal de Saulx-Tavannes, the Cardinals du Bellay, Richelieu, de Retz and de Noailles, de Peiresc, and de Bouillaud; collections of letters from Francis I., Henry IV., Louis XIV.; the original manuscript of the Telemachus of Fénelon. There also is a choice selection of signatures by men of every kind of celebrity, affixed to receipts and other instruments on parchment, among which are three or four signed by Molière, and discovered a few years ago. This is all that remains of the handwriting of our most illustrious comic author. Several thousand pounds' weight of parchments of a similar description have been sold at different times for very insignificant prices to tradesmen, who, after selecting the rarest and most interesting specimens, have sold them again to different amateurs. The rest has been passed off to bookbinders and to glue-makers. Autographs also abound in the archives of the *Palais de Justice*, and the different departments of administration, still more in the archives of the kingdom, where, among rare and curious documents, there is preserved a charter of St. Louis, together with the original of the instrument containing the famous oath pronounced, in the tennis-court at Versailles, in 1789, and subscribed by the great majority of deputies to the States-General. In the same place, also, are preserved the signatures of all the members of the National Convention, and of several other legislative assemblies. However rich France may be in autographs, she is surpassed, not in number, but in antiquity and rarity, by Italy and Spain, if it be true that the library of Florence contains the Gospel of St. John, written by his own hand, and that several autograph manuscripts of St. Augustine exist in the library of the Escurial. The most important collections of autograph letters and signatures in the possession of amateurs in Paris, are those of M. Le Courte de Château-Giron; the late Marquis de Dolomieu; Mons. de Monmerqué, Councillor of the royal court; Mons. Guilbert-Pixérécourt, a professor of literature; Mons. Bérard, a Deputy and Councillor of State; and Mons. Berthevin, formerly keeper of the Royal Printing Establishment. That of Mons. Villenave, more numerous perhaps than the others, contains, it is said, twenty-two thousand signatures of different writings; but the greater part of them were written by persons more remarkable by their rank, their titles, and their offices, than for their actions or productions. For instance, all the French generals of the Revolution, even the most obscure, figure in this collection. We will also refer to the collections of M. de Saint-Gervais, the Marquis Aligre, M. Anatole de Montesquiou, and Mons. Perié, Director of the Museum at Nimes, and husband of Madame Simons-Candeille."

It may be mentioned, as an instance of the extreme difficulty of procuring a complete set of the signatures to the Declaration of Independence, that Mr. Tefft, although an American, and enjoying for many years great facilities in the pursuit of autographs, has been able, with the utmost exertions, to procure no more than thirty-nine out of the original fifty-six signatures. It is remarkable that Dr. Raffles of Liverpool should have been so much more successful in this branch of the pursuit. Mr. Tefft's present list of desiderata is as follows: Braxton, Floyd, Hart, Lynch, jun., L. Morris, Middleton, Morton, Nelson, jun., Penn, Ross, Read, Rodney, Stone, Smith, Taylor, Thornton, Wilson.* Should the present notices ever meet the eye of some happy possessor of any of these lacking signatures, perchance he may be still happier by generously transmitting them to the address of I. K. Tefft, Esq., Savannah, who, we feel assured, would in that instance complete the degrees of comparison, and become in very deed the happiest.

---

* These desiderata have been supplied to Mr. Tefft since the original publication of the essay, and in a great degree, the author is highly gratified to learn, in consequence of its appearance. President Sparks sent him no less than three letters of the Signers.

ESTIMATE OF THE PHILOSOPHICAL WRITINGS OF DR. THOMAS BROWN,

INCLUDING

SOME REMARKS ON MENTAL PHILOSOPHY.

It cannot be regarded as a proof of the superiority of the present age, that comparatively so little attention is bestowed on intellectual philosophy. In spite of the occasional fluctuations of public taste, we are persuaded that the science of mind is still destined to take precedence of all others.

The flippant and superficial remark has been made, and that too by very high authority, that the philosophy of the mind is a useless pursuit, because every one may become his own mental philosopher; that one has only to look within, and he will there find all that the profoundest thinker can acquaint him with. Never was hazarded a bolder or more assailable error than this. Is botany a useless science, because herbs and flowers, enough to fill whole catalogues, may be found within a mile from the cottage of every hard-working farmer? Is astronomy a vain pursuit, because every sailor on the watch, by only turning his head upwards, can count the stars moving over him, and mark the courses which they take? Has one man in a thousand the ability to fasten his attention on the operations of his own mind; and do not the occupations, habits, passions, and characters of a large majority of mankind lead their thoughts away from themselves, and fix them on external things?

Such being the universal and inevitable lot of humanity, we cannot conceive of a more useful, or directly practical employment, than for those individuals whose opportunities and powers of contemplation permit, to sit in the seclusion of study apart from active engagements, and there to fix their thoughts exclusively on the constitution of the mind; to trace action up to its central sources; to take a full survey of the mental phenomena; to estimate especially the extent of the human powers; to analyze, to describe, to classify, every internal property and faculty; to suggest modes of applying them in their proper directions, and to their proper objects; in one word, to unfold before the sight of their fellow-beings that which so very few know,—what they are, and what they can become.

Now, though there are not many men capable of originating these comprehensive, introverted surveys and estimates, yet, after they are made, there are large numbers who can read them with enjoyment and profit. It is no small thing to direct a man's attention to *himself;* yet this is effected by the very sight of a book on the mind. The soul for a moment swells before it with the consciousness of its untried and indefinite powers. The contents of most libraries lead one away from one's self. But take such a work as Cogan on the Passions,—though it is a rather dull book, and the author was not equal to his task, which abler hands might have wrought into a treatise almost unequalled in interest and utility, — we think that any common man who reads this book will become wiser, better, greater, and happier, and will particularly be convinced that every one cannot be his own intellectual philosopher. Passion, habit, prejudice, wild imagination, unprofitable reverie, wrong directions, and mistaken objects of thought, all which, by stealing encroachments or violent incursions, may be fast wearing away the character, are liable to be arrested in their progress even by a prosing treatise, which shall subject them to a cool analysis, and make the mind familiar with comprehensive descriptions and classifications of them.

We feel justified, on the whole, in laying down the following general results, which may be expected from good treatises on mental philosophy. Not to enumerate several advantages of comparatively subordinate value, — such as the mental discipline acquired by the prosecution of the study itself, the very dignity of the subject as a theme of speculation, the accession of a mere appropriate ornament, if nothing more, to a well-furnished mind, and the like, — the *first* unquestionably great advantage is, to make us reflect upon and feel habitually conscious of our powers; a state of mind which necessarily precedes all wise and energetic action. The *second* good result proceeding from this study is, that philosophical self-examination smooths the way directly to moral self-examination, which is the nurse of virtue. A *third* effect is to excite sentiments of piety by the contemplation of the most excellent and wonderful of the known works of God.

Such, we maintain, are the general tendencies of this study. But it may be objected, that these are too indefinite and intangible, being subjects rather of speculation than of clear demonstration. We may be asked to point out the express and particular achievements of the science of the mind, and to enumerate any newly discovered intellectual instruments, so to speak, which have visibly blessed and gladdened the prospects of the species, like the mariner's compass, the chronometer, the safety-lamp, the vaccine virus, the steam-engine; or any which have given new power and stimulus to scientific researches, like some of Newton's theorems, the galvanic battery, or the blowpipe. The Inductive Method of Lord Bacon will, of course, suggest itself here to every reader at all acquainted with our subject; and intellectual philosophers, with the author before us among the number, claim for it the magnificent merit of introducing a revolution not only in their own science, but in every other, and of almost changing the face of the modern earth. But to be candid, we must make a distinction between the inductive method itself, and Bacon's verbal interpretation and proclamation of it. It is the interpretation and proclamation only that truly belong to the science of the mind; the method itself has been more or less operative in all men from time immemorial. It did not depend on a promulgation by Bacon or any one else, whether a right mode of reasoning and philosophizing should, in spite of ancient trammels, occasionally force itself upon inquisitive and strong understandings. Did Locke and Davy, — names which we select to represent improvements in the two departments of intellectual and physical science, — did they rely on a divulged and explicit statute of Lord Bacon for the character and success of their researches? No more, we apprehend, than Napoleon fought his way to empire under the influence of a formula.

In making, however, this large concession, or rather, in drawing this due distinction, we are by no means disposed either to depreciate the actual merit of Lord Bacon's rule, or to disavow the past unequivocal successes of the branch of science in question, or to abandon our hopes of its future indefinite triumphs. Much, certainly, was gained by embodying the inductive method in a preceptive frame, and so suggesting and recommending it to the world. If an earlier start along the true path of science was hereby given to men than they would otherwise have taken, and if, by the same means, an incalculable expenditure of time and talents has in many cases been saved, these are achievements which certainly belong to the science of the mind. For we scarcely need contend, that the investigation and laying down of precepts for the prosecution of general science strictly constitutes one department of intellectual philosophy.

But, to take our stand on still more unquestionable ground: supposing all that has been written and said about the principle of Association of Ideas had been suppressed from the very first, and that men had been left to avail themselves of that principle only as nature prompted and experience dictated, can it be conceived, that every individual in the world at this moment would have been equally wise and skilful, equally happy and virtuous? On the contrary, has not the specification and description of this element of our minds, and the perpetual pressing of its existence and uses upon the attention of men, caused it to become a more constant, systematic, and efficient instrument of thought and practice? Of two orators, in other respects equal, which should we most confidently select for the management of a cause, — one who has been taught the doctrine of association in all its known relations and effects, or one who only instinctively and unconsciously acts upon it? To us there seems a vast accession of power and resources placed at the disposal of the former. Our own convictions are both deliberate and strong, that in the whole body of literature and mental effort at the present day, comprehending alike the speculations of the labored and formal volume, the pulpit, bar, legislative hall, periodical press, ephemeral paragraph, conversation, and solitary thought, no contemptible degree of whatever deep research, true sentiment, accurate rhetoric, and just reasoning are found to prevail, owes its origin, more or less directly, to the influence of what has been *said* and *inculcated* respecting right methods of ratiocination, and respecting the proper application of the associating principle.

Who can doubt that individual virtue has been strengthened, and individual happiness increased, by a scientific acquaintance with the principle of association? When gloomy thoughts overshadow and oppress his soul, the well-educated man, who happily has not neglected the science of the mind, recollects what has come to him from books, and the lecture-room, concerning continued trains of ideas, and the power of the associating principle. He therefore seizes the assistance of this intellectual instrument to lead his attention towards brighter objects of contemplation, and thus to dissipate his gloom. And this he does with much more confidence and effect than the untutored son of sorrow, who, unacquainted with the whole nature and extent of the blessed power within him, makes perhaps, or perhaps not, a few faint, instinctive efforts to turn the train of his ideas and feelings, but soon again desperately yields up his soul to its fixed and haunting agony.

We rejoice to believe that the science we are recommending is frequently found instrumental also in purifying the current of thought, as well as recalling it to its proper channels; that it assists in eluding the suggestions of temptation, in controlling a wayward imagination, in analyzing and dissolving prejudices; and that it produces many other similar effects, favorable to virtue and happiness, which would have arisen less certainly and systematically, had the power of the associating principle been left to its own spontaneous operations, unaffected by former scientific speculations, and unaided by the cultivated habit of self-inspection.

The very nature of the thing, we confess, forbids us to point out, ocularly, the influence of these intellectual instruments acting on the minds of men, as one may show the compass in the binnacle, virtually influencing every motion of a ship, and guiding her safely through difficulties and dangers. All that we can do is, to throw out our suggestions and the results of our own experience for what they are worth, and leave them to elicit the conviction or dissent of our readers, according to *their* views, experience, and modes of thinking. But if there be any truth in the preceding reflections, the claims of intellectual philosophy are vindicated, and she can boast of her specific instruments, that wield as prodigious a power, and are capable of conferring as exhaustless benefits, as certain more tangible discoveries in the sister department of natural philosophy. Observe, we are careful not to claim for this science the principle of association itself, any more than the principle of reasoning, or of memory, or of imagination. It is only the formal recognition, the verbal statement, the didactic exposition, of these principles, which we understand here by intellectual instruments, and for the positively beneficial influences of which we are taking the trouble to contend.

The topical system of the ancients was such an intellectual instrument as has been demanded of mental philosophy, and nearly as palpable as the safety-lamp. The discovery of it strictly belonged to the genuine science of the mind. The art of Mnemonics may be at present only in its infancy. We hold the expectation of new discoveries and methods in this branch of learning to be as reasonable as to look for farther knowledge on the subjects of light and heat. For instance, as an humble example, has a general rule been yet laid down, apportioning the quantity of anything to be committed to memory to the number of times necessary to repeat it, so as to introduce the greatest possible economy of time and labor? If a half-page of letter-press requires to be only six times read over in order to be well fixed in the memory, and a whole page seven times, it is manifestly better to divide the task of a whole page into two portions, and thus to save one reading. If, again, a quarter of a page only requires to be repeated five times, a further economy may be obtained by dividing the task into four portions. It is evident, however, that these divisions may be continued so far as to frustrate the purpose of them; for if the page be broken up into portions so small as one line each, although each portion could be well remembered at one reading, yet the whole page must be read over seven times as at first, and a loss is thus incurred by carrying the divisions too far. But where is the point at which the divisions may cease, and still allow the smallest possible number of repetitions? Now a few patient and attentive experiments and calculations, upon a memory of average strength and quickness, might conduct an inquirer to some result or formula on this subject, which should prove as useful to the world as a new algebraic expression in the general doctrine of chances. Who will pretend to limit the possible multiplication of such facts and rules of every kind, connected with all our mental operations? The time may come when a Grammar or Accidence of the Mind shall be put into the hands of youth, on a very extended and improved plan, like that of some of our easy systems of logic, which shall reveal to the opening intellect the extent of its powers, and early teach it the adroit and perfect use of itself, far beyond what is now practised or conjectured by the most accomplished and experienced men. Should it be incredulously asked, if such things can be expected at this late period of the world, we would inquire in return, how long, on the one hand, the species may yet hope to exist, and, on the other, how long the circulation of the blood has been discovered.

A complete system of intellectual philosophy, in all its abstract perfection, necessarily cannot be executed until the full extent of the human powers has been tried in every art and every science that can possibly develop and employ them. Such a period, it is true, stands at an indefinite distance. But still the remark illustrates and strengthens our position at the outset of this article, that the science of the mind is destined to become the most advanced in rank of all. Approximations to its ideal completeness can be made from time to time, as the mind of man exhibits new achievements and capacities to serve as materials for this last and highest branch of knowledge. When the mathematician has exhausted his skill in numerical combination, and has invented methods by which even the relations of infinite quantities can be managed to his purposes, the philosopher of the mind steps in, looks at the point which has been reached, and records it on some page of the intellectual system. When the natural philosopher has made every possible experiment on matter, has investigated the affinities of atoms, or taken the weight of worlds, or systematized the laws of motion, or measured the long journey of a ray of light from some outer system of the universe, or examined the different properties of opposite sides of that ray, or searched for the lines which divide organized from inorganic substance, and sentient from sluggish life, then the intellectual philosopher comes up to revise the task of his indefatigable agent and forerunner, marking wherein he has triumphed, or wherein he has been baffled, and notes down on the tablet of his own science the strength and the weakness of the human intellect. When the poet, the orator, the scholar, the reasoner, the historian, the painter, the musician, the sculptor, the architect, with the laborers in every other kindred art or pursuit, have exhausted their powers in affecting the souls of men, now moving them with transports of delight, now stimulating and correcting the progress of thought, now impressing a new character on whole generations, and guiding them to new courses of action, the mental philosopher fails not, with observant eye, to follow these varied achievements, and transfers them to his chapter of the influences of mind upon mind. It is equally a branch of his vocation to watch the *spontaneous* movements of individual and collective man; to trace the changes of opinion, custom, character; to observe what is universally pleasing or displeasing; in short, to note and record the operations and affections of the general mind. When hundreds of solitary thinkers have turned their attention inward to survey the operations of their own individual intellect compared with what they know of others, and have classified, as well as the evanescent and impalpable nature of the subject will permit, those laws of thought and emotion that may be gathered from their combined internal experience and foreign observation, at length some master-philosopher of the mind avails himself of the labors of his predecessors, and employs their recorded results to mould into a new frame and aspect this keystone of the sciences. When sciences, which are now unthought of, shall arise and be carried to perfection, calling forth mental powers as yet unexerted and unknown, and when perhaps new combinations and exhibitions of moral excellence shall brighten the face of society, the faithful philosopher of the intellect will stand ready to arrange these freshly created materials in his ever-growing system. Thus, the Science of the Mind, though susceptible of perpetual advances, must necessarily be the last to arrive at perfection. Its materials are drawn from all the other sciences. It is waiting to see what man can do and suffer, for its own business is to record and classify it. We cannot conceive of the final step of its march on earth; its present incipient existence thus constituting a new proof of a future state of being. Like the leading and essential virtue of Christianity, it *never faileth*, not even when prophecies fail, and tongues cease, and subordinate systems of knowledge vanish away.

It is high time to cease confounding the science of the mind with Metaphysics. This word, by common use, has now imperceptibly acquired a new signification, no longer to be found in the dictionaries, and no longer expressive of a distinct science. We will try to explain and fix its present general acceptation. Metaphysics has come to mean something imaginative and hypothetic. It ascribes imaginary and plausible causes to existing appearances, and speculates upon the nature of what is hidden and unknown. We would distinguish it from Philosophy, inasmuch as philosophy *ascertains* the causes of phenomena, and learns from *experience* the properties of things. Metaphysics will be found to enter more or less into every department of learning. When Newton discovered and applied the law of gravitation, he was, strictly speaking, the philosopher. When he ascribed that gravitation to the influence of a subtile, ethereal fluid, pervading all bodies, (though the theory almost prophetically accorded with some things which we now know respecting electricity,) he was only the metaphysician. When Haüy unfolded the mechanical composition of crystals, and even demonstrated the necessary forms of their ultimate particles, he acted the part of a philosopher; but in attempting to account for the transmission of light through them, one might theorize ever so plausibly, and still be nothing more than a metaphysician. When Locke divided our ideas into those of sensation and reflection, although his division might have been incomplete, or even redundant, yet, being a classification of known phenomena, it was perfectly philosophical. But when he accounted for our sensations of different colors by the emission of differently shaped atoms from the surfaces of bodies, he was metaphysical.

Philosophy reasons rightly from right data; the reasoning, or the data, or both, of metaphysics, may be either right or wrong. A spice of metaphysics in a man's mind is a very good thing; in some writers, a slight mixture of it has made many an author popular. It flatters the reader's own consciousness of being profound, and it stimulates his imagination to ascribe uncommon resources to the writer. Most men of genius have somewhat of the metaphysical characteristic. It is the pioneer to discoveries of unknown relations among things. To improve any science, or to break into any original track of thought, one must have some tendency towards this quality. All the great chemists we ever heard of have been endued with the metaphysical impetus. It is conjecture, and fancy, and refined curiosity, which prompt them to experiment, and it is not until they confirm by fact even the most sagacious of their conjectures, that they are honored with the name of philosophers. The science of electricity, if we may strictly call it science, is at this moment half philosophy and half metaphysics. The doctrine of the mind was once almost entirely metaphysics, and rightly bore that name, which it still doubtfully bears, though very much purified from the admixture. Aristotle, however, mingled a good deal of philosophy with his speculation. His followers, and the schools of later date, made the science nearly all metaphysics again. Des Cartes and Malebranche began to restore it to its proper balance, but were still too inveterate metaphysicians to produce the requisite equilibrium. Locke combined the metaphysical and the philosophical attributes to an enviable degree. Hence the improvements which are dated from him. His followers of the French school, together with Berkeley and Hume, Hartley and Priestley, made very few real advances, in consequence of the undue preponderance of metaphysics in their speculations.

The Scotch school, so called, vibrated with too forcible a reaction to the opposite extreme. Reid and Stewart were great philosophers, and it is impossible to rise from the study of their works without large improvement and gratitude; and nature undoubtedly formed them to be also great metaphysicians. They wanted not invention, wing, or acumen. But they fastidiously and conscientiously folded up their excursive powers, or only opened them to brood over the chaos in which the science of the mind lay darkening beneath them. They struck out from the mass no brilliant revolving orb. This peculiarity, we apprehend, is the cause of a considerable depression of their original reputation, and has emboldened the critics to intrude upon Mr. Stewart's weary and honorable retreat, with asking what he has done. An insatiable world is not content with seeing the old cumbrous rubbish removed from the path of science, though the labor is performed, like that of Virgil's swain, in never so elegant a manner. To the disappointment experienced with regard to the Scotch school of mental philosophers, from whom so much was expected, and who were supposed to be making a last grand experiment, we ascribe the unmerited neglect which has been shown towards the works of the late Dr. Brown. But it is a neglect which arose from mere error and misapprehension; for he certainly had the happiness of combining the genius of the severest inductive philosophy with an adventurous metaphysical spirit, which Bacon himself neither by precept nor example condemned. We trust to make all this plainly appear by the following examination of his *Lectures on the Philosophy of the Human Mind*, although, as will be seen, we shall frequently find occasion to dissent from the author's positions. We are persuaded that his reputation as a writer is yet to advance among the votaries of true philosophy.

According to the extensive scope of the views of Dr. Brown, the Philosophy of the Human Mind comprehends the following subjects.

I. Mental Physiology.

II. General Ethics.

III. Politics.

IV. Natural Theology.

We will proceed to unfold, in the first place, the author's favorite science of Mental Physiology.

The object of all physical inquiry is twofold. We either attempt to ascertain the constituent coexisting elements of substances, as we find them at any given moment, and as they compose an apparently continuous whole, or we consider them as the subjects, or as the agents, of those changes which constitute the physical events of the system of the world. What is this piece of glass? If we consider it merely as a continuous whole, our answer will be, that it is a compound of alkaline and siliceous matter. But if we consider it as the agent or the subject of changes, we speak of its refractive powers, its fusibility at a certain temperature, its resistance to solution by the common powerful acids, and the like. In short, we consider the substances into the nature of which we inquire in these two lights alone, as they exist in space, or as they exist in time.

The foregoing views are applied by the author to the physiology of the mind. We know the essential substance neither of matter nor of mind; but the author maintains that the phenomena of thought and feeling have the same relation to the unknown internal essence of the substance mind, which a brittle or a fusible state has to that of the substance glass, or which any sensible properties whatever have to that of the substance in which they inhere. All these various phenomena of thought and feeling he regards as nothing more than modifications, or affections, or states of the mind, which is a simple, uniform principle. They may be complex, like the properties of matter, and so be susceptible of analysis, or they may be the agents and the subjects of innumerable changes among each other, and so sustain the reciprocal relation of causes and effects.

In conformity to these statements, the author proposes, in the first place, to institute a strict mental analysis, a department of philosophy which, he complains, has hitherto been much neglected. Some of our mental phenomena are evidently simple, as the feeling of pain, the sensation of color, and that of sound. Others again are complex, or composed of different simple states of the mind, as we shall soon see to be the case with Appetite, and other feelings. What the chemist does in matter, the intellectual analyst does in mind. His object is to develop the elements of any complex sentiment or emotion, and to show that it virtually bears the same relation of seeming comprehensiveness to those several elements, that is borne by a piece of glass to the various separate constituents to which it is reduced by the chemist.

In commencing his introspective analysis, Dr. Brown seizes hold of Memory as the handle and instrument of all his inquiries. On this faculty itself he scarcely bestows either definition, description, or analysis. He assumes it at once as the Δὸς ποῦ στῶ of his whole system. Let us then for the present grant him memory, if by this single mystery he promises to solve all other mysteries.

The first fortress of old error against which he marches, with this simple talisman, is Consciousness. He attacks this first, since all the varieties of those ever-changing feelings which form the subjects of his inquiry are referred to it. He maintains that it is no distinct power of the mind, as it has always been supposed to be. He rigorously denies that at one and the same moment you can have a sensation or an idea, and also a separate simultaneous feeling of consciousness about it. In the very next instant after the sensation or the idea, however, you have the memory of it. With the memory, moreover, you have an intuitive belief, that you, who just now had the sensation or idea, are the same individual being who have the remembrance of it now. Thus, between the sensation itself, the remembrance of it, and the intuitive belief of personal identity, away slips Consciousness into thin air!

On the subject of personal identity Dr. Brown most admirably argues, that no process of reasoning can ever demonstrate it, because the very essence of every argument consists in the circumstance, that the mind which adopts the conclusion irresistibly believes itself to be the same mind which held the premises. Thus this belief rises above all argument, or rather is the foundation of every reasoning process. It follows directly, that, since no argument can proceed a step without it, the belief itself is intuitive and axiomatic.

We have thus far considered only the phenomena of the mind in general; consciousness and personal identity evidently involving all states of the mind alike. The author now proceeds to consider them in the separate classes in which they may be arranged. Dismissing as incomplete and inaccurate all former arrangements of them into powers of the understanding and of the will, and into intellectual and active powers, and so forth, he proceeds to a new distribution. The following remarks on this design appear to us very just, and constitute at once a powerful recommendation of the author's labors, as well as justification of our own humble efforts in reporting them.

"A new classification, therefore, which includes, in its generic character, those qualities, [which former classifications have neglected,] will of course draw to them attention, which they could not otherwise have obtained; and the more various the views are which we take of the objects of any science, the juster consequently, because the more equal, will be the estimate which we form of them. So truly is this the case, that I am convinced, that no one has ever read over the mere terms of a new division in a science, however familiar the science may have been to him, without learning more than this new division itself, — without being struck with some property or relation, the importance of which he *now* perceives most clearly, and which he is quite astonished that he should have overlooked so long before." — *Lect.* XVI.

The following is the principle of the author's new classification.

The causes or immediate antecedents of the various mental phenomena are either foreign to the mind, or they belong to the mind itself. A change of mental state is either produced by a change in our bodily organs, or, without any cause external to itself, one state of mind is the immediate result of a former state of mind, in consequence of those laws of succession of thoughts and feelings which were established by the Creator himself.

In conformity with this distinction, he makes his first division of the phenomena of the mind, into its external and internal affections. The class of internal affections, by far the more copious and various of the two, he subdivides into two great orders, our intellectual states, and our emotions.

We have sensations or perceptions of the objects that affect our bodily organs; these he terms the sensitive or external affections of the mind. Then again we remember objects, we imagine them in new situations, we compare their relations; these he terms the intellectual states of the mind. Once more, we are moved with certain lively feelings, on the consideration of what we thus perceive, or remember, or imagine, or compare; with feelings, for example, of beauty, or sublimity, or astonishment, or love, or hate, or hope, or fear. These, and various other vivid feelings analogous to them, are our emotions.

Under the external affections of the mind, the author comprehends not only all those phenomena, or states of mind, which are commonly termed Sensations, but also all our internal organic feelings of pleasure or pain, that arise from states of the nervous system, as much as our other sensations. Many of these are commonly ranked under another head, that of Appetites, such as hunger, thirst, the desire of repose, or of change of muscular position, which follows long-continued exertion, the oppressive anxiety which arises from impeded respiration, and various other diseases, the effect of bodily uneasiness. And here occurs a characteristic instance of our author's peculiar powers of abstract analysis; an instance, if we mistake not, equally acute with that which before attempted the resolution of the supposed power of consciousness, and more luminously convincing. These Appetites, he says, evidently admit of being analyzed into two distinct elements, a pain of a peculiar species, and a subsequent desire of that which is to relieve the pain; — states of mind of which one may immediately succeed the other, but which are, unquestionably, as different in themselves, as if no such succession took place. The pain, which is one element of the appetite, is an external affection of the mind, to be classed with our other sensations; the succeeding desire, which is another element of it, is an internal affection of the mind, to be classed with our other emotions of desire. The truth is, we give one name to the combination of the two feelings, in consequence of their being so universally and immediately successive. Still, in every case, the pain is felt before the desire of relief is felt, and two states of mind manifestly compose what an imperfect analysis has hitherto presumed to be but one. All imaginable objections to these views the author arrays and removes, and we recommend the whole of these speculations (Lecture XVII.) as one of the most delightful portions of his Lectures.

Besides those particular feelings of bodily uneasiness, which, as attended by desire, constitute our Appetites, there are other affections of the same class, which, though not usually ranked with our external sensations or perceptions, because we find it difficult to ascribe them to any local organ, are unquestionably to be arranged under the same head; since they are feelings which arise as immediately and directly from a certain state of a part of the nervous system, as any of the feelings which we more commonly ascribe to external sense. Of this kind is that muscular pleasure of alacrity and action, which forms so great a part of the delight of the young of every species of living beings; and which is felt, though in a less degree, at every period of life, even the most advanced; or which, when it ceases in age, only gives place to another species of muscular pleasure, — that which constitutes the pleasure of ease, — the same species of feeling which doubles to every one the delight of exercise, by sweetening the repose to which it leads, and thus making it indirectly as well as directly a source of enjoyment.

With respect, further, to our muscular feelings, the author observes, that, though many of them may be almost unnoticed by us during the influence of stronger sensations, they are yet sufficiently powerful, when we attend to them, to render us, independently of sight and touch, in a great measure sensible of the position of our body in general, and of its various parts; and, comparatively indistinct as they are, they become in many cases, (as in the acquired perceptions of vision, for example, and equally too in various other instances, in which little attention has been paid to them by philosophers,) elements of some of the nicest and most accurate judgments which we form.

On the whole, although our author does not formally lay down a sixth sense in addition to the ancient enumeration, he certainly presents some very strong considerations in favor of ranking our Muscular Feelings as a distinct, peculiar, and independent order of sensations.

The pains of appetite, our muscular feelings, and all other mental states of this class, the author appropriately denominates, in his system, the Less Definite External Affections of Mind.

Having treated of these, he proceeds to what he ranks as the More Definite External Affections of Mind, which comprehend the feelings more commonly termed Sensations, and universally ascribed to five particular organs of sense.

On this subject our author transfers the celebrated theory of Berkeley, as to our acquired perceptions of vision, to the information given us by our other senses. In the case of sound, there is a very evident analogy to our acquired visual perceptions; since a constant reference to place mingles with our sensations of this class, in the same manner, though not so distinctly, as in our perceptions of sight. We perceive the sound, as it were, near or at a distance, in one direction rather than in another. But what should originally inform the infant that the voice he hears in the next room is nearer than the voice which sounds to him from the distance of five hundred feet? Experience, derived from his other senses, alone teaches him, in process of time, to judge with immediate and unfailing precision. The other senses the author also holds to be more or less under the same influence.

Respecting the corporeal part of the process of Perception, all that is known of it, the author acknowledges, is, that certain affections of the nervous system, including the brain, precede immediately certain affections of the mind. As to the nature of the connection between these antecedents and consequents, he thinks it never will be ascertained, and he dismisses the consideration altogether from his philosophy. The various specific affections of the nervous system, as it is spread from the brain to all the organs of sense, and indeed through every part of the body, are known; the various and corresponding affections of the mind, which follow them, are also known. With these facts taken for granted, the author proceeds in his task of analyzing these complicated, organic and corresponding mental, affections, and discovering and estimating the whole degree and body of knowledge (together with the intricate and often fugitive process of acquiring it) which they furnish of the External World, — in which external world he includes even our organs of sense themselves.

He argues at great length, that our five senses alone are in themselves insufficient to give us any knowledge or belief of an external world of matter. In justice to him, let it be borne in mind that he lays down the essential and constituent elements of our idea of matter to be only two, namely, Resistance and Extension. Sight, sound, smell, taste, touch, meaning by touch only the sensation connected with the superficial exterior integument that surrounds the muscular system, he contends, are nothing more than states of mind, which we might experience for ever, without thinking of ascribing them to anything foreign from ourselves, in like manner as we never ascribe any of our internal joys or sorrows to an external cause. Whence, then, do we obtain our notion of something out of ourselves, and whence do we obtain a knowledge of matter? All our information on these points he would derive, originally, from our Muscular Feelings alone. With the experience gained from these muscular feelings, the operations of the five senses are so perpetually, universally, and intimately associated, as to make the senses appear the original sources of the knowledge in question. We decline going over the grounds on which Dr. Brown undertakes to remove the delusion, attacking each sense by itself, particularly that of simple touch, and stripping them all of their long asserted and allowed pretensions on this score.

But though we are so indulgent as to spare our readers this merely preparatory discussion, they need not think to resist, while we lead them, as we now shall do, into the very central labyrinth of the speculations of our metaphysical Dædalus. Assuming that he has proved the senses to have no original concern in conveying to us the idea of an external world, he transfers at once the seat of discussion to the very region of the muscles themselves, leaving the five senses far behind, in the custody of Aristotle, Mr. Locke, Dr. Reid, and the rest of the whole body of his pondering predecessors. With a species of indagation altogether characteristic of himself, or, we might say, of himself and Dr. Darwin, he carries us back to the first semi-instinctive movements of an infant's muscles. He watches its repeatedly and gradually opening and closing fingers, until a solid body is interposed within its little grasp, which impedes the accustomed muscular contractions. It is now that the infant acquires, as our author maintains, the first real and original notion of "outness," of something foreign to himself, of something which is not himself. Those petty muscular motions he feels to be all his own; but the moment that resistance to them takes place, he ascribes the new sensation to a foreign cause.

Here we pause to interpose a stricture. Dr. Brown appears to us not to have carried his analysis quite far enough to be perfectly consistent with himself. If an interruption of the child's muscular motions is sufficient to give it a notion of outness, why, for a like reason, is not an interruption of its gazing on a bright object sufficient to give it the same notion? But this the author will not allow; since, as we have seen, he denies that from mere sight alone we can acquire the least belief or idea of an external world. Now, he has not told us what there is peculiar to the child's muscular feelings, the interruption of which should draw its thoughts out of itself, more than an interruption of the exercise of its visual faculties. He does indeed in one place, we believe, obscurely hint, that, as the muscular motions of the child originate from himself, and continue by his own will, whereas the sight of the bright object comes without any effort on his part, continues without his volition, and is withdrawn without resisting his will at all, this difference between the two kinds of interruption is sufficient to account, in the former case, for the child's having a notion of something foreign from himself, while in the other there is nothing more than a mere succession of natural feelings or states passing through his mind. But the author neither places much emphasis on this distinction, nor brings it forward frequently, which he would certainly have done had he relied much on it. Nor are we willing to admit it as a sufficient explanation of the difficulty in question. For aught we can discern, the child's muscular motion may be stopped, and even his will resisted, and yet the feelings resulting from such interruptions shall still be nothing more than so many simple states of mind succeeding one another, like phantasmagoric pictures, without the necessity of his referring them to anything abroad.

How, then, shall this chasm be filled up in our author's investigation? We would say thus. The child, we apprehend, never begins to adopt the belief of anything external to himself until he perceives that some accustomed object of gratification is *out of his immediate reach*, and requires him to originate a voluntary locomotion in order to recover it. Indeed, all that can be understood of an external world, at any period of our lives, is simply that which we cannot reach, and over which we can have no control, except by moving the body or the hand from its usual position. We allow, with our author, that muscular pressure gives even to the almost new-born infant a perfect notion of one element of our complex idea of matter, that is, Resistance. But we think Dr. Brown should not so gratuitously have coupled the notion of Outness with that of Resistance. The former we conceive to be attained even not until long after the idea of Extension, the other element of our idea of matter, is attained. We conceive our author to be thus misled in the very way against which he is constantly guarding his readers, and to be betrayed into that defective analysis which he complains of in former philosophers. In subsequent life, the perpetual and close connection between our ideas of something resisting and of something external has induced him to suppose that they both spring up together in the infant's mind. But we have learned in his own school to question our teacher, and to discern another source of the peculiar notion in question.

The etymological meaning of the word *external*, and indeed every meaning which is ever attached to it, implies a change or difference of place. As long as the child is locally at rest, sensations of a thousand varieties, "states of mind" both internal and external, may throng upon him in successive waves, and yet all appear to be as much parts of himself as any spontaneous pain or pleasure within. No matter whether it be a smell, or a sight, or a sound, or a feeling of resistance, or a thwarting of his will, or any other feeling which begins and terminates at or in himself; we regard all these feelings as exactly on the same level with respect to the point under consideration. But it is the *separation* of the resisting and extended object from himself, it is the *withdrawal* of something from his power, it is the *dropping* of the rattle out of his hand, it is the *removal* of the fount of infant life from his lips, that reveals to him the secret of something foreign to himself, and convinces him that all existence is not involved in his own, and teaches him the first of that long series of lessons, which he is to be learning through life, comprehending the whole variety of local relations in which he stands to outward things, from the spoon that moves towards and recedes from his mouth, to the remotest star whose distance can be scarcely reached even by the imagination.

But to go back on the track of Dr. Brown. The infant has now acquired his notion of Resistance. It remains to be seen how the other element of our idea of matter, namely, the notion of Extension, is obtained by this miniature metaphysician.

The little fingers before mentioned gradually and repeatedly close and open, until the child has a notion of the length of time it requires to shut his finger down upon the palm of his hand; meaning by length of time, the accustomed succession of different feelings attendant upon each gradual contraction of the muscle. On the interposition of the resisting object, as before described, and the consequent interruption of the muscular contraction, the child, according to our author, has a notion of the remaining length of time which it would have taken for the finger to arrive at the palm of the hand. Immediately the interposed object becomes a representative of this remaining length of time. If the diameter of the object interposed be small, the remaining length of time will be proportionably small, and consequently the infant's notion of the length of the interposed object corresponds. If the diameter be large, there is a corresponding reverse in the infant's idea, in consequence of the larger remaining length of time. Thus Length, with our author, in its true, original, and significant acceptation, indicates only Time, and is transferred metaphorically from time to longitudinal extension. This doctrine he confirms by a number of reasonings, facts, and experiments.

Allowing, then, that the infant derives his notion of the length of an object from the remaining time which that object intercepts, as above described, the next question is as to the origin of his notion of Breadth, which is the other element of our author's idea of extension. When, after obtaining an idea of a particular length from one finger alone, a second closes, or rather the two close together, and are interrupted by the same object, the infant has an idea of two separate, concurring, coexisting lengths. When three, when four, close together, he has the idea of three, of four separate, concurring, coexisting lengths. And what is this but the idea of breadth?

Dr. Brown allows that nothing can be more vague, indistinct, and imperfect than the earliest notions which the child thus acquires of the elements of extension. But every instant that he is awake, he is making new experiments; his muscles never are at rest; the imperfection of one experiment is corrected by the next; and, particularly, other muscles besides those of the hands and fingers are put in motion; the experiments of the arm in every direction extend and confirm those of the smaller members, and the mere muscular perceptions of the child are thus growing more and more distinct and definite every day.

All these muscular operations and feelings are, by

the constitution of our frames, so closely connected with accompanying *tactual* sensations, that the latter habitually become representatives of the former, and we are led to believe that we measure dimensions by Touch alone, when it is only a secondary and subordinate instrument in the business.

We are mistaken if every reader will not concede much truth and originality to these speculations, whatever may be thought of the accuracy of some of the details, and however nearly they may occasionally seem to border on the ludicrous. We have no hesitation in ascribing new and important discoveries to Dr. Brown, in this department of mental physiology. We fear not frankly and gratefully to avow our obligations to him for extending and enlightening the domain of our knowledge, with respect to subjects that must necessarily be near and familiar to us through the whole course of life. Let any one, after becoming familiar with these speculations upon the instrumentality of our muscular system, in conveying to us a knowledge of the external world, betake himself to Dr. Reid's "Inquiry into the Human Mind," particularly to his chapter on Touch, and he will at once be convinced of the extraordinary meagreness of his own former views, and be gratified with the new and permanent light which has here been thrown on the intellectual economy.

From these speculations on the manner in which we acquire a belief of the external world, a very natural transition is made to the theory of Berkeley, who denies the existence of matter, and holds the universe to be only a combination of ideas. The sceptical systems which have been erected on this doctrine owe their plausibility to his assumed fundamental error, that ideas can exist separately from the mind. Dr. Brown's simple principle, that ideas are nothing more than the mind itself existing in certain states, would have saved a world of perplexing scepticism and unprofitable controversy.

Several lectures are devoted to the refutation of Dr. Reid's pretensions, who, as many of our readers know, has enjoyed the glory of irrefragably demonstrating the existence of an external world against the sceptical reasonings of Hume and other Pyrrhonists. As to the main point of dispute between Dr. Reid and Mr. Hume, our author declares it to be entirely imaginary, since the sceptic himself, after all his refined reasonings to the contrary, allows it to be impossible not to believe in an external world, which very proposition is the grand artillery that Dr. Reid leads against his opponent with so much parade; both the disputants maintaining with equal earnestness, for their own purposes, that the existence of an external world can never be proved by argument.

In the course of these discussions, we have another instance of the same acute analysis which we have already seen exhibited on the subjects of Appetite and Consciousness. Dr. Reid had made great use of Perception, which, with former philosophers, he considered a distinct and unique faculty of the mind, that, immediately upon sensation taking place, acquaints us with the objects without. Dr. Brown proves this to be a cumbrous addition to the mental apparatus. The two elements to which he reduces this supposed faculty are, first, a sensation, and, next, a mere reference by the associating principle to some extended, resisting substance, which we have before known only by sensation. Thus, between sensation and association, Perception escapes into impalpable shade! The author, however, allows it to be a convenient term to express the complex process above analyzed, but denies that there is any such separate and single faculty of the mind. Whoever chooses to see Dr. Reid's fame still farther lowered in several particulars, may be amply gratified in consulting the relentless pages of our author.

In analyzing the feelings ascribed to Vision, Dr. Brown claims to have made considerable extensions and improvements upon the wonderful discoveries of Berkeley. That philosopher, together with his successors, had confined his demonstrations to the distance and magnitude of objects alone. They still thought that we perceive the visible figures of bodies by an immediate and original shape, that presents itself to the "mind's eye" as well as the body's. Our author, however, maintains, that our only immediate sensation in the case is that of Color, and nothing more; color, without even extension. This color is by long and varied experience intimately associated with our tactual and muscular feelings of extension and figure, and therefore suggests them. It is true the rays of light form images on the retina; and so do odorous particles from a small flower undoubtedly form a distinct figure as they reach the olfactory organ. But the author maintains, that in neither case does the mind immediately perceive the figure of the external object. He also exhibits many incongruities and inconsistencies involved in the common belief, and we recommend his twenty-ninth Lecture, in which these speculations occur, as a rare piece of delectably hard reading, and of ingenious and staggering argumentation.

We have now exhibited a sketch of our author's remarks on the class of our External Affections of the Mind considered simply. But it is not always simply that they exist. They often occur in combination with other feelings. It is therefore to these complex states of the mind that he next proceeds.

He applies his penetrating analysis here to Attention, which has been supposed to be a separate and simple faculty of the mind. This too dissolves at the touch of his wand. What is Attention? It is but a *continued desire* to know more vividly and distinctly than before any objects of our perception, accompanied always by such a voluntary, fixed contraction of the requisite muscles, as shall enable the object to act with the greatest power on whatever sense we are employing. Now, Desire is only one of the simple emotions of the mind. The author lays it down as an ultimate law of our mental constitution, that all our emotions tend to give the objects of perception an increased vividness and distinctness. And it is to this law, therefore, that he traces the peculiar effects of what is called Attention in making objects more vivid and distinct. But between the desire, which is a common and well-known emotion of the mind, and the consequent muscular contraction, which is an affection of the body, what becomes of the unique *faculty* of Attention? It is not, as has always been supposed, a simple mental state, but a process or a combination of feelings.

Here closes the consideration of the External Affections of the Mind. Next in order of discussion follow the Internal Affections. These were before subdivided into Intellectual States, and Emotions.

The Intellectual States are reduced into two classes, the Phenomena of Simple Suggestion, and the Phenomena of Relative Suggestion.

By Simple Suggestion is meant the readiness of certain feelings or conceptions to arise, after certain other feelings or conceptions, in trains of longer or shorter continuance. Thus a house suggests the person who lives in it; that person suggests the profession that he follows; the profession suggests a multitude of men; the multitude suggests a whole country; the country the government, and so forth. Such a train of indefinite length may evidently take place in the mind, without any relation being observed between its successive links Our Emotions may also constitute links in this train. The author gives good reasons for preferring the term Suggestion to Association.

Next, by the phenomena of Relative Suggestion are implied our feelings of a different order, that arise when two or more objects are contemplated together, feelings of their agreement, or difference, or proportion, or some one or other of the variety of their relations. Though at first sight this classification of our Intellectual States may appear to be excessively simplified, yet the author is confident, that all the intellectual powers of which writers on this branch of science speak are only modes of these two, as they exist simply, or as they exist in combination with some desire more or less permanent.

The laws which regulate simple suggestion are reduced to three: Resemblance or Analogy, Contrast, and Contiguity in time or place. If one feeling or idea resemble another, it may suggest it. If it be of an opposite description to another, it may suggest it. If it has been felt by us before in local or momentary contiguity with another, it may suggest it. Whoever will watch the trains of thought and feeling that pass through his own mind, will perceive that they follow each other in endless succession, only according to one or another of these three laws. By a refinement of analysis, the author believes that he might reduce them all to one; but he retains this obvious and tangible division, for the purpose of more distinctly exhibiting the various characteristics of the mind.

The difference between genius and mediocrity he places in this: — the simple suggestions of genius are those generally of resemblance or analogy; but if a man's suggestions are commonly those of proximity in time or place, he is but a creeping, ordinary person. We cannot give the author's splendid, varied, and extended illustrations of this distinction.

The three primary laws of simple suggestion are, however, very much modified and affected in their operation by several circumstances, which the author denominates the Secondary Laws of Suggestion, and which he reduces to the nine following classes. He finds that our Suggestions are various accordingly as the original feelings which they revive were, — first, of longer or shorter continuance; secondly, more or less lively; thirdly, more or less frequently present; fourthly, more or less recent; fifthly, more or less pure from the mixture of other feelings; sixthly, that they vary according to differences of original constitution; seventhly, according to differences of temporary emotion; eighthly, according to changes produced in the state of the body; and, ninthly, according to general tendencies produced by prior habits.

The illustration of these secondary laws, occupying the thirty-seventh Lecture, presents an elegant specimen of original, true, and beautiful philosophy.

In defence of his substitution of the word Suggestion for Association, the author objects to the latter, as implying some previous link or bond of connection between the mental feelings said to be associated. His greatest and plainest argument against such a supposition is, that an object, seen for the first time, suggests many new conceptions; which renders the notion of any former association purely absurd. His philosophy pretends to go no farther than the simple fact of the rise of one mental feeling from the occurrence of another, while the common phraseology introduces a new mystery, and even involves, as he shows, unavoidable absurdities. That our suggestions do not follow each other loosely and confusedly is no proof, he contends, of prior associations in the mind, but merely of the general constitutional tendency of the mind to exist, successively, in states that have certain relations to each other.

Then follows a series of some of his most brilliant achievements. Former philosophers have been at considerable pains in enumerating and describing various intellectual powers, such as Conception, Memory, Recollection, Fancy, Imagination, Habit, and the like. Dr. Brown proposes to show, that this variety of powers is unnecessarily and unphilosophically devised. He would reduce them to the principle of Simple Suggestion; or, at least, to this simple principle, in combination with some of those other principles which were pointed out as parts of our mental constitution, in his arrangement of the phenomena of mind.

First, the power of Conception, so called, where the perception of one object excites the notion of some absent object, he allows to belong to the mind; but he maintains that this is the very function which is meant by the power of Suggestion itself, and that, if the conception be separated from the suggestion, nothing will remain to constitute the power of suggestion, which is only another name for the same power. There is not, in any case of suggestion, both a suggestion and a conception, more than there is, in any case of vision, both a vision and sight. What one glance is to the capacity of vision, one conception is to the capacity of suggestion. We may see innumerable objects in succession; we may conceive innumerable objects in succession. But we see them because we are susceptible of vision; we conceive them because we have that susceptibility of spontaneous suggestion by which conceptions arise after each other in regular trains.

The next supposed intellectual power to which he calls our attention is Memory. This, he very acutely maintains, is not a distinct intellectual faculty, but is merely a suggestion, and a feeling of relation, the relation of priority in time. When we think of a house, without any relation to former time, or any other relation, we have only a simple suggestion of it; but when we think of it as the abode where we *formerly* lived, the suggestion receives the name of memory. Now, between the power of simple suggestion and the general power of feeling relations, hereafter to be considered, what becomes of such a faculty as Memory? It vanishes before the analytical magic of Dr. Brown.

So Recollection, which is conceived to be a kind of voluntary memory, and particularly under our control, he reduces to "the coexistence of some vague and indistinct *desire* with our simple trains of suggestion." As long as the desire of remembering a particular event or object continues to exist, a *variety* of suggestions, more or less directly connected with the event or object, spontaneously arise in the mind, until we either obtain, at last, the remembrance which we wish, or, by some new suggestion, are led into a new channel of thought, and forget altogether that there was anything which we wished to remember.

Next, Imagination is reduced to its component elements. The momentary groups of images that arise, independently of any desire or choice on our part, and arise in almost every minute to almost every mind, constitute by far the greater number of our imaginations. Here is evidently only a process of simple suggestion. But there are cases in which desire, or intention of some sort, accompanies the whole or the chief part of the process, and it is of these cases that we are accustomed to think, in speaking of this supposed power. By Imagination, in the common use of the word, is meant the creative power of the imagination. But is even this a separate and peculiar faculty of the mind? The following is the process by which the author shows that it is not. First, there arises to the mind of any given Imaginer some conception, or *simple suggestion* of a particular subject; next, this subject excites in him a *desire* of producing by it some beautiful or interesting result.

This desire, like every other vivid feeling, has a degree of permanence which our vivid feelings only possess; and, by its permanence, tends to keep the accompanying conception of the subject, which is the object of the desire, also permanent before us; and while it is thus permanent, the usual spontaneous suggestions take place; conception following conception, in rapid but relative series, and our judgment, all the time, approving and rejecting, according to these relations of *fitness* and *unfitness* to the subject which it perceives in parts of the train.

Such is the author's picture of the state, or successive states, of the mind, in the formation of every species of production which goes by the name of a work of imagination. It is not, he insists, the exercise of a single power, but the development of various susceptibilities, — of *desire*, — of *simple suggestion*, by which conceptions rise after conceptions, — of judgment or *relative suggestion*, by which a feeling of relative fitness or unfitness arises, on the contemplation of the conceptions that have thus spontaneously presented themselves. The results of this process will, of course, be different in value according to the constitution of different minds, and also according to the various influences of those secondary laws of suggestion which were before pointed out as modifying the primary. In the mind of inventive genius, conceptions follow each other, chiefly according to the relations of *Analogy*, which are infinite, and therefore admit of constant novelty; while in the humbler mind, the prevailing tendencies of suggestion are those of former *Contiguity* of objects in place and time, which are, of course, limited, and by their very nature confined to conceptions that cannot confer on the mind in which they arise the honor of originality. The forty-second Lecture, containing the full development and illustration of the foregoing principles, is one of the finest, one of the most interesting, in the series. Imagination and fancy, however, seem to be used throughout as synonymous, or at least with no attempt at distinguishing them. Where the author endeavors to show the spiritual mechanism, as it were, by which, in conducting a work of imagination, some images are selected in preference to others, the train of discussion is peculiar to himself, and contains a full condensation of some of his most original doctrines.

The next Lecture contains two very curious speculations, in opposition to the doctrine that Habit is an ultimate and peculiar law of the mind, and explaining all its phenomena by the mere operation of simple suggestion; after which, the absurdity and incompetency of the Hartleian system of vibrations and vibratiuncles are in various ways exposed and refuted.

We now proceed to describe the other class of internal affections of the mind, comprehending our feelings of Relative Suggestion, that is, all our feelings of relation. There is an original tendency or susceptibility of the mind, by which, on perceiving together different objects, we are instantly, without the intervention of any other mental process, sensible of their relation in certain respects, as truly as there is an original tendency or susceptibility of the mind, by which, when external objects are present, and have produced a certain affection of our sensorial organ, we are instantly affected with the primary elementary feelings of perception. These relations we recognize both among external objects and our mental feelings of every kind, and they are divided by our author into two general classes. We perceive relations among them as they coexist at any given instant in groups, without any reference to succession in time. Thus, you feel that two is to twelve, as twelve is to seventy-two, and you feel this, merely by considering the numbers together, without any regard to time. No notion of change or succession is involved in it. This is the first general class of relations. Next, we perceive relations among objects and among our feelings, considered with reference to time, as successive. Thus you perceive the relation of effect and cause between the bloom of summer and the warmth of its sky.

The first of our classes of Relations, those of which the subjects are regarded without reference to time, are subdivided into five different kinds. First, there is the relation of Position. Mark the furniture standing about your room; one article on your right, another a little farther on, another directly opposite, and so forth. Secondly, the relation of Resemblance or of Difference. Observe in your path two flowers of the same tints and forms, or of different odors. Thirdly, the relation of proportion. Think of the equality between the vertical angles formed by two straight lines, which cut one another; of the pairs of numbers four, six,—five, twenty,—and your mind exists immediately in that state which constitutes the feeling of Proportion. Fourthly, the relation of Degree. Listen to one voice, and then to a voice which is louder; smell one flower, and then another which is more or less fragrant. Fifthly, the relation of Comprehension. Consider a house and its different apartments; a tree and its branches, stems, and foliage; a horse and its limbs, trunk, head, — and you have the feeling of the relation of parts to one comprehensive whole. By some subtilty and refinement of analysis, these divisions might be made fewer, but they are sufficiently distinct for every purpose of arrangement.

Passing over the first of these five classes, the author directs our attention to the relation of Resemblance. To this principle he ascribes all *classification*, and consequently everything which is valuable in language. It is the use of *general terms*, that is to say, of terms founded on the feeling of resemblance, which alone gives to language its power, enabling us to condense, in a single word, innumerable objects, which, individually, would be utterly impossible to be grasped by us in our conceptions. It would be unjust to refuse to Dr. Brown a chaplet of glory for the masterly penetration with which he has treated the subject of general ideas, and the unrivalled degree of light and simplicity diffused by him through dark, tangled difficulties, amid which all former philosophers, without exception, had been hopelessly groping. Time was, when, if we had wished to make a common man tremble, and a wise one appear foolishly profound, we could not have devised a more successful method, than to ask them how they would explain an *abstract general notion.* The very phrase is even now bewildering and distressing, in consequence of old associations involved with it. Yes, even now, when our admirable author has revealed to the world, — what the world may well wonder it never clearly and scientifically knew before, though all, down to child and idiot, must have felt and practised upon it every day, — that the feeling of *similarity* is that which constitutes a general notion. "The perception of objects, the feeling of their resemblance in certain respects, the invention of a name for these circumstances of felt resemblance,—what can be more truly and readily conceivable than this process! And yet on this process, apparently so simple, has been founded all that controversy as to *universals*, which so long distracted the schools; and which, far more wonderfully, (for the distraction of the schools by a few unintelligible words scarcely can be counted wonderful,) continues still to perplex philosophers with difficulties which themselves have made; difficulties which they could not even have made to themselves, if they had thought for a single moment of the nature of that feeling of the relation of similarity which we are now considering." (*Lecture* XLV.)

The point in dispute was shortly this. One party maintained, that, besides all the objects which we can know individually, there are in existence certain universal forms comprehending whole classes of objects. What does the word *triangle* represent? Surely not a triangle of three equal sides only, nor one of two equal sides only, nor one merely of three unequal sides. If it signify anything, they contended, it must signify a universal triangle, comprehending all possible properties of all possible triangles. So of the words man, tree, horse, flower, and other common substantives. The phrase Universals *a parte rei*, which they gave to these supposed general essences, was expressive of real existences, and they who maintained the doctrine itself assumed the appellation of Realists. Pythagoras, Plato, and their followers in the schools and closets of two thousand years, held this doctrine with more or fewer modifications. The last lingering relic of its influence in England probably died with Dr. Price.

On the other hand, their opponents contended, that there is nothing in existence but particular and individual objects alone; and that the *names* which we give to whole classes of them are entirely creatures of our own arbitrary invention, employed, for the sake of convenience, to comprehend many particulars under one general term. These philosophers, for an obvious reason, were called Nominalists. Their doctrine dates from Roscellinus, a native of Brittany, who lived in the eleventh century. Abelard, Occam, Hobbes, Berkeley, Hume, Dr. Campbell, and Dugald Stewart, have been among the most celebrated of its defenders. The Emperor Louis of Bavaria, and Louis the Eleventh of France, took sides on the question, and led to the field the usual arguments of kings.

The great stumbling-block of the Nominalists has been, the *principle* according to which we conduct the classification of objects, and the comprehension of many under one general term. They have considered it as purely a matter of arbitrary performance on the part of men; and have never formally explained what constitutes those classes of objects to which we give a common name. They have not allowed that there is any other mental operation in the business of classification, besides the perception of objects, and the immediate employment of general terms. Dr. Brown has satisfactorily developed the true intermediate operation of the mind between these two; that is to say, *a perception of the relation of resemblance* among whatever objects we rank under one general term. The consideration of this relative suggestion elucidates all the mystery, and reconciles nearly every difficulty. It allows to the Realist, not indeed his universal forms and universal ideas, but a real operation of the mind, which fills up the hideous chasm that offended him, when persuaded to believe that there was nothing in existence to correspond with a name or order. It grants to the Nominalist the whole absurdity of Universals *a parte rei*, but it presses upon him the existence of that which he denied, though he needed it; namely, a general notion in the mind, as the ground and reason for the employment of general terms. If it were the *name* only, which, as they say, forms the classification, and not that previous relative *feeling*, or general notion of resemblance of some sort, which the name denotes, then might *anything*, insists Dr. Brown, be classed with *anything*, and be classed with equal propriety.

Dr. Brown is far from claiming to be the first who conjectured, that there is some intermediate operation of the mind serving as a transition between the ideas of particular objects and the generalization of them by universal terms. There was formerly the sect of "Conceptualists," who maintained that we *conceive* of universal ideas, and give corresponding names to them though they do not exist in reality. Locke and Reid were the more modern disciples of this school. But this argument has been successfully wielded against them, that it is as impossible for us to *conceive* of a triangle, or a man, comprehending in their respective natures the various and contradictory properties of all possible triangles and all possible men, as that there should be in existence the universal forms of such monsters of thought.

Adam Smith had expressly pointed out, indeed, this principle of resemblance used in generalization. But when Dr. Brown took the field, the victory was considered to be in the hands of the Nominalists. How he has snatched the prize away from them, and become at once umpire and conqueror, may be learned from the foregoing sketch, and more at large and satisfactorily from the author's own extended speculations, which he concludes, along with the minor work, by saying: "There have been Realists, Nominalists, Conceptualists. It is as a Relationist that I would technically distinguish myself."

On recurring to Professor Stewart's Elements of the Philosophy of the Human Mind, to see whether *resemblance*, as the principle of classification, could have escaped so acute and profound a thinker, we find that he does suggest it, in his introductory observations on the faculty of abstraction, though unwarily and by chance as it were; and that he seems altogether unconscious of the extensive influence which it possesses in the operations of the mind. That, in the progress of his inquiries, he loses sight of this principle, and ascribes omnipotent influence to the arbitrary use of names, must be evident to all who peruse his fourth chapter.

If Dr. Brown has left anything to be desired in this part of his philosophy, it is a more exact and distinct description of what he means by Resemblance. Perhaps the notion is not to be defined, but must be left to the consciousness of the inquirer, like the explanation of a color or a sound. Yet we can easily conceive that an obdurate Nominalist, before he yields his ground, might demand some definition of this mysterious and flexible cement, which unites into one class objects so unlike in some respects as an acute angle and an obtuse angle, or a man and an insect, an elephant and an animalcule, or a globular atom and the world. Is it possible to hit upon an explanation of Resemblance, which shall comprehend the infinitely multiplied cases in which it exists among objects, forms, motions, and conceptions, that involve at the same instant infinitely multiplied diversities? We decline entering now upon so shadowy a speculation, wishing, however, that our author had devoted a Lecture or two to its prosecution.

Among the five species of relations before enumerated, of which one, that is, Resemblance, has just been treated, the reader must recollect that of Comprehension, or the relation of a whole to its parts. To this our author next proceeds. The relative suggestion, which involves this relation, is considered by him as the great single and simple instrument of our reasonings; nay, its continued operation is that which, according to him, involves the whole process of reasoning. He begins with single propositions. In every proposition, he says, that which is affirmed is a part of that of which it is affirmed. Snow is white. *White* is one of the many feelings which constitute your complex notion of snow. For a proof that reasoning consists of a number of propositions of this kind, each involving this relative notion of comprehension, we give an example, in the words of the author, of a somewhat extended, abstract, moral argument, as an extreme case.

"When I say a man is fallible, I state a quality involved in the nature of man, as any other part of an aggregate is involved in any other comprehending whole. When I add, he may therefore err, even when he thinks himself least exposed to error, I state what is involved in the notion of his *fallibility*. When I say, he therefore must not expect that all men will think as he does, even on points which appear to him to have no obscurity, I state that which is involved in the possibility of his and their erring even on such points. When I say, that he therefore should not dare to punish those who merely differ from him, and who may be right even in differing from him, I state what is involved in the absurdity of the expectation, that all men should think as he does. And when I say, that any particular legislative act of intolerance is as unjust as it is absurd, I state only what is involved in the impropriety of attempting to punish those who have no other guilt than that of differing in opinion from others, who are confessedly of a nature as fallible as their own." —*Lecture* XLVIII.

Granting, then, that the process of reasoning is nothing but the perpetual evolution of successive parts, by which, at each new step, that which was just now a part takes its turn to be considered as a whole, and some one of its own parts to be detected by the reasoner, and so onward, till he has arrived at some desired or unexpected end of his investigations,—yet it is evident, that, for the purpose of successful ratiocination, the propositions should follow each other in a certain order. How is it, then, that they arrange themselves, as they rise in succession, in this necessary order?

Mr. Locke's and the common opinion is, that we have a certain *sagacity*, by which we find out each successive step that occurs in a rightly ordered course of reasoning. But this is only explaining the difficulty by the difficulty itself. The question still remains, what the order of propositions is, which some persons have more, and some less sagacity, or rather facility and readiness, in seizing upon than others. The whole seeming mystery of this order, in the propositions which form our longest processes of reasoning, depends, according to Dr. Brown, on the *regularity of the laws* which guide our *simple* suggestions. In the first place, it is necessary that we should have a *continued desire* to come to some conclusion on any given subject. This continued desire, the nature of all our emotions being more permanent than our flitting and restless intellectual states, keeps the subject itself constantly before our minds; then, by the primary laws of suggestion before described, the conception of the original subject suggests various other *conceptions*. This is the second of the three stages in the process. Now to different minds the conceptions suggested are notoriously different. A man cannot *will* any new conception in a train of reasoning, for that would be to suppose the conception already in his mind. Nor does the same man reason equally well, nor even in the same manner, on a given subject, at different times. To-day you can arrive by five steps of reasoning at a certain conclusion, which yesterday more circuitously cost you ten. Another man perhaps might never arrive at your conclusion, in consequence of his conceptions obstinately taking a different course, even when starting from the same subject with yourself. Yet his reasoning may be perfectly correct, as well as yours; the difference between the conclusions arising from the difference between the conceptions suggested. We must, however, remember that there is a third stage in the process, which is, to feel the relation of Comprehension, as above stated, between any conception as a whole and some one of its parts.

And different men are also worse or better reasoners accordingly as they have a less or greater tendency to feel this relation.

In the foregoing subtile speculations, which we have taken much pains to represent in the most intelligible and favorable manner that a severe abstract would allow, the author has indeed ingeniously accounted for the various opinions existing among mankind, and has thus taught a philosophical lesson of comprehensive charity. But we must confess we looked for more. Is it come to this? Does reason depend for its authority on the accidental conceptions of men? We want a rule, that shall decide between the two opposite conclusions at which equally acute reasoners may, and do so often, arrive. We do not like that there should be *occasion* for charity. We are anxious for uniformity, though not in the way by which legislative theologians would enforce it. Perhaps such a rule is never to be discovered in our imperfect world, where, from unavoidable circumstances, different conceptions must necessarily arise in different minds. But this is the very point, if it must be so, on which we regret that Dr. Brown did not more emphatically dwell. Was he unwilling to confess the weakness of that very instrument with which he has wrought so many triumphs? No man could have illustrated the subject more happily. He too, with his rare union of penetration and philosophical devotion, might have pointed out, with perhaps unrivalled felicity, what consolations mankind still possess in the absence of an infallible and convincing test of true reasoning, and what limits the Almighty himself has established for our safety in the very constitution of our minds, when he placed us in this dark, agitated, and doubtful state.

Perhaps an interesting sketch of the various orders of intellects might be taken in connection with Dr. Brown's views and classifications of the simple and relative suggestions. A mind, for instance, which has a peculiar tendency to feel the relation of Comprehension between any whole subject and all its possible parts or properties, is happily adapted, according to the theory just given, to logic, reasoning, and demonstration in general. If the tendency of a mind be to feel the relation of Proportion, (though with some subtilty this relation may be reduced to the former,) its inclination is to mathematical demonstration. If it be chiefly inclined to perceive the relation of Resemblance or Difference, it deals in the generalizations of philosophy or in the distinctions of wit. If its habit be to look for the relation of Degree, or comparison, it will be likely to excel in exquisite taste and judgment. If its leading tendency be to feel only the relation of Position, it is of an humbler order. There are a few minds which seem to be blessed with equal and decided capacities for all these five relative suggestions; and if the same minds also are gifted with tendencies towards the higher order of simple suggestions, that is to say, the suggestions of Analogy, before dwelt upon, which will almost infinitely multiply the resources of new conceptions among which relations are to be felt; and if also their simple suggestions of proximity in place or time be unusually abundant, meaning thereby, apart from the author's nomenclature, only a strong and ready memory, — on such minds nature has conferred a singular and enviable pre-eminence. Of course, the infinite diversities among different minds will follow the corresponding distributions which nature or circumstances may make of the foregoing tendencies, modified also, be it observed, by the secondary laws of suggestion already enumerated.

Dr. Brown skilfully overthrows the thrice-slain syllogistic system, robbing it even of the little reputation it still possessed as a mode of communicating knowledge. He shows that it is in this light, if possible, still more defective than as a mode of acquiring it.

Besides the Relations of Coexistence, the five classes of which have been now considered, there is one more order, which involves the notion of time, or priority and subsequence, and these the author denominates Relations of Succession. They are of two classes. "They are relations either of *casual* or of *invariable* antecedence or consequence; and we distinguish these as clearly in our thought, as we distinguish any other two relations. We speak of events which happened after other events, — as mere dates in chronology. We speak of other events, as the effects of events or circumstances that preceded them. The relations of *invariable* antecedence and consequence, in distinction from merely *casual* antecedence and consequence, is this relation of *causes and effects.*" Our notions of the fitness or unfitness of objects to produce certain results are ascribed by the author to our Relative Suggestions of Succession. "All practical science is the knowledge of these aptitudes of things in their various circumstances of combination, as every art is the employment of them, in conformity with this knowledge, with a view to those future changes which they tend to produce in all the different circumstances in which objects can be placed. To know how to add any enjoyment to life, or how to lessen any of its evils, is nothing more in any case than to know the relation which objects bear to each other, as antecedent and consequent, some form of that particular relation which we are considering."

The faculty of Taste the author analyzes into two separate elements, one of which he refers to this feeling of the Relation of Succession. One of these elements is the existence of certain *emotions* of admiration or disgust that arise in the mind at the perception of various objects in nature and art. The other element, which involves the feeling of the Relation of Succession, is the knowledge of the particular forms, colors, sounds, or conceptions that are most likely to be followed by those emotions.

The last specimen of Dr. Brown's analytical achievements of this kind which we shall now present, is his explanation of Abstraction, a faculty by which we are supposed to be capable of separating in our thought certain parts of our complex notions, and of considering them thus abstracted from the rest. But the whole mystery of this supposed faculty is nothing more than the perception of the relation of resemblance between two or more objects in certain common properties, without voluntarily or even consciously separating or regarding those other properties in which the objects are unlike. If we are capable of perceiving a resemblance of some sort when we look at a swan and on snow, why should we be astonished, he asks, that we have invented the word *whiteness* to signify the common circumstance of resemblance? Or why should we have recourse, for this feeling of whiteness itself, to any mysterious capacity of the mind, but that which evolves to us the similarity which we are acknowledged to be capable of feeling? Thus dissolves the last *horrida crux* that has tormented so many metaphysical as well as unmetaphysical inquirers.

We have now exhibited Dr. Brown's outlines of the External Affections of the Mind, and its purely Intellectual States; two of the three leading divisions into which he distributes all our mental states or feelings. His peculiar and prominent claims to originality here may be suggested in one word, by mentioning his exhibition of the predominant share of influence which the Muscular System exerts in the first class of feelings, and his analytical reduction of the whole of the second class to Simple Suggestions and Felt Relations.

The Emotions remain now to be considered, before completing the author's system of the Physiology of the Mind. He declines venturing on a definition of Emotions, affirming that the attempt would be as truly impossible as to define sweetness, or bitterness, a sound, or a smell, in any other way than by a statement of the circumstances in which they arise.

The author's general principle of arranging the Emotions is their relation to time. They are, —

Immediate, or involving no notion of time whatever;

Retrospective, or relating to the past;

Prospective, or relating to the future.

Admiration, remorse, hope, may serve as particular instances to illustrate this distinction. We admire what is before us; we feel remorse for some past crime; we hope some future good.

Were they considered only as elementary feelings, without any regard to time, the emotions, he says, might be reduced to the following: joy, grief, desire, astonishment, respect, contempt, and the two opposite species of vivid feelings, which distinguish to us the acts or affections that are denominated virtuous or vicious. Such a consideration of them, however, would be much more abstract, uninteresting, and inapplicable to human life and conduct, than the method which he has adopted.

The immediate emotions are subdivided into those which do not involve any feeling that can be termed moral, and those which do involve some moral affection.

The following are our immediate emotions of the former kind: cheerfulness, melancholy, wonder, mental weariness, the feeling of beauty, disgust, our feelings of sublimity and ludicrousness. To the latter subdivision may be referred the vivid feelings that constitute what we distinguish by the names of vice and virtue, considered apart from the mere intellectual judgments we form respecting actions; our emotions of love and hate; of sympathy with the happy and with the miserable; of pride and humility.

The retrospective emotions are subdivided as they relate to others and to ourselves. Those which relate to others are anger and gratitude. Those which relate to ourselves are simple regret and satisfaction, without the mixture of any moral feeling; and, finally, remorse and self-approbation.

The prospective emotions comprehend all our desires and all our fears. Of the former, the most important may be considered as enumerated in the following series. "First, our desire of continued existence, without any immediate regard to the pleasure which it may yield; secondly, our desire of pleasure, considered directly as mere pleasure; thirdly, our desire of action; fourthly, our desire of society; fifthly, our desire of knowledge; sixthly, our desire of power, — direct, as in ambition, or indirect, as in avarice; seventhly, our desire of the affection or esteem of those around us; eighthly, our desire of glory; ninthly, our desire of the happiness of others; and, tenthly, our desire of the unhappiness of those whom we hate." The following paragraph on this subject is a happy specimen of the author's analytical skill, and of the gracefulness and facility with which he makes the common nomenclature of our mental feelings fall into his own philosophical arrangements.

"I must observe, however, in the first place, that each of these desires may exist in different forms, according to the degree of probability of the attainment of its object. When there is little of any probability, it constitutes what is termed a mere wish; when the probability is stronger, it becomes what is called hope; with still greater probability, expectation; and with a probability that approaches certainty, confidence. This variation of the form of the desire, according to the degrees of probability, is, of course, not confined to any particular desire, but may run through all the desires which I have enumerated, and every other desire of which the mind is, or may be supposed to be capable." — *Lecture* LV.

In the spirit of the foregoing paragraph, the reason why no peculiar place is set apart for the Passions in this classification is, that our passions are truly no separate class, but merely a name for our desires when very vivid or very permanent.

Dr. Brown, also, goes into no separate classification of

our Fears, since it is evident that they are excited by precisely the same objects which excite our desires. We desire to obtain any object, we fear that we shall not obtain it. We dread any pain or calamity; we wish, we hope, that we may escape it. Thus, our fears and our desires are correlative feelings, and whatever is said of the one may be referred, by a contrasted application, to the other.

We have thus given a mere rough synopsis of the author's arrangement of the Emotions. He devotes to them twenty-one of the hundred lectures. This portion of the book will probably be found the most popular and interesting of the whole. It is generally rich and delightful writing, with the exception of some commonplace prosing, and a little occasional declamation. The author separately considers each article in the foregoing ample catalogue, metaphysically, morally, and theologically. His speculations on this department of his science would well bear dividing into a number of profound and elegant essays. They are adorned with a variety of apposite and beautiful illustrations, from a rather limited but very select range of reading. Perhaps the most felicitous and striking traits in this busy picture of the emotions are the luminous explanations of the *final causes* for which each of them was introduced into our mental constitution. The wisdom and goodness of the Creator are here very impressively vindicated. Even anger, hatred, and other passions, most generally liable to abuse, are shown to bear their necessary part in that harmonious arrangement which provides for the happiness of the species. But this consideration leads the author to establish safe lines of distinction, and to deduce from an enlightened view of our whole nature a body of excellent moral rules. To attempt even a slight sketch of the acute and profound disquisitions, the exquisite analysis, the fine sensibility, the sterling good sense, the eloquent and earnest recommendations of morality, the examination and confutation of many opinions and theories of Alison, Hutcheson, Smith, Stewart, and other philosophers, which these twenty-one Lectures exhibit, would be a task agreeable indeed to ourselves, and profitable to our readers, but far too disproportioned to other purposes for which this essay is designed.

Among the very few topics here treated, on which we have found reason to dissent from the ingenious author, is that of Avarice. It will be seen, in his enumeration of the Desires above represented, that he regards avarice as only a modification of our desire of power. We are persuaded that this is an inaccurate reference of the real and original principle of the emotion in question. Avarice is often exercised without regard to the attainment of any kind of power whatever. It loves money and property purely as such, and not for the gratifications they can purchase. Dr. Brown was aware of this phenomenon, and felt its inconsistency with the above classification of the desires. He labors at great length, and quite unsuccessfully, to account for this obvious anomaly in his system. He falls into a maze of his own creating, by first ranking avarice as an indirect desire of power, and then finding that it is not always a desire of power. He wonders, through a whole Lecture, why the miser should be so eager to deny himself all kinds of gratifications for the sake of that money whose only real value is that it can purchase, and is the representative of, those very renounced gratifications! Would not our author's perplexity and inconsistency have been very easily prevented, by only adding an eleventh class of desires to the ten already laid down? Does not avarice flow from a distinct, original, and independent emotion, namely, a love of hoarding, or, as our author would have called it, the Desire of Acquisition? The child hoards its shells and pebbles, the virtuoso his curiosities, the collector his books, the scholar, often, his intellectual stores, and the miser his gold, almost entirely for the gratification of this simple and separate propensity, with a comparatively faint and fortuitous influence of other motives. And to pursue a favorite train of the author's speculation, before alluded to, it is well for us that our Creator has implanted in our minds this particular desire. In His prospective benevolence, indeed, it was intended to be a direct means of acquiring power, as instrumental to our improvement and happiness. But man often fulfils this intention blindly. An inattention to the distinction here pointed out misled the author, we doubt not, into his defective classification. Were it not for the strong operation of the instinctive propensity we are suggesting, man must often have perished through want, the consequence of carelessness and improvidence. We were not left to calculate the benefits resulting from frugality, nor to wait until we should smart from privations, occasioned by lavishness and inexperience. A desire of mere acquisition, therefore, seems to be a compensation as beautiful as it is indispensable in this fluctuating and precarious world. A too great indulgence of the feeling, of course, becomes, like an abuse of any other desire, criminal and mischievous.

It was probably in consequence of not adverting to this indubitable law of our mental constitution, that Dr. Brown, in endeavoring to account for the unreasonable excesses of avarice which are sometimes witnessed, was led to lay a very disproportionate stress on the *regret* that arises from early prodigality. Indeed, he would seem at times to regard this regret as the original foundation and main ingredient of the passion. We are constrained to question the correctness of this theory. Who has not known instances of a decided bent towards avarice, which could be traced up to the earliest period after infancy, when it was impossible that the little miser could have felt any inconvenience or regret arising from prodigality or extravagance? Fasten down the cover of a box, make in it a small aperture, persuade your child to drop into it every coin that is given him, tell him to search for money on the parade-ground early in the morning after each muster-day, instruct him to bargain away his cake and his toys for cash, deliver to him perpetually short solemn lectures and cautions on the propriety of saving and hoarding his money, and such discipline, acting on the native desire for which we have been contending, will soon convert him into a sordid wretch, long before he has experienced one feeling of pain at the loss of that cake which in fact he has never enjoyed. Regret for squandered means, we allow, is often one among the many other circumstances which Dr. Brown has so happily enumerated as enhancing and aggravating the force of the avaricious principle, and may sometimes awaken and develop it when it has slept for a long time. But we cannot believe it to be the main-spring of the passion itself, nor sufficient, especially, to remove the embarrassment which the author has encountered in the exposition of his theory. Even should the separate desire on which we insist be denied, still we would account for most of the workings of avarice on principles far different from this regret. But we cannot trust ourselves now with the discussion.

Dr. Brown has with great felicity assigned several reasons for the paradox in common life of a person's parting tranquilly with large sums, while the loss of a small one is sufficient to destroy his happiness for a day. He might have accounted for this latter case, in some instances, not so much from merely avaricious feelings, as from the shame of being overreached in a bargaining transaction. To many persons it is an intolerable thought that the tradesman with whom they are dealing will wink, in halfpenny triumph, at his brother tradesman, as soon as their backs are turned. Many, also, contend long for a trifle, from a pure sense of justice.

We come now to the consideration of our author's Ethical System. The Science of Ethics, he observes, has relation to our affections of mind, not simply as phenomena, but as virtuous or vicious, right or wrong.

What, then, is the virtue which it is the practical object of this science to recommend? Why do we consider certain actions, says Dr. Brown, and, we would add, certain feelings, as morally right, and others as morally wrong? The only test, according to him, is a simple emotion of *approbation* or of *disapprobation*. We are so constituted, that we cannot help approving certain classes of human actions, and disapproving certain other classes. God himself, who gave us a relish for wholesome food, and a distaste for what is injurious, has, for analogous, but far higher purposes, created us subject to such immediate moral feelings.

These emotions, our author contends, are uniform in all men, but occasionally modified by three circumstances. First, the influence of *passion* obliterates for a time, in many minds, the emotions that ought to arise on the contemplation of moral or immoral actions. Secondly, individuals, and even whole nations, have sometimes partial and imperfect views of the true tendencies of certain actions, in which there is *a mixture of good and evil*, and this is the cause why morality appears to fluctuate in different times and places. Thirdly, *association*, in various ways, exerts considerable influence in modifying and perverting the emotions which would otherwise be naturally produced by particular kinds of actions. The author insists, that these three limitations still leave unimpaired the great fundamental distinctions of morality itself, — moral approbation towards the producer of unmixed good as good, and moral disapprobation towards him who produces unmixed evil for the sake of evil.

He refutes the sophistry and scepticism which pretend that, in consequence of the foregoing limitations, the science of morality is unsettled, and virtue itself but a precarious and fluctuating name. He maintains, that, where one instance can be found of disagreement among men in approving certain actions and disapproving certain others, there are millions of instances, all over the world, of a perfect uniformity of moral sentiment.

The author next proceeds to examine other theories of morality which have been broached by different writers. Hobbes, who makes virtue to depend on political enactment; Mandeville, who reduces it to a corrupt love of praise; Clarke and Wollaston, who identify it with the fitness and the truth of things; Hume, who measures it solely by the standard of general utility; the ancient and modern disciples of Aristippus, who resolve it into the pursuit of selfish gratification; Paley, who defines it to be "the doing good to mankind, in obedience to the will of God, and for the sake of everlasting happiness"; and Dr. Smith, who allows it no other standard than our sympathy with the feelings of others, — are successively met by elaborate confutations. In these strictures we see displayed an instinctive acuteness in seizing the points at issue, and an unrivalled power of argument. The author, of course, throughout the whole speculation, says many things to justify and illustrate his own system of morality, and mode of treating it. We, also, have a few remarks to suggest.

The great defect of Dr. Brown's ethical theory is, that he has confined his attention entirely to *actions*, which are only the occasional signs and representatives of virtue and vice in moral beings. We admire his discovery, as it may well be called, and on which another superior mind of our own country,* by a remarkable coincidence, has lighted, that certain feelings of vivid approval and disapproval are the true and original tests of right and wrong. As the physical qualities of substances can only be properly known, distinguished, and described by their effects on our senses, and not by vain attempts to ascertain their abstract nature, so the moral qualities of thinking and responsible agents are to be designated by their *effects* on other minds. This, indeed, is an ingenious, a

* The late Professor Frisbie. See his Miscellaneous Writings, edited by Andrews Norton, p. 144, et seqq.

noble principle; it is a bright-eyed offspring of the Baconian philosophy; it is the pioneer to satisfactory conclusions on the subject before us; it throws at once a flood of light upon this hitherto perplexed and obscure discussion. But having seized on the mighty instrument itself, Dr. Brown seems to have failed to apply it with his usual comprehensive energy. In inquiring what objects, when contemplated by us, excite the approving or disapproving emotion, he has strangely omitted the consideration of those mental feelings, or rather *states* of mind, which, in the first place, give to actions their entire moral character, and, in the second place, constitute, by themselves, more than nine tenths of the vice and virtue of the world, without ever being brought into action. Thus, simple indifference to the welfare of others we disapprove as vice. A mere intention, a wish, is often virtuous or vicious. *Refraining* from action is frequently virtue or vice. Mere purity of mind we regard with the approving glow which is paid to active virtue. Regret, shame, anger, joy, and other emotions, are regarded as right or wrong, according to the occasions on which they arise. It is not the blush that we admire and approve; but the modesty, of which that meteor-like tinge is the enchanting signal. It is not the mere phantasmagoric sight of a man, exposing his life to save a drowning enemy, that excites within us the vivid feeling of approbation; it is the sublime state of his soul at the moment, which the action itself is only instrumental in making known.

Now, in consequence of not adverting to these essential considerations, Dr. Brown has left this part of his ethical discussions in no little imperfection and perplexity. He all along states it as an ultimate law of our constitution, that certain *actions* excite within us the approving or the disapproving feeling, by which we distinguish them as virtuous or vicious. He speaks as if the moral nature of every action were immediately and intuitively known, as right or wrong, in the same manner as a color is immediately recognized as green or yellow. He takes no account of that long and varied thread of experience, observation, acquisition, reflection, deduction, culture, admonition, discipline, and example, by which moral feelings and ideas are developed in the mind of the child, and by which alone it comes at length to form its judgments of the character of moral actions. This, certainly, is a loose handling of the question, a very imperfect analysis of the matter under discussion.

If, therefore, the foregoing reflections are just, the true and amended theory of Dr. Brown, the really ultimate law of our moral institutions, for which he sought, would be this.

Certain *emotions*, *desires*, *intentions*, or *states of mind*, in other men, which are made known *sometimes* by actions, sometimes by other sensible signs, and sometimes by verbal information, more or less direct, excite within us the vivid feeling of approbation, or disapprobation, corresponding to which we are accustomed to denominate those states of mind, and the actions they produce, virtuous or vicious, right or wrong, moral or immoral. We are the more confirmed in this amendment of our author's philosophical views, from its coinciding with the principles of morality inculcated in the Sermon on the Mount.

It is from this point, we humbly think, that all ethical

science must properly begin. Its adoption, we are persuaded, would have supplied a palpable defect in the work before us, and saved some readers many an hour of wistful dissatisfaction and perplexity. It is no more correct to confine the question to *actions*, than to the *looks* of the countenance. A tolerably plausible system of morals might be built on the latter, as well as on the former species of exterior manifestations. Would that theory of dialing be complete or scientific, which confined the inquiry to the shape of the gnomon and the motions of the shadow alone, while the primary consideration of the sun's movements and rays remained untouched? Our author, in the outset of the discussion, seems to have had a glimpse of the principle we have been urging, but certainly lost sight of it afterwards. He defines the Science of Ethics, as having relation to our affections of mind, as virtuous or vicious, right or wrong. Then why not proceed, and erect the science upon this broad and true foundation? Why abandon it almost immediately, and say, "One inquiry alone is necessary, — what actions excite in us, when contemplated, a certain vivid feeling," &c.* We trust we have sufficiently shown the very narrow and incomplete relation which this particular inquiry bears to ethical science as a whole.

In inquiring what constitutes the sense of moral obligation, Dr. Brown appears to us to be aiming at a theory of too much simplicity. "To feel," says he, "the character of approvableness in an action which we have not yet performed, and are only meditating on it as future,

* Edin. Ed., Vol. IV. p. 148.

is to feel the moral obligation, or moral inducement to perform it." The late Professor Frisbie seems to have been dissatisfied with this explanation, but in his criticism upon it has not, we think, exactly approached the difficulty. "Are there not many actions," he asks, "which seem to us to have very little virtue or merit, yet by which the feeling of obligation is very strongly excited? nay, is not the obligation often inversely as the merit, as, for example, in regard to the payment of honest debts?" * To these interrogatories we reply, that the obligation which Professor Frisbie instances is not properly or entirely a moral obligation. Apparently without being conscious of the fact, he has shifted the very point in question. In regard to the payment of honest debts, there is something more than the sense of moral obligation; there is the sense of legal obligation; there is also the dread of offending society, creating enemies, and thus injuring one's general interests. Let a law be passed exonerating the debtor; let public opinion too coincide with the law. There will then be *merit* in paying the debt, and a merit exactly in proportion to the moral obligation.

In what respects, then, may it be said that Dr. Brown's theory is deficient? According to our opinion, he has, undesignedly, however inconsistently with himself, suggested the precise and true theory in a subsequent part of his speculations. "When I say," he remarks, "that it is my duty to perform a certain action, I mean nothing more than that, if I do not perform it, I shall regard myself, and others will regard me, with moral disapproba-

* Miscellaneous Writings, p. 157.

tion."* Here, we are convinced, he has fallen upon the right key to the nature of moral obligation. It is not enough for us simply to approve an action, in order to feel the whole force of such obligation; the very word *obligation* implies some conditional *compulsion*, *constraint*, apprehended *penalty* in case of our neglecting the duty. Now, what is the penalty implied in the idea of moral obligation? Surely, as our author suggests above, the pain which all moral beings feel in disapproving themselves, or being justly disapproved by others. It is this which we dread; it is this which constrains us. The moment we allow a fear of any other nature than this to operate upon us, such as a dread of corporal punishment, or bodily pain of any other kind, or an injury to our general interests, the moral changes into the character of physical obligation.

Dr. Brown's distribution of the Duties is the old and obvious one of duties to others, to ourselves, and to God. His treatment of this subject completes the work, and, on the whole, deserves a similar tribute of praise, and similarly modified, with that bestowed on his treatment of the more general subject of the Emotions. Curious speculations are pursued, current errors are refuted, novel and valuable ideas are advanced, magnificent commonplaces are unfurled and waved about, and over the whole is diffused a vivid glow of moral and religious feeling.

* Edin. Ed., Vol. IV. p. 395. Just to show the author's inconsistency with himself, above alluded to, turn over one leaf of his book, and there will be seen the following sentence: "It is, as I have said, on the one simple feeling of moral approvableness, that every duty, and therefore every right, is founded." But in the sentence in the text, has he not said that the sense of duty arises from a fear of disapprobation?

A few Lectures, perhaps, in this portion, require a little bracing up of the attention; one needs a perpetual recollection, that one of our immediate duties is to read Dr. Brown's inculcation of the duties, and it requires some resolution steadily to move on. In all probability, these few Lectures were written under the influence of a similar exhausted feeling. Yet, somewhat tedious as they are, they will repay a studious perusal. Nor is any considerable number of them fairly liable to the foregoing stricture. On the contrary, several will be found to exhibit the author's peculiar vivacity, originality, and other excellences. We instance the beautiful and ingenious Lecture on friendship and gratitude, and one on the goodness of the Deity.

In treating of our duties to God, the author takes occasion to demonstrate the existence and attributes of the Almighty Being. He rightly discards the argument *a priori*, which for ever assumes the very point to be proved. He relies altogether on the short, simple, but irresistible argument drawn from the appearances of benevolent design, so profusely scattered over every part of the universe. We are dissatisfied with his attempted demonstration of the unity of God, and never yet have *felt* the force of the same point of reasoning when urged by other writers. It is founded on the unity and simplicity of design everywhere exhibited in the works of the Creator. Two objections to this argument we cannot conquer. The first is, that it would be not very difficult to make out a case of irreconcilable contrariety and multiplicity of design, apparent in the works of nature. For instance, in one point of view, what tender care seems to be taken of the happiness of all living creatures, while, in many respects, they seem to be left, with utter indifference, to their miserable fate. The second is, that, even if a perfect unity of design, without the slightest apparent exception, could be pointed out as prevailing in the universe, it would not absolutely or satisfactorily prove a unity in the power which produced it. A million of deities might conspire in the most complete uniformity of operations. A stranger to this earth would find a certain uniformity of design, nay, thousands of different operations and results harmoniously conspiring to a single end, amidst all the works of men. But it is unnecessary to say how illogical would be his conclusion, that one being was the author of the whole. He might, perhaps, properly infer, that one *genus* of beings had been at work in the construction of our edifices, canals, cities, and other products of art. The mythology of the Greeks, which peopled every department of creation with presiding deities, was built on such an inference. And this, we are persuaded, is as far as human reason can legitimately advance, in settling the point of the simplicity or complexity of the divine nature. It is a matter as far removed from positive, abstract demonstration, as the Deity himself is removed from man. It is true, the idea of the unity of God is now embraced in the world with more or less distinctness and purity; there is nothing in nature to contradict or refute it, since even an actual contrariety of design might be consistent with it; nay, it is almost a self-evident truth; philosophy can defend it by most plausible arguments; but philosophy must not, cannot, assume the triumph of originally establishing and making it known. Every attempt to that effect which we witness, concurring with our inability to trace it so clearly to any other quarter, only drives us back with increased conviction to the leading representation of the Hebrew Scriptures, that the idea in question was originally and directly communicated from Heaven, in one way or another, to men of Asiatic origin.

When Dr. Brown comes to consider our duties to ourselves, he takes up the question of the Immortality of the Soul. He advances in the affirmative some arguments that are of the highest value, and others that appear feeble and untenable. We will give an instance of each kind. They who hastily infer the destruction of the mind from the destruction of the body, will find it difficult to evade the force of the following reasoning, which has all the weight and acuteness characteristic of the author.

"When the body seems to us to perish, we know that it does not truly perish, — that everything which existed in the decaying frame continues to exist entire, as it existed before; and that the only change which takes place is a change of *apposition* or *proximity*. From the first moment at which the earth arose, there is not the slightest reason to think that a single atom has perished. All that *was*, *is*; and if nothing has perished in the material universe, — if, even in that bodily dissolution, which alone gave occasion to the belief of our mortality as sentient beings, there is not the loss of the most inconsiderable particle of the dissolving frame, — the argument of analogy, far from leading us to suppose the destruction of that spiritual being which animated the frame, would lead us to conclude that *it*, too, exists, as it before existed; and that it has only changed its relation to the particles of our material organs, as these particles still subsisting have changed the relations which they mutually bore. As the dust has only returned to the earth from which it came, it is surely a reasonable inference from analogy to suppose, that the spirit may have returned to the God who gave it." — *Lecture* XCVI.

Nothing was ever better said. But Dr. Brown was well aware of an argument, which the obstinate questioner of the soul's immortality still has in store; namely, that all the mental operations, and consequently what the spiritualist gratuitously calls the mind itself, may be nothing more than phenomena resulting from the union and organization of material particles in a certain manner. So that when this organization is dissolved by death, the soul itself must cease to exist. Now to this, our author offers the following feeble argument: —

"If any one were to say, the Sun has no thought, Mercury, Venus, the Earth, Mars, Jupiter, Saturn, and all their secondaries, have no thought, but the Solar System has thought, — we should then scarcely hesitate a moment in rejecting such a doctrine; because we should feel instantly that there could be no charm in the two words, solar system, which are of our own invention, to confer on the separate masses of the heavenly bodies what, under a different form of mere verbal expression, they had been declared previously not to possess. What the *sun and planets* have not, the *solar system*, which is nothing more than the sun and planets, has not; or, if so much power be ascribed to the mere invention of a term, as to suppose that we can confer by it new qualities on things, there is a realism in philosophy far more monstrous than any which prevailed in the Logic of the Schools.

"If, then, the *solar system* cannot have properties which the sun and planets have not, and if this be equally true, at whatever distance, near or remote, they may exist in space, it is surely equally evident, that an organ, which is only a name for a number of separate corpuscles, as the solar system is only a number of larger masses of corpuscles, cannot have any properties which are not possessed by the corpuscles themselves, at the very moment at which the organ as a whole is said to possess them, — nor any affections as a whole, additional to the affections of the separate parts. An organ is nothing; the corpuscles, to which we give that single name, are all,—and if a sensation be an organic state, it is a state of many corpuscles, which have no more unity than the greater number of particles in the multitudes of brains which form the sensations of all mankind."—*Lecture* XCVIII.

This reasoning will never do. To show its absurdity, let us follow it up for a moment in its own style. "If any one were to say, the Sun has no" mutual attraction, "Mercury, Venus, the Earth, Mars, Jupiter, Saturn, and all their secondaries," each separate and alone, have no mutual attraction, "but the solar system has" mutual attraction, "we should then scarcely hesitate a moment in rejecting such a doctrine." Thus, by our author's course of argument, we could disprove one of the most obvious facts of natural philosophy. So, again, What an acid, when alone, has not, and an alkali, when alone, has not, the combination of acids and alkalies never can have; and therefore such a phenomenon as *effervescence* between acids and alkalies, according to our author, can never take place. The truth is, Dr. Brown is here guilty of begging the question. The very argument of the materialist is, that although the particles of matter, when separate, are not able to think, yet, when brought together in a certain way, which the Deity may appoint, the result of their influence on each other may be the phenomenon which we express by the word *thought*. This our author denies, maintaining that what one particle cannot perform in a separate state, a multitude of particles cannot perform in any sort of combination. It is plain, however, that this is no answer, but only a flat denial of the materialist's argument, and, moreover, involves some most careless general positions, which are immediately disproved by an appeal to ordinary experience.

Before quitting this topic, we would just ask the author, Why so strenuous in maintaining the immateriality of the soul, when, in his noble argument quoted above, he assumes the imperishableness of matter?

On the whole, we cannot claim for him the merit of having placed the immortality of the soul on new and stronger vantage-ground than it occupied before. His reasonings on the subject appear to us to be full of assumptions. As might be expected, the discussion leads him too far from the track of pure philosophy into the entanglements of metaphysics. In defending the unity and indivisibility of the thinking principle, qualities which he regards as essential to its immortality, but which we do not, he is betrayed into arguments quite inconsistent with other statements in different parts of his work. For instance, he vigorously maintains that the mind can exist only in a single state at once. But according to his whole philosophy elsewhere, and even according to the most common experience, that very mind is capable of existing in an intellectual state, and in an emotion, simultaneously; and when, before explaining the soul's personal identity, he allowed that, along with the memory of a sensation or an idea, we have an intuitive belief that we are the same individuals who had the sensation or idea before. One would suppose that in these cases there are two states in which the mind exists at the same moment. But our author endeavors to surmount the inconsistency, by denominating them one complex state. Now, we confess ourselves quite as unable to conceive how the single mental principle can exist in what the author defines as a complex state, as how it can exist in two different states at once. If the latter be incompatible with its nature, why is not the former also? There is certainly something within us which *compares* one intellectual state with another, — one emotion with another, — and intellectual states with emotions. The self-active immortal principle seems to stand, as it were, out of the immediate region of the thoughts and emotions, and to scan, communicate with, and in some measure to guide and control them. But these are shadowy speculations. The truth is, that the phrase "complex state," or the still more impalpable and metaphysical phrase, which is sometimes a favorite one with the author, "a state of virtual comprehensiveness," is but a wordy covering for an unconquerable difficulty, and leaves the real nature of the mind in as much obscurity as ever. Amidst all his horror for rash hypothesis and gratuitous assumption, we are astonished at finding him everywhere asserting, as if it were an axiom of Euclid, that "the mind is not composed of parts that coexist, but is simple and *indivisible*." Now this is unwarrantable. According to the true spirit of the new philosophy, we have nothing to do with this question. Much can be said plausibly in favor of the compound nature of the mind, without furnishing any fair triumph to scepticism, or exciting any necessary alarm among modest philosophers.

Indeed, we have no hope of gaining higher assurances of the soul's immortality from any new speculations on its internal structure. Be it simple, or be it compound, we do not despair. We doubt whether all the philosophy in the world can either improve, or set aside, the lucid and truly Baconian argument of the Apostle to the Gentiles, founded on the analogy between the germination of a perishing seed and the revivification of the human soul. The story left to us by the Galilean fishermen, which we are not ashamed to avow is far easier for us to believe than to doubt, needs no support from the visions either of a Plato or a Priestley; and while we look down into the vacant tomb, that once belonged to Joseph of Arimathea, we are little swayed, either one way or another, by the ingenuity and strength, or by the feebleness and inconclusiveness, exhibited in the reasonings even of Dr. Brown.

Our abstract terminates here. As an abstract, it is of course imperfect, and must convey a faint idea of the work. We have rather dwelt upon those topics which seemed to require critical remark, than attempted to give a systematic sketch of all the author's achievements. We shall now exact, from various quarters, a few contributions to the illustration of our author's character and writings. We regret that an essay on his life and genius, by the Rev. Mr. Welsh, of Edinburgh, has never reached our hands. The following notice is from a volume of the Edinburgh Magazine, for the year 1820.

"Dr. Brown's character was one of extreme, and, I might almost say, of fastidious refinement. The habits of speculative philosophy and abstract thought had not destroyed the vivacity of his imagination, or chilled the warmth of his heart. He was by nature an enthusiast, and the prominent features of his mind in early youth were sensibility and ardor. At school he was distinguished by extreme gayety and sweetness of disposition, and his contemporaries remembered how much he delighted and excelled in the recitation of dramatic poetry. Soon after he engaged in philosophical studies, he distinguished himself for acuteness of reasoning; and his answer to Darwin's Zoönomia demonstrated the discriminating powers of his mind. It is not for the writer of this letter to presume to analyze the subtilty, and profound originality, of his metaphysical inquiries. Among those who attended his lectures, some complained of a certain vagueness and refinement that bordered on obscurity; but when he entered on the moral part of his course, he excited the highest degree of enthusiasm for all that was elevated and noble in human nature. It was then he gave full scope to the lofty conceptions of his mind, and displayed an energy and devotion in the cause of moral truth that could not be surpassed, and can never be forgotten.

"Dr. Brown's manners might be considered somewhat artificial, and yet no man had more simplicity and singleness of heart, if that term belongs to one uninfluenced in his opinions, tastes, inclinations, and habits, by the caprices of fashion, or the calculations of a worldly mind. He never sought the society of the fashionable, the rich, or the high-born, on account of any of these adventitious circumstances. He carried the independent purity of his political principles into the morals of private life. His habits were abstemious, simple, and self-denied. His liberality to those who needed his pecuniary assistance was as frank as it was unostentatious. But his benevolence was not of a kind to content itself with the cheap indulgence of almsgiving. Long after he had given up medical practice, he gave his time and attention to the sick friends who required his advice; and what Burke said of Howard, in a sense restricted to the particular objects of his attention, might be said of Dr. Brown universally: 'He attended to the neglected, and remembered the forgotten.' There are many persons, wholly unknown to the circles of fashionable life, who received constant proofs of his cheering and kind attention. One instance of this is so characteristic of his turn of mind, that I cannot omit mentioning it. Two Ayrshire peasants, who had made considerable progress in languages as well as in botanical and mathematical science, were recommended to his notice. After presenting them with gratis tickets for his lectures, he invited them to breakfast; the conversation turned on botanical drawing. One of them proposed to show the Doctor some specimens of his performance in that art. 'I was pleased,' said he, on relating this circumstance, 'to see the progress I had made in the confidence of these young men during the hour of breakfast. They first came to my low door, but when they returned with the drawings, they rang at the front door. I had inspired them with the feeling of equality.'

"The political principles of this excellent man were those of genuine Whiggism, untainted with the asperity of party prejudice. His reprobation of tyranny and oppression, wherever it was exercised, will be remembered by those who have heard him express his satisfaction at the overthrow of Napoleon Bonaparte, whose despotism he execrated. He took a deep interest in the political events of his own country. The five restrictive bills, passed during the winter session of 1819, excited his warmest indignation; and in a meeting held by the Senatus Academicus, on the occasion of condoling with and congratulating his present Majesty, he expressed his opinion of those measures very strongly. The most minute circumstances, favorable to civil and religious liberty, interested him to the last; and, as an affecting instance of the sincerity of his feelings on subjects connected with the freedom of his country, I may mention, that, during his last illness, he daily inquired into the state of the Middlesex poll, an event deeply interesting on a moral as well as political principle, as being the grateful effort of a generous people to reward the son for the virtues of the father; and when he was told, two days before he died, that it had closed in favor of young Whitbread, though unable to speak, his countenance and manner expressed the liveliest satisfaction.

"He had returned in the autumn of 1819 to Edinburgh, in remarkably good health, and engaged with much ardor in the composition of his class-book. He had even sketched out great literary designs for his future execution, but that fatal disorder, which terminated in pulmonary consumption, seized him during the Christmas recess. He only lectured twice after the vacation. During the last lecture he delivered, he was greatly affected when he read some lines on the return of spring from Beattie's Hermit. He wished to persevere in his course. But his affectionate friend and physician, Dr. Gregory, forbade it, and strongly recommended him to try the effects of a warmer climate. His reply was: 'No, I must die at home; you have no idea how miserably I am afflicted with the *maladie du pays.*' His decline was rapid and alarming. As long as he had strength to hold a pen, he continued to give unremitting labor to the writing of his class-book. In February, 1820, he received a short visit from his revered friend, Mr. Dugald Stewart, though at that time he scarcely admitted any one but his medical friend, and the members of his own family. On taking leave of Mr. Stewart, he said gayly, but emphatically, 'I hope Moral Philosophy will live long in *you.*'"

In addition to the above gratifying sketch, an American correspondent has obligingly furnished us with the following interesting particulars, which the numerous admirers of Dr. Brown in this country will receive much pleasure in perusing.

"In compliance with your request, I send you the following very general statements. With Dr. Brown I was personally acquainted, and occasionally spent an evening at his house. I experienced much of his hospitality during my stay in that country. Immediately upon my arrival at the city of Edinburgh, after the opening of the session of the University, I called upon Dr. Brown, and procured a ticket of admission to his class. Interpreting the intent of your request in the sense in which I believe you designed me to do, I have been led to adopt the following simple plan. *The personal appearance* of Dr. Brown seems first to draw my attention. His was in a very especial degree that of an intense student. He was of ordinary stature; of a pale and wan physiognomy; careless and inattentive in his dress. The character of his countenance was highly attractive, and none could meet him in the streets without noticing it in a particular manner. Profound thought was engraven on every feature. There appeared to be a great mind at work within, and absorbed in the most abtruse speculations. The outward aspect of Dr. Brown evinced to the observing mind, that his trains of thought were those of a high order. Next, as to *the mode which he adopted in delivering his lectures.* In the class-room he appeared in the most advantageous point of view. His manner was grave and dignified. He commanded profound silence, marked attention, and a high expression of regard. He read, or with more propriety I should say he recited, his lectures in an animated strain. He appeared himself to feel the importance of those intellectual views which he had created and was delivering, and was solicitous that the value of them should be perceived and appreciated by those who heard them. He read the poetical quotations, occasionally introduced, in a distinct and impressive manner. I was accustomed to hail with delight the returning toll, which summoned us; and regarded the lecture as a philosophical treat. Dr. Brown did not permit his students to take notes during the time of lecturing, owing to a fact with which you are doubtless familiar, namely, that, a few years preceding, some of the lectures of Mr. Stewart were presented to the public in a garbled form, before the author himself had issued them. Dr. Brown was desirous that his students should, at the close of the lecture, apply to him for the solution of those doubts of a metaphysical kind that might arise. With such he would freely converse.

"He was intensely *studious*. Although surrounded by such a host of social attractions as Edinburgh presents, he allowed not his studious habits to be violated. I heard him state, that he set apart two evenings during every week, either for the reception of his company, or for his own personal relaxation. The rest of his time he considered as sacred to study. The *manners* of Dr. Brown were interesting and rather refined. He was full of conversation; very vivacious, and remarkable for the versatility of his information and diction. He could instantly enter upon any topic, however remote, and in his usual happy strain. In *private life* he was truly amiable. Two sisters lived with him, whom he supported. The most marked affection appeared to exist between them. He was devoted to the gratification of their slightest wishes. His feelings as a man were generous and noble. He possessed more than an ordinary share of sensibility, and would indulge, in the hour of conversation, in the most sympathetic strain, on any scene of distress which he had either witnessed or of which he had heard."

A glimpse into Dr. Brown's lecture-room, as most of our readers will remember, is furnished in the saucy but entertaining "Letters of Peter to his Kinsfolk."

Having collected and presented the foregoing testimonials of the peculiarities of our author's genius, and some notices of his life, a few desultory remarks on the former subject, and on the work before us, are all that we now feel justified in attempting.

The prominent capacity in which Dr. Brown offers himself to our minds is that of a fearless, minute, and ultimate *Analyst*. This is the characteristic that distinguishes him from every other author on record. We are not disposed to vindicate his absolute superiority in many other striking qualifications. His style is far from being faultless, his scholarship is neither exquisite in choice nor extensive in its range, nor are his observations on life and manners peculiarly rich or original; though in all these, as well as in many similar valuable requisites for a public instructor, he is not only not deficient, but is much more than respectable. But in the art of looking into the elements and finer relations of things, in detecting the action and reaction between mind and matter, in reducing all human knowledge to its first principles, we boldly pronounce him to be without a competitor in our language. The true focus of Dr. Brown's mind, the mark at which its most intense power acted, was fixed by nature for microscopic inspection. His more comprehensive surveys and larger classifications, though often imposing and magnificent, are sometimes dim, unwieldy, and incomplete. Witness his original arrangement of Politics and *Political Economy* among the peculiar branches of the Philosophy of the Mind, an arrangement, however, which he did not subsequently follow. For another instance to the same purpose, we refer to his Inquiry into Cause and Effect, which wants distinctness in its general management and outline, though all the separate details of the argument are conducted with wonderful acuteness and power. Again, while we follow him along the track of his curious speculations, or peruse his more splendid and ambitious compositions, we seldom or never meet with those happy generalizations of expression, which so frequently astonish and delight us in the French school of the last century. Indeed, if a generalization of this kind had struck him, he would not have been content to state and leave it simply to his reader. He would have indulged his favorite habit of tracing out all the particulars that went to form it, thus appearing to arrive by gradual steps at a conclusion, on which Voltaire or Diderot would have alighted at once.

But they, on the other hand, displayed little of his peculiar faculty and strength. Whoever will gaze, through the medium of Dr. Brown's representations, at the objects of his analysis, will perceive them clothed with unwonted brilliancy and distinctness, and new points of vision starting up which were unsuspected before. All nature crumbles into infinitesimals before his glance. No man is a warmer adorer of the aggregate beauty and glory of the universe, but no man was ever so prone to regard it as a world of atoms. So too, while he is an impassioned admirer of roses and beautiful faces, he cannot avoid reducing them, by a kind of stereographic projection, into plain surfaces of colored rays. He gazes with a poet's delight on the splendid embroidery which nature hangs around us, but traces the involutions of every thread with still more of the eagerness of a metaphysician. He has erected new landmarks between the regions of illusion and those of reality. He has dissolved much of the influence which names exert on our ideas of things. The study of his writings produces on the mind a similar effect with the study of chemistry. We look round upon creation with almost newly furnished optics; every incident suggests matter of philosophical speculation; the motions of an infant, and the actions of an adult, "all thoughts, all passions, all delights," assume unaccustomed aspects, and exhibit interesting relations in the varied system of things. It is worthy of remark, that, at the same moment when Davy was accomplishing some of his greatest achievements in the analysis of matter, Brown was arriving at some of his most brilliant results in the analysis of mind. Both natural and intellectual science seem to have attained a point of equal progress, when these two contemporaries arose, to push further analogous discoveries respectively in each.

The next most remarkable characteristic that distinguishes our author is the undisguised warmth of his moral sentiments. It is rather out of fashion, with existing literature, to seem very much in love with virtue. The phantom reproach of cant lowers in the distance, and frightens the moralizer into a well-dissembled indifference. The public is a kind of good company, whose feelings must not be hurt by declamations against its favorite peccadillos. The whining sentimentality of some authors, which was carried to a disgusting extreme about the end of the last century, and which received its death-blow from Sheridan's character of Joseph Surface, has undergone the usual reaction of other human extravagances, and writers and talkers are now almost ashamed to testify any enthusiasm in favor of the parlor every-day virtues. Rousseau's delightful declamations, too, were mingled with so much that was unprincipled and false, that they contributed not a little to the same effect. Dr. Brown has been one of the first to break this chill spell of assumed apathy. He comes forward, without fearing the charge of mawkishness or of hypocrisy, and pours out his whole soul in ardent praise of whatever is good and lovely. He appears as the unshrinking advocate, especially, of all the domestic and gentler virtues. The seriousness of his enthusiasm is well calculated to put to flight the sceptical and profligate smile of the scoffer. His works, in this respect, might be recommended as an antidote to the poison of Byron. Unlike most moral philosophers, he treats not of the virtues and of our moral feelings with the same cold and scientific interest that he would inquire into the affinities of a salt or a metal. His inmost sympathies keep pace with his subject, and impart light to it. Several indirect testimonials to the truth and inspiration of Christianity are scattered throughout his Lectures. He is thus shielded from a charge, often urged against the productions of his illustrious predecessor. But we wish that he were more than so shielded, and that Christianity had been more directly, explicitly, and formally introduced into his moral system. We lament the miserable mistake, into which so many moral philosophers have been betrayed, in declining any assistance from the New Testament. How might Dr. Brown have added light, sanctity, and authority to his own doctrines, while he in turn would have contributed no small support to the cause of Christianity! Can it be doubted, that Dr. Chalmers is at this moment supplying the defect on which we have been animadverting? May his attempts be wise and successful.

We have but a few words to say respecting our author's style. We remember hearing reported a happy *jeu d'esprit* on this subject, from the admired writer of Letters from the Mountains. When asked how she was pleased with Dr. Brown's poetry, she replied, that it had too much metaphysics for her; and when immediately again questioned how she liked his metaphysics, she pronounced it too full of poetry. There is at least some foundation for this smart antithesis, though not enough to raise a serious objection against the writings in question. Dr. Brown published several volumes of poetry at different times, but, in our opinion, scarcely a line of it was sufficiently metaphysical or respectable to deserve reading over, with the single exception of the Paradise of Coquettes. This work, published anonymously, was immediately, by the unanimous consent of the critics, pronounced to be second of its kind only to the Rape of the Lock. There are metaphysics in it, but we cannot think it too metaphysical. That portion of it particularly entitled to this epithet is one of the most ingenious and original efforts of the English Muse. It is a description of the heaven of coquettes, and we have always regretted that so very lofty a flight of the imagination should have been introduced into a work of a design so gay and humorous. It is difficult to read it without feeling religiously, rather than facetiously, disposed. It somewhat resembles an inspired glimpse into the possibilities of a future state of being, and, with due modifications, would have been much more worthy of occupying a place in Baxter's Saints' Everlasting Rest, that gorgeous and delightful poem in prose, than of serving as a rhapsody in an heroi-comic effusion.

With respect to the other point of the above-mentioned antithesis, we allow it to be better founded. There is a little too much of poetry in Dr. Brown's metaphysics, or, more exactly speaking, his general style as a writer is over-poetical, — ornamented in excess. We are very far from recommending it as a model, and should be sorry to see it adopted as such, with the same facility with which our young men copied the less ambitious, but still somewhat too measured, flow of Mr. Stewart's periods. We have sometimes thought that, having written his Lectures when comparatively young, and adopted at that time a florid and towering manner, Dr. Brown was afterwards the less likely to correct it, in consequence of retaining, repeating, and laboring upon the same course from year to year. He often indulges in solemn parade and emphatic preambles, while approaching the discussion of his topics, and talks much of the difficulty of his tasks. We know of no better way to characterize his style, than to denominate it ultra-Ciceronian. Coming short of the perfections attained, on the one hand, by the Roman orator, it leans, on the other, rather towards his faults. It is too elaborate, tumid, and redundant. It is like Akenside's verse turned into prose, except that it sends out not the slightest Grecian savor; and this last circumstance, coupled with the rarity, amounting almost to absence, of quotations from the Greek, convinces us that the author must have been very superficially versed in the literature of that language. It may seem a hard and rash judgment to estimate a person's scholarship from the number of his learned quotations; and so in general it is. But when one is a professed, and, as we may say, an inveterate quoter, filling his productions with extracts from English and Latin authors, we may fairly conclude, that a line or two from Euripides, and a sentence now and then from Plato, if they had been "familiar to his ear as household words," would have embellished his moral declamations, or given point to some of his philosophical statements and conclusions.

Notwithstanding these negative peculiarities, it must not be denied, that our Lecturer deserves to be ranked among the classical writers of the language. He is wanting only in a kind of Augustan perfection; yet still he is classical, in the same way as that epithet belongs to Ammianus, to Statius, and to Seneca. The last author, by the way, is a god of his idolatry, and is quoted by him, we remember, alone of all others, five times in one Lecture. No man ever wielded the resources of the English tongue more elaborately than Dr. Brown, or wrote it in more perfect purity. Yet it was the general European standard of its perfection at which he aimed, and not at its idiomatical properties and graces. His style has all the effort and completeness of a well-executed movement by some scientific composer, but little of the indescribable and native charm that pervades the beautiful melodies of his own country. He is full of brilliancies, while he has few felicities, and it is this defect which will lose for him the greatest number of readers. There are no easy, sweet, and playful turns in his diction, to relieve the strained and everlasting *nisus* of scientific disquisition. He hammers everything to the last degree. There is not a thought shown us just as it came into his mind. Though we admire the productions of his skill, yet we almost hear the workman panting and striving at his labor, and the whole atmosphere of his book is redolent of oil.

A favorite figure of speech with the author, which he very frequently carries to a fault, is the climax. There is scarcely a Lecture that does not contain one. To set off some leading idea, or to give force and splendor to an illustration, circumstance is heaped upon circumstance, and clause mounts over clause, till the breath of the stoutest reader gives way, and the dizzy train of his thoughts often goes with it.

We must acknowledge that, in the writings of Dr. Brown, there are too many obscure and difficult passages. After making due allowance for the imperfect state in which his manuscripts may have been left,* for the abstruse and shadowy nature of many of his topics, and even for an occasional mysticism and unattainable aim in some of his thoughts, there still remain too many sentences to remind us, by contrast, of the unabating transparency of Mr. Stewart's diction. On the whole, we must allow that our author's is often a hard style to read, and, as we should have thought, a much harder one to hear. He seems frequently not to have adapted his sentences to the capacity of the ear. The attention is stormed and borne along, rather by the force and brilliancy of the expressions, by the earnest energy of the writer, and by the novelty, splendor, and importance of his well-selected topics, than by the clearness and dis-

---

* We take the liberty of mentioning here a confused and erroneous arrangement of a few of the Lectures, at the end of the first and beginning of the second volumes of the Edinburgh edition, and in the latter portion of the first volume of the Andover. To any one who will examine the matter with ordinary attention, there will, as we think, appear so many undeniable reasons for a substitution of the following arrangement, that we shall not take the trouble to enumerate them. It is certain that, as the Lectures now stand, nothing can be more perplexed and ill concatenated. To introduce order among them, we recommend these six movements.

1. Lecture XXIV. as now numbered should unquestionably be Lecture XXIII.

2. But the *recapitulation* prefixed to Lecture XXIII. as it now stands, including pp. 511, 512, Edinburgh edition, and p. 345, Andover edition, should remain as it is. Then the body of the true Lecture XXIII. will properly begin near the bottom of p. 537 Edinburgh, or on p. 362 Andover: "That we now seem to perceive," &c. This, if we are correct, should be continued to p. 563 Edinburgh, or 376 Andover, where Lecture XXIII. will properly end.

tinctness of each successive position, and a certain smooth and resistless current of language, of which Adam Smith, Paley, and Godwin in his philosophical works, occur to us just now as three of the most remarkable instances. It would be unfair, of course, to refer for this point of comparison to historical or narrative writing.

Though it is impossible to deny to Dr. Brown the possession of very extensive attainments in polite literature, yet sometimes there occur passages which seem to indicate a want of familiarity with subjects that are at the fingers' ends of every general reader. In one place he condescends to impart, with much display, the information, that Abelard, besides his well-known connection with Eloisa, "was distinguished for his talents and attainments of every sort"; and somewhere else he tells us, as a perfect novelty, the whole story

---

3. The recapitulation prefixed to Lecture XXIV. stands where it ought, ending near the close of p. 375 Edinburgh, or on p. 362 Andover, thus: "boundaries from the other." The body of the true Lecture XXIV. will begin at p. 513 Edinburgh, or p. 346 Andover, thus: "Though the notion of extension," &c., and continue to the end of p. 530 Edinburgh, or p. 357 Andover, where the true Lecture XXIII. terminates.

We know no way of accounting for the disorder here pointed out, except by supposing that Dr. Brown wrote his recapitulations on sheets of paper separate from the bodies of his Lectures, and thus that the bodies of Lecture XXIII. and Lecture XXIV. have accidentally changed places, while the recapitulations continued in their proper order.

4. The whole of Lecture XXVII., recapitulation and all, should take the place and number of Lecture XXV.

5. Lecture XXV., recapitulation and all, should take the rank and place of Lecture XXVI.

6. Lecture XXVI., in like manner, should entirely assume the place and rank of Lecture XXVII. A slight inspection will demonstrate the correctness of these last alterations.

of the sympathetic needles from Strada's Prolusions. Mr. Stewart touches upon such things in a quite different manner.

The remarks hitherto made apply to the general characteristics of Dr. Brown as a writer. We have a few more specific criticisms to offer on the particular Lectures before us. Their posthumous publication is a warrant for gentle treatment, of which, however, they little stand in need. It is enough to secure Dr. Brown the highest praise to say, that he has well discharged the vast responsibility of being the successor of Mr. Stewart, or rather, of taking up the Philosophy of the Mind where Reid and Stewart had left it. He enjoyed, indeed, some peculiar advantages in coming after such men, and inheriting a certain general excitement and respect toward the science, to which they had been instrumental in raising the public mind. The era in which he wrote, too, was one of remarkable intellectual development. Poetry, and every branch of natural science, were daily accomplishing wonders, and our author's condition was precisely such, that he must either produce corresponding achievements in the Philosophy of Mind, or encounter the mortification of failure and obscurity. To these arduous advantages he was equal. Certain it is, that during his life he sustained the highest reputation as a Lecturer, and that on every individual who witnessed his performances, without, as far as we are aware, a single exception, he made a favorable impression, unusually profound and permanent.

A very valuable, if not the most valuable, feature of this great work, consists in the contributions which it furnishes to the science of Natural Theology. Paley had already collected, from every part of external material nature, the most striking proofs of benevolent design in the Deity. Brown has effected precisely the same object, with respect to the various phenomena of our intellectual frames. A volume might, with great ease, be extracted from different portions of these Lectures, which would completely fill up the chasm in Paley's outline, and deserve a place in every library on the same shelf with his celebrated treatise. Its plan might be consistently extended and improved, by the addition of such extracts as most directly contribute to the cause of religion, morality, and right thinking. One recommendation, at least, of the proposed work would be, that it would present a body of the most clear, original, popular, and least exceptionable passages that occur throughout the Lectures. Its tendency to higher utility can as little be doubted.

The general plan of the Lectures is, perhaps, too unwieldy and encyclopedic for a single work. We have no right to complain, indeed, of any author, for giving to the public, at whatever length, a series of delightful and improving compositions. The statutes of his professorship might also have enjoined upon this writer a very comprehensive range of subjects, more or less connected with the mind. His original scheme, as we have before seen, included Politics and Political Economy. Why it might not also have embraced Languages, Rhetoric, and Grammar, with equal propriety, we cannot divine. We are of opinion that the proper science of the mind, if treated with the requisite compactness, would be limited to the investigation and description of our mental operations alone. Legitimately it cannot branch out into

Moral Philosophy, nor into Natural Theology. Each of these should form a system by itself. The philosopher of the mind ought, indeed, to trace the connections which his subject bears with these and all other sciences. But he has no particular business with erecting systems of moral, theological, political, or historical philosophy. For instance, he may, with Dr. Brown, attempt to investigate the true nature of Moral Obligation. This is a sentiment of the mind. But as a mental philosopher, his task stops there. He departs from his particular sphere, when he proceeds to enumerate and enforce the personal, social, political, and religious duties arising out of our sense of moral obligation, since he thus encroaches on the real domain of the moral philosopher.

Among the inconveniences to which the form of posthumous lectures subjects this work, are the innumerable recapitulations and repetitions which everywhere occur. Probably all the leading ideas and arguments are stated, to a greater or less extent, three times over; and many of them even more. So that, were the Lectures reduced to a regular treatise, and these repetitions omitted, we should have a book little exceeding in size two thirds of the present. It should be remembered, however, that what is thus sometimes an annoyance in perusal, must have been attended with some advantages to those who originally had the privilege of hearing the Lecturer. And even now, the reader will find much assistance in comprehending and appreciating the author's arguments, by studying the recapitulations, in which former statements are frequently placed in better points of view, and altogether new considerations are sometimes presented. Nor, on the whole, do we regret that the identical Lectures themselves have been published as they were delivered, with all those little incidental appeals to the honor and good feelings of the students, those occasional compliments to the author's colleagues in office, and those other allusions to circumstances of time and place, which take much from the abstract nature of the work, and invest it somewhat with the charm of local reality.

Although, as we before intimated, our author's style is the very opposite to the sententious, yet the vastness of his philosophy, and acuteness of his mind, have caused him to scatter many weighty maxims throughout these Lectures. We subjoin a few as morsels for reflection.

"Science is the classification of relations."

"The form of bodies is their relation to each other in space,—the power of bodies is their relation to each other in time."

"The power of God is not anything different from God."

"The philosophy of the mind and the philosophy of matter agree, in this respect, that our knowledge is, in both, confined to the mere phenomena."

"We pay Truth a very easy homage, when we content ourselves with despising her adversaries."

"The difficulty of ascertaining precisely whether it be truth which we have attained, is in many cases much greater than the difficulty of the actual attainment."

"Philosophy is not the mere passive possession of knowledge; it is, in a much more important respect, the active exercise of acquiring it."

"Happiness, though necessarily involving present pleasure, is the direct or indirect, and often the very distant, result of feelings of every kind, pleasurable, painful, and indifferent."

"When absolute discovery is not allowed, there is left a probability of conjecture, of which even Philosophy may justly avail herself without departing from her legitimate province."

"To know the mind well, is to know its weaknesses as well as its powers."

"There is always in man a redundant facility of mistake, beyond our most liberal allowance."

"All the sequences of phenomena are mysterious, or none are so."

"National ridicule is always unjust in degree."

"If we had been incapable of considering more than two events together, we probably never should have invented the word *time*."

"That men should not agree in opinion, is a part of the very laws of intellect, on which the simplest phenomena of thought depend."

"Objects, and the relations of objects, — these are all which reasoning involves."

Three or four Lectures are occupied in giving the substance of the author's doctrine of Cause and Effect. It is an objection to the doctrine, when urged in his broad and unqualified manner, that it must tend to the discouragement of scientific inquiry. In pressing his particular views, he unguardedly represents it as a fruitless task to search for any other cause of a given effect, than the obvious and apparent one. But this would keep us back in the ignorance of infancy. The author could not have intended such a conclusion; but he should have provided better against it. Another thought that has struck us, in our perusal of these arguments, is, that they do not come much short of asserting, that the Deity himself cannot know why a particular cause produces its immediate effect. One more remark connected with this topic. When Dr. Brown asserts, that nothing can exist in nature but all the substances that exist in nature, what would he say of motion? Is this nothing, or is it something? If it be something, can it be called a substance? In short, the existence of motion, particularly spontaneous motion, though more intimately connected than any other phenomenon with this subject, and perhaps involving its essential difficulty, receives not in these speculations its due share of notice.

The author loses himself in a criticism on Hume, at the end of the thirty-fourth Lecture. Hume does not speak of the annihilation of an idea, as Dr. Brown represents him, but of the idea of annihilation. This mistake destroys the whole reasoning.

We were disappointed in seeing no attempts to draw the characteristic lines of distinction between man and the brute creation. The subject is nowhere hinted at. It was admirably adapted to the peculiar powers of the author. He does not even encounter the obvious objection, that most of his arguments for the immortality of the soul would as well apply to faithful Tray as to his master.

We are not satisfied with the liberties everywhere taken in quoting the English poets. Scarcely a passage from them occurs, that is not altered, apparently with a direct intention, though, we are not always fortunate enough to perceive, with a happier adaptation to the subject in hand.

From the author's ambition to say something of every subject more or less connected with his particular science, we were surprised that he has interwoven no remarks upon Delirium, Hypochondriasis, Liberty and Necessity, and a few others. An evident vein of Necessitarianism runs through all his speculations. That doctrine may be pretty directly deduced from his views of Cause and Effect, as well as from his favorite statements of the operations of the mind. Amidst his loftiest declamations, upon the immortality and other attributes of the soul, we never hear a word of its freedom, although such a topic would have thrown a characteristic lustre on many a splendid paragraph.

Perhaps it may be wrong to assert, that the author was under obligations to the late Dr. Cogan, as that gentleman's name, unaccountably in any view, is alluded to nowhere in the Lectures. Yet it cannot be denied that a strong general coincidence exists between the two writers in their treatment of the Passions and Emotions, and several ethical questions, and particularly in regard to the *final causes* of the actual arrangement of many mental phenomena.

Dr. Brown, more frequently than any other writer, goes back to infancy, childhood, and savage life, for the decision of philosophical points.

He seems to have possessed little sense of the ludicrous. He never undertakes of himself to combat an error with satire. When he has need of this weapon, he constantly resorts to large quotations from Martinus Scriblerus, or Fontenelle. There is in this respect a striking contrast between him and Dr. Campbell, whose ridicule was as irresistible as his serious argument.

We were going on to particularize our favorite Lectures, and to transcribe abundance of other pencil-marks with which we have cumbered the margins of the author's pages; but there is no end to this kind of critical chitchat, and we forbear.

1825.

THE MAN OF EXPEDIENTS.

Φοίτα δ' ἄλλοτε μὲν πρόσθ' . . . . ἄλλοτ' ὄπισθεν.
HOMER'S *Il.*, E. 595.

"All means they use, to all expedients run."
CRABBE.

"It is a fine subject.

"Button-holes! there is something lively in the very idea of them, — and trust me, when I get among them, — you gentry with gray beards, look as grave as you will, — I'll make merry work with my button-holes. I shall have them all to myself, — 't is a maiden subject, — I shall run foul of no man's wisdom or fine sayings in it." — *Tristram Shandy.*

THE Man of Expedients is he who, never providing for the little mishaps and stitch-droppings with which this mortal life is pestered, and too indolent or too ignorant to repair them in the proper way, passes his days in inventing a succession of devices, pretexts, substitutes, plans, and commutations, by the help of which he thinks he appears as well as other people.

Thus the man of expedients may be said only to half live; he is the creature of outside, the victim of emergencies, whose happiness often depends on the possession of a pin, or the strength of a button-hole.

Shade of Theophrastus! spirit of La Bruyère! assist me to describe him.

In his countenance, you behold marks of anxiety and contrivance, the natural consequence of his shiftless mode of life. The internal workings of his soul are generally a compound of cunning and the heart-ache. One half of his time he is silent, languid, indolent; the other half he moves, bustles, and exclaims, "What's to be done now?" His whole aim is to live as near as possible to the very verge of propriety. His business is all slightingly performed, and when a transaction is over he has no confidence in his own effectiveness, but asks, though in a careless manner, "Will it do? Will it do?"

Look throughout the various professions and characters of life. You will there see men of expedients darting, and shifting, and glancing, like fishes in the stream. We will give a few tests by which they may be recognized. If a merchant, the man of expedients borrows incontinently at two per cent a month; if a sailor, he stows his hold with jury-masts, rather than ascertain if his ship be seaworthy; if a visitor of those he dislikes, he is called out before the evening has half expired; if a musician, he scrapes on a fiddle-string of silk; if an actor, he takes his stand within three feet of the prompter; if a poet, he makes *fault* rhyme with *ought*, and *look* with *spoke;* if a reviewer, he fills up three quarters of his article with extracts from the writer whom he abuses; if a divine, he leaves ample room in every sermon for an exchange of texts; if a physician, he is often seen galloping at full speed, nobody knows where; if a debtor, he has a marvellous acquaintance with short corners and dark alleys; if a printer, he is adroit at *scabbarding;* if a collegian, he commits Euclid and Locke to memory without understanding them, interlines his Greek, and writes themes *equal* to the Rambler.

But it is in the character of a general scholar, that the man of expedients most shines. He ranges through all the arts and sciences — in Cyclopædias. He acquires a most thorough knowledge of classical literature — from translations. He is very extensively read — in title-pages. He obtains an exact acquaintance of authors — from reviews. He follows all literature up to its source — in tables of contents. His researches are indefatigable — into indexes. He quotes *memoriter* with astonishing facility — the Dictionary of Quotations; and his bibliographical familiarity is miraculous — with Dibdin.

We are sorry to say, that our men of expedients are to be sometimes discovered in the region of morality. There are those who claim the praise of a good action, when they have acted merely from convenience, inclination, or compulsion. There are those who make a show of industry, when they are set in motion only by avarice; there are those who are quiet and peaceable, only because they are sluggish. There are those who are sagely silent, because they have not one idea; abstemious, from repletion; patriots, because they are ambitious; spotless, because there is no temptation.

Again, let us look at the man of expedients in argument. His element is the sophism. He is at home in a circle. His forte, his glory, is the *petitio principii.* Often he catches at your words, and not at your ideas. Thus, if you are arguing that light is light, and he happens to be (as it is quite likely he will) on the other side of the question, he snatches at your phraseology, and exclaims, Did you ever weigh it? Sometimes he answers you by silence. Or if he pretends to anything like a show of fair reasoning, he cultivates a certain species of argumentative obliquity, that defies the acutest logic. When you think you have him in a corner, he is gone, — he has slipped through some hole of an argument, which you hoped was only letting in the light of conviction. In vain you attempt to fix him, — it is putting your finger on a flea.

But let us come down a little lower into life. Who appears so well and so shining in a ball-room as the man of expedients? Yet his small-clothes are borrowed, and as for his knee-buckles, — about as ill-matched as if one had belonged to his hat and the other to a *galoche*, — to prevent their difference being detected, he stands sideways to his partner. Nevertheless, the circumstance makes him the more vivacious dancer, since, by the rapidity of his motions, he prevents a too curious examination by the spectators.

Search farther into his dress. You will find that he very genteelly dangles *one* glove. There are five pins about him, and as many buttons gone, or button-holes broken. His pocket-book is a newspaper. His fingers are his comb, and the palm of his hand his clothes-brush. He conceals his antiquated linen by the help of close garments, and adroitly claps a bur on the hole in his stocking while walking to church.

Follow him home. Behold his felicitous knack of metamorphosing all kinds of furniture into all kinds of furniture. A brick constitutes his right andiron, and a stone his left. His shovel stands him in lieu of tongs. His bellows is his hearth-brush, and a hat his bellows, and that too borrowed from a broken window-pane. He shaves himself without a looking-glass, by the sole help of imagination. He sits down on a table. His fingers are his snuffers. He puts his candlestick into a chair; — that candlestick is a decanter; — that decanter was borrowed; — that borrowing was without leave. He drinks wine out of a tumbler. A fork is his cork-screw. His wineglass he converts into a standish.

Very ingenious is he in the whole business of writing a letter. For that purpose he makes use of three eighths of a sheet of paper. His knees are his writing-desk, his rule is a book-cover, and his pencil a spoon-handle. He mends his pen with a pair of scissors. He dilutes his ink with water till it is reduced to invisibility. He uses ashes for sand. He seals his letter with the shreds and relics of his wafer-box. His seal is a pin.

When he takes a journey, his whip-lash — But I shall myself be a man of expedients, if I fill ten pages with these minute details.

O reader! if you have smiled at any parts of the foregoing representation, let it be to some purpose. There is no fault we are all so apt to indulge, as that into which we are pushed by the ingenuity of indolence.

1818.

DESULTORY THOUGHTS ON LEXICOGRAPHY AND LEXICONS.

LEXICONS being the right-hand, or rather the very eyesight, of the scholar, all pertinent discussion in regard to them should have a certain interest. Lexicography is, in fact, well entitled to be raised to the dignity of a science. In order to create and advance it, copious inductions might be formed from works of the past laborers in this field, of every age and nation. The successive developments and improvements, which from time to time have been introduced into the art, would contribute further materials. Other aids might be derived from the observations suggested to scientific inquirers by the nature of language, and from the obvious uses, of various kinds, to which lexicons may be applied.

If such a science could be constructed, it would form a foundation for far more useful and complete dictionaries than we have yet known. I am acquainted with no essay or treatise which aims to place Lexicography on a scientific basis. My present purpose is not so ambitious. I propose merely to throw out a few desultory suggestions, that have occurred within my own limited experience, in the hope of eliciting, from better-instructed quarters, contributions to a subject so wide-reaching and prolific.

To say nothing of other languages, have we at this moment a model English Dictionary, such as might be fairly demanded by the general scholar, or the ordinary reader? In the first place, what we require in a perfect dictionary for ordinary purposes is, I think, neither a bald glossary on the one hand, nor a cyclopædia on the other, but something of an intermediate character. In this respect, Webster's Dictionary is admirable. It contains many thousand articles, in which the thing represented by a word is not merely expressed by a synonyme, or even by a neat, adequate, logical definition, but a brief description tells you something of the nature and relations of the thing itself. This is particularly the case with objects in natural history, with the technical language of the law, and with terms in the various arts and trades. Webster is, also, very happy in pointing out instances of the several shades of meaning which the same word sustains in its different applications. Doubtless his book will be susceptible, with the lapse of time, of continued improvements in both these particulars. Perhaps he carries to a fault the descriptive habit I have mentioned, and sometimes, in this respect, causes his Dictionary to approximate too nearly to the character of a cyclopædia. His rule of giving the derivations of his words is excellent, however he may have failed of accuracy in particular instances, or fallen short of the modern stage of development in scientific etymology. But all dictionaries ought to present the etymologies of words, as often the best means of enabling the student to judge for himself as to their true signification.

A satisfactory dictionary of the English language should give, systematically, the pronunciation of the words, after the manner of Walker. This is particularly desirable for the use of foreigners. It is not sufficient to show how the roots of derivative words are pronounced. The foreigner should at once be enabled to perceive the sound of each individual vocable. I am aware of the great difficulty of carrying out this whole system to universal satisfaction. Something like the phonetic signs, which have attracted so much notice in England and America, would seem to be available for this purpose. In that system, each articulate utterance of the human voice, at least every elementary sound employed in the English language, amounting, as it is said, to thirty-six (short, I should think, of the reality), is represented by a distinct character. The supporters of the system are very sanguine in the hope of substituting it for our existing orthography, and thus producing a universal change in the drapery of literature, whether in writing or typography. If, however, they can succeed in employing it only for the purpose above suggested, namely, to teach the true pronunciation of established current words in the existing modes of spelling, they will probably render it as useful and popular as it is capable of being made.*

We need a system of this kind for dictionaries of the French language more than of any other. It is impossible for any combination of our alphabet to represent the nasal sounds, so peculiarly enunciated by that nation, in distinction from every other on earth. Whether those sounds can be traced to the Frank or the Celtic element

---

* Since this article was written, a work has been published in Cincinnati, entitled "Smalley's American Phonetic Dictionary of the English Language." 8vo. pp. 770.

of that people, I am not aware. In their purity, so far from being disagreeable, they are ranked by some among the noblest and most musical sounds uttered by man. Some writers suppose them to be identical with the utterances recorded of a very ancient tribe of Etruscans, who were said to have emitted a vocal sound resembling the clarion cry of an eagle. How far different from that, or from anything heard within the precincts of Paris, are those villanous attempts to represent the nasal tones of France in such dictionaries as that of Meadows, where page after page is loaded with abortions like *kong-pang-sai*, to illustrate the true pronunciation of *compenser!* How must such representations mislead the learner! Might he not as well give a downright English pronunciation to the French vocables before him? Thousands of pupils, all over the English and American worlds, may at this moment fancy that they are attaining a correct French pronunciation from this Mr. Meadows, when, in fact, they are learning barbarisms, worse than nothing, and enough to agonize every genuine Frenchman who hears them. If, now, some distinctive character could be adopted, instead of these deplorable *ongs* and *ungs*, which should represent the nasal sounds, and if the pupil were taught that it is impossible for any alphabetic combination to express them, but that they must be imparted originally by oral communication alone, and then mentally connected with the characters, a great advance might be made in conveying the knowledge of French pronunciation.

But supposing some phonetic system of this kind adopted for all dictionaries, another Alpine difficulty immediately arises before the practical lexicographer,—

I mean, the establishment of an authoritative standard of pronunciation. That Walker has been extruded from the throne on which he sat with absolute sway for thirty years, is no fair ground for concluding that no man or body of men may rightfully aspire to wield the sceptre that has fallen from his hands.* There certainly can be laid down some general principles of pronunciation, such, for instance, as would be that of shortening the antepenult in a derivative word of three syllables, when the same syllable is long in the corresponding primitive; as *pātron*, *pătronage*, &c. By the way, I observe that this rule, though much may be said in its favor, is not practically recognized by Worcester, Smart, or Webster. Whether they are right or wrong in this particular, a body of principles *can* be established, which would organize and fix, to a very great extent, the general pronunciation of our language. Then, however, would come the exceptions and anomalies, to be upheld by inveterate custom or by the usage of good society, or perhaps to be strangled by the bold hand of the lexicographer himself, and forced to give way to more legitimate and analogical forms of speech.

But where is the man competent to this whole task? Where is the man who, having told me whether I must say *purfect* or *pĕrr-fect*, shall instantaneously receive from me as implicit obedience as the tax-gatherer whom the legislature sends to my door? I long for such arbitrary rule. I sigh for the repose and certainty of so benign a

* The present standard in England is believed to be Smart, editor of the dictionary known as "Walker Remodelled." He is said to have been teacher of elocution to Queen Victoria.

despotism, as much as I desire the Papal infallibility, which shall direct me, amidst the sinkings of extreme unction, whether to say, *I die*, or *I am dying!*

Now, to establish such an authority, we naturally turn our thoughts first to the political, legislative powers in any country. Could they effect the object desired? No. Not all the wealth and political power of the state is equal to the task of giving currency to a new expression, or exterminating an old one. Even although we could attract the attention of any legislature to such a project, — which we could not do if we tried, — we should find these matters quite beyond their authority. They cannot even legislate a coin out of circulation. I receive almost every day, even from our great federal post-office, those old English Brummagem coppers, which should have disappeared half a century ago, but which still retain their vitality, and more than their intrinsic value, in spite of laws, and mints, and Presidents, and national pride and jealousies. And even so, and more also, would it be with *winged words*, which, flying aloft in disdain and defiance from the grasp of power, nestle down on the lips, in the habits, in the hearts, around the hearths, and in the markets of the whole people, among whom they are cherished as an essential, ingrained portion of the national existence itself. Look at the unavailing attempt of the affluent, dictatorial Harpers to alter the orthography of a few words in American books, in conformity with some of the peculiarities of Webster. With all their millions embarked in the book-trade, with their tempests of steam, and mountains of stereotype, with their monopoly of whole markets, they can scarcely constrain or influence a single press besides their own to omit even a little *l* in the word *traveller*.* Noah Webster himself had tried the experiment on a large scale, some forty years ago, in an attempted radical improvement of the whole orthography of the English language. His example was followed by a single person only,—the late lamented Grimké of South Carolina; and the valuable writings which they both published in that new drapery, fell almost dead-born from the press, in consequence simply of their outlandish, repulsive garb. The retaining by Webster, in his great Dictionary, of a few of these new-fangled peculiarities, constitutes, I conceive, the prominent defect of that excellent work. Although he might have had good reasons for altering the ordinary spelling of some words, yet his reforms were only partial and capricious. If he began this task, he should have made thorough work of it. But, as we have seen, he had tried the thorough work and failed. No valid reason could be assigned on his part why his few changes in orthography should not have been multiplied, so as to reach the full claims of the phonetic system itself, which requires the spelling of every word to correspond uniformly to its oral enunciation. Even Macaulay, in his letter to the Harpers, while he acquiesced in these innovations in their edition of his history, had not a word to advance in their favor, but passed their merits over, in ominous, half-smiling, mystifying silence, although they were the main topic in the controversy before him, between the Harpers and the other publishers.

The true principle on this subject I take to be, that

* I refer to the book-press. The New York Tribune, with its vast circulation, adopts Webster's later orthography.

lexicographers, as such, ought rarely of themselves to initiate any improvements or alterations in the current forms of a language, written or vocal, but only to be faithful reporters of what is existing and recognized. When general custom has stamped with its seignorial approbation any new form introduced by individuals, the lexicographer's duty is to range it in the cabinet of his faithful columns. Webster, by his attempted innovations in orthography, has transcended this rule, and so far failed in his function, since he did not succeed in carrying the public with him; thus rendering his Dictionary, in this respect, the dictionary of one man, instead of the dictionary of a nation.

Such, then, being the powerlessness of any single man, or body of men, however strong in wealth or political authority, to enforce modes of orthography and pronunciation on the public acceptance, as well as to authenticate the employment of individual words, might we not look with hope of success to some moral or intellectual authority, to whom should be referred the verbal usages and exigencies of a country? I am unable to state with accuracy the influences, in this point of view, which were exerted by the French Academy in France, and the Academia della Crusca in Italy. But I have sometimes thought, that if there could be a standing convention of scholars, assembling annually, or perhaps oftener, who should be delegated from all our colleges, universities, courts of law, ecclesiastical bodies, literary and scientific societies, and other kindred institutions, whose duty it should be to discuss and decide every doubtful point in orthography, etymology, syntax, prosody, rhyme, orthoepy, purity, obsoleteness, new proprieties, substantive value of individual terms, and the like, I, for one, as a good citizen of the literary republic, would yield obedience to their decrees, even though pronounced against my own philological conscience. I have mentioned *rhyme* among the objects of consideration, because it is very well known that usages and authorities in regard to it are subject to as many vicissitudes as in respect to anything else. Rhymes which were constantly employed by Pope and Dryden as legitimate, would not at present be tolerated, and are regarded in no better light than mere assonances.* Some are still dubiously endured. But the tendency, both of the poetical and public ear, is evidently towards exactness of rhyme. The world seems to say to the trembling poet, If you will inflict rhyme upon us, let it indeed be rhyme, the genuine article, and of no mongrel description. Thus the range of poetical license is limited, and whole pages and volumes of innocent verses are sacrificed in advance. Already the bard shudders in fear of being bereaved of such facile but inexact resemblances as *give* and *thrive*, *bough* and *owe*, *improve* and *love*, *past* and *taste*, *fear* and *there*, *afford* and *lord*.

Now, if a convention of the kind just supposed could be established and generally submitted to, how easy, comparatively, would be the task of the lexicographer! He would but have to register the decrees of that literary parliament. His function would be simply that of the codifier. Then how free from perplexity would writers

* Take as an example the closing couplet of Pope's Temple of Fame: —

"Unblemished let me live, or die unknown;
Oh! grant an honest fame, or grant me none!"

and speakers, both in public and private, pass their responsible existence! For as Talleyrand used to class blunders in a more atrocious category than crimes, so have I known persons, who, I verily believe, were almost as charitable to a moral obliquity as to a mispronounced syllable or a suspected solecism. How readily, too, might those who, like myself, are passing off the stage, guard themselves from indulging in antiquenesses and obsoletenesses of phrase or enunciation, which might have been the height of fashionable propriety in our youth, but which now, perhaps, extort the same smile from our juvenile hearers as we once bestowed on similar infelicities in our too-little-venerated predecessors;—even as the smooth-shaven chin probably excites among our juniors the same wistful speculation as did, in our own young imaginations, the huge, bushy, phenomenal wigs of those septuagenaries who glided off the stage of our early life.

But, ah me! in the proposal submitted above, am I not dreaming fondly of an impossibility? How could we secure steadfastness and consistency in the very legislative tribunal I am imagining? "Quis custodiet ipsos custodes?" How prevent dissensions and deviations among those subjected to their sway? If I mistake not, the history of the two foreign academies above mentioned, with their surrounding contemporaries, is replete with accounts of parties and factions in all matters subjected to their jurisdiction. And so it might be with us. Boileau, in his wonderfully ingenious satire, *Sur l'Equivoque*, represents the peace of the whole world, and the high interests of orthodox Christianity, as having been at times suspended on some pun or word of doubtful meaning. In like manner, might not the peace of our own America, already too often disturbed by our characteristic wordiness, be still more jeoparded, if the matters in dispute were veritable words?

On all these accounts, I am constrained to confess, that, since there is as yet no tolerable science of lexicography, and since the art and task of the lexicographer are environed by so many practical difficulties and impalpable perplexities, I feel incompetent to present a satisfactory estimate of any particular lexicon or dictionary, and can but throw a few empirical random observations into the general reservoir of ideas on the subject.

Webster's Dictionary must be acknowledged by all as an inestimable treasure. What a dear friend in need it is, whenever we meet with any sort of word which we hardly fancied to exist in the heavens above or the earth beneath! It is not twenty years since the London Quarterly Review pronounced the number of terms in any language, necessary for the exigencies of modern civilization, to be only about forty thousand. But behold, Webster and Worcester have more than doubled the number, and who will venture to deny the possible or probable utility of any of their articles? Yet, to evince how much the task of compiling such a work transcends the powers of any single man, however industrious and eminent he may be as a philologist, I will here mention that my own very limited reading, during the last twenty-five years, has supplied me with a list of one hundred and eighty-five words which are wanting in Webster's quarto of 1828. How to account for such a deficiency will, I apprehend, appear difficult to my readers, especially when it is remembered that his assistant in preparing the work for publication was the poet Percival, the range of whose erudition is scarcely surpassed among the living scholars of any country. A few of the omissions were probably accidental, but by far the greater number must have occurred through the limited knowledge or the still stranger intention of the compilers. Before the author's death, I communicated to him my list of missing words as far as it had then grown, — a circumstance which may in part account for the appearance of over one hundred of them in the revised editions. The following are among those still wanting. I record them chiefly as matter of curiosity, and would not be understood to vouch for the entire list, or for the uniform accuracy of the annexed definitions.

Arreed, — used by Milton.
Barbican, in fortification.
Bothy, a hut or small building.
Branchial.
Busheller, one who repairs garments for tailors.
Calavance, a fruit.
Calceolus, a flower.
Carapace, perhaps the same as Callipash.
Cassoon, an architectural decoration.
Clabbed.
Clinker, refuse of coal.
Clinker-built, in marine architecture.
Clow, in draining.
Conacre, in husbandry.
Crinkets, a disease.
Cruives, fishing implements.

Cult, a worship. — Vestiges of Creation.

Debmised, in heraldry.

Dian, — not for Diana. — Andrew Marvell's Poems.

Dipod, in prosody.

Dispasted, in physiology or surgery.

Dochmaic, in prosody.

Doller, a machine for lifting.

Dyslogism, false reasoning.

The Fancy, sporting world.

Feuars, a kind of tenants.

Finite, applied to verbs.

Flexion, the same as Inflection, in grammar.

Forefaulter.

Gradine.

Guttery, part of a soldier's equipment.

Hobble, an instrument of confinement.

Indicial, in arithmetic.

Intarsiated, checkered?

Lagerstræmia, a plant.

Laura, a collection of separate cells, in distinction from a monastery. — Curzon's Monasteries of the Levant; Lord Lindsay's Christian Art.

Marrionate, in angling.

Mill, to travel under water, as a whale or fish.

Mosarab, Spanish Moor?

Navvy, an English laborer.

Obsequience, — used in the London Quarterly Review.

Odic, — the Odic Force of Reichenbach.

Ozone, in chemistry.

Paræmiac, in prosody.

Paul, an Italian coin.

Peschito, an ancient copy of the Scriptures, as Syrian Peschito.

Pinder. — George à Green was, in olden time, the Pinder of the town of Wakefield.

Predella, in Romish church-furniture.

Previous Question, in deliberative bodies.

Reiver, a robber.

Rolster, — London Quarterly Review, No. 180, p. 249.

Sarcel, in falconry.

Senachy, — in London Quarterly Review, June, 1841, *Art.* Whewell.

Sennet, a musical term in Shakespeare.

Slub, to prepare wool for spinning.

Smolt, a young salmon.

Sockdologer, — used in Mrs. Howe's "Passion-Flowers."

Spinney, in hunting.

Theotisc.

Toril, — in Andrew Marvell's poems.

Triptic, a utensil employed in a monastery or church.

Water-brash, a disease.

Willock, a sea-fowl. — Kingsley's Glaucus.

Zymotic, a class of diseases.

The great rival of Webster's Dictionary, in our country, is Worcester's Universal and Critical Dictionary, published in royal octavo, in 1846. It is a monument of learning and ability, and must be considered as indispensable to every well-furnished library. I understand that in New England it is recognized as a paramount authority. By the kindness of the author, I have been favored with an opportunity of examining the valuable manual, published in 1855, compiled from his great work. Of course, it cannot present the vast variety of shades and modifications of meaning exhibited in the significations given by

Webster, or in Worcester's own larger work; but those which it gives are exceedingly full, compact, and intelligible. Dr. Worcester's Dictionaries, hitherto published, are destitute of one valuable characteristic of the rival work, in withholding the etymologies of the words. But his latest abridgment possesses a new and redeeming feature, in exhibiting the peculiar forces of nearly synonymous expressions.* This must have cost the author much thought and labor, and evinces in its execution a high degree of discrimination and skill. The work, also, has the high recommendation of presenting the pronunciation of every word, on its face, without exception. In fact, vast care seems to have been expended on the department of pronunciation, and it is hard to conceive of any authority, on that point, more complete or satisfactory. The adjuncts, prefixed and subjoined to the body of the work, are all appropriate to such a production, and must be very useful in the practice of daily literary life. Indeed, they suggest rich materials towards such a science of lexicography as has been insisted on in the former part of this essay. It is but fair to judge of the execution of any work according to its own plan and pretensions. Judged on this principle, very great merit must be assigned to Worcester's Dictionary. But perhaps a further approximation towards perfection is yet

* The author must have experienced some difficulty in devising a rightly descriptive title for his late work. He calls it "A Pronouncing, Explanatory, and *Synonymous* Dictionary," &c. Now a book which treats of synonymes can hardly be entitled on that account a *synonymous* book, as the word has generally been received. The occasion might have justified the daring creation of some such new term as *synonymic*. But it seems the able author chooses to justify himself by the equally daring creation of a new *definition* for *synonymous*, which he explains as sometimes signifying, *Relating* to synonymes.

to be attained, by combining the plans of both Worcester's and Webster's.

As an instance of the virtual impossibility of any one man's mastering and exhibiting the whole vocabulary of any language, I have already presented a list of the words omitted in Webster's Unabridged Dictionary, so far as detected by the casual and limited reading of a single student, in the course of twenty-five years. On consulting Worcester's Universal and Critical Dictionary, I find that he supplies only five of Webster's omissions, given above; namely, Bothy, Clinker, Dipod, Dochmaic, Obsequience; — while, of my original list of 185 words, Webster has the following, which are not to be found in Worcester: —

Alignment, adjustment to a line.
Antispast, in prosody.
Catafalque, in funeral solemnities.
Cob, clay mixed with straw.
Cufic, ancient Arabic characters.
Force, a water-fall.
Gopher, the wood of the Ark.
Intention, in surgery.
Plant, of a tradesman.
Proper, in heraldry.
Quintet, in music.
Septet, ditto.
Stertorous, snoring.

I feel sure (and I say it without any affectation) that my reading has been of a more limited extent than that of almost any man, of any literary pretension; although to exact and careful reading, as far as it has gone, I am ready to confess. Now, if I, within my short range, have discovered so many omissions in these two industrious, faithful, and learned lexicographers, how large would probably be the catalogue, if one hundred of the most extensive readers in England and America had taken notes similar to mine? Doubtless, also, I have met with many other words in the same predicament, which I failed to verify or record.

In early life, I commenced, and worked for some time, on a task which, if well and thoroughly executed, might result, I apprehended, in considerable literary utility. Other cares and necessities withdrew me from its continued prosecution. The object was a classification of all the words in the English language, according to the various ideas which they represent. All epithets, for instance, implying good moral qualities, were arranged under one division, and those of the opposite kind under another. Words representing mental action, of any kind formed one class; words representing bodily action, another; words representing the bodily sensations, a third, &c. I can well conceive that writers and speakers may often be essentially aided by such a work, in the proper treatment of their themes. Fortunately, Roget's Thesaurus of English Words and Phrases, constructed mainly on the principle in question, has appeared. It constitutes, unquestionably, one of the richest treasure-houses of our vernacular philology.

An abridgment of Webster, with its peculiarities in orthography, has been adopted for the public schools in the State of New York. How far this was effected by its essential merits, and how far by the overshadowing influence of the Harpers, I presume not to say. Washington Irving has written and published a letter, complaining of a grossly unfair use made of his partial recommendation of the work.

The struggle for public favor between Worcester's and Webster's Dictionaries has been more or less active for some years past. Into the merits of that controversy, I do not propose further to enter; but I cannot forbear remarking upon the absurdity of charging Dr. Worcester with having borrowed from Webster's vocabulary. Who can charge another with stealing *ἔπεα πτερόεντα* out of his *battue*, when the winged creatures themselves are wild game, flying all about the country, — animals *feræ naturæ*, in which no man can claim private property?

Richardson's Dictionary of the English Language is admirable for tracing the history of English words; and is, therefore, peculiarly valuable to persons of philological tastes; it is little suited for ordinary purposes.

But the highest hopes of the students of English undefiled are now fixed upon the appearance of the great Lexicon of the English tongue, announced by Dr. Worcester. He has, undoubtedly, brought to its preparation unsurpassed industry, accuracy, capacity, and conscientiousness; and we may, with much confidence, look to its publication as the most promising means of gaining clear and consistent information as to the character, construction, derivations, meanings, and resources of the English language, which are likely to be enjoyed in our generation. Not the least important and interesting feature of this vast projected work will probably be the illustration, by neat and well-drawn cuts, of all those terms whose meanings can be rendered clearer by such accompaniments. Although illustrative designs have been more or less employed in books, both before and ever since the dawn of printing, yet their increasing use, at the present day, and the important place they now hold, are of auspicious omen for literature, as well as art. Clear, exact, copious, satisfactory, and often delightful conceptions of objects are thus imparted to the inquirer, who obtains by a glance what might otherwise cost him hours of research. The improvement in question constitutes a new era in verbal lexicography, and must go to enrich the science itself with a choice element. Of course, it cannot be claimed to have originated here. Setting aside technical glossaries, we believe that a recent English work, Ogilvie's Imperial Dictionary, on the basis of Webster, has the honor of being the first "illustrated" dictionary of the English language.

To make a transition from our own to the classical languages. It must be gratifying to Americans, that Pickering's Greek Lexicon and Leverett's Latin Lexicon, prepared by the hands of two of our own countrymen, are, or at least were at the time of their publication, unsurpassed, even if equalled, by any other works of the kind. I have used them both from the beginning, and feel that I can almost say a *Nunc dimittis*, whenever I lay them down. John Pickering, no doubt, was the most erudite man our country has ever produced. Of this fact the sketch of his life and attainments, executed and published, at the request of the American Academy of Arts and Sciences, by Judge White, of Salem, Mass., must establish a clear conviction. When shall we see the more formal and complete monument of his vast acquisitions and achievements, which was invoked by the hopes of Judge White in his admirable little memorial? Pickering's Lexicon, in its matter, structure, and arrangement, is of extraordinary excellence. In reading the classic writers of Greece, one finds it a blessed help, pouring all desirable light, and distinguishing the exact shades of meaning in the very passages under examination. Perhaps it is not so full and satisfactory for the Greek Testament, — not at all superseding the use of Schleusner. And even Schleusner, although a very great assistance, must not be depended upon without an independent exercise of one's own judgment, since his definitions of words and classifications of meanings are necessarily more or less tinged with the foregone conclusions of his own peculiar faith and views of the context.

The English rival of Pickering's Lexicon would be Donnegan's, — which I have seen subjected to some rather withering criticisms, — or perhaps Liddell and Scott's, which has been admirably reprinted, and in some respects edited, by Professor Drisler, of Columbia College, New York. This Lexicon embodies, to a great extent, the best results of modern criticism, up to the time of its publication (1846), and (as the highest compliment I can pay it, or any other Greek and English dictionary of foreign origin) is not unworthy of a place by the side of the second edition of Pickering. Before procuring Pickering, my great aid in reading the Greek classics, when obliged to abandon Schrevelius, was a noble and splendid improvement of Budæus's Thesaurus, printed in 1554. Since Pickering commenced his reign, the Budæus has slumbered very much on the shelf, though its assistance would probably be required if a kind destiny should ever lead me much amongst the Alexandrian writers and the Greek fathers. These matters stir up in my mind a pleasant reminiscence. Paying a visit once to the elder

President Adams, when he was between seventy and eighty years old, our talk, or rather *his* talk, as it swept over a very wide range of subjects, lighted at last upon Greek lexicons; when up jumped the venerable sage, like a sprightly young man, and actually ran up stairs to his library, from which he brought down in his arms a huge folio *Constantine*, which he exhibited as his favorite companion in his Greek studies.

To all Greek lexicons I feel thankful, in contrast with all Latin dictionaries that I am acquainted with, inasmuch as they give, in their alphabetical places, the various inflexions and irregular oblique cases of all words, as well as the original roots and leading forms. Why should it not be so in all sorts of vocabularies? One valuable principle in our proposed science of lexicography would be, that every inflexion of a word at all irregular, or not obvious to the merest tyro, should be introduced in its place, as well as the root. For instance, in every Greek Lexicon, when I look for *οἴσω*, the future of *φέρω*, or for *ἤνεγκα*, the perfect of the same word, I find them waiting for me as faithfully as the root *φέρω* itself. But in looking into a Latin dictionary, even into my favorite Leverett, for *tuli*, the perfect of *fero*, I find it absent, and I am driven back to my grammar knowledge of the word, if I wish to proceed any farther with *tuli*. In like manner, you will find *εἶς*, the second person of *εἰμί*, in a Greek lexicon, but never *es*, the second person of *sum*, in the Latin dictionary, although the words precisely correspond in the two languages, and although the Latin *es* is more irregular than the Greek *εἶς*, and more difficult to be traced by one not well acquainted with the language. The same inconvenient practice, probably the relic of some antiquated pedantry, is also adopted in most dictionaries of modern foreign languages. I have been perplexed by it in using French, Italian, Spanish, German, and Danish dictionaries, and have often been obliged to hunt through the grammars of those languages for certain forms, which, if they had been inserted, as they ought to have been, in their alphabetical places in the dictionaries, would have saved numberless fragments of precious time in a life too short and crowded to be thus wasted. I am happy to say that most English dictionaries are free from this monstrous delinquency, and that Webster and Worcester respect the individuality of *went* and *gone* as much as that of their radical *go*.

The Latin Lexicon of Leverett professes to be chiefly compiled from the great work of the Italians Facciolati and Forcellini, and from the German works of Scheller and Luenemann, of which it is a much slighter modification than Pickering's Lexicon is of Schrevelius. But in its translations, methodical arrangements, and accurate execution throughout, it shows consummate scholarship and industry. I cannot but feel something of the complacency of the sexton who "rang the bell" for the great orator, when I remember that two little boys who began the Latin grammar together, at the age of nine years, under my humble tuition in the morning of my own life, were Frederic P. Leverett of Boston, and William H. Furness of Philadelphia.

Whenever our contemplated science of lexicography shall utter its decrees, let it abolish from its practical systems all such pedantry as, I am sorry to say, still adheres to Leverett, in confounding together in alphabetical arrangement the letters *I* and *J*, and also the letters *U* and *V*. The truth is, there is now no more identity or affinity between *I* and *J*, or *U* and *V*, than between *M* and *N*. *I* is in all cases a vowel, and *J* is in all cases a consonant. So, respectively, with *U* and *V*. Why should the young be perplexed, and all ages be annoyed, by the unnecessary tribulation of distinguishing by an effort of memory what are really distinguished in the nature of things, and ought to be equally distinguished in the columns before their troubled eyes?

Let our imagined science also decree that Greek lexicons for proper use shall present their definitions in the vernacular language of the country where they are published. This will facilitate the study of that incomparable tongue far more than enough to counterbalance the little advantage gained by an increased knowledge of Latin, on the antiquated plan.

In connection with this point, may I not suggest the inquiry, whether there has not been, in time past, and is not still, too much that is formal, superstitious, mechanical, and pedantic, in insisting that youth shall commence and pursue the study of a language with no other aid than the eternally twirled, tumbled, and dog-eared dictionary? Is not this scheme as unnatural as it is unnecessary? Does nature send the little bright and inquisitive learner to a big vocabulary? Does she not immediately teach him words from the lips of a superior? I am therefore for teaching languages by the judicious but not exclusive use of translations, or at least of closely accompanying vocabularies, and copious, clear annotations, carried on from lesson to lesson. The quick and active memory of youth demands something of this kind. The importance of saving time demands it. When a large foundation of knowledge is thus naturally supplied, then let the mind be disciplined, and the powers exercised, by the study of pure originals and the use of the dictionary. In this way, I feel persuaded that less disgust at learning would be engendered than has darkened the annals of the past, far higher enjoyment secured, and a vastly greater amount of ripe scholarship developed.

To revert for one moment to our main topic;—I am happy to know that Professor Guenebault, who has resided for many years in Charleston, as an eminent teacher of the French language, has long been engaged in a peculiar and (so far as I am informed) quite untrodden path of the field of lexicography.* He has compiled, and is soon to publish, a Vocabulary of such French words and phrases as have originated in cant, or slang, or some provincial or other idiosyncratical sources. Such a task, if executed with the industry, tact, and fidelity which the public have a right to expect, will unquestionably furnish many curious and valuable results in the study of philology and social science.

---

* I speak here of French literature only. The English works of Francis Grose, among others in the same department, are well known.

1855.

A DAY OF DISAPPOINTMENT IN SALEM.

BY AN ADMIRER OF "TWICE-TOLD TALES." *

I HAD completed my Northern summer tour, and was lingering through a few days at the Tremont House, in Boston, for the arrival of a party of friends from Canada, in order that we might all start together on the journey to our Southern homes. To beguile the tedious and vacant hours of my delay, I had resorted to the various expedients which suggest themselves to a solitary stranger. I had made numerous excursions on foot to the enchanting environs of the American Athens. I had paid a sweet and solemn pilgrimage of several hours to Mount Auburn. I had gone up to the dome of the State-House, on two different sunshiny afternoons, and drank a full flow of delight (no less intense for arising from a twice-told tale) from the wonderful landscape around, more gorgeous and varied than an Achilles-shield, — those distant, slumbering, yet shining towns, — those hundred steeples, scattered, like the religion they represent, in all quarters of the horizon, — those graduated hills far off at the south, along which I could not

* Soon after the appearance of Hawthorne's "Twice-Told Tales," the author of the present volume, desirous of rendering his testimony to the excellent promise they contained, published the above *jeu-d'esprit*, in the assumed character of a Southern Planter.

help faucying that Neptune sometimes ascended, as up a flight of stairs, when, tired of the storms and calms of his own ocean, he was desirous of refreshing himself with a glimpse of the works of the demigod man,— that beautiful harbor with its small green islands,— the winding, glistening Charles, with its bridges, and bays, and causeways,— the venerable group of edifices at Cambridge, glowing amidst the picture, as if Learning and Religion had said to each other, Sit we down here together and form a part of the bright glories of this mysterious emblem-world,— that vast city at my feet, with its palaces, halls, camera-obscura squares, winding streets, autumn-brown gardens, mirrored roofs and towers, leafless forests of dim-receding masts, and hazy-blue atmosphere, penetrating, overspreading, and harmonizing all,— itself also harmonizing exquisitely with the gently lessening sounds of a busy population as the shades of twilight deepened,— and last, in still nearer perspective beneath my downcast eye, that extensive Common, crossed by numerous footpaths, in which I could discern now and then a couple of saunterers of different sexes, but too minute by reason of distance for me to distinguish whether they were lovers mutually dreaming away a too short happy hour, or a little brother and sister returning leisurely home from school. I had several times strayed to the Athenæum (impressive exponent of united intellect, refinement, and munificence), had wandered and paused through its encyclopedic range of apartments, had skimmed the world's periodical literature on the tables of its reading-room, and amidst the favoring silence of the visitors had beheld, with a feeling of almost terrific enchantment, the cast of

> "Laocoön's torture dignifying pain,—
> A father's love and mortal's agony
> With an immortal's patience blending."

The shops of the booksellers, also, presented their resistless attractions in my daily walks. What charming lounges! How invariably polite and kind, both masters and clerks! How willing that I should gratuitously entertain myself for hours amidst their "treasures new and old," and how especially welcome was I made to the full enjoyment of their luxuries, when it was perceived that I was a rather liberal purchaser of their choicest publications! A chair in the quietest corner of the shop, yet not too remote for a gentle and unoffending glance at the fair customers who applied, at almost every moment, for pocket-books, gold pencils, annuals, tablets, and the last new novel, was always secured for the gentleman who, on a single day, could select and order to his lodgings a parcel containing Prescott's Ferdinand and Isabella, Bancroft's United States, Sparks's Franklin and Morris, Everett's and Story's Miscellaneous Writings, the works of Thomas Carlyle, Furness on the Gospels, and other novelties of like commanding interest.

One morning, while ruminating somewhat vacantly in my privileged nook in one of these favorite haunts, the graceful and obliging shop-boy brought me a volume, which he said he should have certainly offered me before, had he not believed that every copy had long since been disposed of. He was sure I should be pleased with it, and begged me to give it a cursory inspection. The title of the book, "Twice-Told Tales, by Nathaniel Hawthorne," put me at once upon a train of musing speculation. I knew not whether to consider it attractive or repulsive. Generally speaking, a twice-told tale is a tedious affair. Some tales, however, will very well bear repetition, and who knows, thought I, but such may be the case with those before me? Twice-told tales, moreover, are often fresh and new to some portion of the audience; and as I learned from my active little Mercury that this compilation of narratives and fancies acquired their existing title from having nearly all appeared previously in various periodicals, I acknowledged that they at least must possess the charm of novelty for those who, like me, could indulge but sparingly in that sort of reading. Thus, the reasoning of a moment or two (would that all prejudices might be as easily surmounted!) dispelled the unworthy prepossessions I had been induced to entertain. On the other hand, a little further reflection awakened me to a sense of the peculiar beauties and merits of this singular title. Like all new converts, I was now inspired with an inborn zeal for what I had just before repudiated. *Twice-Told Tales!* How simple, how antique, how purely Saxon, these three little alliterative words! How they transport us at once to the enchantments of the Middle Ages and of minstrel utterances! Then, again, what a frank and sturdy honesty there is about them! The author of the book seems to say: "I give the world fair warning that these tales have been published before. It is possible you may have dined on the same fare yesterday. If, gentlemen, you can tolerate a picked-up dinner, here are the fragments of former entertainments, collected and served to the best of my ability. So, walk in! But if you can put up with nothing short of a fresh-killed and entire turkey, and a new batch of pies and puddings directly from the oven, you must go your ways and be entertained elsewhere." I perceived also in the same circumstance a noble self-reliance, — a modest confidence that the book had merits and would win its way, notwithstanding the unpretending and even self-disparaging character of the title.

Thus inspired with favorable inclinations, I opened the volume, and glanced rapidly over the first two articles. The result of this hasty inspection was, that I threw a half-eagle on the counter, waited impatiently for the change, and hurried home to my lodgings with the book, which, before I slept on my pillow that night, deserved, at least from *my* experience, the title of *Thrice-Read Tales.*

On the next day, my mind was full of Nathaniel Hawthorne. I felt rejoiced that a first-rate book was added to our scanty American library, — a first-rate classic to our incipient literary galaxy. I hailed the appearance of another genuine *original* on this threadbare earth; and, better still, I hailed the appearance of one of the rarest productions of human nature, — an original, devoid of almost every exceptionable or offensive quality. For alas! thought I, originality is too often attended with some enormous evil genius, some outrageous affectation, some perilous error, some frightful absurdity in taste, opinion, or morals. Not so with Nathaniel Hawthorne. He is as good, as delicate, as pure, as old-fashioned, as sensible, and as safe, in all his sentiments and conceptions, as the most timid worshipper of established proprieties could desire. One of the greatest triumphs, indeed, of his genius, is to have mingled so much genuine humor, so much keen, flashing wit, with a taste so exquisitely fastidious and refined. Nor does it detract from his originality, that he occasionally reminds us of the quaintness of Lamb, or of the almost feminine lusciousness of Washington Irving's picked and perfect English. These things are merely extraneous and accidental, — just as if Shakespeare should have made a bow like Sir Philip Sidney, or Lord Byron unconsciously imitated the tone of his friend Rogers. Enough is left behind to constitute him one of the most original of American writers. A single paper of his, "Rills from the Town-Pump," for instance, is enough to give any man a lasting reputation. It is one of those unique and fortunate productions that genius sometimes throws off to excite wonder and delight, and to defy imitation, — such as Horace's Visit to Brundusium, Boileau's Third Satire, Pope's Rape of the Lock, and Irving's Rip Van Winkle. O that respectable, sensible, humorous town-pump! Who would have supposed it possible to elevate a pump to all the dignity and interest of a living personage? Who can read the paper, without feeling a loving sympathy for that worthy, eloquent, and slily satirical piece of wrought timber, shall I say? or may I rather call it that fragment of oaken humanity? Surely, the inhabitants of Salem, where Hawthorne resides, if they rightly appreciate such an author, would be willing to appoint him their essayist-laureate, with a handsome salary. They would *settle* him, as a parish settles a minister, with the understanding that he should furnish something periodically for the gratification and instruction of the town. I should like, at some time or other, as a mere *jeu-d'esprit*, to try my hand at imitating him. Yet how impossible to catch his felicities! How difficult to strike like him first into an unbeaten track of imagination, and then to strew it with characteristic flowers of wit, fancy, fact, humor, eloquence, and wisdom, as I went along!

Thus I ran on in my reflections at different times and places through the day, admiring the depth and felicity of my own criticisms almost equally with the qualities of my new favorite, — till at length I wrought myself up to such a pitch of enthusiasm, that I resolved on the morrow to visit Salem, and obtain, if possible, before I left New England, a sight of the author of Twice-Told Tales.

Accordingly, I found myself at the appointed hour among the crowd on board the steamboat, which was to transport us over the ferry to the commencement of the new railroad between Boston and Salem. Just before starting, an acquaintance introduced me to two ladies, whom he placed under my charge for the journey, as it was out of his power to accompany them himself.

"Take care of your heart," said he in a whisper, as he led me aside for a moment. "Between that lovely widow and her daughter, there is but a slender chance of your getting back to Boston entirely unscathed, and the result may be, either that one of them will attend you next fall to grace your Southern plantation, or that you will be induced to transfer your interest to New England, and form a connection and residence among the Yankees. Yet, in either case, I shall congratulate rather than pity you, for they have every sort of recommendation one can imagine or desire."

A caution so abrupt and pointed had, I confess, a singular effect upon my mind. Instead of fortifying me against the charms to which I was to be exposed, it only rendered me more vulnerable to their power. There are certain cases in which, if you inform a man of his danger, you do but increase the risk of his losing himself. A calm and unconscious feeling of security is sometimes a better guide through perils, than the exciting terrors of admonition. Cruel and almost insulting inconsistency! To awaken one's anxiety and interest respecting his companions for a pleasure-jaunt, at the very moment that you warn him to beware of losing his heart! So I shall not dwell upon my emotions as I rejoined the two ladies, by whose side I remained until I conducted them to the door of their friend in Salem.

They were both very beautiful. The widow was two or three years older than myself, while her daughter was just on the verge of sixteen. Their conversation was animated, intellectual, and *spirituelle;* bearing marks of the highest female cultivation for which their city is renowned, yet modified considerably by the age and character of each party. The daughter was full of enthusiasm; imbued with the transcendental philosophy just springing up; inclined to doubt the utility of all forms; familiar with Wordsworth and Carlyle; and bent upon a certain philanthropic project of establishing schools for adults, of which the teachers should be children, as being nearer the Source and Centre of all spiritual Light. In short, what with her loveliness and extravagance, I could not avoid perpetually regarding her as a sort of delightful dream. Her mother, with equal, though different attractions, I may call, not a dream, but a waking vision. She, too, had her high hopes and aspirations, her large, kindling views, her enthusiastic schemes of improvement; but amidst them all, she seemed to have solid ground to tread upon. She reverenced, though she did not worship, the spirit of the Past. She believed there was a desirable medium between slavish routine and vague extravagance. She quoted the Edinburgh Review; and once, I remember, when a little excited by her daughter's inveighing against all forms, she with some warmth expressed her hope that the young ladies of the present day would not take it into their heads to get married after the manner of the turtle-doves.

Take the two ladies together, however, they were a truly fascinating pair. The very points of contrast in their characters and sentiments did but inspire me with a more vivid interest. The suggestion of my friend, as to one of them accompanying me to the South, irresistibly intruded itself on my mind. On him be all the burden of so presumptuous an idea. Of myself, I should not probably have ventured to entertain and cherish it. But the spark had caught. My imagination was kindled. And, to my surprise, I found myself silently inquiring, "Which of them will go?"

On bidding them farewell, their cordial smiles, their expressions of gratitude for my attentions, and their frank solicitations for my protection on our expected return the next morning, absolutely banished from my mind for a few moments the object of my visit to Salem. I wandered at random a short time through one of the streets of that beautiful city, without inquiring for the residence of Nathaniel Hawthorne; but as I mused and strayed along, I involuntarily revolved the questions,—"Which of them will go? Will either of them go? Would not both be pleased with a residence at the South? Shall I take the enchanting dream? or shall I invite the more solid waking vision?"

But the surrounding novelties of a strange city now dispelled these pleasant reveries, and recalled me to my original purpose. I discovered the way to the lodgings of my favorite author. He was not within, but would probably be at home some time in the course of the day. I inquired respecting his haunts. They were the Athenæum, the booksellers', the streets occasionally, or North Fields, or South Fields, or the heights above the turnpike, or the beach near the fort; and sometimes, I was told, he would extend his excursions on foot as far as Manchester, along the wave-washed, secluded, and rocky shore of Beverly.

It was out of the question for me to explore all these places, as I could not prudently spare more than a day on my present adventure. I resolved, however, to do what man and my limited time could do for the accomplishment of my design. I first visited every bookseller's shop in town, and inquired with an air of assumed indifference if Mr. H. had been there that morning. He *had*, I was told, lounged a few moments at one of them, and taken away the last number of the Democratic Review. But in none of these resorts was he at present to be found. I next inquired my way to the Athenæum, or public library of the city.

On my asking a gentleman if the person I was seeking were present, he replied: "It is scarcely a quarter of an hour, sir, since Mr. Hawthorne was mounting that ladder, to return to its shelf a book he has had out some time, on the early history of New England. If you are very anxious to see him, he may possibly be found on the Neck below the town, where he sometimes walks on so fine a morning as this." So down to the Neck I hastened, and although I was still unfortunate in my search, since I saw no human being along those solitary fields and shores, yet I was half repaid for my trouble and disappointment by the distant views of Beverly on the one side, and of Marblehead on the other, and the larger and nearer city in my rear, while in front the harbor exhibited its islands, and the rolling and glistening of its cool waves.

I returned and dined at a hotel; after which I made another attempt to surprise my quarry at his lodgings, but in vain. He had not been seen since the morning, and in fact was sometimes known to pass a whole day abroad, without communicating his intentions to the household. Still undiscouraged in my pursuit, I inquired the location of some of the most retired, romantic, and beautiful scenes in the vicinity of Salem. When Orne's Point was described, I determined to direct my course thither, thinking it possible I might there discover the interesting object of my pursuit. Passing up Essex Street, in the stillness of the early afternoon, when scarcely a citizen was yet returning from dinner to his place of business, I came to its intersection with Washington Street, where I immediately recognized my old friend, the Town Pump; just as Andrew Jackson or Queen Victoria would be recognized by one who had for some time been in possession of a faithful, living portrait of either of those eminent personages. I could not pass the spot without stopping, for I felt as if on classic soil. All was silent and solitary around. The beams of the autumn sun came down upon the dry, warm iron basin affixed to the pump's venerable nose. I quaffed a generous draught of the cool beverage, partly for my own bodily gratification, partly as a token of respect to my inanimate friend, and partly in honor of the felicitous reporter of his speeches. I then said within myself, "I will wait here awhile, for I may be amused by some of the visitors who have already amused me in description before;—and who knows but the very man I am in search of may, on his return home to a late and solitary meal, pass this way, and, observing a well-dressed, bookish-looking stranger gazing with fervent admiration on his own glorified pump, betray by a conscious smile his authorship and identity?" So there I stood for half an hour; but of the forty or fifty persons who passed during that time, though many stared at me with some astonishment, yet none appeared to exhibit the slightest sympathy with my situation, nor should I have judged from their physiognomy or carriage, that any one of them was at all capable of composing a book like the Twice-Told Tales. As for the pump itself, it remained all the while untroubled, save by one fair little girl, who filled her pitcher from it, and then retired, gazing with a fond but pardonable vanity into the liquid mirror in her hands,—the very child, I have no doubt, who was immortalized for the selfsame act in the original "Rill from the Town-Pump."

I reached Orne's Point by the middle of the afternoon. It is one of the loveliest retreats imaginable, and lies at the distance of a short two miles from the centre of Salem. A hill covered with trees overhangs a small and beautiful secluded bay. A mile or more down this bay, where it widens towards the sea, one of the longest bridges in the State connects Salem with Beverly. On a calm day, as you stand upon the rocks at Orne's Point, you will hear the frequent tramp of horses and carriages traversing the bridge, and you will scarcely be able to conceive how so loud and rapid and near a noise could proceed from the little black spot which your eye discerns moving like a slowly creeping insect over the distant bridge. I paused for a full half-hour enjoying in solitude the perfect beauty of this delightful scene. Its picturesqueness was not a little heightened by the appearance of two cranes stalking silently in the shallow water, and at length simultaneously rising and soaring slowly away over the trees. Their departure was the signal for my own. After idly skipping a few stones over the smooth surface, and looking round in vain through the trees and on a neighboring cliff for my desired companion, I retreated lingeringly towards the main road. "Farewell, unrivalled spot!" said I, almost aloud. "Worthy art thou of the tasteful and observing visits of a being like N. H., and next to the pleasure of seeing himself, I at least feel indebted to him for indirectly and unintentionally giving me this glimpse of thee!"

Falling into company with a teamster on the Danvers road, who gave me a very interesting account of a Lyceum which he subscribed for and attended, I was shown by him the hill on which were executed the Salem witches of old. Listless and disappointed, I rambled thither, and felt my mind somewhat excited by the reminiscences incident to the spot. I then pursued my way westwardly across many fields and hills and hollows towards a populous-looking settlement, and found myself in an ancient and extensive graveyard. I examined a few of the inscriptions, of which one happened to be the epitaph of poor Eliza Wharton, whose sad history I had read and wept over when a youth. What an eventful and fruitful walk, thought I, would this be for Hawthorne himself! How would trains of historical incidents, and heart-touching reflections, be awakened in his mind, to constitute, perhaps, a choice portion of the second volume of Twice-Told Tales!

The westering sun reminded me that I must rapidly direct my course to the city. On arriving at the corner where the turnpike leads off to Boston, I remembered that the heights above it had been mentioned as one of the resorts of my favorite author. There was still enough of sunlight left to encourage me in exploring this spot also; while the prospect, which I should at all events enjoy, presented a strong temptation to the enterprise. I clambered the rocky precipice, and, as I turned round to view the city, the setting luminary threw a strong golden glare on all its steeples and windows and waters, together with the populous villages that spread far out towards the northern horizon. I stood entranced with this new vision. Less magnificent and imposing than the view from the Boston State-House, it exhibited a repose, a oneness, a gem-like completion, which the other does not possess. The noise of Boston was wanting, scarcely a sound being heard except the striking of the "North clock," which was immediately and faintly echoed by the striking of the more distant "East." I permitted the prospect to fade away before my eyes, one tinge dying out after another, — one object or group hiding quietly behind a nearer, — till the sombre curtain of a gathering twilight left me just glimpses enough to commence finding my way back to town.

On turning to look for an eligible path down the precipice, I observed a gentleman standing at some distance from me, eyeing the same scene with an interest as deep as mine, and lingering longer than myself, as if more unwilling to depart, or better acquainted than I was with the method of descending from the height. I immediately approached him, delighted with the belief that I had not undertaken my somewhat romantic pilgrimage in vain. We exchanged a few words on the exceeding beauty of the prospect we had just been surveying. The stranger was accessible and companionable. I told him I was from a distant part of the United States, but was not ignorant of the reputation sustained by Salem in reference to the past progress and present elevation of the country. "With no common emotion," said I, as we descended the cliff, and entered the outskirts of the city, "have I trodden the streets and gazed on the scenes where a BOWDITCH passed so many years of his life, — and a HOLYOKE calmly turned his hundredth year, — and the venerable and gentlemanly PRINCE pursued his scientific improvements to so late a period, — where a jurist and a philologist,* who are still living, and have done so much for their favorite sciences and for their country's reputation, long resided, — and may I not add, without flattery, where so many admirable effusions have perhaps proceeded from him whom I now have the honor to address?" The gentleman smiled and bowed, as if pardoning the compliment, observing, it was true he had written a few things that had been favorably received by the public, but that he was far from arrogating the distinction I had assigned to him. "However," continued he, as we passed along through

* Hon. Joseph Story and Hon. John Pickering, since deceased.

Chestnut Street, whose beautiful avenue of trees and elegant residences on each side was now illumined by the rising moon, "I have often, like yourself, been impressed by the constellation of eminent minds that have shone in our little town since the commencement of the present century. The list you have enumerated might easily be enlarged. You may not have heard of the learning of our BENTLEY, — nor the masterly and comprehensive, but subdued spirit of our WORCESTER, who lies in his grave among the missionary stations on the Mississippi, — nor of several of our learned, cultivated, and *sui generis* physicians, — nor of some of our "merchant princes," whose sagacity, enterprise, and good generalship established our connections with India, and introduced a flood of wealth and prosperity into the land. I have sometimes entertained the design, as topics connected with this city are always favorite ones with me, of composing a volume which might be entitled, *The Worthies of Salem in the First Quarter of the Nineteenth Century.* Such a volume, if properly executed, would, I believe, be very acceptable in this vicinity, as well as to the public at large, and throw a desirable light on the intellectual progress of our country. But as the task could not perhaps be delicately performed during the lives of some of the subjects, an approximation to its completion might be effected by compiling memorials for a future opportunity."

"And by whom," exclaimed I, as we arrived and stopped at the door of my lodgings, "could the task be so well executed as by yourself, Mr. Hawthorne?"

"*Mr. Hawthorne!*" replied my companion, with much astonishment. "I have not the honor, sir, of bearing that name." Then, with a good-natured smile and a pleasant voice, he abruptly bade me good night, and departed hastily down the street.

Petrified with disappointment and surprise, I had not the presence of mind to go after him, to apologize for my mistake, and learn his real name. After standing some time on the steps, I slowly turned and walked into the house, where the creature-comforts of a generous tea-table afforded me some refreshment from my fatigue, and some diversion to my mortification.

When half of the evening had passed away, and I had paid a proper attention to my toilet, I visited with some eagerness my two fascinating companions of the morning car. Having briefly related to them my adventures and chagrins, and provoked a due admixture of their pity and their smiles, I was invited by the lady of the house to accompany them all to a large party in the city, which they were on the point of attending, and where she assured me I might confidently expect an interview with the object of my search. I need not say with what alacrity I accepted the invitation, and made a fourth in the precious-freighted carriage, which bore us rapidly off to the more brilliantly lighted and brilliantly crowded mansion in the vicinity of the Mall.

After presenting me to the hostess of the evening, my fair and kind introducer proceeded to acquaint her with the object I had at heart, and to inquire in what room or corner we might find the gentleman in question. "Sad enough!" said the hostess, "Mr. Hawthorne left us half an hour ago, having just made his appearance, and told us that he must return home to his bed, since he was completely worn out with one of the longest day's walks he had ever taken."

For the remainder of the evening, as my name was unknown to the generality of the company, I believe I must have been distinguished by them as the gentleman with the long face. I was silent and abstracted, with the exception of a half-hour's secluded and agreeable conversation with my accomplished companion of the cliff. Gleams of precious consolation, however, were occasionally afforded me by glances and smiles from the widow and her daughter, as they floated down the whirlpool of attentions, which usually absorb creatures like themselves in a fashionable party.

As destiny itself appeared to be against me, I resolved to brave it no more, and to resign the hope of seeing a person who seemed to escape me like the foot of the rainbow. On the next morning, leaving him to his probable repose after his fatigues of yesterday, I was punctual to my appointment with the ladies, and placed myself between them on the back seat of one of the crowded cars.

As we waited a few minutes before starting, a gentleman sitting on the front seat held a conversation with a friend who had accompanied him to the car, and who was pausing outside until the departure of the train, but whose person I was prevented by my position from seeing. He seemed animated and inspired by the presence of his friend, and conversed in the tone and manner of one who is desirous of expressing sentiments agreeable to the person he is addressing. I give the substance of his remarks. "I heard last evening," said he, "that, after you had gone to Boston yesterday in the car, you came home on foot along the old road through Malden and Danvers. I heartily sympathize with you for so doing. For although the railroad is sometimes a convenient evil, yet this condensing of time within a nutshell, and filling up the whole of life with nothing but urgent business, will make sad work, I am afraid, with the best parts of our character. The turnpike was bad enough in this respect, whirling us off to Boston, as it did, in an hour and a half, and whirling us back again on the same day, as if in mockery of the good old leisurely practice of the last generation. Give me the blessed times when a journey to Boston occasioned a week's thought and preparation, and occupied a long summer's day in the performance. That circuitous ride through Danvers, Lynnfield, and Malden exerted a blessed effect on our merchants and citizens. It gave them a breathing-spell from care and toil. It afforded them refreshing glimpses of the beauties of nature. It was a kind of week-day Sabbath for the weary soul. Many a match, too, was made in that way by our young grandfathers and grandmothers. I declare I think I shall in future, as often as once a month, hire a horse and chaise and go to Boston on that route, just to keep up the memory of the days gone by. If the hotel at Lynnfield were only still open, where I could stop two hours and take an old-fashioned dinner at my leisure, the charm would be complete. Nothing makes men so worldly-minded as the calculation of the business value of every instant as it passes. When I can afford to let the minutes roll unconsciously away, I seem to escape from the slavish, mechanical, monotonous tyranny of Time, and to partake beforehand of the glorious absolute liberty of Eternity. Soon after the railroad opened, I went to Boston in the car, because that hubbub Everybody said that I must. The finest thing I perceived about the road was, that it had rescued from the marsh and the salt spray some patches of land, which, they say, produced last summer beautiful flowers. But I found that it had entirely banished from the earth those far lovelier flowers, Patience and Resignation. An accidental detention of four or five minutes threw almost the whole two hundred passengers into a fever of complaint and agitation. You would have supposed that the country was on the verge of ruin, and the Union about to be dissolved, simply because our precious and almighty selves would arrive at Boston at five minutes past nine o'clock, instead of precisely at nine. Surely the old method of travelling was more favorable to the cultivation of Christian virtue. If you had not a long day of pleasure before you, you had one at least of resignation, and you did not look for the sky to fall, if you happened to be ten minutes, or even an hour, behind your time. Ah, sir, you must have seen yesterday what we lose by abandoning that excellent route. Now there is a gentle rise, then a gentle descent, then a smooth level. Here the road winds round a half-mile, to take you by a pretty though antique dwelling, or to avoid a lofty hill, and there it proceeds a short distance with a straightness that gives you the pleasure of contrast and surprise; and then again it abruptly turns a corner, where a quince-tree is growing over the fence, and presents you below its branches with a new prospect. All is charming variety. Don't you remember the willow-thickets, and the precipices in Lynn on the left hand of the road, and the frequent and beautiful glimpses of the sea away off to the right? And then, when you have endured just fatigue and absence enough to prepare you for the change, how great is the pleasure of approaching and entering the town! But what pleasure of this kind does the railroad give us? There is no anticipation about it, no gentle transition, no blending interchange and succession of feelings, but the only sensation attending it is that of a hard, uniform, concentrated, iron-beaten *Now*. I only wish that circumstances this very day permitted me to practise what I preach. But I am whirled along with the multitude and the age, and the locomotive's bell has just done ringing for the last time. So good morning, Hawthorne."

"Hawthorne? Hawthorne?" said I, as I jumped suddenly from my seat to the window of the car, where, on looking out, I caught a dim glimpse of a person who had just turned to make his way into the town. At that instant the train started, and threw me back into my place. One of my feet came with an almost crushing violence on the foot of the younger of the two ladies, who involuntarily uttered a shriek. My confusion and disappointment prevented me from tendering her the apology which was her due. I sat in a moody and sullen silence for the remainder of the trip. The ladies in vain tried to rally me into good humor. The younger condescended even so far as to beg my pardon for what she called her uncivil shriek. Kind and generous spirit! It was I who ought to have volunteered concession. My foot had no business even with the gentlest pressure against hers, — much less with a momentum that resembled the hard tread of a horse. But there was a point of forbearance and politeness beyond which their feminine dignity would not permit them to go. They became retired and reserved in their turn, or rather, they opened a most spirited conversation with the friend of Hawthorne; and when we alighted from the carriage that conveyed us from the ferry to their mansion in Summer Street, I received a civil farewell, but nothing like an invitation to walk in, or to visit them in future.

My chagrin was somewhat softened by finding that the expected party from Canada had arrived at the Tremont House. We set out the next day on our journey South. New York, Philadelphia, Baltimore, Washington, Richmond, and Wilmington, delayed us each a day or two as we advanced. My Boston disappointments faded from my memory, as an ascending balloon fades from the eye, or as one of the well-known "dissolving scenes" lessens and disappears before the spectator. This result may have been hastened by the presence of a fair member of our party, a native of the South, who was placed under my immediate protection, and in whom I found myself cherishing an increasing interest, as we visited the museums, and curiosities, and various places of relaxation on our route, or were exposed to the usual calms and incidents of a journey. By the time we had arrived in Charleston, I was very nearly induced to make to *her* the proposition of becoming an ornament to my plantation, — a proposition which I have reason to believe she would have graciously entertained. But some evil genius or other provoked me from time to time to delay the proposal, until a bolder and more fortunate hand conducted her to a sphere which was worthy of her graces and virtues. This very incident, however, together with my New-England experiences as above narrated, well exemplifies my usual destiny, which never allows me to look perfect satisfaction directly and permanently in the face, but only, like Moses in the wilderness, to behold its departing skirts.

1838.

POEMS.

PLEASURES AND PAINS OF THE STUDENT'S LIFE.

A COMMENCEMENT POEM.

1811.

WHEN envious Time, with unrelenting hand,
Dissolves the union of some little band,
A band connected by those hallowed ties
That from the birth of lettered friendship rise,
Each lingering soul, before the parting sigh,
One moment waits, to view the years gone by;
Memory still loves to hover o'er the place,
And all our pleasures and our pains retrace.
The Student is the subject of my song; —
Few are his pleasures, — yet those few are strong;
Not the gay, transient moment of delight,
Not hurried transports felt but in their flight.
Unlike all else, the student's joys *endure*, —
Intense, expansive, energetic, pure.
Whether o'er classic plains he loves to rove,
'Midst Attic bowers, or through the Mantuan grove, —
Whether, with scientific eye, to trace
The various modes of number, time, and space, —
Whether on wings of heavenly truth to rise,
And penetrate the secrets of the skies,
Or, downward tending, with an humble eye,
Through Nature's laws explore a Deity, —
His are the joys no stranger breast can feel,
No wit define, no utterance reveal.

Nor yet, alas! unmixed the joys we boast;
Our pleasures still proportioned labors cost.
An anxious tear oft fills the student's eye,
And his breast heaves with many a struggling sigh.
His is the task, the long, long task, to explore
Of every age the lumber and the lore.
Need I describe his struggles and his strife,
The thousand minor miseries of his life?
How Application, never-tiring maid,
Oft mourns an aching, oft a dizzy head?
How the hard toil but slowly makes its way,
One word explained, the labor of a day, —
Here forced to search some labyrinth without end,
And there some paradox to comprehend, —
Here ten hard words fraught with some meaning small,
And there ten folios fraught with none at all?
Or view him meting out, with points and lines,
The land of diagrams and mystic signs,
Where forms of spheres, "being given" on a plane,
He must transform and bend within his brain?
Or, as an author, lost in gloom profound,
When some bright thought demands a period round,
Pondering and polishing? — Ah, what avail
The room oft paced, the anguish-bitten nail?
For see, produced 'mid many a laboring groan,
A sentence much like an inverted cone!
Or, should he try his talent at a rhyme,
That waste of patience and that waste of time,
Perchance, like me, he hammers out one line,
Begins the next, — there stops ——

Enough! no more unveil the cloister's grief; —
Disclose those sources whence it finds relief.
Say how the student, pausing from his toil,
Forgets his pain 'mid recreation's smile.
Have you not seen, beneath the solar beam,

The winged tenants of some haunted stream
Feed eager, busy, by its pebbly side, —
Then wanton in the cool, luxurious tide?
So the wise student ends his busy day,
Unbends his mind, and throws his cares away.
To books where science reigns, and toil severe,
Succeeds the alluring tale, or drama dear.
Or haply, in that hour his taste might choose
The easy warblings of the modern muse.
Let me but paint him void of every care,
Flung in free attitude across his chair.
From page to page his rapid eye along
Glances and revels through the magic song;
Alternate swells his breast with hope and fear,
Now bursts the unconscious laugh, now falls the pitying tear.
Yet more; though lonely joys the bosom warm,
Participation heightens every charm;
And, should the happy student chance to know
The warmth of friendship, or some kindlier glow,
What wonder, should he swiftly run to share
Some favorite author with some favorite fair!
There, as he cites those treasures of the page
That raise her fancy, or her heart engage,
And listens while her frequent, keen remark
Discerns the brilliant, or illumes the dark,
And, doubting much, scarce knows which most to admire,
The critic's judgment, or the writer's fire;
And, reading, often glances at that face
Where gently beam intelligence and grace,
And sees each passion in its turn prevail,
Her looks the very echo of the tale, —
Sees the descending tear, the heaving breast,
When vice exults, or virtue is distressed;
Or, when the plot assumes an aspect new,
And virtue shares her retribution due,

He sees the grateful smile, the uplifted eye,
Thread, needle, kerchief, dropped in ecstasy, —
Say, can one social pleasure equal this?
  Yet still even here imperfect is the bliss.
For ah! how oft must awkward learning yield
To graceful dulness the unequal field
Of gallantry? What lady can endure
The shrug scholastic, or the bow demure?
Can the poor student hope that heart to gain,
Which melts before the flutter of a cane?
Which of two rival candidates shall pass,
Where one consults his books, and one his glass?
  Ye fair, if aught these censures may apply,
'T is yours to effect the vital remedy;
Ne'er should a fop the sacred bond remove
Between the Aonian and the Paphian grove.
'T is yours to strengthen, polish, and secure
The lustre of the mind's rich garniture;
This is the robe that lends you heavenly charms,
And envy of its keenest sting disarms;
A robe whose grace and richness will outvie
The gems of Ormus, or the Tyrian dye.
  To count one pleasure more, indulge my Muse; —
'T is Friendship's self, — what cynic will refuse?
Oh! I could tell how oft her joys we shared,
When mutual cares those mutual joys endeared;
How arm in arm we lingered through the vale,
Listening to many a time-beguiling tale;
How oft, relaxing from one common toil,
We found repose amid one common smile.
Yes, I could tell, but the dear task how vain!
'T would but increase our fast approaching pain, —
The pain so thrilling to a student's heart,
Couched in that talisman of woe, *We part!*

SEQUEL

TO THE COMMENCEMENT POEM.

1852.*

I, WHO once sang the Student's Joys and Woes,
Would chant, to-night, their *retrospective close.*
Nay, start not, classmates, at such theme of gloom,
Nor charge that I anticipate your doom.
'T is true, some rare vitality seems given
To the lithe graduates of Eighteen Eleven,
Since but a third of our whole corps appears
Stelligerent † in the lapse of forty years;
A proof, perhaps, that, spite of youth's elation,
We shunned the fault of over-application!
Yet, though our fated summons be not soon,
We 're wearing down life's lessening afternoon;
Not sullenly nor seldom do we hear
The lisped cognomen of "Grandfather dear,"
And, startled, bear as bravely as we can
That graphic title, The Old Gentleman;
Not having reached that period when the old
Seem pleased and proud to hear their ages told.
So, your indulgence I shall no more ask,
But straight commence my retrospective task.

---

* Delivered on the evening of Commencement day, at the residence of the Hon. Edward Everett, in Boston, whither the Class had been invited to celebrate the forty-first anniversary of their graduation.

† A star is prefixed, in College Catalogues, to the names of deceased graduates.

Still for the Student-Man, as Student-Boy,
Varied has rolled our course with pain and joy.
O those long boding years of work and care,
For our embraced Profession to prepare!
And then those longer years, still doomed to see
No "call of Providence," nor grateful fee!
But, in due time, hope cheered the patient heart;
In life's grand duties we have borne our part, —
Have laid our shoulders to the social wheel,
In all that man can do, or think, or feel, —
Have sometimes triumphed with a favorite cause,
And sometimes wept to see it droop, or pause.
Amid these storms and outward cares of life
Came the dear sunshine of a home and wife.
Not ours the *selfish* scholar's huge mistake,
That household ties rude interruption make.
From those same ties a finer zest we catch,
For every studious moment we can snatch!
If in our ranks some Benedicks there be,
They scarcely muster more than two or three;
And I feel sure their fault it has not been,
But rather of the world's capricious queen!
As down the Past our grateful memory looks,
Let us confess the bliss we drew from books;
Those mute companions of the dear-bought hours,
Those quickening Mentors of our dormant powers.
Our inward life how favored, to have found
Such various nutriment spread all around!
Yet, as no good is pure from some alloy,
This rank abundance has impaired our joy.
How hard the choicest reading to select,
And specious dulness in advance detect!
Into what tomes of nonsense have we dipped,
What modest, solid pages have we skipped!

'T is pain to think that we must quit this world,
With myriads of the brightest scrolls yet furled.
We snatch but half a life, to leave unread
Great utterings of the living and the dead.
Yes, *I* shall die, before I have looked o'er
Montaigne, and Marlowe, and unnumbered more.
May we not hope, that, 'midst the heavenly rest,
One of the "many mansions" of the blest
Shall be a spacious LIBRARY, arrayed
In spirit-volumes from the earth conveyed?
There all that Omar burned shall be restored,
And bright gold bindings clothe the priceless hoard;
New series of celestial works pour in,
Never to end, and ever to begin;
Some sainted Russian shall the books perfume,
A softened heaven-light shall the place illume,
Sweet mystic silence mantle all around,
Just broken by the outward choral sound;
One glance a volume's contents comprehend,
And leisure last whole æons without end!
  That heaven of heaven those men may enter in,
If washed, I mean, from other stain of sin,
Who, in this world, a book with smiles laid down,
At the intrusion of some friendly clown; —
All those, in short, who lettered sweets resigned,
To give their powers in person to mankind.
  'T is pleasure for the student's thought to trace
The advance of Art, and Science, and the Race.
Blest are the eyes that see what we have seen,
In the brief lapse since our unfledged nineteen.
Within that handbreadth have been crowded more
Of marvels than ten centuries knew before;
While life, and man, and all things here below,
Show a changed world from forty years ago.

Who would have thought dear Harvard's walls had stood,
In our young days, had her imperilled brood
To witching Boston been enticed to stray
Four times an hour, instead of twice a day?
Yet of such wonders this is far the least:
We sit at an Arabian-Nights' strange feast;
We witness metamorphoses, that seem
Less like reality than some wild dream.
Through every range of current life extend
Increasing lights, and comforts without end;—
School-books so plain that babes can understand;
Two morning papers in a cabman's hand;
Mammoth gazettes, each day, as full of new
Fine matter, as the old Critical Review;
Stone-coal, ignited, conquering wintry glooms,
And western lakes upgushing in our rooms.
One fount of lighted gas a city serves,
One whiff of ether calms the frantic nerves;
Steam in a month conveys us round the globe,
Weaves for the nations their protecting robe,
Prints off ten thousand sheets within an hour,
And clothes mankind with preternatural power.
Yet Steam's may be but a Saturnian reign;
The Electro-Magnet seeks that throne to gain.
Antipodes demand the talking wire;
Portraits are painted by the solar fire; *
New planets ferreted before perceived,
And facts established almost ere believed.
Here, animalcular creations ope,
There, heavens draw near us through the telescope,
And Berenice sees, 'mid polar cars,
Her nebulous locks unbraided into stars.

* Speaking with prosaic precision, the photograph acts only by means of the rays of *light* in the solar beam.

Nor less in public life have marvels reigned;—
Thrice our torn land its wholeness has regained;
Our strip of States a continent has grown,
And Europe risen, to circumscribe the Throne.
Yet o'er this wonderful Achilles-shield,
The trembling student's tear is oft unsealed.
Amid such strides of vast material power,
He sees new evils lurk, new dangers lower;
He asks for some great moral engine's force,
To speed man's *spirit* on an equal course.
As civilized achievement rises high,
Mounts the dread tide of vice and misery.
Has Education yet the secret gained
Of Youth restrained, yet not too much restrained?
When will young people cease to play the fool,
And take some warning from their parents' school!
Alas! cigars and oaths, I shrewdly fear,
Get nearer to the cradle every year.
And even in mental discipline alone,
With all its lights, has Learning raised its tone?
Is riper scholarship developed now,
Than when an Abbot * smoothed the school-boy's brow?
Is intellect more patient and profound,
Than when it delved in harder, narrower ground?
Books also might improve by quarantines;
Thought oft cries liberty, but license means;
The Press, sometimes a foul prolific sty,
Makes the land noisome with its numerous fry.
Opinion's leaders rival Shakespeare's Puck,
Pert Speculation fairly runs amuck;
Fantasy questions all established things,
Tired Reverence folds her once face-covering wings,

* The former distinguished Preceptor of Exeter Academy.

And, with some lightning truths by Genius given,
His daring apothegms shake earth and heaven.
So, if again to politics we turn,
Dark futures for our country we discern,
With parties, aims, machineries, and ways,
Undreamt of by our Hamiltons and Jays;
None knowing, too, if our gigantic state
Will fall, or hold its own by sheer dead-weight,
Of heterogeneous elements composed,
To the world's dregs our flood-gates all unclosed;
While far across the vexed, ship-fevered main,
Reactionary Europe hugs her chain.
Yet let us own, amidst the general taint,
Proud Liberty endures some wise restraint;
The flood prevails not every place above,—
Lights on some resting-spots the wandering Dove;
The germ that bourgeoned at our nation's birth,
Nobly assimilates the very earth;
Unchecked democracies the Sabbath keep,
Fierce parties o'er a dying statesman weep,
And (civic self-control unknown before!)
Whole States resolve to pass the Cup no more;
The blessed *School* embowers Youth's flexile tree,
And Faith burns brighter, as it burns more free.
Science blasphemes no longer, as she pores,
And Comte, his Titan Law relaxed, adores! *
Classmates, we know not where this maze shall end;
To our own work we know that we must bend;
On other hands the task must be devolved,
Before these mighty problems can be solved.

---

* M. Comte, in his "Système de la Politique Positive," recently published, at length recognizes, with considerable personal sensibility, the moral and religious element in man as a legitimate object of philosophical speculation.

For us, though welcoming each hopeful plan,
I deem our class conservative, to a man.
So, with a prayer that all may yet be right,
Let us indulge in apter themes to-night.
One heart-born pleasure for our student race
Is to behold a classmate's well-known face.
We do not meet him like another man;
He starts emotions that no other can.
Whether in throngs or wastes our footsteps bend,
Meet but a classmate, and we meet a friend.
Certes, if one *my* distant home but greet,
The door flies open for his welcome feet.
Our classmates know us as few others do,
Kind to our failings, to our merits true.
Hence our unfading, our unique delights,
When our "Fair Mother" holds her festal rites.
Who can forget that famed centennial year,
When Harvard hailed her sons from far and near?
What joy, what beckonings, what exchanged surprise,
As at each other flashed inquiring eyes!
How changed, yet how the same, ourselves we found,
Since last we parted on that classic ground!
The same old joking and peculiar ways,
That marked the intercourse of fresher days;
And yet the experience deep we could but see,
Ploughed by one quarter of a century!
To-night again such greetings we renew, —
O'er life's slant pathway memory's roses strew,
Light with fresh tints our lingering sun's decline,
And closer draw the invaded circle's line.
Ah yes! such pleasures have their dark reverse;
Through flowery beds rolls on the ruthless hearse;
Of those familiar forms we miss to-night,
Most are for ever sundered from our sight.

Oft have I passed a mournful day, when came
The new Triennial, starred with many a name.
It seems but yesterday since Harvard's shade
Saw us as Freshmen, curious and afraid.
Erelong, what salient characters there sprang,
What life and fire from our collisions rang!
And now, a cohort of that valiant band
Knows us no more beneath the spirit-land.
What is the meaning of this shadowy scene?
Where are the meteor-friendships that have been?
Pause we a moment o'er each name, and see,
Even in these few, mankind's epitome.
BAKER, of generous, independent haste;
FARNHAM, of graceful phrase, and polished taste;
STORY, that youthful miracle of Greek;
HILDRETH, intent on politics to speak;
COOPER, Refinement's many-cultured child;
REED, meekly pious; WESTON, still and mild;
PRENTISS, the spotless and the studious youth;
Lone WATERHOUSE, through nature following truth;
HUNT, like his own geometry, upright;
OTIS, the glass of fashion, frank and bright;
Good-natured WELD; and unassuming GRAY;
ROGERS, with happy laugh, and merry play;
PUTNAM, wise, learned, and old enough to teach;
DAMON, of open heart, and fluent speech;
PERKINS, the social; WILLIAMS, the retired;
And all with true class-fellowship inspired.
ONE grave and name we pass, — but tremble still
At passion's force, and self-indulgent will;
Owning the need of Heaven's restraining grace,
To curb and sanctify our erring race.
Brethren, that grace, in its abounding scope,
Shed on *your* path faith, peace, content, and hope!

May children's children lead you down the way
Of cheerful, useful, unperceived decay;
Not forced to toil too late for wearied self,
And not too early laid upon the shelf!
Blest with keen bodily and mental sight,
May books still prove your solace and delight;
And duly may your search be there where lies,
Imbedded near, the pearl of richest price!
Stay yet, dear friends; the Minstrel bids you toast,
In pure, bright water, our accomplished host;
Who gives, one need not say, our class its name,
Tinged with the lustre of his well-earned fame.
Health for his labors, for his cares relief,
To him, our first and last unenvied chief!

HUMAN LIFE.

Life, Human Life! Such is the theme to-day,
Which kindles hope in you, in me dismay,* —
A theme to me, unpractised wight, yet new,
A theme enjoyed, adorned, and filled by you.
Life is but tasted at threescore and ten;
What can green twenty-three accomplish, then?
Life is an ocean, where whole myriads sweep, —
How can a minim comprehend the deep?
Or atmosphere, where countless insects glance, —
Can one poor fly survey the immense expanse?
Who shall direct me on this shoreless route?
Where enter? rather, at what point come out?
How o'er these fluctuating spaces range?
How sketch one trait of this eternal change?
How, dreaming, can I reason on my dream?
How take the soundings, as I glide the stream?
But why thus ready in despair to sink,
When smiles like yours forbid my heart to shrink?

---

* This poem was delivered in 1815, at Cambridge, Mass, on the anniversary of a literary society (the Phi Beta Kappa), before a large audience composed of both sexes. Though widely circulated in manuscript, it has never before been published. Many portions were necessarily omitted in the delivery, while several local and temporary allusions are at present suppressed. Other retrenchments and modifications have been made, without, however, impairing the identity and integrity of the piece.

Urged by those smiles, my trembling spirit burns,
And each dread wave of difficulty spurns.
  Whirled though we are around life's giddy tide,
Some steadfast views by care may be supplied.
Could Newton, wiser Archimedes, show
How the world moved, without a δὸς ποῦ στῶ,
If Locke the secrets of the mind unsheathed,
If Priestley analyzed the air he breathed,
Why may not we, with philosophic eye,
The laws that guide our *moral* sphere descry?
Why not transcend the range of chemic strife,
And decompose this circumambient life, —
Detect the good and evil blended there,
Like oxygen and nitrogen in air?
  Two grand and primal characters we find
By Nature's God impressed on all mankind,
In Age and Sex. First let us ponder these,
For method's show, then ramble where we please.
  Mark, then, what wisdom shines in that decree,
Which, varying life, ordained our ages three, —
Youth, manhood, and decline. In these we trace
A fine proportion and harmonious grace.
Deprived of either, life would cease to charm, —
A passion-chaos, or a deathlike calm.
If all were youth, and this a world of boys,
Heavens! what a scene of trifles, tricks, and toys!
How would each minute of the livelong day
In wild obstreperous frolic waste away!
A world of youth! defend us from a brood
So wanton, rash, improvident, and rude!
Truants from duty, and in arts unskilled,
Their minds and manners, with their fields, untilled,
Their furniture of gaudy playthings made,
Sweetmeats their staple article of trade,

No fruit allowed to ripen on the tree,
And not a bird's-nest from invasion free!
In public life, there still would meet your sight
The same neglect of duty and of right.
Go, for example, to some stripling court,
And see which there would triumph, law or sport.
"Adjourn, adjourn!" some beardless judge would say;
"I'll hear the trial, when I've done my play."
Or, should the judge sit faithful to the laws,
Hear how the counsel would defend his cause:
"May it please your honor, 't is your turn to stop;
I'll spin my speech, when I have spun my top."
Meanwhile the jury pluck each other's hair,
The bar toss briefs and dockets into air,
The sheriff, ordered to keep silence, cries,
"O yes! O yes! when I have caught these flies!"
Such were the revellings of this giddy sphere,
Should youth alone enjoy dominion here;
All glory mischief, and all business play,
And life itself one misspent holiday.
Now let us take a soberer view again,
And make this world a world of full-grown men, —
Stiff, square, and formal, dull, morose, and sour,
Contented slaves, yet tyrants when in power;
The firmest friends, where interest forms the tie,
The bitterest foes, when rival interests vie;
Skilled to dissemble, and to smile by rule,
In passion raging, but in conduct cool,
Still, with some deep remote design in view,
Plodding, yet wanting ardor to pursue;
Still finding fault in every fretful breath,
Yet dreading innovation worse than death;
In arts unwieldy, but too proud to learn,
In trifles serious, and in frolic stern;

Selfish in love, — conceive to be alive
A tender, timorous pair at forty-five!
What sighs and wishes — for a thousand pound!
What killing glances — at a manor-ground!
True sighs and looks are better understood
By hearts of fresh, uncalculating blood,
And sure the stream of life must sweeter stray,
The nearer to the source its waters play.
Besides, there glows such raciness in youth,
Such touches come of innocence and truth,
We love the things, how full soe'er they be
Of jocund mischief or disturbing glee.
If they require man's strong, experienced rein,
Man's darker vices they in turn restrain.
From youth the profligate their sins conceal,
And feign that virtue which they cannot feel.
Before his son what parent is profane?
What outcast dares a filial ear to stain?
Who does not check his conduct and his tongue,
In reverence for the yet untainted young?
O yes! in tender age, a holy charm
Breathes forth, and half protects itself from harm.
Bereft of that, and to mid-age confined,
The life of life were ravished from mankind;
The same mill-wheel of habits would prevail,
Vice wax inveterate, folly would grow stale,
And life's fair task of active bliss become
A long, dark fit of hypochondriac gloom.

Thus youth's and manhood's fierce extremes contend,
With wholesome war, each other's sins to mend.
Waging a sort of elemental strife,
They raise and purify the tone of life,
The light and shade that fix its colors true,
The sour and sweet that give it all its *goût*.

But shall Old Age escape unhonored here, —
That sacred era, to reflection dear, —
That peaceful shore, where Passion dies away,
Like the last wave that ripples o'er the bay?
Hail, holy Age! preluding heavenly rest!
Why art thou deemed by shallow fools unblest?
Some dread, some pity, some contemn thy state,
Yet all desire to reach thy lengthened date;
And of the few so hardly landed there,
How very few thy pressure learn to bear,
And fewer still thy reverend honors wear!
He who in youth hath fed the pure desire,
And rode the storm of manhood's fiercer fire,
He only can deserve, and rightly knows,
Thy sheltering strength, thy glorious repose.
As some old courser, of a generous breed,
Who never yielded to a rival's speed,
Far from the tumults of Olympic strife,
In peaceful pastures, loiters out his life,
So the wise veteran crowns his strenuous race,
Breathing, released, in dignity and grace.
What though the frost of years invest his head?
What though the furrow mark time's heavy tread?
There still remains a sound and vigorous frame,
A decent competence, an honest name.
In every neighbor he beholds a friend,
Even heedless youth to him in reverence bend,
Whilst duteous sons retard his mild decay,
Or children's children slope his weary way,
And lead him to the grave with fate-beguiling play.
Thus, as the dear-loved race he leaves behind
Still court his blessing, and that blessing find,
And, since they must survive the good old man,
Tread on his heels as softly as they can,

Their tenderness in turn he well repays,
And yields to them the remnant of his days.
For them he frames the laughter-moving joke,
For them the tale with pristine glee is spoke,
For them a thousand nameless efforts rise;
To warn, to teach, to please, he hourly tries,
Nor ever knows himself so truly blest,
As when purveying comforts for the rest.
His hands in timely duties never tire,
He grafts the scion, points the tendril's spire,
Or prunes the summer bower, or trims the winter fire.
  Nor is this all. As sensuous joys subside,
Sublimer pleasures are to age allied.
Then pensive memory fondly muses o'er
The bliss or woe impressed so long before;
The sinking sun thus sheds his mellowest ray
Athwart those scenes he brightened through the day.
Then, too, the soul, as heavenly prospects ope,
Expands and kindles with new beams of hope;
So the same parting orb, low in the west,
Dilates and glows before he sinks to rest.
Yes! if Old Age were cancelled from our lot,
Full soon would man deplore the unhallowed blot;
Life's busy day would miss its tranquil even,
And earth must lose its stepping-stone to heaven.
  Thus, every age by God to man assigned
Declares His power, how good, how wise, how kind;
And thus in manhood, youth, and eld we trace
A fine proportion and harmonious grace.

  But Life a richer aspect still supplies:
Sex is the theme to which my pencil flies.
How Life exulted at that glad decree,
When Nature said, Let man, let woman be!

'T was kindness all, 't was Heaven's redundant grace,
That wove this blest distinction for our race.
If men had started from the teeming earth,
Or, like Deucalion's sons, disdained a birth;
If tribes of women from the deep had sprung,
As she of old, by dreaming poets sung;
Had life, with fatal independence, known
Mere Benedicks, or Amazons alone,—
Woe worth the gloom of that untoward scene,
With no redeeming joys to intervene,
These tranquil duties and bland cares denied,
Which now so finely checker and divide!
The toils of either sex devolved on one,
Life's crowded business must be half undone.
Men, torn between the household and the field,
Must now the spade and now the bodkin wield;
Hands, by long rigid labor callous grown,
Must plait the muslin, or adjust the gown,
And hordes of uncouth lubbers you might see
Stalk from the plough (ye Gods!) to pour out tea.
Not such the picture of our present state;—
No tasks oppress with disproportioned weight.
Exempt from pains absurd, and awkward cares,
Each willing sex a separate burden bears.
The one, adapted and inured to toil,
Roves the wide earth, or tills the stubborn soil.
The other sways the still domestic sphere,
More circumscribed, though not to life less dear.
Yet think not thus their interests blend the worse:
Identity of sphere would prove their curse.
Relation, contrast, makes their being one,
As Day consists of morn and evening sun.
Scarce a more vital, binding union feel
The centre and the circuit of a wheel.

Life lives on both; their contrast simply this,
Man is its glory, woman is its bliss.
Joint pilgrims onward through this rugged road,
Their best relief to ease each other's load;
He clears the way, and guards it with his powers,
While she that pathway strews with choicest flowers.
If he must brave the hardships of the storm,
'T is she at least that keeps his shelter warm.
If he with fortune wage perpetual war,
'T is she that makes his lot worth fighting for!
But ah! my laboring fancy strives in vain
For some apt semblance of the human twain.
Nature has no two webs so closely joined
As their conspiring influence on mankind.
Like the glad breeze that animates the air,
He is the health, and she the music there.
Or, shining like the sun's compounded blaze,
He darts the bright, and she the melting rays.
And can it be that men should e'er combine
To frustrate Nature in this wise design,
And with a rival's malice dare degrade
A sex, their pride, their bliss, their equals made?
Yes, such there are, who hope themselves to raise,
As woman sinks beneath their base dispraise.
One class traduces her material frame,
Others her mind, the last her morals, blame.
These three I meet, the sex's champion,
And, like Horatius, smite them one by one.
First, then, some sinewy heroes boast their strength,
And cry: "This difference you must own at length,
Woman is not so muscular as man,
And hence inferior, even on Nature's plan.
She is not strong, — she cannot bear such shocks."
True, but I tell you, sir, what can, — an ox.

Go, then, and rate your merit by the stone ;
Woman wars not for cartilage and bone.
  Next comes a railer of a higher kind :
Not woman's size offends him, but her mind.
Methinks I hear some dapper wight exclaim,
Whose sex confers his only right to fame :
"Thanks to my stars, I 'm not a woman born !
Learning and science hailed *my* natal morn ;
Nature on me no gifts or graces spared,
She gave omniscience, when she gave a beard.
Let them whose wonder still on woman doats
Produce a Newton hooped in petticoats, —
A Doctress Johnson, in her cap and ruff,
Or kilted Stewart, deep in thought and snuff."
  Before I answer this right witty spark,
His merry charge deserves one grave remark.
Where are the schools and colleges designed
To train and discipline the female mind?
Would Newton's name, or Johnson's, loom as great,
Had they been trammelled in a woman's fate, —
Condemned through life to ply the eternal thread,
Or bake some hapless scholar's daily bread, —
Toils, from which learned ideas flit away,
Like the scared ghosts that fly the coming day ?
Think, then, how base, preposterous, and unfair,
A woman's mind with Stewart's to compare !
You shut the gates of science in her face,
Then publish that exclusion her disgrace !
  But while reluctant I the palm concede
Which fortune, and not nature, has decreed,
Think not I mean to parley with the foe,
Or quit the field without one parting blow.
O ye profound monopolists of mind !
To whom all wit and wisdom are confined,

Who aim to rule the lettered world alone,
And cannot bear a sister near the throne,
Who still at every female effort rail,
And brand their thoughts as feeble, trite, and stale,
Pray condescend sometimes to leave your lore,
And be as shallow as De Stael or More.
But of this triple host, who forms the arriere?
A foe indeed! yet let not woman fear.
Though rudely he assassinate her heart,
Yet shall her injured fame repel the dart.
Come on, maligners of the sex, declare
How weak, how false, how faithless, are the fair.
I grant you all, — and yet I'll win the field;
So woman conquers, when she seems to yield.
Allow she has a soft and ductile soul;
Is gold the hardest metal of the whole?
Allow she has a fickle, wavering mind;
Do we not breathe and live on fickle wind?
Allow she has a wily, treacherous heart;
Are you, O man, inveigled by her art?
What! her superior? you, her better part?
Besides, have you not had the upper hand? —
Six thousand years of absolute command!
Then why not mould and train, ye sovereign kings,
Your pliant subjects into nobler things?
Yourselves, too, will the page of history find
Such perfect patterns to frail womankind?
Has your example ruled in life's affairs,
More pure, peace-loving, and devout than theirs?
I could pursue the triumph, but forbear, —
Even woman generously bids me spare, —
Content if I have placed in fairer light
Her claims of equal dignity and right.

Still on my mind a few inquiries press,
That urge reply, — our theme demands no less.
What makes the nuptial pair most truly blest?
'T is this, — just so much worth must fill each breast,
That, when they wake from love's romantic dream,
Their eyes may open on a fixed esteem.
Again, what constitutes the choicest wife,
Next to the praise that she abhors all strife?
'T is this, — identity of bliss and woe,
Of hopes and fears, of what they wish or know.
Have you not seen an honest, gracious dame,
Alive to all her husband's pride or shame?
Have you not visited their generous board,
And watched her anxious interest in her lord,
Heard the long story, in his hackneyed strain,
Told and retold, (ah me!) and told again?
No matter, — she enjoys it quite as well,
And would till doomsday, did he live to tell.
Her appetite and relish for the jest
Return as punctual as the dinner 's dressed.
And see her speaking eye of you implore,
"Do laugh — though you have heard it all before."
What churl at this his muscles would restrain?
Let yours relax, — it shall not be in vain.
She looks and acts ten thousand thankful things,
And helps you to two luscious capon's wings!
Fie on the odious doctrine, somewhat rife,
That marriage profits by a tinge of strife;
That life would grow, without some stringent jar,
Tasteless as salad without vinegar.
A savage creed! gilding with phrase ornate
Domestic jargon, hymeneal hate.
There shall not come betwixt our model pair
More than some transient difference, mild and rare.

When mutual faults or shades steal in to show
That both still wander in these vales below,
He reprimands by glancing with his eye,
And she inflicts her soft reproach, a sigh.
That is abundant feud for man and wife,
More potent than whole Iliads of strife.
Why need invective to make error smart,
When gentle signs as deeply touch the heart?
One question more the marriage theme demands:
How may a husband best adorn the bands?
How can a man that mystic secret find,
To keep his partner ever true and kind?
To virtue's laws how make his offspring bend?
How fill the spheres of parent, master, friend?
In short, how spread a heaven above his dome?
Five words shall answer, — he must keep at home.
And who from *Home* could ever wish to rove,
That tranquil sphere of peace, and joy, and love?
Search Life's whole map, — of all its scenes so fair,
Home is the brightest spot that glistens there.
'T was there the light, first falling on our eyes,
Gladdened our young existence with surprise.
There, too, the smile, which met our infant view,
Straight to our lips with sweet contagion flew.
Such were the lessons home could then instil;
Such heaven-like lessons it exhibits still.
There flourish, where no envious arts encroach,
Praise without flattery, blame without reproach.
If you have virtues (and all men have some)
Where can they find so kind a soil as home?
Your faults, though conned, are conned to be forgiven;
Each frown is mercy, and each smile is heaven.
No outward trappings there deceive the eyes;
The native heart bursts through, and mocks disguise.

There you may stroll, attired in dishabille,
And be allowed some share of merit still;
Nor blast your character (believe it, pray!)
Should you go slipshod for a chance half-day.
  Of all the varying scenes that life can boast,
Home suits the growth of wit and wisdom most.
Besides its calm retreats and noiseless shade,
Which lend philosophy the choicest aid,
'T is there that *Converse* bids its glories roll,
Converse, that choral interchange of soul!
Whatever else in social life we find
Is but the body, Converse is the mind.
Come, join the circle, — bid the language flow,
Pluck from time's wings the blossoms ere they go;
Let every friend, undaunted, bear a part,
To swell the fund of intellect and heart.
But let us banish from this blest pursuit
The shameless prater, and the shame-faced mute;
The one who talks, and talks, and talks, and talks,
The other walks and sits, and sits and walks;
The one, a long obstreperous cascade,
Usurps those beds where many rills had strayed;
The other, like a stagnant pool, is found
Not only dull, but spreads contagion round.*
  I own there is a better kind of mute,
Who cannot yield his share of common fruit.
Poor souls! they silent sit the evening long,
At length risk something, and that something wrong.
From these let Satire's shaft divert its aim,
They need our sympathy, but not our blame.
  But who is she, retiring and alone,
That makes her thoughts by sign and gesture known?

* The author was unconsciously anticipated in these two characters by Boileau, in his Satire on Woman.

No sound can vibrate on her barren ear,
No voice escape those lips in accents dear;
'T is one dead silence all from year to year.
Yet let not pity too officious rise,
Nature requites the blessings it denies.
The expressive look, the motion fraught with grace,
May rival language, and supply its place:
And, for that senseless ear, perchance are given
Ethereal sounds, and intercourse with heaven.
But hark! the envious clock proclaims the hour,
And friends glide off, as leaves forsake the bower.
Nor are you desolate, though left alone;
Home still has pleasures, pleasures all its own.
There, as you loll beside your waning fire,
And, like the embers, feel each care expire,
Your dog, spoiled favorite! slumbers on the floor,
And, whimpering, dreams his day's adventures o'er;
While Puss, with fond, insinuating purr,
Rubs by your ankle with her silken fur.
And when the elastic frame's worn powers are fled,
Home has a pillow for your drooping head,
Where, as your drowsy thoughts, in broken train,
Announce the approach of fancy's fairy reign,
This is the last that floats upon the brain,—
Search Life's whole map, of all its scenes so fair,
Home is the dearest spot that glistens there.

But endless questions start on every side:
Let not your sweet forbearance be denied,
While I discuss, with all consistent haste,
Where shall the home we love so well be placed?
Shall rural scenes alone extort our praise?
Or shall the town engross our gliding days?
To show how rural scenes with me prevail
I weave my notions in a simple tale.

A weary laborer hailed the setting sun,
And wandered home, — his long day's work was done.
A rippling stream, that crossed his stony road,
With broken gleams and tempting murmurs flowed;
He stooped to meet its pure and cooling brim,
And gratefully refreshed each dusty limb.
Then fared he on, with joy and freedom gay,
And felt such raptures as departing day
Yields to the child of nature. All the west
In one calm, unrepulsive glare was dressed.
Far to the north, clouds long and black were seen,
And streaks of sky fantastic shone between.
The south a heap of splendid vapors bore,
Which every moment differing colors wore;
While through the paler chambers of the east,
The silvery moon her gradual pace increased.
Oft did our laborer pause amid this scene,
Forgetful of his supper on the green;
Forgetful even of his partner's smile,
That could his utmost weariness beguile;
Forgetful of those little prattlers gay,
That wont each eve to meet him on his way,
Received the promised kiss, and strove for more,
And gambolled round him till he reached the door,
Then, when the well-conned prayer was duly said,
With sighing resignation shrank to bed.
Though joys like these were to his heart full dear,
Yet pleasures more sublime allured him here.
The lingering pace, and oft-uplifted eye,
That traced quite round the variegated sky,
The half-burst exclamation, all expressed
The blissful transports that usurped his breast.
But ah! delight so thrilling cannot last:
This ravished ecstasy at length was past,

And trains of milder contemplation stole,
By reason's hand directed, o'er his soul.
To childlike wonder manly thought succeeds,
And God's own work to God's existence leads.
"What generous power has all this beauty given?
And whence this rich 'magnificence of heaven'?
Who sends the balmy fragrance of this air?
Who decks out Nature in her drapery fair?
Could harmony so perfect e'er combine
Without the guidance of a wise design?
And whence did I my powers of thought acquire?
Who lighted up this sacred inward fire?
Who made my frame? and who my feeling soul,
Kindly diffusing pleasure through the whole?
'T was thou, great God! I own thy power divine;
Such acts of wonder can be none but thine.
To thee alone my happiness I owe;
Thou bidst my cup of blessings overflow;
And since thy mercies thus profusely pour,
How can I aught but love thee and adore?"
Such were the musings of a rustic mind,
Nature's plain dictates, simple, unrefined;—
And thus the lowliest hind that turns the sod
May look through nature up to nature's God.
Now view awhile the city's murky glare,
Where noise and dust and smoke infest the air,
Where works of man on every side arise,
And scarce one trace of God salutes the eyes.
"Sermons in stones!" some pious poet sings;
"Sermons in stones!" right-edifying things!
If so, in yonder well-paved town, I fear,
Where every step their eloquence may hear,
More homilies are trodden under foot,
Than Chrysostom or Gregory ever wrote.

But let us fairly grant the town its due :
With faults, it has redeeming virtues too.
Those splendid arts that lend to life a zest,
Those darling charities that make it blest,
Fly from the country's rude, ungenial air,
In quest of social haunts, to nestle there.
Hence, though all shapes of meanness swarm in town,
Scarce are incorrigible niggards known.
Where luxury's ten thousand channels flow,
Where want obtrudes the ceaseless tale of woe,
The frequent shilling from the pocket parts,
And keeps the issue open of their hearts.
Next, to the city's *intellect* must yield
The vegetative wisdom of the field.
As knowledge floats and shifts from ear to ear,
The swelling mass becomes an atmosphere.
The meanest artisans who trudge the street,
The poor *canaille*, who delve for present meat,
Derive from frequent converse with mankind
Much tact of character, and liberal mind.
I should indulge more hope, by reason's light,
To set a truckman than a ploughman right ;
Though when by both the path of duty 's found,
Then, I confess, my preference changes round.
The truckman's head is sounder than his heart,
The peasant's bosom is *his* better part ;
The former oftenest yields to tempting things,
The latter to his sturdy conscience clings.
Thus, let your home be planted where you will,
Expect, around you, blended good and ill ;
Your door, thank Heaven, can still admit the good,
And from your inner shrine the bad exclude.

But ceaseless home is not for social man ;
Duties abroad must share Life's mingled plan.

And when the youth first quits his native nest,
What doubts and cares annoy his fledgling breast,
As the vast range of public life he views,
And trembling asks, Which calling shall I choose?
Choose the pale author's, — and behold my books
Mangled by critics, and by pastry-cooks?
Choose the attorney's, — feast on breach of laws,
Batten on quarrels, and subsist on flaws?
Choose the sad patriot-politician's lot,
And by my grateful country — be forgot?
Choose the poor pedagogue's, and wield the rod?
Alas! not mine the patience of a god!
Choose the physician's, and inflict the pill,
And get on well, as others get on ill?
Choose the divine's, and spend my strength to show
My listening flock the way they will — not go?
Or choose the merchant's, sport of every wave?
O how superbly wealth shall heap — my grave!
  Such is the gloom by public life displayed,
To him who views it only in the shade.
But if we scan it o'er with kinder eyes,
From each profession happier tints shall rise.

  First, be the *Author* in the balance weighed.
'T is true, he plies a thorny, thankless trade;
Condemned beneath the public beck to move,
And pander to the taste he would improve,
And who, to place his fame in decent light,
Must write down malice, and make dulness bright.
Yet he has pleasures, large, secure, unbought:
No power can rob him of the bliss of thought.
A few still smile, though all the world deride;
A few still smile, he cares for none beside.
How well deserving of a nation's praise,

Who gives to lettered toil his studious days;
Who, far abstracted from the rude world's din,
Expatiates o'er that greater world within!
'T is his to stamp his country's rank and name,
To fix her language, and extend her fame.
No drudge in science, 't is his godlike fate
To guide like Bacon, or like Scott create.
His mind, o'erflowing with conceptions bright,
Writes what it thinks, not thinks what it shall write,
Pours its whole genius on the enchanted page,
Adorns, improves, refines, exalts, the age.
We own such giant spirits are but rare, —
Yet do they languish in our country's air?
Or must we traverse the Atlantic o'er,
To find that greatness on a foreign shore?
Not so! such excellence can flourish here, —
Does flourish, — brightens, moves our lettered sphere, —
Though half adored, from affectation free,
And fled from pedants, Kirkland,* dwells with thee.

Next, to the *Lawyer's* labyrinth draw near,
Threading from maze to maze his dark career,
By varying rules and precedents perplexed,
Pushed by opponents, and by clients vexed.
What wear and tear the harassed drudge must find,
I do not say of conscience, but of mind!
Yes, lost to all that shame and truth demand,
Who pour reproach on this much injured band!
Their short-eyed malice rashly represents
The law mere subtlety and impudence!

---

* John Thornton Kirkland, D. D., late President of Harvard University. The estimate presented of him in the text was but the echoed sentiment of the surrounding literary community.

Calumnious tongues! as if the world ne'er saw
A modest, upright steward of the law!
Whose faithful zeal, by no restraint outdone,
Makes his own interest and his client's one;
Whose manful reasonings, lucid, fair, and sound,
No wiles can match, no sophistry confound;
Whose stainless honor none suspects of blame,
Pure as the tablet of a virgin's fame;
Whose fruitful wit can make law's barren field
A harvest of exotic fancies yield;
In fine, who *can* sometimes defend the oppressed,
And pocket for his fee — a quiet breast.
Such is the face the slandered law presents;
Looks this like subtlety and impudence?
Ah! at that bench in cypress hung so late,
Where almost more than mortal wisdom sat,
How justice reigned, — how prompt, exact, and pure!
How trembled vice, how virtue felt secure!
There Parsons,* like the sun, sank down to night,
In full-orbed glory, majesty, and light;
Soon did the shadow into darkness grow,
When Sewall,† bright twin-lustre, ceased to glow.
Wherefore were both not destined to attain
The long, sweet, tranquil twilight shed by Paine? ‡

Now shall I launch you on that stormy sea,
Where loud-voiced *Politics* its rage sets free?

---

* The justly celebrated Theophilus Parsons, LL.D., the foremost lawyer of his time.

† Hon. Samuel Sewall, LL.D., who succeeded Judge Parsons, for a very short time, on the bench of the Supreme Court of Massachusetts.

‡ The Hon. Robert Treat Paine, LL.D., one of the earliest judges of Massachusetts after the Revolution, had recently died at a very advanced age.

Do I not hear a general murmur burst,
"In mercy save us from that theme accurst!
Cling to Life's poetry, nor look behind,
Where veering principle outstrips the wind.
One day embargo, with its colors furled,
The next, free intercourse with all the world!
Mobs, murders, patriots, factions, feathers, tar,
With cabinets, and embassies, and war,
Chaotic horror, and eternal gloom,
Where truth and bliss and virtue find their doom!"
A truce with picturés pencilled by despair!
'T is not so dark and sickening everywhere.
Does not, sometimes, a nation, nobly wise,
On her best sons, instinctive, fix her eyes,
Cheering them on, while, struggling in her cause,
They weave her righteous, life-inspiring laws?
What though, along the lapse of twenty years,
One Bonaparte hath whelmed the world in tears.
In the same space one Wellington hath shone,
One Alexander, and one Washington.
That name, for ever blest! for ever dear!
How can it pall upon a free-born ear?
Shall our spent souls with feebler tumults glow,
To hear the hallowed sound oft echoed? No.
Pilgrims may kiss their marble saints away,
But his dear image never shall decay,
Though still our grateful hearts unceasing homage pay.

But turn from politics and public rule,
To view the humble *Teacher of a School.*
Hark! as yon low-roofed mansion you draw near,
What miscellaneous tumult strikes the ear!
The wholesome rod, perhaps too often swayed,
The busy murmurs memory calls to aid,

The unlawful whisper, and the bolder tongue,
The tedious task, monotonously sung, —
The tricks of mischief, which defy restraint,
The mock apology, and mock complaint, —
Genius too wild and confident to learn,
Dulness too deep and sluggish to discern, —
Whilst the whole scene, beneath its master's care,
Seems like young Chaos, tutored by Despair.
  Yet though the pedagogue's dark lot be hard,
Think not from pleasures he is quite debarred:
Each crowded hour its special comforts brings.
He sits in potent state, like other kings;
Sees many a subject reverently obey,
And marks improvement grow from day to day.
He doats, with something of a father's pride,
On infant worth, close nestling by his side, —
Sweet youth! o'ercome by one forbidding look,
Who hides his mournful face behind his book,
But, when applauded for his task well said,
Pulls down his waistcoat, and erects his head.
  Whilst thus the teacher glories in his boys,
Another sex may still enhance his joys.
Imagine, then, some pupil nymph consigned
To you, the guardian of her opening mind,
In all the bloom and sweetness of eleven,
Health, spirits, grace, intelligence, and heaven;
While still from each exuberant motion darts
A winning multitude of artless arts.
Withal, such softness to such smartness joined,
So pure a heart to such a knowing mind,
So very docile in her wildest mood,
Bad by mistake, and without effort good,
So humbly thankful when you please to praise,
So broken-hearted when your frown dismays,

So circumspect, so fearful to offend,
And at your look so eager to attend,
With memory strong, and with perception bright,
Her words, her deeds, so uniformly right,
That scarce one foible disconcerts your aims,
And care and trouble — never name their names!
Yes, I forget, you have one anxious care,
You have one ceaseless burden of your prayer:
It is, — Great God, assist me to be just
To this dear charge committed to my trust.
  Such are the comforts of the teacher's lot,
And if with these but blest, he murmurs not,
But bears contentedly, as bear he must,
The mixed renown of usefulness — and dust.
  And yet I cannot quite dismiss him here;
One word I 'll whisper in the Public's ear:
Why on the teacher of our youth must wait
A menial's wages, and a menial's fate?
Behold the man who all day long for years
Moulds your child's life, — yes, even his smiles and tears!
His bosom's close companion why not hail
Your own companion in the social scale?

  Now to the *Healing Art* one moment turn; —
And first the empiric we condemn and spurn,
Who on the blindness of his brethren thrives,
Tampering with their credulity and lives, —
Unlike those angel-ministers of health,
Who boast no "cure-alls," hoard no "patent" wealth,
Distrust themselves, and follow nature still,
Or compass science to complete their skill.
Yes, when we find such men with healing powers,
Soothing this miserable world of ours,
Whose piercing eye can read your inmost frame,
Whose mystic tact can gauge a fever's flame,

Who with a smile your illness can rebuke,
And make you convalescent by a look,
It seems as if some more than mortal brood,
On busy message of dispensing good,
Had come, like pardoning legates from the sky,
And half revoked the sentence, "Thou shalt die."

Perhaps the ambitious youth, whose earnest aims
Explore life's mingled periscope, exclaims:
"I 'll be no jaded minister of health,
But seek the *Merchant's* glittering prize of wealth."
Beware! that prize a thousand blanks surround;
Crowds of competitors usurp the ground.
Commerce, I own, waves her enlightening hand,
And in one wreath weaves every distant land;
But dire collapses and revulsions rush
The wisest speculator's plans to crush.
How often, too, may trade's low maxims wrest
Truth, honor, right, from thy bewildered breast!
Yet, if the thought still fires, cast in thy lot,
Some pass the quagmires, and contract no spot.
Go, march to fortune's summits, and sit down
With "merchant princes" in yon classic town.*
Crowning, like them, the long, hard, tempting strife
By unimpeached integrity of life,
Serve, with thy treasures and thy liberal heart,
Religion, Learning, Charity, and Art.

Thus having roved o'er life's less hallowed round,
Now may we venture upon holier ground?
One sacred task remains, though last, not least,
To sketch the ideal of a *Christian Priest;*

---

* Boston.

That bright example Heaven so rarely gives,
Which died in Eliot,* but in Lowell † lives.
  The minister of God! thrice awful name,
Ah, who may dare its vital functions claim?
Yet, would you serve your God with zeal sincere,
Approach and act, — naught frowns forbidding here.
How blest, who spends his consecrated days
In alternations sweet of prayer and praise,
Who now soars high, in heaven-aspiring mood,
Now treads his earthly round of doing good!
No scene of life by Providence is given,
But he comes near to join that scene with heaven.
With pure baptismal rite, and lifted eye,
'T is he who drowns in prayer your infant cry;
'T is he who seals your holy marriage doom,
Soothes your sick bed, — nor quits you at the tomb.
Thus with life's every phase he mingles in,
And strives, by word or deed, your souls to win.
Hence, smiles from Heaven, from man esteem, he gains,
And every house for him a home remains.
Where'er he goes in duty's toilsome hours,
Soft marks of friendship strew his way like flowers;
The kind inquiry, and the smile sincere, —
The look respectful, and the attentive ear;
Even the rude boy, who bursts upon his sight,
Bows, as he stops the trundling circle's flight.
And should he sometimes glance at fashion's shrine,
Where gay coquettes salute, defame, and shine, —
Where nice gregarious fops together link,
Talk, laugh, eat, play, and anything but think, —

---

* Rev. Dr. Eliot, then recently deceased, minister of the Second Church in Boston.

† Rev. Charles Lowell, D. D.

At his approach their wanton trifles fly,
And cards and dice are reverently laid by.
But men are men, — and, be the truth confessed,
The pastor shares his troubles with the rest.
His ways and means are sometimes hugely few,
And his black coat is often threadbare too.
Yet to such trifles cheerfully resigned,
Graver and life-long cares o'erwhelm his mind.
Hunting the whole first half-week for a text,
To spin therefrom two sermons in the next,
His sinking spirit craves some heavenly guide,
To search the truth, and rightly to divide,
To smite perennial waters from the rock,
And rouse and charm and save his various flock.
And who the pang can tell that cuts his heart,
When some fond pastor tries his tenderest art
To show an erring soul the path to heaven,
And lo! that flint-like, dumb return is given,
A strange, half-sanctified, sarcastic look,
Which mocks instruction and defies rebuke?
Less sad than this, — when, on the week's last night,
He seeks his desk, the homily to write,
Some thoughtless neighbor slowly shuts the door,
And runs the stock of village gossip o'er.
Our good divine the fretful smile reserves,
And breathes a prayer for patience and for nerves.
Then when he roves abroad in freer air,
And pays the willing visit everywhere,
The jealous, kind complaint 't is his to hear,
And guilt of wasted seasons wakes his fear.
He and his flock his visits may condemn
As profitless alike to him and them.
"Cases of conscience" form not all their themes:
He must partake in news, tales, whims, and dreams,

To every claimant yield attention due,
Salute Tryphœna and Tryphosa too.
"But must not books and study soothe his care?"
Somewhat, — yet is not peace unmixed even there.
As o'er fell controversy's page he bends,
Where truth lies bleeding from the wounds of friends,
Sees Campbell lay Castalio on the rack
And countless jokes on poor Montanus crack,
Sees Lardner with his gravity dispense
To torture Wetstein into truth and sense,
Sees Calvin's system even with Calvin clash,
And sparks of ire from Christian bosoms flash,
Sees saintlike foemen into sophisms fall,
And pens of almost angels dipped in gall,
He casts his eyes despairingly around,
And asks, Perfection, where canst thou be found?
"But, if his study must unquiet be,
Is not the pulpit from vexation free?"
The pulpit, friends? alas! 't is often there
The sad quintessence dwells of his despair.
Who would desire the pulpit for his sphere,
When Gallios slumber, and when critics sneer?
There as he stands, with arguments arrayed
No vice could front, no unbelief evade,
Line upon line, precept on precept plies,
Some dozing hearer dreams how bank-stocks rise!
Show me the church who love their guide so well,
His manner they o'erlook, and on his matter dwell.
The veriest trifle in his dress or mien
May mar the whole devotion of the scene.
So Alcibiades a bird let fly,
And caught each frivolous Athenian's eye.
A lock misplaced — too long, too short, too sleek —
May blast the labors of a studious week.

In vain he urges their eternal good,
His toilet first must win their serious mood.
Nay, though his language in such lustre shone,
As Blair or Buckminster were proud to own,
Yet all in vain. Should he have chanced to tie,
In haste his band unluckily awry,
No Providence could more disturbance give —
(I speak of things that on the record live.)
If the brass serpent healed old Israel's pain,
This fatal tie no less diffuses bane;
The sly contagion lurks from pew to pew,
And taints the tittering congregation through.
Strange, on the threshold of the heavenly ground,
That earnest minds so seldom can be found!
But thus it is. Some give their hearts to gold,
Some for a fatal appetite are sold,
Some for a song; and weaker still than that,
Some perish smiling at a wry cravat!
Saddest, that this regard for outward form
Pervades that sex with souls most pure and warm!
From one calamity Heaven shelter me,
A fair, fastidious, critic-devotee!
Though to her church each Sabbath she repairs,
And deeply loves its homilies and prayers,
Nothing quite suits or edifies her there,
If not propounded with a graceful air.
This seems the touchstone of each word and deed,
The Alpha, you would fancy, of her creed.
If Enoch with a gait ungainly trod,
She scarce believes he ever walked with God;
Would doubt the powers ascribed to Moses' wand,
If wielded by a cramped or awkward hand;
To the true faith her heart would fain be won,
If but the act may be genteelly done;

To all religion's laws devoutly yield,
Just where religion chimes with Chesterfield.
I give with pity, and no wish to mock,
The spirit of her Sabbath-evening's talk.
"How well that preacher moved along the aisle!
What holy gestures, what a reverend smile!
Did ever periods so devoutly roll?
Did ever cadence so convict the soul?
How piously the handkerchief was waved!
Sure such a nice man's audience must be saved!
The afternoon beheld a different treat;
Bare were the walls, and vacant many a seat.
Nor strange that shepherd found so thin a fold,
Who was so plain, so awkward, and so old;
Too antique-fashioned to be understood,
Too unrefined to work our highest good.
I own that he is faithful, worthy, true,
But what can such insipid virtues do?
His earnestness repels, — his unction shocks,
And one may be too strictly orthodox."
O ye who deal fantastic praise and blame,
Whose nimble tongues dispense and tarnish fame,
Why thus the transient and the eternal blend?
Why make religion to a shadow bend?
Lo! stern reality is brooding near;
Will sorrow, conscience, change, regret, and fear
Give heed to fantasy's capricious breath?
Will outward graces charm the hour of death?
The hour of death! I may not lift the screen,
Which darkly mantles o'er life's closing scene;
Here end its folly, wisdom, pleasure, pain,
Here too must cease my desultory strain.

Yet, patient friends, before I bid adieu
For ever to the lyre I strung for you,

Indulge me still a momentary stay,
To glean some scanty moral from my lay;
Nor, as a fond bequest, will you refuse
The parting tribute of a grateful Muse.
  You all, my friends, a line of duty see,
Drawn by the hand divine, that made us free.
This line observed, promotes our being's aim,
But this transgressed, our wretchedness and shame.
Small wanderings make the fault, — the whim; meantime
Large deviations constitute the crime.
The former move contempt, as weak or droll,
The latter justly rouse the indignant soul.
Custom, society, and law assign
To each offence its punishment condign.
The censor's lash, the poet's angry pen,
Suffice to check the minor sins of men,
While bold and flagrant misdemeanors draw
A weightier vengeance from the offended law.
This stern tribunal I may not approach,
Nor on its high prerogative encroach.
Enough for me to satirize the times,
And prosecute your Liliputian crimes, —
Gibbet some vice, detect some follies' gang,
Flog scoundrel freaks, or private whimsies hang,
And scourge the small atrocities of man;
'T is all I aim at, — all that Satire can.
  Now Satire has a double list of foes,
Some to conciliate, others to oppose.
One class deem all is levelled at their head;
They chafe and fume at everything that 's said; —
Poor self-made scapegoats, men without a skin,
Who suffer penance for their neighbors' sin.
  The other tribe, of these the exact reverse,
But who yet try the Satirist's patience worse,

Are they whom no rebuke can touch with shame,
No sarcasm rouse, — though much the fairer game.
If the most general vices you condemn,
They join the censure, but you can't mean them!
Pursued themselves, they mingle in the hunt,
And, though the arrow rankles in their front,
With keen and charitable zest look round,
To see their neighbor twinge beneath the wound.
This pair of portraits have their places here,
To guard us from the extremes we all should fear.
Ye, whose sore vengeance I have braved to-day,
Chancing your peccadillos to display,
Pray be not angry if the coat suits true,
For I protest I did not measure *you*.
And let us all that worse extreme beware,
To relish satire, and disdain to share.
Why should we fondly think, complacent elves,
The shaft hits anywhere but our dear selves?
Unfair it is to join the bantering laugh,
And yet refuse to take our rightful half.
No, no! thou honest and thou liberal soul,
Whom candor and humility control,
Thou art not quite that monster of a saint,
That claims exemption from the general taint.
Thou ownst thy failings, since imperfect made,
As every solid wears its following shade.
But even these shadows wouldst thou brush away,
And quicken virtue toward the perfect day,
In duty's vital sphere be ever found,
And strive to make that sphere not large but round.
Perfection in the humblest globule lies,
As in the bulkiest globe that decks the skies;
And thou mayst find among the narrowest streams
The richest murmurs and the sweetest gleams.

Then be content to range life's lowliest vale,
Nor rashly breathe ambition's dangerous gale.
Careless though rivals for a day excel,
Polish thy little diamond talent well.
Aim to *do* good, and good will surely flow;
Aim to *be* good, and Heaven will make thee so.
But striving to complete thy little sphere,
Study *His* will who kindly placed thee here,
Nor from that sacred guide presumptuous stray,
Who is himself the Life, the Truth, the Way.
Walk in that way, and live that life divine,
Believe that truth, — obey, and heaven is thine!
Heaven! where our foibles and our faults shall close,
And care and sorrow smile into repose.
There, though no eye hath seen, nor ear hath heard,
Nor heart conceived the mystic-meaning word,
Yet, as once sang a brother, we may find
"The grand Phi Beta Kappa of mankind." *
New friendships there shall knit our growing powers,
And happier warblings charm the bliss-winged hours;
The expanded soul shall breathe immortal air,
And live indeed! for Life is only there.

* I once found this line, as descriptive of the future state of the blest, in a manuscript poem delivered by some predecessor at one of the anniversaries of the Phi Beta Kappa Society.

UNION ODE,

COMPOSED FOR THE UNION PARTY OF SOUTH CAROLINA, AND SUNG JULY 4, 1831.

AIR. — "Scots wha hae wi' Wallace bled."

Hail, our country's natal morn!
Hail, our spreading kindred-born!
Hail, thou banner, not yet torn,
Waving o'er the free!
While, this day, in festal throng,
Millions swell the patriot song,
Shall not we thy notes prolong,
Hallowed Jubilee?

Who would sever Freedom's shrine?
Who would draw the invidious line?
Though by birth one spot be mine,
Dear is all the rest:
Dear to me the South's fair land,
Dear the central mountain-band,
Dear New England's rocky strand,
Dear the prairied West.

By our altars, pure and free,
By our Law's deep-rooted tree,
By the past's dread memory,
By our Washington,

By our common parent tongue,
By our hopes, bright, buoyant, young,
By the tie of country strong,
We will still be ONE.

Fathers! have ye bled in vain?
Ages! must ye droop again?
Maker! shall we rashly stain
Blessings sent by Thee?
No! receive our solemn vow,
While before thy throne we bow,
Ever to maintain, as now,
Union, Liberty!

NEW-ENGLAND ODE,

FOR THE UNIVERSAL SONS OF THE PILGRIMS, ON THE TWENTY-SECOND OF DECEMBER.*

NEW ENGLAND! receive the heart's tribute that comes
From thine own Pilgrim-sons far away;
More fondly than ever our thoughts turn to thee,
Upon this, thine old Festival Day.
We would rescue, with social observance and song,
Awhile from oblivion's grave
The loved scenes of our youth, and those blessings recall
Which our country and forefathers gave.

---

* Composed for the New England Society at Charleston, and the Sons of the Pilgrims at Plymouth.

We have gazed on thy mountains that whitened the sky,
  Or have roved on thy tempest-worn shore ;
We have breathed thy keen air, or have felt thy bright fires,
  While we listened to legends of yore.
We have gathered thy nuts in the mild autumn sun,
  And the gray squirrel chased through thy woods,
From thy red and gold orchards have plucked the ripe store,
  And have bathed in thy clear-rolling floods.

When thy snow has descended in soft, feathered showers,
  Or hurtled along in the storm,
We have welcomed alike with our faces and hearts
  Its beauteous or terrible form.
We have skimmed o'er thine ice with the fleetness of wind,
  We have reared the thick snow-castle's wall,
And have acted our part in the combat that raged
  With the hard-pressed and neatly-formed ball.

We remember the way to those school-houses well,
  That bedeck every mile of thy land,
We have loved thy sweet Sabbaths, that bade in repose
  The plough in its mid-furrow stand.
We have joined in thy hymns and thy anthems, that swelled
  Through religion's oft-visited dome,
We have blest thy thanksgivings, that summoned from far
  The long-parted family home.

Can distance efface, or can time ever dim
  Remembrances crowding like these,
That have grown with our growth, and have ministered strength,
  As the roots send up life to the trees ?
Then be honored the day when the May-flower came,
  And honored the charge that she bore,
The stern, the religious, the glorious men
  Whom she set on our rough native shore.

New England! speed yet in thine onward career,
  With thine inborn, all-conquering will:
Still triumph o'er Nature's unkindliest forms,
  By thine energy, patience, and skill.
Thou shalt grow to thy height, as thou ever hast grown,
  O'er the storms of ephemeral strife,
And thy spirit, undying, shall cease not to be
  The deep germ of a continent's life!

FAIR HARVARD.

SUNG AT THE CENTENNIAL CELEBRATION OF HARVARD UNIVERSITY, SEPTEMBER 8, 1836.

Air. — "Believe me if all those endearing young charms."

Fair Harvard! thy sons to thy jubilee throng,
  And with blessings surrender thee o'er,
By these festival-rites, from the age that is past,
  To the age that is waiting before.
O Relic and Type of our ancestors' worth,
  That hast long kept their memory warm!
First flower of their wilderness! Star of their night,
  Calm rising through change and through storm!

To thy bowers we were led in the bloom of our youth,
  From the home of our free-roving years,
When our fathers had warned, and our mothers had prayed,
  And our sisters had blest, through their tears.
Thou then wast our parent, — the nurse of our souls;
  We were moulded to manhood by thee,
Till, freighted with treasure-thoughts, friendships, and hopes,
  Thou didst launch us on Destiny's sea.

When, as pilgrims, we come to revisit thy halls,
  To what kindlings the season gives birth!
Thy shades are more soothing, thy sunlight more dear,
  Than descend on less privileged earth:
For the good and the great, in their beautiful prime,
  Through thy precincts have musingly trod,
As they girded their spirits, or deepened the streams
  That make glad the fair City of God.

Farewell! be thy destinies onward and bright!
  To thy children the lesson still give,
With freedom to think, and with patience to bear,
  And for Right ever bravely to live!
Let not moss-covered Error moor *thee* at its side,
  As the world on Truth's current glides by;
Be the herald of Light, and the bearer of Love,
  Till the stock of the Puritans die.

ODE,

SUNG AT A PICNIC OF THE CHARLESTON WASHINGTON LIGHT INFANTRY.

AIR.—"The Fine Old English Gentleman."

O WHO are they that formed their ranks, a self-devoted band,
When insult rude and lowering war assailed their native land,—
Who bear inscribed upon their helms the world's most honored name,
And wave their little Eutaw flag, baptized in blood and flame?
  The Washington Light Infantry, old Charleston's loyal sons!

And who are they that boast a line of leaders brave and true, —
The mighty LOWNDES, — the gifted CRAFTS, — and CROSS, with eagle view, —
And SIMONS, warm, — and MILLER, bland, — and others yet on earth,
Whose lengthened years God grant may prove co-equal with their worth?
The Washington Light Infantry, old Charleston's loyal sons!

And who are they, when trumpet-call and martial duties cease,
Who gladly ply their civic toils, the gentle arts of peace, —
Who love the social gathering too, in nature's green retreat, —
The mossy shade, the woodland breeze, and friendship's cosy seat?
The Washington Light Infantry, old Charleston's loyal sons!

And who are they that find their most delightful task and care,
In peace or war, to serve, protect, and gratify the fair, —
From whom one smile of tender faith can largely overpay
The fiery perils of the camp, or labors of the day?
The Washington Light Infantry, old Charleston's loyal sons!

And who are they that know full well each wild excess to check,
And throw the rein of self-control round festive freedom's neck, —
Who listen to the friendly words by age and wisdom given,
And pause amid life's swift career to lend a thought to heaven?
The Washington Light Infantry, old Charleston's loyal sons!

And who are they that will, while time shall urge his onward flight,
The soldier and the citizen thus faithfully unite, —
Who will, should e'er their ranks be thinned, more close together grow, —
Who never can a friend forget, nor quail before a foe?
The Washington Light Infantry, old Charleston's loyal sons!

ODE ON THE DEATH OF J. C. CALHOUN,

SUNG AT A CELEBRATION OF HIS OBSEQUIES IN COLUMBIA, S. C.

AIR. — German Hymn.

FARE thee well! From storms below,
Tried and mighty spirit, go!
Worker! to thy high reward;
Faithful servant! to thy Lord.

Son and type of thy great time;
Prophet, with the eye sublime;
Statesman, in thyself a host;
Martyr, dying at thy post!

Rarest gifts in thee we saw;—
Thought — that probed each hidden law;
Presence — like a felt control;
Speech — that awed a nation's soul;

Mind of giant; heart of child;
Quickly roused or reconciled;
Braving, but forgiving foes;
Stirred, that others might repose.

Thou wast proud, confiding, free,
Like thy State's own chivalry;
Moral stain couldst not endure,
Like thy State's own daughters, pure.

Thundering 'neath the Federal dome,
Turning fondly to thy home,
Feared, extolled, or disapproved,
Still thou wast revered and loved.

Falling at thy noon of fame,
Thou, with ripe and world-wide name,
Needst no more from life; but WE,
Darkling here, have need of thee.

God of nations! quench the brand
Cast on our imperilled land;
Bid our patriot's honored grave
Speak the word which yet may save.

LINES,

WRITTEN AFTER THE FUNERAL OF MRS. PARSONS (MARY WENDELL HOLMES), IN CAMBRIDGE, MASS.

A BITTER silence reigned around that bier,
  Where fairest youth and brightest genius slept;
The grief we felt knew no relieving tear;
  Our hearts *within* — our bleeding *bosoms* — wept.

Not there was heard the careless, idle talk
  So oft exchanged above the common dead;
Humbled and soft we took our graveyard walk,
  And neared that tomb with vague, reluctant tread.

She was the wonder of her native green,
By rich and poor, by high and low, beloved;
Transplanted thence, she knew no change of scene, —
There were no strangers where her presence moved.

Mary! what power has stayed thy happy breath?
Sure thine elastic spirit sprang on high;
We deemed thee not a creature formed for death;
Religion tells the truth, — thou couldst not die.

Who ever heard or witnessed thee but praised?
Age, learning, softened at thine artless wile;
Even rival loveliness unenvious gazed,
And childhood caught from thee its sweetest smile.

Thou dazzling grace of beauty's sparkling halls,
Thou early votary of the studious cell,
Glad visitant of poverty's cold walls,
And, most, thou ornament of home, farewell!

Wide was the circle by thy loss bereaved,
All seemed to mourn a *sister's* life-star set;
And one, a passing pilgrim, sadly weaved
This funeral wreath of friendship and regret.

HYMN FOR AN ORDINATION.

Father! thy rich spirit shed
On this youthful suppliant's head;
Soothe his self-distrusting tears,
Temper his abounding fears;

Guide his vast and high desire;
Touch his lips with coals of fire;
Pour thy truth upon his soul,
O'er the thirsting Church to roll.

In thy vineyard called to toil,
Wisely may he search the soil;
Sinners may he love and win,
Whilst he hates and brands the sin;
Give him boldness for the right,
Give him meekness in the fight;
Teach him zeal and care to blend;
Give him patience to the end.

Seal, this day, the vows that hold
Flock and shepherd in one fold;
May he well those mandates keep,
Feed my lambs, and, Feed my sheep.
Bless his home, his watch-tower bless;
Guide him, with thy gentleness,
In the path once taught and trod
By the enduring Son of God.

Grant him, in his charge, to find
Listening ear and fervent mind,
Helpful counsels, deepening peace,
Earnest life, and glad increase.
May they, by each other led,
Grow to one in Christ their head;
And at last together be
Ripe for Heaven, and meet for THEE!

THE PLEDGE,

FOR A TEMPERANCE SOCIETY.

WHEN Sin invites with aspect fair,
And Misery broods beneath the snare,
And Habit clasps with fell control,
We pledge — for the Immortal Soul!

When Man, imbruted, can despise
His fond wife's tears, his children's cries,
The care of self, the social plan,
We pledge for hee, thou Brother-Man!

And since on us the future fate
Of myriads yet unborn may wait,
Though small the sacrifice will be,
We pledge, Posterity, for thee!

Since thou, Creator, dost prefer
The meek and stainless worshipper, —
From pride and self-reliance free,
We pledge, O God! we pledge for thee!

THE WHOLE WORLD KIN.

A SAILOR's cheek is browned, a lady's white;
The *tear* on each has equal warmth and light.

BETHLEHEM'S GREATNESS.

"And thou, Bethlehem, in the land of Juda, art not the least among the princes of Juda." — Matt. ii. 6.

Wherein, O Bethlehem, doth thy greatness lie?
In warlike host, proud tower, or palace high?
"No! a sweet babe's first slumber I have seen,
And hence the cities own me for their queen."

CHARACTERISTICS OF A PUPIL.

I can describe thee in one half a line,
Dear Susan, thus: — *completely feminine.*
'T is this that makes thee self-possessed and meek;
This drives those lights and shades across thy cheek;
This gives thy flexile soul, and flexile form;
Makes thee, with feelings delicate and warm,
Quick, faithful, patient, accurate, prepared
In Memory's tasks, however light or hard.
'T is this, too, Susan, (ah, true woman's fate!)
Deepens the puzzling mysteries of thy slate!

THE SILENT GIRL.

She seldom spake; yet she imparted
Far more than language could;
So birdlike, bright, and tender-hearted,
So natural and good!

Her air, her look, her rest, her actions,
Were voicc enough for her;
Why need a tongue, when those attractions
Our inmost hearts could stir?

She seldom talked, — but, uninvited,
Would cheer us with a song;
And oft her hands our ears delighted,
Sweeping the keys along;
And oft, when converse round would languish,
Asked or unasked, she read
Some tale of gladness or of anguish, —
And so our evenings sped.

She seldom spake; but she would listen
With all the signs of soul;
Her cheek would change, her eye would glisten;
The sigh, the smile, upstole.
Who did not understand and love her,
With meaning thus o'erfraught?
Though silent as the sky above her,
Like that, she kindled thought.

Little she spake; but dear attentions
From her would ceaseless rise;
She checked our wants by kind preventions,
She hushed the children's cries.
And, twining, she would give her mother
A long and loving kiss;
The same to father, sister, brother, —
All round, — nor one would miss.

She seldom spake. She speaks no longer;
She sleeps beneath yon rose; —

'T is well for us that ties no stronger
Awaken memory's woes,
For oh! our hearts would sure be broken,
Already drained of tears,
If frequent tones by her outspoken
Still lingered in our ears.

THE SUNBEAM ON MY PATH.

Late a wanderer far from home, and subdued by pensive care,
I lighted on a stranger form, young, feminine, and fair.
"I will bring for you, O pilgrim!" the vision seemed to say,
"A sunbeam on your path, a blessing on your way."

And soon we grew acquainted, though we wist not how or why:
She divined my tastes and moods with her quick, sagacious eye;
Giving and winning confidence, — gay, but serenely gay, —
A sunbeam on my path, a blessing on my way.

She was a gracious listener, but when discourse declined,
She filled the threatening pauses with her sprightly bursts of mind.
One week we dwelt together, but she made it seem a day, —
That sunbeam on my path, — that blessing on my way.

By quiet ministrations of a thousand nameless deeds,
She averted my mishaps, she supplied my hourly needs;
Ever studious, like a daughter, to comfort and obey, —
A sunbeam on my path, a blessing on my way.

A hundred damsels pass me, without one look or smile,
From whom the gray-haired gentleman no deference can beguile;

Then why did *she* so fancy me? and why so strangely lay
A sunbeam on my path, a blessing on my way?

I *must* somewhat believe in those famed mesmeric spheres,
By which heart recoils from heart, or heart with heart coheres.
One man you loathe, you know not why; another pleases, nay,
Is a very sunbeam in your path, an angel in your way.

At length, when Duty beckoned us, our separate ways we took,
With the firmly pressing hand, and the silent, farewell look;
But very oft, from home's dear bowers, will grateful memory stray
To that sunbeam on my path, that blessing on my way.

And when, as soon must happen, my worn head in dust lies low,
And she, still blessing others, through this mingled world shall go,
Grant her, my Heavenly Father, I here devoutly pray,
Such sunbeams on her path, such angels on her way.

THE HISTORY OF A RAY OF LIGHT.

The hint for the following composition was derived from a recent discovery by a Swedish botanist; namely, that there are certain flowers which emit, in the darkness of evening, the rays of light imbibed from the sun during the day. A thought hence occurred to the writer, that each individual ray of light may possibly in this manner perform a variety of successive functions, and even be efficiently darting about from object to object, and from one quarter of creation to another, for an indefinite number of years. Should the idea be questioned, as not strictly philosophical, it must be content to aspire no higher than to the character of fanciful.

"Let there be light!" creation's Author spoke,
And quick from chaos floods of splendor broke;—
On that magnificent, primeval morn,
Myself, an humble ray of light, was born.

Vain were the task to guess my native place;
Rushing, careering, furiously through space,
Plunged amid kindred rays and mingling beams,
These are my first of recollection's gleams.
O, with what joy we rioted along!
Darting afar, in young existence strong,
Onward we poured the unaccustomed day
Through tracts, the length of many a milky way.
(For know, we rays of light are living things,
Each with ten thousand pair of brilliant wings:
No wonder, then, when all those wings are stirred,
We flit it so much faster than a bird.)
At last, when youthful years and sports were done,
Choice, chance, or duty, brought me to your sun;
And while my brother pencils fled afar,
To swell the glories of some viewless star,
'T was mine to fly about this nook of heaven,
Where one huge orb gave light and heat to seven; *
Although short visits now and then I make
To distant spheres, for recreation's sake.
Ah! ne'er shall I forget the eventful day
When to this planet first I sped my way:
To many a twinkling throb my heart gave birth,
As near and nearer I approached the earth.
What was to be my fate? for ever lost
In some dark bog? or was I to be tost,
In wild reflection, round some narrow spot,
Then sink absorbed, inglorious and forgot?
No, reader, no, — far different the career
Which fate designed me to accomplish here:
Millions of splendid scenes 't was mine to grace,
Though my first act brought ruin to your race.

---

* Our luminous autobiographer seems to take no account here of the Asteroids in the solar system.

Trembling, I reached the serpent's glistening eye,
Then glanced, and struck the apple hanging by,
Then to your mother Eve reflected, flew,
And thus, at one exploit, a world o'erthrew!
O scene of woe! the mischief I had wrought,
Those quick successive shocks, that stunned my thought,
The poisonous magic from that sire of lies,
The keen contagion in that woman's eyes,
All were too much for one poor ray of light,
New to his task, and meaning only right.
Distressed in heart, at once myself I hurled
Far to the outside of this injured world,
Wishing to wear my wretched life away
'Mid scenes where solitude and chaos lay.
At length, while wandering o'er those realms of woe,
I heard a small, sweet voice, that whispered low,
In tones of soothing, — 't was a brother ray
Sent from the hand that first created day.
"No longer mourn," the darting angel said,
"The hopes of man are not for ever fled:
From his own race a Saviour shall arise,
To lead him back to his forbidden skies;
And hark! when Bethlehem's beauteous star shall shine,
Its first and freshest radiance shall be thine!"
 Cheered by these words, I longed to gain once more
This lovely world, and try my fortune o'er.
Just then a globe, new struck from chaos out,
Met me, and turned my headlong path about;
Back to the sun with breathless speed I flew,
And thence rushed down, where bright to Noah's view
The glorious rainbow shone, — a lingering stop
I made within a small pellucid drop,
Glazed its internal concave surface bright,
Back through the globule travelled, and outright
Darted through air to glad the patriarch's sight.

Glancing from thence away, I sported on
Where'er by pleasure or by duty drawn; —
Now tipping some bright drop of pearly dew,
Now plunging into heaven through tracks of blue,
Now aiding to light up the glorious morn,
Or twilight's softer mantle to adorn,
Now darting through the depths of ocean clear
To paint a pearl, — then to the atmosphere
Again reflected, shooting to the skies
Away, away, where thought can never rise;
Then travelling down to tinge some valley-flower,
Or point some beauty's eye with mightier power,
Or to some monarch's gem new lustre bring,
Or light with fire some prouder insect's wing,
Or lend to health's red cheek a brighter dye,
Or flash delusive from consumption's eye,
Or sparkle round a vessel's prow by night,
Or give the glowworm its phosphoric light,
Or clothe with terror threatening anger's glance,
Or from beneath the lids of love to dance,
Or place those little silver points on tears,
Or light devotion's eye while mercy hears; —
In short, to aid, with my poor transient flings,
All scenes, all passions, all created things.

Few rays of light have been where I have been,
Honored like me, or seen what I have seen:
I glowed amid the bush which Moses saw,
I lit the Mount when he proclaimed his law:
I to that blazing pillar brought my mite,
Which glared along old Israel's path by night:
I lent a glory to Elijah's car,
And took my promised flight from Bethlehem's star.

But not to holy ground was I confined;
In classic haunts my duties were assigned.
I primed the bolts Olympian Jove would throw,

And Pluto sought me for his fires below;
Over and over gallant Phœbus swore,
I was the finest dart his quiver bore;
Oft was I sent, a peeping, anxious ray
From Dian, hastening where Endymion lay;
When Iris shot from heaven, all swift and bright,
Thither I rushed, companion of her flight;
From Vulcan's anvil I was made to glare;
I lent a horror to the Gorgon's stare;
I too have beamed upon Achilles' shield,
And sped from Helen's eye when Paris kneeled;
Faithful Achates, every school-boy knows,
Struck from a flint my whole long year's repose;
Ten wretched days I passed in sobs and sighs,
Because I could not dance on Homer's eyes:
I once was decomposed from that pure oil
Which cheered the Athenian sage's midnight toil;
I from the brazen focus led the van,
When Archimedes tried his frightful plan;
'T was I from Cleopatra's orb that hurled
The fatal glance, which lost her slave the world:
I struck the sweetest notes on Memnon's lyre,
And quivered on the Phœnix' funeral pyre.

Nor ancient scenes alone engrossed my pranks,
The moderns likewise owe me many thanks.
Straight in at Raphael's skylight once I broke,
And led his pencil to its happiest stroke;
I sparkled on the cross Belinda wore,
And tipped the Peri's wing of Thomas Moore;
To Fontenelle I glided from above,
When whispering soft astronomy and love;
And know, whene'er the finest bards have sung
The moon's sweet praises with bewitching tongue,
Or that blue evening star of mellow light,
'T was always after I had touched their sight.

Nor yet have Poetry and Painting shared
My sole regards, — for Science I have cared.
When Galileo raised his glass on high,
Me first it brought to his astonished eye;
When Newton's prism unloosed the solar beams,
I helped to realize his heaven-taught dreams;
When Herschel his dim namesake first descried,
I was just shooting from that planet's side.
At all eclipses and conjunctions nigh,
Of sun, or satellite, or primary,
Oft have I served the longitude to fix; —
And heavens! in June of eighteen-hundred-six,
How all New England smiled to see me burst
Out from behind her darkened sun the first!
I formed a spangle on the modest robes
Of Doctor Olbers' new-discovered globes;
I from the comet's path was downward sent,
When Bowditch seized me for an element.
Once travelling from a fourth-rate star to earth,
I gave the hint of aberration birth.
I led the electric flash to Priestley's sight,
And played my sports round Franklin's daring kite;
Absorbed in copper once I long had lain,
When lo! Galvani gave me life again.
I taught the Swede that, after sunny days,
Lilies and marigolds will dart forth rays;
And when polarity made *savants* stare
For the first time, be sure that I was there.
When iron first in oxygen was burnt,
When Davy his metallic basis learnt,
When Brewster shaped his toy * for peeping eyes,
And Humboldt counted stars in Southern skies,
'T was I that moved, while bursting on their sight,
The flush of wonder, triumph, and delight.

* The Kaleidoscope.

Nor scarce does history boast one splendid scene,
Or deep-marked era, where I have not been.
The sky-hung cross of Constantine, which turned
All Rome to truth, by my assistance burned;
When the Great Charter England's rights restored,
I scared her monarch from a baron's sword;
When pious Europe led the far crusade,
Did I not flash from Godfrey's wielded blade?
Did chivalry one tournament display
Of dazzling pomp, from which I kept away?
Was I not present at that gorgeous scene,
Where Leicester entertained old England's queen?
Did I not sparkle on the iron crown
Which the triumphant Corsican took down?
Did I not revel where those splendors shone,
When the fourth George assumed Britannia's throne?
And last, not least, could I refuse to hear
The summons of the Atlantic Souvenir? *
No, gentlest reader, trust your humble ray,
'T is here at length I would for ever stay,
If to and fro I could descend and rise
'Twixt these bright pages and your brighter eyes;
Absorbed, reflected, radiated, bent,
With force emitted, or for ages pent,
Through the wide world so long and often tost,
The excursive passion of my youth I 've lost.
I wish no more in my six-thousandth year,
Than just to take my peaceful mansion here,
To deck these limnings with my happiest art,
And 'mid these leaves to play my brightest part.

---

* First published in the Annual of that name.

1822.

THE END.

Milton Keynes UK
Ingram Content Group UK Ltd.
UKHW010659220124
436466UK00007B/387